Crash *and* Burn

KP Evans

Author Bio

Lawyer by day and romance author by night, KP Evans splits her time between Chicago, IL and Madison, WI with her wife and two ludicrous cats. When not writing about grumpy women and the rays of sunshine who love them, she spends her time drinking tequila, handicapping the Academy Awards, and agonizing over Wisconsin sports teams.

Bella Books, Inc.
P.O. Box 10543
Tallahassee, FL 32302

This is a work of fiction. Names, characters, businesses, places, events and incidents are either the products of the author's imagination or used in a fictitious manner. Any resemblance to actual persons, living or dead, or actual events is purely coincidental. The publisher does not have any control over and does not assume any responsibility for author or third-party websites or their content.

First Edition - 2025

Editor: Heather Flournoy
Cover Artist: Joanna Estep

ISBN: 978-1-64247-666-8

PUBLISHER'S NOTE

Crash *and* Burn

KP Evans

Acknowledgments

This book would not be possible without the love and support of so many people in my life.

To my GCLS Writing Academy crew—thank you for all your feedback and kind words, especially beta readers Kate R., Dillon, and Jayne. Your creativity, encouragement, and enthusiasm makes the writing process a little less lonely.

To my dear friend and fellow writer Kat, whose maniacal pace and inhuman productivity is constantly inspiring me to go higher, further, faster, baby.

To Jo, for creating the perfect cover. Get ready for the next one.

To Heather, for shepherding this to the finish line with grace and precision.

To the folks at Bella, who decided to take a chance on this. Your work as an indie publisher is vital and important, and I'm honored to play a small part in that.

To my parents, who fostered in me a love of reading and writing at a young age, and gave me the confidence to pursue this project.

To Kelsey and Tim, for always being the best cheerleaders.

And finally, to Rae, whose love, support, and incisive edits made this book come to life. I will never be able to thank you enough.

To Rae,
Who always knows what I'm capable of before I do.

CHAPTER ONE

"This is a terrible idea." Parker Mandli kicked at the floor of the empty store, creating a plume of dust that hovered around her ankles. A distinct odor followed, a mix of must and pine shavings that made her nose wrinkle. She sighed and stared down at the dirt now settling on her shoes—a pair of Jordan Ones, the Retro Patent Leather in shiny red, black, and white Bulls colors that always brought her good luck. They didn't seem to be working.

"This is all you can afford," Josie said, looking up from her phone. She raised an immaculately groomed eyebrow and tucked a strand of hair behind her ear. "The lease terms are reasonable. You don't want any more rentable square footage than this. Trust me."

Parker bounced lightly on her toes for a few moments, ejecting more puffs of dust from under her heels, then took another lap around the store. She'd met Josephine Beaumont through her brother, Rob, right when she first moved to Mayville and was crashing on his basement couch. Josie had found Parker an outstanding deal on her downtown loft, even though she was only renting, and was attacking Parker's newest project with equal gusto—though it was proving to be more challenging.

As a realtor and a self-proclaimed small-business expert, Josie was probably right about this place. With her tailored suit and tanned skin,

Josie reminded Parker enough of her ex, Sophia, to be both unsettling and alluring at the same time. The look she was leveling at Parker was eerily similar as well. Thankfully, Josie turned out to be nothing like Sophia, which is probably why they quickly became friends.

"What the hell was in here?" Parker scrunched her nose up even more.

Josie returned to her phone. "A pet store."

Well. That explained the smell.

Parker groaned and yanked open the front door, stepping out into the late-afternoon sun. It was mid-April and spring had taken hold, but the mild, pleasant weather did nothing to improve her opinion of the store's location. She looked up and down the block lined with lush green trees and began to sulk. Josie followed her outside.

She had toyed with the notion of opening her own sneaker resale shop for years, but it never really coalesced in her mind until she moved. Here, the idea of a fresh start in a new town and building a business of her own had grabbed hold almost instantly, and having something to focus on lessened the sting of her unplanned relocation. The actual reality of such a venture soon hit home like a bucket of cold water dumped on her head.

Parker had convinced herself that a spot downtown, right on the square, would be the perfect combination of foot traffic and prestige for the higher-end sneakers she was planning to sell. Josie swiftly disabused her of the notion. The rents were astronomical, the lease terms onerous, the spaces too big. Although she'd pouted about it, Parker listened when Josie steered her toward Tomlinson Street, a quirky, artsy neighborhood on the east side of town. So now she found herself seriously considering renting a former pet shop that still smelled like ferrets, sandwiched between a run-down four-unit apartment building and a tattoo parlor.

What a strange neighborhood. What a strange *town*. None of this was what she had expected when she moved to Mayville. Then again, she had never expected to end up here in the first place.

"All right, look." Josie appeared on the sidewalk next to her. Still gripping her phone in one hand, she grabbed Parker's shoulders and spun her around so she stared down the street. "Just past that bar I know you were judging is a bakery, a pizzeria, and a bike shop. Up here"—Josie wrenched her around in the opposite direction—"are two coffee shops and an honest-to-God butcher. I also have it on very good authority that a bespoke furniture store is set to go in two doors down. This neighborhood is primed to explode."

Parker shrugged her off. She looked up and down Tomlinson again, struggling to see the potential Josie described. Old, dilapidated houses extended down the block, mixed in with small storefronts. A marquee dangled precariously over the entrance to a bar, advertising weekly karaoke. The general appearance of both the bar and the hazardous marquee suggested it had been hosting karaoke since the early seventies, and no one had been brave enough to change out the lettering. "On my way over here, I saw a barefoot guy walking his dog," Parker said.

"It's a colorful area."

Frustration mixed with a healthy dash of anxiety seeped into Parker's chest. She raked a hand through her hair as she started bouncing on the balls of her feet again.

Josie gestured with her phone. "I know it doesn't look like much right now, but when summer really hits, the foot traffic is incredible. There are street festivals, too. There's opportunity here, I promise."

The emphasis on the word *opportunity* made Parker's heart unclench slightly. Still, she groped for more objections. None came to mind. Her eyes flicked across the street, and she changed the subject. "Is that a fire station?"

"Yep. That's the oldest fire station in the city, actually, which is why it's in the middle of the neighborhood like that. Everything sprung up around it. All the firefighters who work out of Station Two are really involved in the community. Usually a group of them sit outside after dinner and talk to whoever comes by, offer tours, stuff like that. It's become kind of a tradition."

Parker had gotten used to Josie's brochure-ready speeches; she doubted there was a single neighborhood in town that Josie didn't know top to bottom, as per her reputation as Mayville's preeminent real estate agent. As if on cue, the fire station's garage door opened, and two white firefighters ambled out, carrying lawn chairs.

Josie tapped her phone against her chin, brow furrowed. "You know, you might be able to make it part of your marketing. 'Come to Remix Footwear, where the shoes are fire' or something like that. Maybe even a collaboration? The MFD does a charity calendar every year, I wonder if..."

Parker stopped listening.

The first firefighter was a trim man with wavy blond hair and an obviously affable manner, wearing a broad smile as he moved. Parker's eyes swept over him and instead locked on his companion.

The woman was tall and broad-shouldered, her athletic build emphasized by a tight T-shirt. She moved with a strong grace, opening her chair with a practiced, one-handed snap. Leaning back, she crossed her legs and clasped her hands on the back of her head, ruffling her short pixie cut. Intense eyes stared across the street. The power in that gaze seemed to part the traffic on Tomlinson by sheer will alone, gluing Parker to the sidewalk. All she could do was stand there and dumbly stare back.

A buzz from Parker's back pocket broke the spell. She fumbled for her phone. It was a text from her brother reminding her about dinner that night for what had to have been the tenth time—like they hadn't been having dinner every Sunday since she moved to town. Two missed call notifications also glared up at her. Parker grumbled to herself and dashed off a curt reply. Out of the corner of her eye she saw Josie wave across the street. The firefighters each raised a hand in acknowledgment. She kept her face buried in her phone, scrolling through her favorite auction sites to check on several sneaker pairs she had outstanding bids on. Jesus, even from a distance the woman was stunning. There was also something familiar about her that Parker couldn't place. "You know them?" she asked, trying to sound casual.

"Sure I do. I've been friends with Alex and Cate for years. I know most of the firefighters at Station Two. They're all super fun. They take over Crystal's on Thursday nights and absolutely kill at karaoke—well, most of them. Cate just kind of drinks whiskey and scowls."

Parker stopped herself before suggesting that she wouldn't mind seeing that scowl up close. Another notification came through, distracting her from the thought. Apparently, Rob hadn't appreciated the tone of her last text. Parker skimmed the response and tapped out a snarky rejoinder about his receding hairline.

"Holy hell, is she the one that rescued those kids from that house fire?" Although Parker didn't usually pay attention to local news, the story had been inescapable last week. She'd seen the newspaper's breathless front-page layout at Rob's house. The main picture showed a duplex engulfed in flames and a firefighter running from the blaze carrying a hysterical child in each arm. A file photo was included in the article, a headshot of the heroic firefighter in her formal uniform. Those dark eyes had nearly stopped her dead in Rob's living room.

So not only was she a hero, she was a devastatingly beautiful one at that. Seemed unfair. Josie let out an aggrieved sigh. "Don't ask her about it, okay? She hates the attention."

"Who said I wanted to ask her about anything?" Parker replied a little too quickly.

Josie arched her brow again and cocked her head like she was conducting an examination. Parker squirmed and returned to her phone. Rob had sent a paragraph-long retort about her chicken legs, complete with citations. That's what she got for picking a fight with an attorney.

"So? What do you think?" Josie nudged her and gestured at the store, still wearing a curious look.

Parker abandoned any attempts at eloquence and decided to tell Rob to go choke on a Lego. The hair rose on the back of her neck, and she knew instinctively that the firefighter—*Cate*—was looking her way again. Parker tucked her phone away and turned to face the store, putting her back to the fire station. She started another round of pacing as she focused on the decision before her. The biggest decision she'd ever make, really.

Fear trickled in, seeping through the cracks of the external confidence she worked hard to maintain. She tried to ignore it.

This was going to be different. She wasn't going to run or give up at the first hint of difficulty. She would see this through to the end. After all, she'd been buying and selling sneakers for years. She knew the brands, the pricing, the margins. Even Rob had to admit her business plan was solid, and through his help, she was able to obtain a small loan with a minimal amount of fuss. A brick-and-mortar store was a natural next step.

Parker took a breath. "Send me all the paperwork, and I'll have Rob look it over tonight."

Josie clapped her hands together and gave a little jump despite the dangerous height of her heels. "I'm so excited for you!" She reached over and hugged Parker's shoulders. "This is going to be amazing, I promise. And don't even worry about the smell."

Parker couldn't help but smile at Josie's enthusiasm. "Thanks a lot for all your help, Josie. I appreciate it."

"Absolutely. We'll be in touch."

They parted after another hug, and Parker walked over to her Harley Sportster Iron 1200 parked in front of the store. Her eyes flicked over to the fire station. Cate had looked away. Her phone vibrated in her back pocket, but she ignored it. Probably Rob again. Parker snapped her black-and-white Supreme varsity jacket up to her neck and straddled her bike. She gave it a kick start and slipped on her full-face helmet, black with bright-red racing stripes down the middle in the same shade as the color of the bike. Fire-engine red, her dad had called it when he presented it to her as a college graduation present. Of course, Parker would have preferred it if he'd actually shown up to the ceremony in person, but she'd known better than to expect that.

She couldn't help glancing across the street. That powerful gaze caught her again, and her cheeks burned under the helmet.

Parker gunned the accelerator and roared off down the street.

* * *

Cate Wildman cocked her head, more curious about what was going on across the street than she really ought to be.

The woman Josie was trying to corral appeared incapable of standing still. Or paying attention. Alternating between pacing in front of the store and bouncing on her toes, she played on her phone while Josie spoke. Thick brown hair, cropped short on the sides but longer on top, fell onto her forehead with each raking pass of her fingers. Despite the fidgeting, she exuded an easy, boyish energy that was palpable from yards away. In spite of herself, Cate found it compelling.

The woman looked up suddenly, catching Cate staring, and froze like a deer in headlights. Cate shook her head and looked away.

"Huh." Next to her, Alex Rutherford shifted in his seat. "Looks like Josie's finally getting someone in that old pet store."

The store had sat vacant for the better part of a year. While that wasn't necessarily unusual for the Tomlinson neighborhood, there was a fair amount of curiosity about who the new tenant would be.

"Guess so," Cate said. The woman had jammed her hands into the pockets of her ripped jeans and was frowning. Cate wondered what magic Josie was trying to work. A pang of sympathy struck her. Cate had also found herself at the receiving end of Josie's formidable talents, and the last time that happened she'd almost put a down payment on a lakefront condo on the north side she absolutely could not afford. The woman kept bouncing on the balls of her feet as Josie spoke. Nervous habit, most likely.

"I heard the guy who ran that shop wasn't evicted. He skipped town," Alex said.

Cate frowned. "Really."

"Yeah." Alex grinned and gestured with his hands. "Illegal imports. Like, poisonous snakes and shit."

"I think you mean venomous."

"What?"

"Snakes are venomous, not poisonous. Good Lord, man, you're a paramedic."

Alex's eyes narrowed. "Sorry, I must've missed zoology day during training. Anyway, the point is, I pity the person who has to clean up whatever mess that guy left."

Cate's gaze drifted across the street again. The woman stopped pacing and made a gesture that suggested surrender. Josie wrapped her up in a big hug, the rumble of a passing 4x4 truck unable to drown out the excited squeal that followed. When Josie finally released her, the woman dipped her chin shyly and waved before hopping on the motorcycle parked in front of the store. Cate's chest clenched involuntarily at the sight. The woman revved the engine and peeled away, shiny helmet gleaming in the late-afternoon sun.

"Hey, Wilds?"

Cate turned, almost annoyed by the intrusion. Morgan hovered outside the open bay door. She hitched a thumb over her shoulder. "Captain wants to see you."

Cate stood and walked back into the firehouse, giving the younger woman a once-over as they fell into step beside each other. Morgan Cook was a probie—a probationary firefighter fresh out of the academy, assigned to Station Two a few months ago. She was like most other probies Cate had worked with: strong, bristling with potential, eager to the point of resembling an overgrown Labrador. Except that now Morgan's shoulders were slumped forward, her face pale. Cate was certain she knew the reason for the shell-shocked look.

The job earlier that morning was the most difficult Morgan had faced yet. Due to its central location, the crew at Station Two were often dispatched to two of the most precarious areas of Mayville: dark, winding McChesney Road, and the four-lane county highway outside of town. Out on the highway, a semi driver had clipped a motorcycle while changing lanes to make the offramp. The rider had gone under the trailer's back wheels. Medic Two and Ladder Two were the first on the scene, but when they arrived there was nothing to be done. Even Syed Kirmani, the senior paramedic on Medic Two and a twenty-five-year veteran, had been unnerved at the sight.

Wordlessly, Cate pulled Morgan aside, ducking around the back end of Ladder Two. Freddie, one of the two other firefighters on duty, glanced up from near the ladder truck's front wheel, then continued checking the emergency medical equipment stowed in the side compartment. He offered Morgan a kind smile.

"Munoz! Get your dirty mitts off my rig!" Alex yelled from the sidewalk. Freddie answered with both middle fingers.

Ignoring the exchange, Cate crossed her arms and waited. Morgan let out a long breath. Her stocky frame trembled. "That was a rough one earlier."

"They won't all be like that. You find ways to manage the worst of it."

"I thought I had an idea of what to expect coming out of training, but…" Morgan looked up at her, bright-blue eyes imploring. "How do you do it, Wilds?"

"What do you mean?"

Morgan's eyes widened, almost in disbelief. "Are you serious? It's like nothing fazes you. There was that school bus accident last winter, and that apartment complex fire, and hell even last week—" Morgan shut her mouth and glanced away.

Cate patted her shoulder. The gesture felt awkward. She was terrible at conversations like this, but it seemed to offer Morgan some comfort. "You did a good job today. And you can talk to any of the guys about this stuff. They're all here for you."

Morgan nodded and stepped back as if she had sensed she crossed an invisible boundary. Freddie's head poked out from around the engine, and he gestured for Morgan to join him, going over yet again how to properly store the equipment after a call. He nodded at Cate, a look of understanding passing between them. When it came to technical and procedural training, she was second to none, but anything deeper than instruction on proper forcible entry techniques or maintenance on their breathing apparatus was strictly off-limits. It had to be. Focusing on everything but her emotions was the only way she got her job done. And the job was paramount.

Captain Jamie Cordell's office was located near the back of the firehouse, in a side alcove right before the kitchen. Out of habit, Cate checked the whiteboard in the common area outlining A Shift's duty assignments. Syed and the other paramedic on duty, Omar, were starting on dinner—stuffed peppers, according to the elaborate sketch taped to the board. Salt, another firefighter, had flopped into one of the brown recliners set up in front of the TV and was flipping through a training manual. He gave Cate a mock salute as she passed. Her eyes narrowed. It was supposed to be his night to clean the bathrooms, and Cate suspected he was putting off the chore yet again, hoping for another job to get him out of it. She also suspected he dodged it to annoy her.

Cordell wore her usual frown when Cate knocked, waving impatiently at the seat across from her desk. She flipped through a stack of papers, pausing occasionally to scribble a hasty signature on the bottom of the pages. Cordell's office wasn't much more than a glorified closet, and Cate always felt claustrophobic whenever she was called in to speak to her superior. She glanced around as she waited for Cordell to finish, eyes trailing over the bland white walls decorated with various memorabilia commemorating the history of Station Two.

A pennant emblazoned with the station's logo hung above the captain's left shoulder, celebrating the oldest working firehouse in the city. To the right was a framed picture of the first crew assigned to the house. Awards and ribbons and newspaper clippings told the history of the Mayville Fire Department and the heroes who served the community, including those who had died in the line of duty. Cate could recite the tales from memory. The only personal touch was the Gold Glove necklaces dangling from the corner of Cordell's monitor, trophies from her time as a back-to-back state champion boxer.

Cate looked to her right. The annual charity calendar hung directly at eye level, prominently displaying Sam from Station One. And his abs. Cate bit back a groan.

Applying for that damn thing had *not* been her idea, and she regretted the decision more and more with each inexorable turn of the month. She'd only done it after the organizers put out a sincere plea for more diversity, and Alex spent an entire night at Crystal's eventually whittling down her objections with shots of Jameson and an unyielding belief she had been called upon to "give the gays what they want." Cate knew everyone was counting down the months until her appearance. She shuddered to think what she would encounter walking into the firehouse on the first day of November. It was not the kind of legacy she had hoped for.

"How's the probie?" Cordell didn't look up.

"She'll be fine. Just shaken up."

"Understandable. Brutal one today." Cordell gestured with her pen. "Make sure she has the info for the department therapist."

"Absolutely."

For some reason, Cate's thoughts went back to the woman Josie was talking to outside the vacant store. She hoped that, wherever she had taken off to, she was riding carefully. The idea of her hurt sent Cate's stomach twisting into knots, even though she had no damn idea why. Before she could interrogate her reaction further, Cordell completed her paperwork and looked up, hitting Cate with a steely gaze. After a beat, her lips curled into a crooked smile.

"So, any update on the case of your missing coffee creamer?"

Cate huffed. Station Two's coffee came from an ancient, belching machine as old as the firehouse itself, and the only way to make that sludge palatable was decent creamer. Everyone else swore the coffee was fine, and the fact that the machine probably had never been cleaned added to its character. Cate had stopped arguing with them. If they all wanted to drink motor oil, that was their business, but the least they could do was leave her creamer alone. She'd even labeled it this time.

"No. Probably someone from B Shift. You know they never pay attention."

Cordell nodded. "Indeed. A full investigation is obviously warranted."

"Well, if my request for a new coffee machine had been included in the budget this past fiscal year, then we wouldn't have to monopolize resources on such an investigation." Cate straightened in her seat. "Ma'am."

Cordell snorted. "We don't have the money to buy a fresh pack of pencils, let alone a coffee machine." She rummaged through another huge stack on her desk, eventually coming up with a folded newspaper. She tossed it over to Cate and leaned back in her chair, putting her boots up on the desk with a loud *thump*. It was the latest edition of the *Mayville Reader*, the city's premier independent newspaper.

"What's this?"

"Marching orders from above. Apparently, you're good PR." Cordell clasped her hands behind her head. The crooked smile grew even more cockeyed, and Cate realized that she was in trouble.

"No."

"Yes."

Cate sighed. "Jamie, I—"

Cordell held up a hand. "With this latest round of budget talks, the department needs all the good press it can get. You know how this game is played. Enough people see the good work we do, the more public outrage at the lack of funding, the less likely the Common Council is going to vote for more cuts. It's the circle of life."

Cordell was right, as usual, but it didn't stop Cate's shoulders from slumping forward or a dull ache from building behind her eyes. "What do you need me to do?"

"This reporter is supposed to reach out to you to set up an interview." Cordell leaned forward and tapped the byline with her finger. "Nothing too intrusive. Just talk about life as a firefighter, what it's like working for the department, stuff like that. With your naturally sunny disposition, you should be fine."

Cate grumbled under her breath.

"It's a great opportunity to put in a plug for next month's benefit and the Butler Center." Cordell gave her a knowing look.

Cate cocked her head, her building irritation abruptly halted. She hadn't considered that. Maybe it wouldn't be so bad after all.

"Okay, I'll do it."

"Good." Cordell sat forward and slammed both boots to the ground, the long-suffering desk chair creaking in protest. "That's all I had. Make sure Salt does the bathrooms today."

"Yes, ma'am." Cate stood, but just before she turned, Cordell spoke one more time.

"Hey, did I see Josie working her magic across the street? Someone finally going to rent that store?"

Cate shrugged, trying to remain casual. It was harder than she realized. "Maybe."

CHAPTER TWO

Mayville curled around the banks of Lake Hinz, a small inland lake roughly fifteen miles in diameter. Parker zipped up the section of McChesney Road that ran along the lakeshore, revving her bike as she darted in and out of traffic. She'd always loved how quick and responsive the Sportster handled underneath her, and the sudden turns when the road dropped from four lanes into two were an absolute joy to navigate. She gunned the accelerator and darted past a slow-moving Subaru, ignoring the driver's aggrieved horn blast.

Rob lived on the north side of the lake with his wife, Meagan, and their son, Tyson. Their finished basement had more than enough room to accommodate Parker when she'd unexpectedly moved to town two months ago and needed a place to stay.

Parker pulled into the drive and killed the engine. Perching her helmet on the bike seat, she freed the case of Modelos strapped to the back. The loud clanking of bottles announced her presence as she shoved through the front door without knocking. She was met by a savory and familiar smell coming from the kitchen. Rob's specialty—green chili pulled pork. Her earlier annoyance at his texting evaporated.

"Auntie Parker!"

Tyson stood on a chair pulled up to the counter as he helped Meagan use the tortilladora to press homemade tortillas. A round-faced and eager five-year-old, he had brown skin like his mother and thick, curly black hair like his father. He'd also been blessed with Meagan's markedly sunnier disposition.

"What's up, squirt?" Parker ruffled his hair and greeted Meagan with a peck on the cheek.

Rob was at the stove, cooking the tortillas in a cast-iron pan. Parker pulled out three of the Modelos and shoved the rest into the fridge. Placing one at Meagan's elbow, she handed another to Rob. They slapped hands, then reached around to pound each other on the back. Rob quickly turned back to the tortillas.

"Hey," he said.

"Hey." Parker leaned against the kitchen table and sipped at her beer, watching the small family work in practiced efficiency. Tyson yelled in triumph every time he successfully muscled over the press, earning a song of praise from Meagan. Rob pointed at the skillet with his tongs, and Tyson dropped the tortilla in. A high five, then they would start the process over again.

She glanced away and found her thoughts drifting back to Cate. Christ, she was gorgeous. If she was that attractive from across the street and in a grainy newspaper photo, Parker couldn't begin to fathom how shattering Cate would be up close. Her apprehension about setting up shop on Tomlinson Street turned into a sudden thrill. Taking a chance on that odd storefront in an even odder neighborhood was now pretty appealing if she got to look at Cate on a regular basis.

Parker took a long swig of beer, forcing the excitement away. She thought about Sophia instead. Her chest tightened.

She did that occasionally—unearthed the wound and prodded at it to see how much it still hurt. The relationship had been a mistake; with the benefit of both time and geographic distance she could see that now, but she had been too caught up to realize she was drowning.

Mayville could be a fresh start. An opportunity. She'd fucked around long enough. Maybe if she kept herself focused on one thing, she wouldn't repeat those same mistakes.

No matter how many hot firefighters she encountered.

"Park? Hello?"

Parker blinked. Meagan was looking at her quizzically. Parker realized she was thinking about the stupid sexy way Cate had snapped her chair open with one hand.

"You checked out another location today, right?" Meagan asked. "How'd it go?"

Rob cut in before Parker could answer. "You finally listening to Josie?"

"I am." Parker's jaw tightened. "She showed me a shop on Tomlinson."

"Tomlinson? That's a weird neighborhood." Rob flipped a tortilla.

"Josie said it's up and coming, though. There's been a lot of new development in the area. It's primed to go off," Parker said, dutifully repeating the sales pitch from that afternoon.

"What block?" Meagan asked.

"One thousand."

"By the fire station?"

That same thrill ran through Parker again. She chugged more of her beer. "How did you know that?"

"Tyson has a field trip there in a couple of weeks. He hasn't stopped talking about it." Meagan looked down at Tyson, placing a guiding hand over his on the lever of the tortilladora.

"I'm gonna see the fire trucks!" he announced after successfully pressing the last of the tortillas.

"That'll be fun." Parker wondered if Cate would be leading the tour.

Rob snapped his tongs, like he suddenly remembered something. "Wait, are you talking about the vacant shop that used to be a pet store?"

Parker nodded. "Josie sent me the lease info. Will you look at it?"

"If you want. Still seems like an odd location to me."

Parker rolled her eyes. "First you get pissed when I don't listen to Josie, then you get pissed when I do listen to her. Make up your mind."

"I'm not pissed, it's just weird. I'm allowed to have an opinion."

"You have an opinion on most things I do."

Rob turned and opened his mouth but was met by Meagan shoving his son into his arms and ordering them both to wash up. She then spun on Parker and handed her a stack of plates and silverware.

"Let him be. He's in a mood." Meagan shooed her toward the open dining room, lips pursed.

Parker wanted to point out that her brother was always in a mood but decided against it. She went about setting the table. "What's going on?"

"Your dad called today."

Parker almost dropped the plates. "Seriously? What did he want?"

"Just to talk, apparently." Meagan was bristling with anger and doing a poor job of concealing it.

"Shit." Parker kept her eyes trained on the table as she arranged the place settings.

Meagan sighed in response. Rob came back into the kitchen, Tyson hanging upside down in his arms, both laughing madly. Parker forced a smile and sat down next to Tyson's seat. She made exaggerated faces at her nephew throughout dinner, grateful for the distraction provided by his squeals and giggles, which rose by at least one octave every time Parker pretended to steal a piece of tortilla from his plate.

After she had stuffed herself full of spicy pork and avocado and black beans, Parker helped Meagan clean up while Rob settled Tyson for bed. Meagan asked a few more questions about the store, but Parker demurred, her enthusiasm waning with each passing moment. Her stomach twisted when Rob finally reappeared. He grabbed two more beers and nodded at the patio door. Parker followed.

The early spring night was cool, the breeze off the lake enough to give Parker a chill. Even though their Cape Cod-style house was smaller than any of the other surrounding homes, the property still had direct lake access with a dock and a boat lift. A line of oak trees shaded the backyard, the largest of which cradled Tyson's treehouse, and a fair portion of the sprawling stone patio was dedicated entirely to Rob's grill. They sat next to each other in a matching set of Adirondack chairs, both looking out over dark water. City lights flickered from across the lake. Rob handed her a beer and leaned back in the chair with a sigh.

Parker took a long pull from the bottle, then started plucking at the corner of the label with a thumbnail. "So, what did Dad want?"

Rob's eyes flashed. "The usual. He bitched about Mom, went on and on about Skylar's grades. I'm guessing Charity wasn't around, so he didn't have his usual captive audience. Barely asked about Meagan or Tyson. But, of course, he wanted to know if we needed any money."

Parker grimaced at the mention of their half sister and stepmom. She hardly knew either of them. "What'd you say?"

"That we were fine, thank you." Rob downed half his beer in one go. "He also asked about you. He still doesn't get why you moved."

"Nice of him to inquire. Not like we saw each other that much when I lived out there, anyway."

Rob shrugged, looking out over the lake.

"Heard from Mom?" Parker asked.

"Nope."

They'd been raised in Chicago until their parents' divorce. Their father worked in finance and now managed a hedge fund worth an ungodly amount of money, which he threw at the children from his first marriage with impunity, probably because he felt guilty about cheating on their mother with Charity, his assistant at the time. When Parker was younger, she'd enjoyed the benefits of a rich daddy—an unlimited credit card came in handy while in college, especially when it came to impressing girls. Now, when she looked back on it, she felt nothing but shame. She wished that, instead of paying for everything without question, her dad would have made her work for it a little more. Or, even better, paid even the slightest bit of attention to her.

Parker looked over at Rob as he raked his fingers through his hair. She felt bad about her earlier jab about his receding hairline; his widow's peak was barely noticeable compared to the rest of his thick brown hair. He was eight years older than her and had done what he could to shield Parker from the fallout of their parents' separation. He looked the most like their father, with the same deep-set blue eyes and wide jaw, thick shoulders, and a broad chest. Parker always felt like nothing more than a wisp of a thing next to him. She had taken after their mother, Elizabeth.

They remained silent until Rob held out his hand. "Let me look at that lease."

Parker pulled up the documents and passed her phone over. She watched Rob's face as he read, the light of the screen illuminating the deep creases of his frown.

"It's all in order." He handed it back. "Josie got you a good deal."

"So you think I should go ahead?" Parker bit her lip. She had involved Rob from the outset as she developed her business plan, shoving articles and investment notes about the emerging sneaker market into his face until he finally admitted that it wasn't the worst idea she'd ever had. Her research and uncharacteristic thoroughness had also impressed him enough that he and Meagan agreed to cosign her business loan. Parker had refused to ask her father for the money.

"You really want to do this?" Rob asked.

Parker took a deep breath. "Yeah. I do."

Rob looked out over the lake again. This time, the silence irritated her, which she concealed behind a swallow of beer. She hadn't necessarily expected a full-throated endorsement, but a little enthusiasm would've been appreciated. Maybe he was reconsidering their entire arrangement. While Rob had always supported her, he hadn't necessarily approved of her decisions. Which was fair, to be honest. But at least she was trying.

She knew she shouldn't care so damn much. She was twenty-seven, for fuck's sake. She didn't need to go chasing her big brother for hugs anymore.

The thought struck her. A few years away from thirty and with nothing tangible to show for it.

Parker took back her silent apology about his hairline. "Your excitement is palpable."

"Sorry. It's been a long day." Rob dragged a hand down his face, and Parker knew she was being petty. Talking to their dad always killed his mood for the rest of the day, mostly because it just made him sad.

Parker twisted in the chair so that both of her feet were flat on the patio. Rob did the same. Their knees were almost touching. He reached out and placed a palm on her shoulder.

"Look, this is a big deal. You've never done something like this. *I've* never done something like this. I appreciate your ambition, but if you sign this lease, you're not only locking yourself in, but Meagan and me, too." He paused, brow furrowing. "You can't walk away this time. And you can't expect Dad to bail you out."

"I'm not expecting Dad to bail me out." Parker jerked away, almost dropping her beer. "I told you, I'm done taking money from him."

"I'm just—"

"I could've called him when Sophia dumped me. I could've asked for a security deposit, rent, all that shit. But I didn't. I'm here." Heat rose in Parker's face.

"I know, I know. I'm proud of you for that. I really am." He spoke kindly, but Parker couldn't help her irritation. "I'm glad that you want to do something substantial. We worry about you. You're smart and talented and you can do anything, but it's almost like you're afraid to succeed."

"Is this another lecture about not living up to my potential?"

"I'm not trying to lecture you. You just get so excited and make all these huge plans but don't exactly follow through." Rob gave her shoulder a squeeze, his smile gentle. "I mean, first it was business school, then art school, then back to business school, not counting those two months you were applying for Teach For America. Or that summer when you were convinced you could make it as a screenwriter. And the less said about that NFT thing, the better."

Parker pointed with her beer bottle. "*That* was a good idea."

"Oh, my God, no it *wasn't*."

Parker turned away, scrunching her nose. She knew Rob meant well, but she still hated when he recited every choice she'd made like he was building a résumé of failure on her behalf. At least he was kind enough not to mention Sophia.

She'd been living in LA, fully engrossed in her postcollege aimlessness, tending bar in West Hollywood. Sophia had breezed in like a vision, leading a pack of coworkers out to celebrate her recent promotion. When their eyes met, Parker had almost dropped the beer she was pouring. The attraction was intense, palpable, and immediately acted upon. Within weeks, Parker had moved in. The fact that almost everyone had told her it was a bad idea only strengthened her resolve, and through pride alone did Parker manage to convince herself it would work.

In the end, her excitement overrode common sense, which was a reoccurring theme in Parker's life. It turned out that Sophia's divorce was not as final as Parker had been led to believe. In fact, it didn't exist at all. Which she found out via text. In a parting act of generosity, Sophia had given her one full week to move out.

She started picking at the label on her beer. Rob never understood how much easier it had been for him, how everything had always been laid out in a clear path from one destination to the next. No one had passed such a map to her.

"I'm trying, Bobby, I really am." The nickname she used to call her brother when she was a little kid slipped out, as it did whenever she was feeling particularly vulnerable. Part of her hated that she lapsed into the old habit—like she needed another reason to feel small in front of him.

Rob gave her a gentle smile, his hand going from her shoulder to the back of her head and delivering an affectionate pat. He didn't mention the nickname. "I know. Just see it through, okay? All the way to the end."

Parker looked away from Rob, toward the dark lake and the twinkling city lights. Moonlight reflected off the smooth, black surface of the water. She let out a long sigh. "I will."

* * *

After she left Rob and Meagan's, Parker didn't go home. Instead, as she rounded one of McChesney Road's sharp bends, she clamped her brake and quickly downshifted, pulling the handlebars into a ninety-degree turn. The back wheel slid out from under her, but she stepped off the footrest and stuck out her leg for counterweight, then gunned the accelerator again and peeled off the road in a spray of dust and gravel.

Parker had discovered the concealed hiking path on one of her first rides around town. For some reason, it wasn't as well maintained as the rest of the paths around the lake, and as a consequence, it was also not as traveled. The path cut through a small cluster of trees and opened to reveal direct access to the water. She eased her bike down the path, engine rumbling in protest as she kept it in a lower gear than what it was used to.

When she emerged through the trees, she parked the bike on a patch of grass, taking a quick look around before she killed the headlight and removed her helmet. Typically, the spot was empty, but sometimes she encountered groups of teenagers smoking and drinking, or a lone wanderer staring out over the water. Tonight, she was alone.

The breeze kicked up as she reached the water's edge, and she huddled deeper into the varsity jacket. She started hopping from boulder to boulder across the breakwater, careful not to scuff her Jordans.

She fought the urge to run.

From a purely technical standpoint, there was nothing keeping her in Mayville. Yet. Her apartment lease was only month to month, and if she didn't open the store, she could pay back the loan. She could start over somewhere else. Maybe the East Coast or back in Chicago. She had no idea what she'd do when she got there, of course, but she would figure it out.

That would prove Rob right, though. But what if she fucked it up like she had damn near everything else?

A familiar, roiling anxiety built in her stomach and climbed up her chest. She continued to bounce across the rocks as the gentle waves splashed against the breakwater. The moon seemed bigger in the sky than it did at Rob's house, and it lit up the whole lake, moonlight dancing across a black canvas. Parker thought about the picture of Cate in the newspaper.

Before she could change her mind, Parker pulled out her phone and opened the attachments to Josie's email. Dry legalese zoomed by in a blur as she scrolled to the bottom and tapped to send her e-signature. An automated reply popped up instantly to confirm acceptance. Parker let out a long breath. Then she searched for the Mayville Fire Department's website.

Past the overview of the department's history and its community outreach programs was a section on that year's fundraising efforts. A bright graphic announced that tickets to the annual fire department charity ball were now on sale, and below that was a link to purchase the department's latest calendar they put out for charity. The proceeds that year were going to Butler Center, a local community center in danger of closing. Parker zoomed in on the calendar preview.

Fucking hell.

Smoldering dark eyes stared back at her. Cate posed in front of a bright-red truck with her arms crossed, baggy uniform pants slung low across trim hips, only the vaguest suggestion of a smile on her face. She wore a black sports bra, displaying shoulders carved from stone and lean, taut forearms. Her abs, like everything else, were perfectly sculpted. In block letters across the bottom of the photo was a simple caption: *Lieutenant Cate Wildman, Station Two.*

Parker nearly dropped her phone in the water. A few frantic taps later, the calendar was on its way to her. Express shipping. After all, it was for charity.

Parker shoved her phone into her pocket with a huff, as if the entire day had all been the device's fault. She looked out over the water, then made one more pass across the rocks and walked back to her bike.

CHAPTER THREE

"These aren't what I ordered." Jake's voice rose an octave.

Parker jammed the phone against her ear with her shoulder as she stepped around the piles of cardboard boxes, Bubble Wrap, and rolls of packing tape strewn at her feet. She juggled four pristine shoeboxes in her hands, each holding different rereleases of the Air Jordan Eleven— two limited-edition Concords from 2011, a 2001 Playoffs model, and a random 2015 low-top in a citrus color scheme she thought looked interesting. None of the sneakers had ever been out of their original boxes. Parker tried both to listen to the voice on the other line and set the shoes on the wire rack against the stockroom wall without tripping and busting her ass.

"Yeah they are, Jake."

"No, they aren't. I wanted highs. These are mids."

"If you wanted high-tops, then you should have ordered high-tops." Parker was only half listening, staring up at the rack that was filled nearly to the ceiling and already running numbers in her head. She could get over $400 each for the Concords, easy. Same for the Playoffs. Maybe she'd keep those lows for herself. They were pretty cool, actually.

"And that's exactly what I did. Check your messages." An affronted, dramatic huff came over the line. "What the hell, man?"

Parker rolled her eyes. She knew damn well if she went back through her messages, she would find the one Jake was talking about: abrupt, borderline rude, with a picture of a Jordan One in a black/yellow Bumblebee colorway. With a mid-ankle height. She remembered it specifically because not only was it an odd request, but the text had come through at two in the morning on a Wednesday. She'd been awake, but still.

"I got what you asked for. What do you want me to say?" Parker put him on speaker and flipped through her texts. A screenshot would shut him up. "Are you sure you sent me the right thing? It's hard to tell the difference between highs and mids sometimes." Her tone remained neutral, but the implication was there.

"I know the difference!" Jake squeaked. Parker held back a snicker. He always sounded like a squirrel when he got agitated. "You sure you didn't fuck something up?"

Parker's smile faded and she stopped scrolling. What a prick. New York Manni, one of the top resellers on the East Coast and a close friend, had warned her when she'd started doing business with Jake. He was annoying and entitled and didn't know half as much about the market as he claimed he did, but his industry contacts were legitimate. The rumor in her circle was that the reason Jake was so well-informed about new releases was because his mom was high up at Nike. She didn't know how much stock to put into that, but she couldn't deny that Jake's information was usually solid. And since Parker was on the verge of opening her own store, firm intel on the hottest drops was something she couldn't afford to throw away.

She found the text and took a screenshot but held off on sending it to him with a caption of expletives. She'd been right, of course. The differences between a high-top and a mid were obvious once you knew what features to look for. Jake hadn't paid attention, as usual. "No, I'm pretty sure I got it right," Parker said through gritted teeth.

"Hello? You there? I think you're cutting out."

"Dammit, hang on."

Parker stumbled out of the back stockroom, stepping over the assorted cardboard boxes and packing materials all over the floor, past the small desk overflowing with paperwork, and staggered into the front of her small shop where she got a stronger signal.

"Better?" She kicked at a piece of Bubble Wrap tangled around her ankle. When she looked up, she glanced through the glass front door to the fire station across the street. In lieu of the polite response any well-mannered adult would give, Jake started ranting. Actually, it was more like a tantrum, but Parker soon stopped listening.

She inched closer to the door, peering out at the station and its open bay doors. Alex sat outside in a lawn chair, as he had before when Parker had first spotted him, cheerfully talking to a woman who had ambled by with her dog. Sitting next to him was the biggest man Parker had ever seen, somehow wedged into the same kind of chair.

There was no sign of Cate.

The disappointment stung deeper than she cared to admit.

"…so I don't see why I have to—Hey, are you even listening?"

Parker snapped back to the droning still coming out of her phone. "I'm listening," she lied.

"Well, what am I supposed to do with six pairs of mids?"

"I don't know, Jake. Sell them? Like you were planning to do anyway?"

"I can't sell these without taking a huge hit, you know that."

Parker did know that, but her mind wandered back to Cate, imagining her in that tight MFD T-shirt. Or better yet, the picture from the calendar.

"Look, maybe I should call New York Manni," Jake continued. "They can help get this straightened out."

"No, don't call New York Manni." Parker took Jake off speaker and jammed her phone back to her ear. The last thing New York Manni was interested in was mediating a petty disagreement between her and Jake. Parker started pacing around the store, stepping over and around unorganized stacks of shoes, partially unpacked boxes of shelving, and a pile of metal pieces that was supposed to be a clothing rack. She'd get to assembling those. Eventually. "How about this. Why don't I cut you a deal on a couple of pairs of Infrareds and we'll be good?"

Jake paused. "How'd you get those?"

"Trade secret, my man. Yes or no?"

"How many pairs?"

"Two, maybe three. What's your size again? Ten?"

"Yeah. Ten." Another pause. "Okay, fine. Text me when you have them."

"I will." Parker affected an airy accent and performed a mock bow in the middle of the store, still pressing her phone to her ear. "Pleasure doing business with you, sir."

"Fuck off, Park."

She was still grinning after he hung up. What a douche. She headed back to the chaotic stockroom when her phone buzzed. It was a text from Josie, reminding her about their dinner plans tomorrow night. Parker frowned. She thought that was supposed to be the day *after* tomorrow.

Shit, what day *was* it? Her lease on the store had started on the first of May, and she'd been so caught up with getting everything up and running—and getting that goddamn smell out—that the days had flown by. A nagging, itchy feeling crawled up the back of her skull. Was there something she was supposed to do?

Parker pushed through the swinging door, stumbling over the mess of boxes to the small desk shoved in the corner, knocking over the stack of Air Force One Supremes she had just finished organizing. She rummaged through pricing history reports, design sketches, and copies of *Sneakerheadz Magazine*, almost spilling a half-full Starbucks cup before coming up with the to-do list she had scribbled out a week ago.

At the top, in all caps, she had written *FIRE INSPECTION!!* Beneath were additional notes, linked by arrows: *inspection → retail permit → insurance*. And beneath that, underlined twice, were the words *responsible business owner*.

Wait a minute.

Behind her came a knock, followed by the creak of the front door. A deep, rich voice echoed through the store.

"Hello?"

When she poked her head out of the stockroom, Parker's jaw almost dropped.

Oh shit.

She'd been right. In person, Lieutenant Cate Wildman was brain-meltingly attractive.

Cate stood in the center of the store holding a tablet in one hand, the other casually in her pocket. Instead of the T-shirt that Parker had been daydreaming about all afternoon, Cate wore a more formal, dark-navy button-up shirt with a Mayville Fire Department crest over the left chest pocket. Somehow, Cate made the standard unassuming uniform look like designer wear. The sleeves were rolled up to her elbows, displaying her lean forearms, and the top two buttons were undone, showing off the curve of her collarbones. Dark eyes once again pinned Parker in place.

"Um, hello," Parker managed to say.

A small furrow appeared between Cate's brows. She glanced around the store quickly before looking back at Parker. "I'm Lieutenant Wildman with Mayville Fire. I have a two o'clock appointment for a fire inspection with"—she consulted the tablet—"Parker Mandli. Would that be you?"

Willing her legs to move, Parker shoved aside another pile of boxes and stepped out of the stockroom. She brushed her palms down the front of her loose black T-shirt, realizing both the shirt and matching jeans were covered in dust. Her hair was probably a mess, too. Granted, her hair was always a mess, but she hoped it conveyed more of a rakishly disheveled vibe, as opposed to a haven't-showered-in-three-days kind of look.

She extended a hand and smiled, praying she didn't appear like someone who had completely forgotten about a very important appointment. "That's me. Good to meet you."

Cate's grip was firm, her hand warm. For some reason, that last part threw Parker. "Likewise." Cate looked around again. "Is now still a good time?"

It definitely *wasn't*, but Parker recalled the urgent arrows on her to-do list. "Absolutely!"

The furrow in Cate's forehead deepened. She stared at Parker for a moment, then flipped up her tablet and pulled out a stylus in one crisp move. "All right, then. This is a retail space, obviously?"

"Trying to be." Parker smiled, but Cate appeared oblivious, stabbing at the tablet with her stylus. For some god-awful reason, Parker kept talking. "I'm opening a shoe store. It'll be resale. Mostly Nikes. And I'll have some clothes and accessories, too." She jammed her hands into her pockets. "You know, basketball shoes."

Cate looked up. The corner of her mouth twitched. The gesture was nearly imperceptible. "I know what basketball shoes are."

"No, I know, I just meant…you know…" Parker's hand flailed as she completely forgot whatever point she was trying to make.

Cate made a noise in the back of her throat, a sort of exasperated grumble, and began walking around the store. Parker followed her gaze, almost choking when it landed on the candles burning in the far corner, hopefully warding off the stubborn stink of small mammals. The floors had been swept and mopped at least three times over, but the smell of pine shavings and musk still lingered. She hadn't thought twice about keeping them lit all afternoon, but that was before she'd invited a goddamn firefighter inside.

"Sorry about that," Parker said. "They're for the smell."

This was a poor time to realize that she had no idea what the hell went into a fire inspection. Maybe she should have rescheduled.

"Technically, burning candles in a retail space doesn't violate any ordinances." Cate wrinkled her nose. "I can't blame you, either. What *is* that?"

"Ferrets, I think."

Cate snorted. She continued her circle around what would eventually be the sales floor but was now almost as messy as the stockroom. Sections of wall paneling were piled in the center of the open room, next to stacks of display shelving and the all-white cash register stand, still waiting to be assembled. Several more piles of shoeboxes were scattered about. Cate crouched down to peer at an outlet in the far corner, and Parker pulled out her phone, distracting herself so she wouldn't be tempted to stare at Cate's ass.

She remembered her to-do list again. Responsible business owners did not ogle dedicated public servants while they tried to do their jobs.

"Those are nice."

Parker looked up from her phone. Cate was pointing her tablet at an open box of Jordan Sixes in a dark-purple-and-yellow Lakers colorway.

"You know sneakers?" Parker beamed.

"Not really." Cate quickly returned to her tablet. "I played basketball in college. A couple of girls on the team were very into their shoes. Always seemed a bit excessive to me."

Parker cocked her head. Was she being insulted? It didn't quite feel that way. Cate's frown deepened, and she was jabbing the tablet harder than she needed to. She probably wasn't very good at small talk. And, as Parker admired the way Cate filled out her uniform shirt, she also guessed Cate wasn't someone who gave in to excess.

"So did you play ball here?" Parker asked.

"Yes." They locked eyes for a moment, then Cate glanced away, craning her neck as she frowned at the sprinkler head above her.

Basketball made perfect sense, of course. She moved like an athlete and sure as hell had the height for it. Parker wondered how tall Cate actually was, or if the boots and uniform pants made her appear larger than life—all she had to do was stretch one arm overhead to reach the sprinkler with the corner of her tablet. She did the same to the emergency light in the back corner, nodding when the light flashed.

"Everything looks good up here. You have a back room?"

Parker led her to the swinging door, shoving past all the packaging material strewn on the floor. There was barely enough room for Cate to squeeze through. Her eyes got even darker at the sight of the boxes and packaging material that stretched the length of the back room. The cascading wave of debris stopped at the back door. Right above the door was a brightly lit sign that said *Fire Exit*.

Parker forced out a laugh. "I've been meaning to clean up back here."

Cate shook her head. "You can't block fire exits. And you definitely can't do it with combustible materials."

"Yep, got it."

Cate jabbed the tablet, checking something off. She turned to the storage rack lining the wall, crammed full of shoeboxes. She pointed to the top shelf. "Storage has to be maintained two feet from the ceiling in nonsprinklered areas of the building."

Parker looked up. Boxes filled the entire shelf in rows of at least three high, shoved so close to the ceiling only a sliver of light peeked through. She shot Cate a wide grin. "What, that's not two feet?"

"No." Another check. "And I would anchor the shelving to the wall if you're planning on keeping it this full." Cate nudged the corner of the rack with a single finger. It swayed precariously.

Parker sighed. "Anything else?"

Cate stepped around the cardboard and shoeboxes toward the back corner, where a fire extinguisher was strapped to the wall. After skimming the tag, she tugged it off the wall and checked the pressure, then put it back and made a note. She eyed the array of pipes that Parker now realized must belong to the sprinkler system, fingers grazing over a small gauge. Parker's throat suddenly became very dry. She grabbed her Starbucks cup off the desk and took a swallow of watered-down cold brew.

Apparently satisfied with the gauge, Cate stepped into the small alcove next to the fire exit and let out a low noise.

"What?" Without waiting for a reply, Parker wedged herself into the alcove, sidling up beside Cate. The space was too narrow for them both to stand shoulder to shoulder, and Parker twisted toward Cate as she edged in closer to see. Now standing chest to chest, their height difference was more apparent. Parker only came up to Cate's chin, allowing a full view of the sharp line of her jaw and the curve of her neck. Heat radiated off her body, and Parker's mind went blank. She caught the hint of a dark vanilla scent, mixed with smoke. All she'd have to do was lean forward ever so slightly and her lips would brush across Cate's skin.

Parker forced the thought away.

Cate cleared her throat. "Look." She pointed at the breaker. Was Parker imagining things, or had Cate's cheeks flushed pink?

The door to the breaker was hanging off its hinges at an awkward angle, lucky it hadn't broken off completely in Cate's hand. A thick layer of duct tape was slathered across half of the switches, anchoring them in the "on" position. It clearly wasn't the first time—underneath the tape was the fraying edges of older pieces stacked on top of one another like tree rings. A dusty cord ran out from behind the box that looked to be half-chewed off, the plug barely connected by a few thin wires. That cord led to another bundle of wires jammed into a square electrical box.

Most of them appeared to have been gnawed on as well. Farther back in the alcove, Parker spied what she assumed to be rodent droppings.

Cate let out a dry laugh. Her hand almost brushed Parker's hip. "You think those ferrets got out?"

The state of the breaker box and its adjacent wiring was enough to snap Parker out of her haze. "Fucking delightful." Parker wondered how this had slipped past Josie's review, but the storefront had sat unoccupied for so long it was possible this would have been missed. Or forgotten about completely.

"At least it's not snakes," Cate muttered to herself.

Parker jerked backward. "Snakes? Where?"

"No, it's just a dumb joke my partner said—"

Parker's brain didn't keep up. She shimmied away and spun around so quickly she tripped over another box. Cate's hand shot out and caught her arm before she fell backward into a sea of cardboard and Styrofoam. Parker looked into those dark eyes. They were hazel, she realized, with a smattering of gold flecks that seemed to glitter.

"Careful now." Cate pulled Parker closer, keeping her steady. Her grip was gentle but still firm enough to hint at the sheer muscle she possessed. "There's no snakes. But you might want to call an exterminator and make sure whatever was chewing on those wires is gone. And an electrician, obviously."

Parker nodded, throat dry again. Her ears started to burn. "Yeah, you're right. Thanks." She swallowed thickly. "I, um, think you can let me go now."

Cate blinked and looked down, like she hadn't realized her hand was still clasped around Parker's forearm. "Of course. Sorry."

Parker pulled away and rubbed the back of her neck, avoiding Cate's gaze. She *definitely* should have rescheduled this. Preferably after she'd cleaned up the store and had a shower and could mentally prepare herself for being in such close proximity to Cate Wildman. Seeing her across the street was one thing. Touching her was something else altogether.

Christ. She needed to get a grip.

"So what happens when you fail a fire inspection?" Parker asked, feeling more than a little defeated.

"You haven't failed yet." Cate picked her way through the boxes. Parker thought she heard a new tension in her voice. "I'm going to issue you a corrective order, not a citation. You'll have up to thirty days to fix everything on the order. Just clean up back here and have an electrician come in."

"A month? But I need to get my retail permit sooner than that."

"Let me know when you get it taken care of. I'll come back over and reinspect."

"Thanks. I really appreciate that."

"It's not a problem. We try to be as accommodating as possible to new business owners." Cate signed the bottom of the inspection form. "I'll email you the order for your records. Do you have a business card?"

Business cards. That's what she had scribbled into the corner of her to-do list. Right next to _responsible business owner._ Her handwriting had always been atrocious.

"They're, um, not here yet." Parker grabbed Cate's tablet and stylus and filled out the inspection form with her information.

Cate slid the stylus into her pocket when Parker finished. "You know where to find me." She took a step toward the swinging door then paused, hand hovering in midair. "It's only May, you know." Cate nodded at the overflowing desk.

Among the scattered papers and magazines, peeking out from underneath the stack of mail Parker had rummaged through earlier, was the Mayville Fire Department calendar, splayed open to the month of November. Cate's dark eyes stared up from the glossy spread.

Parker threw herself on top of the desk, flailing about in a desperate attempt to cover Cate's impossible abs and sculpted shoulders.

"I just was mapping out my lease payments!" Parker squeaked, face burning and no doubt as red as the fire engine Cate was standing in front of in that painfully distracting photo. As she frantically clawed through unpaid utility bills and last week's pricing trends, her hand knocked into the Starbucks cup, sending the remains of her cold brew crashing to the floor and splattering across the white toe of her Jordan Fives.

Cate took a step closer. "Let me—"

"I got it!" Parker fumbled for the roll of paper towels she had left under her desk. She kept her head down and mopped up the mess with fierce determination. If she was lucky, maybe a sinkhole would appear underneath the store and swallow her whole.

What the fuck? Between the less-than-successful inspection, tripping over her own damn feet, spilling her coffee, and getting caught with the calendar, Parker had reached a level of remarkable dumbassery. A mere twenty minutes in the presence of this woman had reduced her to an inarticulate, fumbling idiot. No one had ever done that to her before. Not even Sophia.

Cate waited only a beat. "I'll see myself out."

CHAPTER FOUR

The sound of shoes squeaking on hardwood and teenagers yelling greeted Cate when she entered the Butler Center. The full-size basketball court was a flurry of chaotic activity, with rowdy half-court games going on at each end. To Cate's left were the bleachers that were always filled with an assortment of middle and high schoolers, the mix of kids varying depending on the day and type of activities going on. Today was the typical after-school pickup games, which Cate had supervised at least twice a week for the past ten years. It was a tradition that was dangerously close to ending.

She hadn't even shrugged out of her jacket when an awkward, excitable seventh grader with limbs too long for his torso loped over to her and started complaining that another kid's team wouldn't give up the court. Cate sighed. This was a common occurrence. Arguments over court etiquette and house rules happened pretty much daily, depending on the group of kids present. The alliances and rivalries shifted too fast for Cate to keep up, but usually the grievances that dominated the court one week would burn themselves out the next. Such was the cycle of teen social drama.

Cate bit down on her lower lip and let out an ear-shattering whistle. The play on both half-courts stopped immediately, a sea of wide eyes looking in her direction. She cleared her throat. "We have a lot of players here today, so remember the rules. Your team has to sub out or split up after winning three in a row so everyone gets a chance to play. Understood?"

A half-hearted chorus of "Yes, Miss Cate" echoed through the gym. Satisfied, Cate whistled again, and play resumed. The seventh grader jogged over to court and slapped hands with another gangly boy, the offense quickly forgiven. Cate almost smiled at the sight.

She couldn't help but think of Anthony in moments like these. The gawkiness of preteens that had yet to grow into their bodies, bristling with raw potential. Most, if not all, would go on to play high school ball. She'd even seen a few kids get college scholarships. And if not, they would still have family and friends to build a life around. All chances Anthony never got.

Cate took up her usual position leaning against the wall next to the low bleachers, arms and ankles crossed. She didn't act in any sort of official capacity during the after-school games; mostly she let the kids call the fouls and figure it out on their own, unless she was specifically called in to mediate a dispute. Her years of volunteering had built up her credibility enough that often her mere presence alone was enough to defuse any arguments. By the time the kids got to high school, she'd been presiding over their games for several years. Her paramedic training came in handy as well—she had tended to dozens of twisted ankles and bruised knees. It also helped that despite two knee surgeries of her own, Cate still had a lightning-quick first step and could outshoot most anyone who walked into the rec center.

She shifted her weight against the wall, and as the games continued with no additional drama, her mind wandered. Soon she ended up back on the same subject she'd been stuck on for days now. It was, to put it mildly, getting annoying.

Cate wasn't quite sure what to make of Parker Mandli.

Yes, she could admit that Parker was cute. Maybe even charming, with soft gray eyes and that bright smile bordering on the edge of cocky. Stumbling around the storeroom with her wild hair and dusty pants, she was a skinny little bolt of energy that had struck Cate right in the chest. Usually, such extroversion made her skin crawl, but in Parker's case, it hadn't bothered her. In fact, maybe she had even found it a little appealing.

For what had to be the hundredth time, her brain replayed the moment in the alcove, Parker heedlessly wedging her way in so they were pressed against each other. Her face flushed at the memory. It was very, very distracting. Cate hated being distracted.

She let out an irritated huff, uncrossing then recrossing her arms. Parker had a flightiness about her that worried Cate a little, especially since she was starting a business. Not that it was Cate's place to worry. Or judge. She was only curious. And then there had been the whole thing with the calendar, which had been embarrassing. Cate only meant to mention the calendar as a joke—Alex kept telling her not to take it so seriously—but clearly it hadn't landed right. Parker's flustered reaction had been pretty endearing, though. Maybe she should bring her a fresh coffee when she went over to reinspect.

Which, Cate realized, she was hoping would be soon.

"Afternoon, Cate."

Her thoughts were interrupted by a gentle baritone voice. Jameel Simmons sidled up beside her, wearing a cheerful smile and clutching a cane. He was dressed impeccably, as usual, in a crisp dress shirt, pressed slacks, and two-toned wingtips, as if he hadn't spent the better part of three months in the hospital. Encouraged by the sight, Cate greeted him warmly, but her brow furrowed at the tremor in his hand and obvious fatigue after walking across the gym.

"I thought you weren't supposed to be back working yet." Cate eased him down onto the bleachers.

Jameel waved a hand. "Bah. What do they know?"

"A lot, I would assume. They're doctors."

He waved his hand again and crossed his wrists on top of his cane as he watched the games. He leaned over and gave her a nudge, keeping his voice low so that he couldn't be heard over the yelling and pounding on the court. "I got your message. I wanted to tell you before the committee meeting that the bank gave us a sixty-day extension."

Cate kept her eyes straight ahead. His quiet delivery of what should have been good news made her suspicious. "That's great, but what aren't you telling me?"

"Perceptive as always." Jameel exhaled. "It's worse than I thought. We owe eighty thousand dollars on the mortgage or the bank will start foreclosure proceedings."

Cate's jaw tightened. "What happened to sixty thousand?"

"Why, accrued interest, of course." A rare spike of bitterness edged into Jameel's tone.

Butler Center had been a stalwart presence on Mayville's south side for decades, but this year's state budget cuts slashed into the center's operating budget, and they failed to qualify for a grant from the school district. Amid the budget shortfall, Jameel, the longtime executive director, suffered a stroke last winter and was forced to step away from day-to-day operations. The leadership void created by Jameel's abrupt departure resulted in numerous communication breakdowns between the staff and an absentee board, and within months, Butler Center was in danger of closing permanently.

Cate was one of Butler Center's longest tenured volunteers and the first person Jameel confided in about how dire the financial situation truly was. She and several other volunteers immediately formed a group to start raising funds. Cate came up with the idea of pitching to the MFD's charity ball planning committee, and she'd given the presentation herself, arguing for the proceeds to be donated to the rec center. To her surprise, the committee had agreed. The charity ball was scheduled for the first weekend of June, which was now less than a month away.

Anger surged through her, directed at the inattentive, apathetic board members who'd let things get so bad. Jameel confessed to her in strict confidence the litany of work that had gone undone while he was hospitalized, including a fully completed grant application that, for reasons unknown, was never submitted. The money from that award alone would have easily funded the rec center for half of its fiscal year.

"We'll figure it out." Cate wished she felt as confident as she sounded. "I got some more donations for the silent auction. And ticket sales are steady."

Cate didn't tell him about the distinct lack of energy this year. Past donors seemed more enthusiastic with their support when it went directly to the Mayville Firefighters Foundation or the Humane Society, not a struggling community center in the least affluent part of town. Hopefully, the ball would still raise enough money to fend off foreclosure, but with this latest update, her hopes began fading.

"Thank you, Cate." Jameel gave her a fatherly pat on the shoulder. "I know how much effort you and everyone else has put into this, and I can't thank you enough."

Jameel lowered his hand, the unspoken words hanging in the air between them. Coming up with $60,000 was a stretch but still seemed obtainable. Adding another $20,000 to the tab felt insurmountable.

Another burst of anger coursed through her. Jameel was a man of faith and had always been sanguine about finding money to keep the rec center afloat, the calm in the storm while Cate and the other volunteers scrambled to call local politicians and scour the Internet for grant applications. Cate was hard-pressed to accept his cool, steady approach.

In her experience, there was no grand scheme, no higher power watching over them all. Things just happened, without consideration or fairness or worth. A drunk driver hits a minivan head-on and kills a family of four but walks away unscathed. An otherwise healthy middle-aged man drops dead from a heart attack while shoveling snow. A referendum fails to pass, cutting the school district's budget and dooming a neighborhood institution to permanent closure.

There were no lessons to be learned here. She had seen too much to believe otherwise.

Jameel patted her shoulder again and hauled himself up on shaky legs. "I need to speak with Chris. The plumbing in the boys' room is acting up again." Cate watched him shuffle away.

A tan blur entered her field of vision. Cate reached up and snatched the basketball out of midair before it crashed into some giggling teenagers sitting on the bleachers. She pivoted and sent a textbook chest pass back to Tasha, the girl who was chasing after it. She caught it cleanly, the force of pass making her take half a step back. She gave a quick nod in Cate's direction and ran off.

Cate's eyes roved over the court, as she had ever since college. Yes, there was no lesson here, but that didn't mean she couldn't do something about it.

Cate set her jaw. She couldn't afford any distractions now.

* * *

"Come on! Go go go!"

The squeal of kindergartners echoed through the firehouse, drifting out through the open bay door to Cate's seat near the sidewalk. Inside, the kids on the field trip swarmed the firepole, each clamoring for their chance to slide down. Alex managed the group with practiced efficiency, carefully helping each one grasp the pole and wrap their legs around it, then sending them down gently into Freddie's and Morgan's waiting arms. Crash pads were grouped around the bottom of the pole to cushion any too-sudden impacts. Three parents and the class's teacher stood off to the side and clapped every time one of the kids landed successfully.

Cate craned her neck to look into the firehouse, trying not to scowl. Not that she minded the frequent class trips Station Two hosted, it was just that sometimes kids reached a pitch she didn't think possible for humans to make. She'd led her fair share of station tours until Alex had shooed her away one afternoon years ago, when she bored a group of fifth graders to tears with her detailed lecture on the history of firepoles, and how actually they were not a common fixture in firehouses anymore because of updated safety codes, and that Station Two was the only firehouse in Mayville that still had one due to being grandfathered into the new city ordinance.

Alex took over permanently after that. Not that Cate minded; she was probably better off with the middle and high schoolers at Butler, where her awkwardness came off as cool. Kind of.

"That's cute."

Cate turned back to the perky woman sitting next to her, balancing a notebook on one knee and holding out an iPhone. All things being equal, she'd rather be hanging out with the kids.

"We get a lot of field trips," Cate said.

Sarah DeWitt's smile dropped for a moment, then quickly reappeared. Nothing seemed to dampen the journalist's sunny disposition, not even Cate's reticence. God, she hated stuff like this. Her time was better spent drafting donation emails or finalizing auction items for the charity ball. She'd better be able to wring a favor or two out of Cordell.

"We already covered the broad day-to-day responsibilities of a firefighter, but I'd like to get to know you personally a little better." Sarah made a note and then leaned forward with her phone. "Let's start with that house fire in March. Can you tell me what was going through your mind while you were searching for that family?"

Cate squirmed in her seat. The red motorcycle was parked across the street, but she'd spent most of the morning pretending not to notice. "I needed to get them out."

"Uh-huh. I see you've received several department commendations, including a Distinguished Service medal."

"Yes, that's true."

"Can you tell me a little more about that?"

"Well." Cate paused. "I was honored to receive them."

Sighing, Sarah paused the recording app on her phone. "You know, these profiles go a lot easier when the subject of said profile answers in more than two sentences."

Cate's mouth was already twisting into a frown, and she fought to keep her expression neutral. "I'm sorry. I'm really not good at this."

"This isn't really my thing, either." Sarah moved closer, like she was about to confess something. "I prefer the investigative beat, not fluff pieces. But my editor gave me this assignment, and here I am. So maybe we can both get through this as painlessly as possible?"

Cate chuckled in spite of herself. "That's fair. I just hate talking about myself."

"What *do* you like talking about?"

This was the opening she needed. Cate thought back to Cordell's earlier suggestion, and Jameel's news yesterday. The update about Butler's finances had been delivered matter-of-factly but hit her like a freight train, even though she managed to hide her concern. The ball proceeds could have maybe—maybe—hit the original $60,000 goal. But not $80,000.

"I don't know if you're aware, but every year the department holds a firefighter's ball, and the proceeds are donated to a local charity or nonprofit organization." Cate recrossed her legs, keeping her hands tightly folded in her lap. "The beneficiary this year is Butler Center, and I've been pretty involved in planning the event. Alongside the official planning committee, of course."

"Okay, great." Sarah made another note, clearly grateful that the conversation was gaining steam. "Let's talk about that."

Cate gave a rundown of the rec center's history and emphasized the numerous programs Butler ran, from basketball leagues and the after-school activities, to the community outreach initiatives and career coaching offered to juniors and seniors in high school. She explained how the funding cuts and Jameel's illness had resulted in the center being on the cusp of foreclosure, and—perhaps a little too sharply— commented on the lack of enthusiasm for this year's ball compared to last year's. If it were up to her, she'd hunt down every prior sponsor that had ducked them and hang them upside down until their wallets fell out.

Sarah laughed. "Really?"

"Yes. I was told that was a bad idea."

The kindergarten class spilled out onto the station's driveway. They all clutched matching workbooks containing fire safety information for home and coloring pages full of engines and equipment. In the middle of that pack was a particularly excited dark-haired boy who screamed in triumph at his new coloring book. She'd noticed him before when the class had arrived. He belonged to one of the dads chaperoning the trip, who nodded encouragingly as the overeager kid ran over and began spouting all the new facts he had learned about firefighters.

Cate frowned. Something in the man's eyes or the way he smiled was familiar, even though Cate was certain she'd never seen him before. He took his son's hand and started texting with the other while the kids clustered around the sidewalk and continued bombarding Alex and Morgan with questions.

Seconds later, Parker burst out of the shop.

Cate watched Parker bound across the street, not giving the slightest consideration of the potential of oncoming traffic. A brightly colored T-shirt hung off her slight frame, and tight jeans were slung low on her hips, sporting what Cate assumed were strategically fashionable holes in the knees. Her sneakers were an obnoxious clash of yellow, green, and orange that somehow got even louder the closer she came. Messy, short-cropped chestnut hair was tousled in the breeze.

She was adorable.

"Do you know her?"

Sarah's question snapped her back to reality. "Yes. I mean—no. Not really," Cate answered too quickly. "She's renting the store across the street. She moved in a few days ago."

Thirteen days, to be exact, but it wasn't like Cate was tracking that closely.

Sarah raised an eyebrow. "I'm glad it's finally being rented. I heard that some landlords were deliberately keeping properties vacant for the tax breaks."

"Huh. Really."

Parker stopped midstride and looked right at Cate, eyes wide like the first time they'd seen each other across the street. After a wave and a tight smile, she turned her back to Cate and plopped herself down on the ground in front of the dark-haired boy. He squealed yet again and tore open his workbook, showing off the pictures inside.

Sarah was still speaking. "I talked to my editor about it. I'm convinced it's a story, especially with the city's budget issues…"

Cate tried to listen but kept glancing over to Parker and the boy. Clearly they were related. Whatever genes that passed between them were strong enough for there to be a strong resemblance in all three, although the boy had a darker skin tone.

Parker continued to chat happily with the boy, their excited chirping blending in with the rest of the chattering kindergartners. While they spoke, the man dashed across the street and went into the store. He emerged less than a minute after and rejoined the class.

Parker popped to her feet when he approached. Cate thought she saw a new line of tension running through Parker's shoulders. They talked quietly, but the expression on the man's face changed. Where before he had seemed cheerful and engaged with his son, with Parker he became much more serious. He nodded a few times at what Parker was saying, then ended the interaction with a shrug, patting Parker on the shoulder before he turned away to walk with the other chaperones leading the children back to school.

Parker ran a hand through her hair. She jammed her fists into her pockets, her jeans sinking even lower on her hips, and hung her head. Cate wondered what their conversation had been about, her gaze lingering on Parker's back as she returned to the store, her gait much more subdued on the return trip.

"Lieutenant?"

Cate stiffened, back now ramrod straight in the chair. She looked at the journalist. "Yes. I'm sorry."

"Don't be. I tend to ramble." Sarah waved her hand with a smile. "I have a few more questions, and then we can wrap it up."

"Sounds good."

Cate tightened her hands in her lap, knuckles white, as she imagined brushing Parker's hair off her forehead.

CHAPTER FIVE

Parker yanked on the heavy door to Crystal's and followed Josie into the dimly lit bar. She paused as she crossed the threshold, giving her eyes a chance to adjust and her brain an extra second to process the soft, squishy feeling underneath her feet. She looked down at her Jordan Four Off-Whites, horrified.

"Is. This. Bar. *Carpeted?*"

"Yes." Josie didn't bother looking at her to answer, eyes eagerly sweeping the interior. They'd gone out together a few times, and every time they entered a new establishment, Josie needed to make an appraisal of the crowd before venturing forth. When they first met, Parker had assumed she was nothing more than a typical real estate shark, always moving and circling her nearest prey, but Parker soon realized that Josie was genuinely the most outgoing person she'd ever met. Josie was the only person Parker knew who was disappointed if after a night out she hadn't run into anyone she knew.

Tonight, Josie was introducing her to Crystal's infamous Thursday night karaoke. Several weeks ago, Josie had mentioned in passing that this was a favorite spot of Station Two's firefighters, which made sense given its proximity to the station, and Parker tucked that little piece of knowledge away for future reference. Not that she intended to use said knowledge for any particular purpose. However, if she happened to be enjoying a drink after work and a group of firefighters (or a certain firefighter) happened to also come in, well, she couldn't be faulted for the coincidence. Striking up a friendly conversation was certainly not off-limits. Parker had accepted Josie's invitation earlier in the week without hesitation.

But that was before her fire inspection and the Terrible, Awful, No Good, Very Bad Calendar Incident. It had also been before Tyson's field trip to the fire station and Parker's Not At All Obvious Attempt at ignoring Cate completely. Yet, despite all that, Parker couldn't bring herself to cancel. Josie was the first real friend she'd made since moving to Mayville and had gone out of her way to help with Parker's business and make her feel at home. When Parker called Josie after the fire inspection (once she'd cleaned up the coffee and stopped hyperventilating), Josie sprang into action, reaming out the landlord on Parker's behalf and even negotiating an additional three-month rent abatement for the inconvenience.

Parker had never experienced such instant kindness and concern from someone. The idea of bailing last minute didn't sit well with her. She still had some sliver of pride, wounded as it may be. Canceling felt like an admission she'd done something wrong. It wasn't her fault that Cate and her ridiculous abs decided to pose for the damn thing, was it? What was she supposed to do, *not* look?

Parker raised her foot off the floor and grimaced. She shouldn't have worn the Off-Whites. Shit, she'd be better off in waterproof combat boots. "Seriously? This is nasty, Josephine."

Josie tossed a look over her shoulder. "It's fine as long as you don't spill anything."

Parker made a face.

"Why don't you get us some drinks? I need to talk to someone real quick." Josie waved at a couple tucked into a corner booth near where the karaoke proprietor was setting up his equipment. "I'll have a martini. Belvedere. Extra dirty."

"Uh, I don't think this is the kind of place that does martinis." Parker looked around skeptically, but Josie was already walking away, waving a hand over her shoulder.

"Tell Renee you're with me. She'll take care of us."

Parker sighed. This was certainly a different scene than the craft cocktail bar they had gone to last week, or the brand-new sushi restaurant the week before. Over the course of their short friendship, Parker had learned to trust Josie when it came to selecting the better spots in town, so she relented and stepped farther into the dingy bar, scrunching her nose at the spongy floor.

A clutter of worn tables and chairs were grouped haphazardly in the center of the room, and a row of booths lined the wall across from the bar. Thick orange extension cords ran up the cheap wood paneling and across the exposed cross beams of the ceiling. A series of mechanic lights dangled from the cords like a half-assed renovation project.

The bar itself looked as worn as the rest of the building, accented by a line of stools. Most of them sported matching splotches of duct tape which only partially concealed the tears in the vinyl. Tucked away in the back corner was pool table with a low-hanging stained glass chandelier helpfully labeled *Billiards*.

Clustered at the end of the bar were the same firefighters who'd been hanging around the station—Alex and the larger man she'd seen outside on the day of her inspection. His barstool looked far too small. Two women were shooting pool, and Parker guessed they were also from the fire station, judging by the more serious one's MFD ball cap tugged low over her eyes.

No sign of Cate. Relief and disappointment mingled in her chest.

She eased up to the bar. The bartender, who Parker assumed must be Renee, planted herself in front of Parker, arms crossed, and raised an impatient eyebrow.

"Can I get that ale on tap? And a Belvedere martini, extra dirty." When the eyebrow arched even higher, Parker quickly added, "It's for Josie."

Renee rolled her eyes but didn't say anything. She poured Parker's beer first, then began digging around behind the bar. After peering behind several shelves, she stomped off in a huff, apparently to find the top-shelf vodka. In Parker's opinion, the place was lucky to have any shelves at all.

Her eyes trailed over the wood paneling framing the bar, covered in Mayville Fire Department memorabilia and framed newspaper clippings. Dusty trophies from various sports leagues took up a small ledge. Next to an ancient, tarnished plaque commemorating an achievement that was no longer readable was a flyer advertising the MFD's annual charity ball. And next to that…was the calendar.

Parker took a hasty gulp of beer. Guess she'd avoid Crystal's during all of November. Easy.

"Hey, don't I know you?"

Alex had turned to look at her, wearing a broad smile. The bigger man peered over the top of Alex's head.

"Not really." Parker buried her face in her beer. Shit, was this one of those townie bars where everyone knew each other and someone had to vouch for you and your entire family tree or they'd charge twice as much? While the firefighters seemed friendly, the bartender definitely *hadn't* been, so Parker didn't know what the hell to think.

"Yeah, you're renting the old pet shop, right? You were with Josie the other day?" Alex jabbed his companion with an elbow. "Wilds did her inspection."

Wilds. Even her nickname was hot.

Parker grinned weakly. "That'd be me."

"Welcome to the neighborhood. Come on, we'll buy you a round." The massive firefighter waved her over with a hand the size of a grizzly bear's paw. His voice rumbled like a gravel pit. When Parker approached, he took her hand and nearly wrenched her shoulder out of its socket.

After introductions, Alex asked, "How'd the inspection go?" He was almost obnoxiously cheerful. Kind of like a golden retriever. Parker liked him immediately.

"It went fine."

"Really?" Freddie asked. He and Alex exchanged glances. By the pool table, Parker heard the crack of a cue ball, then a loud curse. One of the women looked especially despondent.

"I guess I sort of failed?" Parker grimaced. "But I can fix it, so no big deal really."

Freddie rolled his eyes. "She's a real hard-ass sometimes. Don't take it personally."

Alex nodded in solemn agreement.

Parker swallowed more of her beer. "What's up with that, by the way? This place looks like a serial killer's garage, but I get in trouble because I stacked a shoebox too goddamn high."

Alex and Freddie both laughed in unison. Parker grinned back, but the moment was interrupted.

"It's above code. Barely."

Parker turned.

Cate stood with her arms crossed, staring at Parker expectantly. She was dressed in tight black jeans and a deep V-neck Henley with the sleeves pushed up to her elbows. Parker couldn't stop her eyes from trailing over the curve of Cate's collarbone and settling on the hollow of her throat, where a small pendant hung from a thin gold chain. Cate gestured at the stool Parker was leaning over. A black leather jacket was draped over the torn seat. "Do you mind?"

"What? Oh. Sorry." Parker stepped aside, forcing herself not to stare as Cate gracefully slid in to reclaim her seat.

"Damn, Wilds, didn't you cut her any slack?" Alex gave Cate a nudge and nodded in Parker's direction.

"It was just a corrective order. She can get a reinspection." Cate paused. "Besides, you should have seen that back room."

Parker puffed out her chest. She still had a point about the dilapidated bar. "And when you come back, everything will be in compliance with state statute chapter 101.14 and Mayville general ordinance 34.307."

Cate leaned back and raised a brow. She looked at Parker the same way she had in the store—not judgmental per se, but coolly appraising. Whatever silent evaluation she was conducting, Parker hoped she passed.

"You've been studying."

"My brother's a lawyer. Really obnoxious about it, too."

"I see." Something flickered in Cate's eyes. "I think I saw him with you the other day."

"Yeah, he took the afternoon off to go on the field trip with my nephew. He hadn't seen the store yet." Parker put her beer down and started playing with the edge of a damp cocktail napkin. Rob was still skeptical, and seeing the actual location had reassured him a little but not to the extent that Parker had hoped. It was probably the smell. Damn ferrets.

"Your nephew is cute. Loud, but cute." Cate drained the rest of her drink and idly circled the rim of the glass with a fingertip, the tendons in her hand flexing.

Parker silently chastised herself for staring at Cate's hand. "Tyson doesn't believe anything is worth saying unless he can scream it at the top of his lungs."

Renee reappeared, depositing Josie's martini at Parker's elbow, along with a fresh beer even though Parker was only halfway through her first. The firefighters' drinks were all replenished as well, and before Parker could say thanks Renee was already at the other end of the bar, favoring another group of customers with her disinterest.

"Um. So." The cocktail napkin was mostly shredded. Parker's hand went to her pint glass. "I wanted to apologize. About the calendar. I didn't mean to make it weird or anything."

Cate sipped her whiskey. Neat. Then, surprisingly, she placed both forearms on the edge of the bar and dropped her head, letting out a defeated sigh. "No, that's not your fault at all. It was a poor joke. I just—" Cate looked over at her. "It's everywhere."

Parker inched closer, brows furrowing. "Why'd you do it, then?"

"That bastard talked me into it." Cate hitched a thumb over her shoulder. Parker wasn't sure if she meant Alex or Freddie, but the descriptor probably could apply to either. The begrudging tone in Cate's voice suggested she was only half serious. It made her seem more approachable, and for a moment Parker was able to forget their awkwardness around the calendar entirely. "There's never been enough women featured."

"I applaud your commitment to diversity." Parker tipped her pint glass at Cate and took a drink.

Cate snorted. "Thank you. It's been a thrill. My crew gets a whole year to plan all the ways they're going to embarrass me for a month."

"No one said being the face of an entire department was easy," Parker said solemnly, as if she were the authority on such matters.

Cate snorted again, although this time it sounded more like a cut-off laugh. Her eyes were still dark and shadowed, but her mouth twitched again. Maybe there was a hint of amusement in Cate's expression. "That picture is airbrushed all to hell. It doesn't even look like me."

Parker feigned shock. "You mean you *don't* have an eight-pack?"

"Hardly."

I doubt that. Parker bit her tongue but couldn't stop her eyes from trailing downward, admiring the way the simple Henley hugged Cate's midsection. She brushed at an imaginary speck on her pants then took a sip of beer, hoping the gesture appeared more causal than it felt. She really, really needed to stop thinking so much about Cate's abs. And her hands. Especially right in front of her.

Parker switched tacks, not wanting to stop talking but physically unable to continue with the subject of Cate with no shirt on. "It's all in the name of charity, though, right?"

At that, Cate seemed to brighten. As much as she was capable of, anyway. "Yes. Exactly. I should thank you for buying it."

Parker pointed at the flyer she'd seen earlier. "What's this Butler Center place?"

"It's a community center on the south side of town. I'm a volunteer coordinator there."

"No shit?" Parker plopped her elbows on the bar and leaned in closer. "What's that like? How's the fundraising going?"

Clearly this was the right subject to bring up. Parker finished her beer while Cate told her all about the center, the fundraising efforts, and all the work she'd been putting in with the department planning committee for the ball. When she was done, a sheepish look crossed her face, and she took a healthy swallow of whiskey. Parker couldn't help but notice the flush in Cate's cheeks.

"I'm sorry it hasn't been going as well as you hoped," Parker said.

"I appreciate that. There's still time, though." Cate finished her drink without so much as a flinch and pushed it away. "I think."

Parker offered her a smile. "You'll do it."

Dark eyes caught Parker in their gaze. Parker remembered how those eyes had reflected the warm afternoon sun, and despite the ill-lit bar they were both trapped in, she was almost certain she saw a flash of heat behind hazel irises.

A burst of swearing from the back corner pulled Parker's attention away from Cate. The combat at the pool table had ceased, and the smaller woman with a blond ponytail collapsed onto a stool next to Freddie, complaining loudly.

"Oh my God, I just got my ass kicked."

Freddie placed a comforting hand on her back. "What did we tell you was the first rule of firefighting, probie? Never play—"

"—pool with Captain Cordell. I know."

"Don't worry," Alex said. "She'll let you win your money back next week."

Cordell ambled over, tugging the ball cap lower over her eyes, and threw two twenties onto the bar. "Drinks are on Morgan tonight," she said with a wink. "You kids have fun." A smattering of goodbyes trailed down the bar as she headed to the exit.

"The captain always leaves before the singing starts." Alex leaned over, almost ending up in Cate's lap.

Cate shoved him back onto his seat with an irritated grumble. Parker went for her second beer, concealing her smile behind the pint glass. In the far corner of the bar, diagonally from the pool table, a man in a full suit and tie finished setting up a karaoke machine, flicking on a cheap plastic disco ball. A line already formed at the table. Parker hadn't noticed how quickly the bar had filled up. Two men sidled up next to her to order from Renee, forcing Parker to move closer to Cate. She thought she heard a sharp inhale come from Cate but quickly told herself she imagined it.

Freddie leaned forward and caught Cate's eye. He jerked his head toward the karaoke machine and its purveyor. "Wilds, your favorite diva is here."

Cate groaned.

"Who's that now?" Parker spun around and leaned her back against the bar, hooking her heel on the footrail. The position brought her another inch closer to Cate. Neither of them moved away.

Freddie pointed to a nondescript man in jeans and a white T-shirt waiting to put his name in. "The guy over there with the ball cap on."

"He seems harmless enough," Parker said.

"He always comes for eighties night," Freddie continued. "And he does have a pretty good voice. Unfortunately, he only sings songs with female leads."

Parker cocked her head. That didn't seem to be a problem. "Okay…?"

"Let's just say that he has the spirit, but not the range."

Alex chimed in. "And our dear lieutenant here has the musical taste of someone fifteen years older and is, shall we say, an aficionado—"

"Snob," Freddie corrected.

"—when it comes to eighties power ballads. She doesn't take kindly to someone mangling Pat Benatar."

"Or Heart."

"Or Roxette."

Freddie reached over, placed his massive palm on the bar for emphasis, and looked directly into Parker's face. "You should have seen it when he tried to do 'Gloria.' She was nearly apoplectic."

Parker laughed, her eyes drawn to Cate's profile. Cate's jaw tightened, another flush working up her sharply angled cheekbones. With Cate sitting and Parker standing, their height difference wasn't so pronounced, but it reminded Parker of that moment in the alcove. It was too easy to imagine leaning forward and brushing her lips against Cate's cheek. She glanced away.

Cate tried to defend herself. "I only think that nothing is worth doing—"

"—unless you do it right," Alex and Freddie finished in unison, bolting straight upright on their stools and snapping off crisp salutes.

"Go to hell," Cate muttered.

Warmth blossomed in Parker's chest, both at Cate's discomfort and the obvious affection behind Alex's and Freddie's teasing. Cate didn't seem like someone who would enjoy cheesy eighties music, but her apparent high standards for karaoke singing struck Parker as being on point. She also didn't mind watching the stoic firefighter squirm a little bit. Despite her tough exterior, Cate seemed to embarrass easily, and her coworkers acted like they knew it.

"Get up there and show him how it's done, Lieutenant." Parker pointed at the spinning disco ball and grinned. She leaned against the bar, the second beer going to her head already.

Cate stiffened. "Absolutely not."

"She just judges everyone," Alex said.

"Exactly." She winced. "I suppose that makes me an asshole."

"Yes," Parker said.

The rest of the firefighters burst out laughing. Cate didn't acknowledge them, though. She took a long, thoughtful sip of whiskey, looking Parker up and down. Parker was positive she saw heat blooming in Cate's dark eyes. Cate licked her lips and turned away, raising her chin.

"Those shoes are ridiculous."

Parker slid closer. Cate shot her a look out of the corner of her eye, a silent challenge. Right as Parker was about to speak, someone edged in between them.

"Sorry, sorry!" Josie appeared out of nowhere, sliding up to the bar to scoop up her martini. Cate turned her head and started talking to Alex.

"I needed to talk to them about—oh no." Josie glanced at the karaoke station, then pursed her lips. "I hope he doesn't try to do 'Gloria' again."

The firefighters all murmured in agreement. Parker let out a shaky breath and didn't say anything.

* * *

It didn't take that long before Parker understood why, despite appearances, Crystal's was one of the best bars in town. The drinks were cheap, the food was better than it had any right to be, and the crowd was cheerful and energetic, no doubt due to the abundance of said cheap drinks. But alcohol or no, there was an earnestness that permeated the entire bar, a distinct lack of pretention that often overwhelmed Parker whenever she went out in LA. Everyone seemed like they were there to enjoy themselves in the purest sense of the term. It was unexpected and, frankly, pretty refreshing.

The man running the karaoke night also contributed to the positive atmosphere. He acted more like an MC than anything else, pumping the crowd up between songs and jumping in with backing vocals whenever the performance was lagging or to gently steer an overenthusiastic singer back on track. Parker noticed he also didn't appear to go in exact order of submission. Instead, he shuffled songs around to match the mood of the room, making sure there weren't too many ballads or slower selections grouped together. And no matter the song, everyone sang along and clapped for each performer.

Her second beer was going down easily, and the anxiety that had clung to her since moving to town unclenched its grip. It had everything to do with the alcohol, of course, but Parker welcomed the respite. She finally stopped worrying about the store, the inspection, her insurance, her father, Rob. Instead, she sang loudly and clapped so hard her palms stung. She cheered Alex and Josie's duet and argued with Freddie over whether *NSYNC or Backstreet Boys had the superior catalog. It was the most fun she'd had in months.

Cate, too, seemed to loosen up, even though she didn't say much. Parker noticed the stiffness in her neck and shoulders ebb, that hint of a smile playing on the corners of her mouth as the boy band debate became more animated. Parker wondered if Cate ever smiled fully, and if so, what it took to make that happen.

Alex let out a warning, and Parker saw the man with the ball cap holding the mic. Parker jokingly planted herself in front of Cate as the opening of the song began to play. It sounded like the theme from *Top Gun*—or was it *Pretty Woman*? Parker wasn't sure, but either way, Cate was already grinding her teeth.

"Please, everyone stay calm." Parker held up both hands, palms out. "It will be over soon."

Cate rolled her eyes, but then caught Parker's gaze. Now Parker was sure she hadn't imagined the heat that had been there earlier. Her heart leapt into her throat.

She excused herself and wove through the crowd toward the restroom. On her way back, spurred on by the look in Cate's eyes and a fair amount of liquid courage, she stopped at the karaoke machine. Parker wasn't a gifted singer by any means but knew that if she didn't stray too far outside her limited range, she wouldn't totally embarrass herself. She reached for a scrap of paper, then paused.

Sophia had disagreed with her on that. They had mostly spent time with Sophia's friends, and one of the last times they'd all gone out, it'd been to one of those upscale karaoke places frequented by *American Idol* finalists. She had a great time, clapping and singing along despite her limited skills, and hadn't thought much about it at all until later when Sophia told her in no uncertain terms that she had made an ass of herself. Parker shot back a shitty comment about how uptight she was. That was start of one of their most explosive fights, and while the makeup sex had been just as explosive, it wasn't enough to plaster over the deepening cracks in their relationship.

Fuck it. Sophia wasn't here. Neither were her cadre of vapid friends. Parker scribbled out an artist and a song and slipped it over to the MC, along with a twenty. He looked at her in surprise. Parker winked.

Josie's eyes narrowed when Parker returned to the bar. Despite the energetic duet with Alex and her second martini, she appeared as put together as she had when they first arrived. She had also been fixing Parker with a knowing look for most of the night.

"What are you up to?" Josie asked.

"Nothing." Parker bounced lightly on her toes. She tried to stop herself from glancing in Cate's direction but failed. Cate had moved to the other end of the bar and was locked in an intense conversation with Morgan, holding both hands in front of her at different angles to demonstrate something presumably related to firefighting. Parker polished off her beer.

Josie leaned in and went right for the jugular. "She's single, you know."

If Parker hadn't finished drinking mere seconds ago, she would have choked. "Jesus, Josie."

"I am merely offering you a piece of information you may or may not find relevant." Josie shrugged. "Especially since you're not being very subtle."

"I don't think that's a good idea."

"Really? Because from what I can tell, Cate's not being very subtle either."

Parker ran a hand through her hair. She'd never been good at subtle. Her chest tightened as she pictured Sophia again. Not only had she been hurt when they broke up, but the embarrassment at having to walk back a very public decision clung to her months later. Her judgment had completely abandoned her when it came to Sophia, and Parker was still staggered by how poorly she'd gauged everything. She thought she could read people better than that. Or, hell, at least realize when someone was lying about being in love.

"I just…I don't think dating is in the cards for me." She still hadn't told Josie about Sophia.

"Oh, come on. You're not *that* busy with the store." When Parker didn't answer right away, Josie paused. "I'm going to guess this has something to do with how you ended up sleeping in Rob's basement."

Parker forced herself to smile. "Women, am I right?"

Josie's brown eyes softened. "If you ever want to talk about it, I'll listen."

Before Parker could respond, the MC called her name. Alex's head popped up like an eager groundhog, and he jabbed Freddie with his elbow. Josie put down her drink and clapped with the rest of the bar. Cate stopped in midsentence, hands still in the air, eyes wide. When Parker took the mic, she realized the shot of tequila she'd taken between beers one and two was about to kick her in the ass, but it was too late to turn back now. As with most things she did, sheer enthusiasm would have to make up for any lack of skill.

"I'd like to dedicate this one to the Mayville Fire Department." Parker pointed to the back of the bar. The crowd erupted in cheers. Both Alex and Freddie pounded on the bar top and raised their glasses. The signature sound of an eighties drum machine boomed through the speakers, followed by a pulsating bass line.

Freddie's massive form rose over the crowd as he cupped his hands to his face and let out a whoop. An ear-piercing whistle followed. The rest of the crowd soon caught on, a ripple of laughter snaking its way through the bar when everyone realized the irony of her dedication. Parker didn't know that much eighties music in general, but luckily her mom was a huge Madonna fan, and both she and Rob had been indoctrinated with Madge's entire catalog. One of her early club hits was the perfect choice, even if it was a bit on the nose.

There wasn't much room to maneuver in front of the karaoke station, but Parker broke out into a smooth little shuffle as she sang the verse. Two blondes at the table right in front of her—who had earlier been responsible for a sloppy yet entertaining performance of a Bon Jovi song—danced in their seats and made eyes at her while she sang. Parker played along for a few lines but looked away when she hit the chorus, belting out that she was burning up, burning up for Station Two's love.

Dark, flashing eyes caught hers for half a breath before melting away into the crowd. Parker threw herself into the rest of her performance, feeling freer and more unrestrained with each cheer. As the synths faded away, she ended on a neat, Michael Jackson-esque spin and brought the house down.

The MC took back the mic. "Give it up for Parker, causing a commotion with that absolute banger! And since she brought it up, now's a good time to mention the MFD's annual charity ball. This year's proceeds go to Butler Center on the south side. See Renee at the bar for more details. I promise, she's not as mean as she looks." After even more applause, he announced the next singer.

Screeching guitars followed Parker as she made her way back to her group. Freddie accosted her as soon as she came into view, throwing a meaty arm around her shoulders. She grunted and sagged under the weight. It was like a tree trunk had fallen across her back.

"We're keeping this one, Josie," Freddie proclaimed, hugging Parker's neck so hard he nearly pulled her off her feet. "David is going to *love* her."

Josie did a half curtsy. "I'll take that as a compliment."

Parker laughed and peered out from under Freddie's forearm. Cate was standing and easing into her leather jacket.

"You're leaving?" Parker asked, spinning out of Freddie's grip.

Cate pressed her lips together. "I have to be at Butler early tomorrow."

"Oh." Parker bit down on her bottom lip, hard. She pulled out her phone to check the time. Almost eleven. She realized she hadn't looked at it all night, and not only had she lost track of time, but a litany of unread notifications also screamed up at her.

Cate nodded over Parker's shoulder. A full glass of water waited on the edge of the bar. "I'll see you around."

"Yeah, totally."

With a small wave, Cate disappeared into the crowd. Parker gratefully reached for the water.

An ache formed deep in her chest, but Parker shoved it aside. Cate's departure was a good thing, she decided. Beer and tequila had weakened her resolve, and now any temptation was removed. For perhaps the first time in her adult life, Parker had a plan, and she was going to stick to it. A plan that Cate was not a part of, no matter how attractive she was. They'd had a good time tonight, and that's where it would end.

Alex and Freddie exchanged glances, Morgan having replaced Parker under Freddie's arm. All three shrugged in unison. Josie swirled the olive around in her glass.

"One more round?" Alex suggested.

A new singer had come to the mic, and suddenly the booming drum intro to "Gloria" filled the bar.

Parker smiled. "One more."

CHAPTER SIX

The chill from an unusually bitter winter still clung to the mid-May night. Cate didn't mind the cold in the slightest, letting out a sigh of relief as cool air brushed against the flushed skin of her neck. She told herself that the bar had just been crowded, more so than typical for a Thursday, and that was why she was overheated and agitated. Nothing to do with the pointed looks Alex and Freddie kept sending her way, or how Josie took every opportunity to surreptitiously elbow her in the ribs. And it certainly had nothing to do with Parker's inescapable, inexhaustible presence.

Cate paused at the corner, inhaling crisp air deep into her lungs while she waited for the light to change, even though there was no traffic on either side of the intersection. She jammed her fists into the pockets of her leather jacket and forced herself to stop thinking about Parker.

Her last significant relationship had been over two years ago. Melissa. A solemn, blond accountant. Their similar personalities had meshed perfectly at first, but the unforgiving reality of dating a firefighter soon made itself known, as it often did. Melissa tried to be patient with the overbearing schedule and dangerous calls, yet she was never comfortable with the inherent demands and chaos of Cate's life. Admittedly, Cate had done little to assuage her anxieties. The breaking point came when

Cate started devoting all her free time to studying for the lieutenant's exam. She remembered Melissa's tears of frustration as she packed up the last remnants of her belongings from Cate's townhouse. When the door closed behind her, Cate felt nothing but relief.

Cate had thought little about dating since then. Sure, she missed sex on occasion, but it often came with conflicts and expectations she didn't have time to negotiate. Anyone she dated seriously would have to come to terms with the job she had committed to and everything that came with it, including the specter of serious injury. Or worse. The woman willing to do that would be someone special, to be sure, but Cate was certain they would eventually find a reason to leave. That's what usually happened, anyway. Better to be on her own and spare herself the pain. She'd already had her fill.

When the light changed, she crossed, headed up Peterson Street toward her townhouse three blocks away. To her right, she could glimpse the dark second story of the firehouse rising over the top of the surrounding houses. A clear view of Parker's shop was over her shoulder. She turned, looking across the quiet street, and froze.

Like the rest of the surrounding neighborhood, the storefront was dark, but inside the building thin beams of light bounced sporadically, like someone waving around a flashlight or cell phone. The light caught against the front window. Broken glass sparkled in the night. A shadow stepped through the window, clutching several boxes under their arm. They turned and gestured impatiently. A second figure emerged, holding a few boxes of their own.

Cate was moving before the thought even formed in her mind. In two full strides she was barreling down the sidewalk like a freight train, arms and legs pumping in perfect rhythm. She barked out a warning as she crossed the intersection.

"Oh shit!"

The second thief dropped their boxes, shoes dumping out onto the sidewalk, and took off down Tomlinson, their companion following closely behind.

The bright lights from the gas station up ahead spilled into the street, the only business still open on the east side of the street. The thieves ran toward the light, their oversized hoodies and jeans coming into view. Just before they reached the parking lot, they split up, each veering off at opposite ninety-degree angles so quickly Cate couldn't catch a glimpse of either of their faces. The one on the left darted across the street without looking, the other disappeared between two small houses. Chest heaving, Cate came to a stop and clasped her hands on top of her head, letting out a long, dissatisfied hiss through clenched teeth. Her boots slowed her down. If she had her running shoes, she would've caught them both.

She turned back the way she came, dreading what needed to happen next. She loathed the idea of walking back into Crystal's and reporting what she'd seen, not only because it was sure to ruin Parker's night, but because she hadn't been able to stop it.

Cate was halfway down the block before she noticed the small figure standing right outside the shoe store, staring with their mouth agape. She recognized Parker immediately. She opened her mouth to call out, but before she had a chance, Parker ducked through the shattered window, heedless of the jagged edges. Cate upped her pace.

Parker flipped on the lights, placing the extent of the ransacking on full display. The store was in shambles. Display shoes lay in a jumbled heap before the slatted wall. The cash register stand had been tipped over, the corner cracked from where it impacted the floor. Shoeboxes and tissue were strewn everywhere, covered in bits of glass. On the floor next to the window was a brick.

Parker paced the length of her destroyed shop, head whipping back and forth, eyes wild. Her sneakers crunched over the broken glass. "What the hell?"

"I saw two kids breaking in and chased them down the block," Cate explained, still a little out of breath. "I hope they didn't take too much. If I had left a few minutes earlier, I might've stopped them. I'm sorry." Even though it wasn't her fault, Cate found herself apologizing anyway. A familiar piece of her reared its head and sent out a plume of guilt, reflexively chastising herself at not having done more.

Parker didn't appear to have heard a single word Cate said. Her pacing increased, her movements erratic. She stopped suddenly, clutched at the back of her head, and spun all the way around, nearly tangling her feet together as she surveyed the damage with growing horror, then scrubbed at her face as if trying to will away the sight. Words tumbled out of her mouth so fast Cate could barely keep up.

"Fuck. Fuckfuckityfuckfuckfuuuuck." Parker pressed a hand to her forehead, the other holding her phone. A blinking alarm app filled the display. "The soft opening is supposed to be next week. What am I supposed to do now?" Parker's breathing turned shallow, and she took a strangled gulp of air. Sweat broke out across her brow. She continued to pace.

Cate could diagnose the beginnings of a panic attack from miles away—she'd seen more than she could possibly count while treating people on calls. She closed the space between them, planting herself right in Parker's path, and carefully placed her palm on Parker's shoulder.

"Breathe, okay? Just breathe." Cate had to duck her head to find Parker's eyes, and when she did, she kept their gazes locked. Parker's shoulder trembled under her hand, the heat of her skin radiating through the thin material of her baggy long-sleeved T-shirt.

Parker nodded. She closed her eyes and inhaled deeply. Once, twice. When she opened her eyes, she'd stopped trembling. Cate kept her hand on Parker's shoulder.

"Are the police on their way?" she asked.

Parker raised her phone. "My alarm has an app. I was outside on a call when it went off."

"Okay. Easy enough. They'll file a report, and you can give a copy to your insurance."

"Insurance." Parker's entire torso sagged, and she let out a groan. "My policy isn't in place yet because I don't have a permit, which I don't have because of that fire inspection. I knew I was going to screw this up somehow. I fucking knew it."

Sadness laced through Parker's words, a stark contrast to the fun, easygoing personality on display at the bar. Cate wondered what could have happened that colored Parker's opinion of herself in such a way. An urge rose in her to argue the point, but she really didn't know what to say. Words always failed her in moments like these. She tightened her grip on Parker's shoulder in what she hoped was a reassuring gesture.

"You'll figure it out, okay?" Cate said softly.

Parker's eyes widened, almost comically so, and for a moment Cate was struck by the expressiveness of her face. She doubted Parker could conceal her emotions if her life depended on it.

Parker sniffed and looked around the wrecked store. "Yeah. Okay."

A squad car pulled up a few moments later, the red lights dancing off the shards of glass at their feet. The police officer was young, probably only in his first or second year on the force. He was polite and attentive, taking detailed statements from both Parker and Cate, even though the odds of catching the people responsible were slim to none without any surveillance footage and only Cate's vague description to go by. However, he did promise to file a report right away for insurance reasons and to investigate thoroughly, departing with a jaunty tip of his ball cap.

When he left, Parker raked both of her hands through her hair, still looking lost. Then, like she had just remembered something, she darted though the stockroom door. Cate followed.

The stockroom had received the brunt of the destruction. The shelving was pulled down and shoeboxes had been dumped onto the floor in massive heaps. Sneakers spilled out everywhere in chaotic bursts of color—bright shades of red and green and yellow and blue shimmered before her like a kaleidoscope. Cate's anger at the thieves returned at full force. This would take hours to clean up. And for what? From what she could tell, they'd only gotten away with a few pairs.

Parker was in the far corner of the stockroom by the fire exit, frantically rummaging through the nearest pile, boxes and tissue paper flying over her shoulder. She came up with an unmarked box and flipped it open. Her shoulders slumped in obvious relief. Parker leaned back against the fire exit and sank down to the floor, surrounded by ransacked shoes.

Remembering her first trip to Parker's stockroom, Cate picked her way over carefully, making sure not to step on or further damage any of the sneakers. She sat down next to Parker.

The shoebox was on Parker's lap. It looked like most others tossed about the room—brown cardboard adorned with a single swoosh on top—and the shoes inside were perhaps the most boring thing Cate had seen in the entire store, only a simple navy-blue high-top with white soles. Yet Parker was staring at them like she had unearthed buried treasure.

"What are those?" Cate asked.

Parker removed one of the shoes with the tips of her fingers, holding it up for Cate to examine. She could see now that blue top was made of suede, with elaborate stitching along the sides.

"These," Parker said slowly, "are the ultimate grails."

"Grails?"

"Like the Holy Grail. Something that you want but is incredibly hard to get."

Cate took the sneaker from Parker, touching it gently like it was as ancient an artifact as Parker implied. As she turned them over, Cate couldn't see what made this pair seem so special.

"What's the story?"

A shy grin crossed Parker's face. "You are holding the limited-edition Air Eleven Retros, released last year to commemorate Cooper Alexander's retirement from the Yankees. There were only five made, and they were only available through a secret pop-up shop in New York City."

"Only five?" Cate arched a brow. "How'd you get one?"

"My friend New York Manni is plugged into the industry. They get intel on all the biggest releases. They texted me the day before the shoes were supposed to drop. I took a red-eye from LA to New York on a Wednesday night, then headed right from the airport to the store. I bought the third pair. Celebrated with Manni until about midnight and then hopped a flight back. Didn't even pack a change of clothes." Parker's grin turned a bit sheepish. "My girlfriend at the time was pretty pissed. Worth it, though."

Cate's brain zeroed in both on the word *girlfriend* and the past tense in which it had been used. She stopped herself from asking more about it and quietly filed the information away, telling herself that Parker's relationship status was of no concern to her. "Your friend's name is New York Manni?"

"How else are we supposed to tell them apart from Boston Manni?"

Cate couldn't argue with the logic. "So how much is a holy grail Air Twelve limited-edition Cooper Alexander retirement shoe worth?"

"Air Elevens," Parker corrected gently, then thought for a moment. "Right now, I could get fifty thousand for them. Maybe more at auction."

Cate threw the sneaker back at Parker like it had burned her. "Fifty *thousand?*"

Unbothered by Cate's reaction, Parker repacked the sneakers and set the box down. "How much is the *Mona Lisa* worth?"

"You are not seriously comparing basketball shoes to the world's most famous piece of art."

"Why not? I bet you more people know who Michael Jordan is than Leonardo da Vinci." Parker's eyes flashed, and she sat up straighter. "It's all about context. Someone dribbles paint all over a canvas, and it sells for a million dollars. Why not sneakers? There's so much more to it than people realize. The designer, the collaboration, the materials, the technology—it all matters."

Parker pointed at an overturned box and the pair of red running shoes tumbling out of it. "Those are Nike's first collaboration with a Dutch artist widely considered the next Keith Haring. There were only two hundred fifty-eight of them made in that colorway with the multicolored sole. And those"—Cate watched Parker's slender hand sweep across the stockroom and come to rest on another pair—"were designed for the employees at NASA's Jet Propulsion Lab. The uppers are made of the same material used for the airbags on the Mars Exploration Rover missions. Right next to that one is a rerelease of Sheryl Swoopes's shoe. She was the first woman athlete ever to have a signature shoe line. And those over there are regular Nike Cortezes. You can get them anywhere.

It's not just about the flex. It's about trying to capture that moment in time when objects are created, and how those objects take on value. How they last."

Parker dropped her hand and scrubbed the back of her neck, eyes shyly downcast. "Sorry. I'm sure that's more than you wanted to hear."

Cate didn't notice the tightness in her throat until she tried to speak. "Don't apologize for being passionate about something." *Passion* seemed like too dangerous a word to use, even if it was accurate. Cate hadn't been able to tear her eyes off Parker the entire time she was talking.

Parker turned her head, looking up at Cate through her eyelashes. Her grin returned. "It's kind of my thing. I've been flipping sneakers for years on Instagram and Twitter, and I started a website last fall. This store was supposed to be—" She stopped herself, teeth sinking into her lower lip. The defeated tone returned. "Fucking hell. What a mess."

Cate's eyes drifted to Parker's profile. Her strong jaw was offset by full lips that seemed to be perpetually quirked into a playful grin, and lush eyelashes brought an edge of femininity to her androgynous presentation. The contrast of her features was undeniably alluring. Cate glanced away before she was caught staring.

Parker's head fell back against the wall with a thud. She drew her legs up to her chest, bony knees sticking out of torn jeans, and quietly surveyed the mess. She shivered.

"I'm sorry I didn't stop them sooner," Cate said softly.

"It's not your fault." Gray eyes met her own, dark like thunderclouds but gentler than any storm Cate had ever experienced. "I'm glad you came by when you did. It could have been a lot worse. Thank you." The corner of her mouth twitched, her irrepressible grin making yet another appearance despite the circumstances. "I suppose I should be glad I chased you out of the bar with my awful singing."

Cate hadn't realized her eyes had flicked down to Parker's lips, and she had to force her gaze upward before responding. "You weren't *that* bad."

"From you, I'm going to take that as a compliment."

Cate chuckled and leaned her own head against the wall. She thought Parker had sounded quite good, actually, and her theatrics had more than made up for any lack of technical skill. Cate swallowed.

She hadn't lied; she did need to be at Butler early tomorrow, although she hadn't meant to leave so abruptly. But when Parker had found her in the crowd while she sang, wearing the same smile she was giving Cate now, an alarm inside her tripped. Suddenly, the bar had closed in on her and she felt hot and claustrophobic, and she needed to escape into the cool night.

That alarm was still ringing within her. A match had been struck and was hovering over a pool of accelerant, flames poised to be unleashed if she didn't get on a line and douse them immediately. And yet, she didn't move from her spot next to Parker on the floor.

Knees still pulled to her chin, Parker shifted onto one hip to reach for her phone. Her shoulder leaned into Cate. A jolt raced down her spine at the contact. Cate felt a shiver ripple through Parker as well and guessed that she was cold. They were sitting on unforgiving concrete, and a draft snaked in from the gap between the fire exit and the floor. The hole in the front window of the store didn't help, either. Although Parker was in long sleeves, the shirt looked woefully thin and was about a size and a half too large.

Cate shrugged out of her leather jacket and passed it over. "Here."

"I don't—"

"You're freezing. Take it."

The jacket was also too big and hung off Parker's slender frame, but she somehow still made it look stylish. She huddled into it, frowning at her phone. "It's Josie. What do I even tell her?" She dipped her chin to brush against the collar of the jacket.

It was a subtle gesture, barely nothing, yet it sent an ache through Cate that she couldn't explain. She remembered the interaction outside the firehouse between Parker and her brother, the way her shoulders fell and how she had dejectedly trudged back across the street after he left. That same crestfallen look had been on her face when she discovered the damage to her store. An urge to protectively wrap her arms around Parker came over her.

The alarm drowned out everything else in her head.

She stood and held out a hand, pulling Parker to her feet. "Tell Josie the truth. And have her ask the crew to come over."

"Why? For what?"

"We're going to get this place cleaned up."

"You don't have to do that. I know you have somewhere to be—"

"Don't. This will take forever by yourself. And you can't leave here without doing something about that window."

"Um, okay." Parker's brow furrowed, like she wasn't sure how exactly Cate was going to solve that problem. She finished the text, then started snapping pictures. As she turned on her heel, something glinted on the top of her head.

Cate caught Parker's upper arm. "Hold on. There's something in your hair."

Her height advantage gave Cate a clear view of the glass shard caught in the swirl of Parker's cowlick. Parker stepped closer and bent her head obediently as Cate plucked it from the thatch of messy brown hair.

"Just can't help being heroic, huh?"

Cate tossed the glass away with a grunt. It was her only response, mostly because she had lost the ability to speak. Gray eyes looked up at her, peering out from under those long eyelashes. Cate put her hands on her hips and hooked her fingers into her belt, not trusting herself to stop from reaching out and running her fingers through Parker's hair. The air hummed in the space between them.

"Parker? Cate?" Josie peeked around the swinging door, mouth dropped open in shock. Behind her were Alex, Freddie, and Morgan, all equally aghast at the sight. Cate couldn't help feeling a healthy burst of pride. She knew they'd show up.

"What happened?" Josie's voice had risen an octave.

"Couple of kids broke in," Parker said. "Cate stopped them before they could steal too much. They mostly trashed the place."

"Nice timing, Wilds," Freddie said. In the far corner, Morgan kicked ineffectually at a piece of tissue paper and declared the perpetrators "motherfuckers."

"Lucky me." Cate turned to Alex. "Is all that plywood still at the house? Those big pieces we used to build that—"

"For the window drills, I know." Alex scratched his chin. "I think so. The nail gun should still be over there, too."

"Think you and Freddie can board up that window?"

Alex didn't hesitate. "On it." He grabbed Morgan's shoulder and shoved her out the front door. Within minutes they were walking back across the street with the plywood and the nail gun. The three firefighters attacked the broken window with gusto. Through her usual magic, Josie conjured up a broom and dustpan, and she and Parker started cleaning up the broken glass. Cate retreated to the back room to stack shoeboxes as best she could, at least creating some small amount of order within the chaos. Parker would have to reorganize it to her standards, but it was a start. She eyed the Coopers as she worked, making sure they remained untouched while she methodically moved through the back room.

After about thirty minutes, the store was in a much better condition and safe to leave for the evening: the window boarded up, the mess in the front cleaned, the shelves in the back room pushed back up against the wall, and a path cut through the stacks of shoeboxes for easy access.

"This is incredible. Seriously. I can't thank you all enough." Parker spun around to survey their work, eyes as wide and disbelieving as when she had first entered the store. Parker rubbed the back of her neck as she spoke.

Damn, she looked really good in that jacket.

"Like I told Josie earlier—we're keeping you." Freddie slapped her back with a dinner plate-sized palm, sending Parker staggering forward one full step. "You're part of the neighborhood now."

"Yep," Alex chimed in. "The group on B Shift caught a nasty job earlier, so most of them were sacked out. I can guarantee they all would've been over here in a heartbeat if they'd heard something."

Parker nodded, captivated by a spot on the far wall. Cate watched the muscles of her throat work as she swallowed. She swiped at her cheek and smiled back at them, her gaze passing over everyone except Cate.

"I appreciate that." Still keeping her eyes trained away from Cate, she began shrugging out of the borrowed jacket.

"Keep it." Cate raised her hand. "I'll get it back from you later."

Finally, the soft gray eyes cast her way. Another nod, and Parker wordlessly slipped it back over her shoulders.

"Well." Alex clapped his hands together. "I think we all deserve another drink after this. Anyone up for a nightcap? I'll buy."

Freddie checked his watch and groaned. "I would, but David and I are watching our niece tomorrow. I need some decent sleep if I'm going to make it through *Encanto* for the eleventy-billionth time."

"I think I'm done, too," Parker said. "Thanks, though."

"Hang on," Josie said to Alex, then looked at Parker. "Are you okay to get home? Can we call a ride for you?"

"I'm good. I got my bike."

"You sure?"

"Yeah. I could use the ride to clear my head. I'll probably take the long way, around the lake."

Something inside Cate's chest clenched, just like the first time she had seen Parker ride off on her motorcycle. She pushed the feeling aside. Parker's preferred mode of transportation was her own business, no matter Cate's personal distaste. Cate shouldn't care about any of that, really. She shouldn't care if Parker was out riding late at night, or how well Parker wore her jacket, or how charming Parker's smile was. Or exactly how far in the past that ex-girlfriend resided.

Except, as she followed Parker out of the store, she realized she very much did care.

Quick goodbyes were exchanged on the sidewalk, and her friends scattered for the night: Freddie down the block toward his pickup, Alex and Morgan and Josie practically skipping back to Crystal's. Their almost-competent a cappella rendition of "We Don't Talk About Bruno" echoed down the otherwise quiet street.

Parker zipped the jacket up to her throat and shuffled her weight back and forth. She tapped her motorcycle helmet against one restless thigh. "Thank you. Again. I'll bring your jacket by the station tomorrow, if that's okay."

"I don't work again until Saturday."

"Oh, sure. Saturday, then."

"Sounds good."

Although it was her favorite jacket, Cate didn't mind waiting an extra day or so before getting it back. Not that she needed it anyway. Despite the cool night, her neck and arms felt flushed, like her body's internal temperature had risen by several degrees. She took a step back, putting some space between her and Parker.

"I'll be seeing you." In one smooth motion, Parker swung her leg over the bike and kick-started it.

"Parker?" Cate raised her voice over the rumble of the motorcycle's engine. The cracked, strained tone that came out of her mouth was completely unfamiliar.

Parker looked over her shoulder, slowly raising her eyes to Cate's face. "Yeah?"

"Be careful."

Parker gazed at her for two full heartbeats. Then a sunny, lopsided grin flashed across her face. "Always." She slipped on her helmet and took off, her headlight beam cutting through the oblong shadows cast down Tomlinson Street.

Cate watched until the bike passed under the farthest streetlamp and disappeared from view. She turned and started to walk home, her skin still flushed in the night air, impervious to the chill. A hot, glowing ember of something she did not want to acknowledge smoldered within her. She locked it away and kept walking.

CHAPTER SEVEN

"Wait, what happened?"

Parker grumbled. She shifted Tyson's weight on her lap and picked up a crayon, adding gentle shading to his drawing of the next-door neighbor's burly dog. Rob stared at her from across the kitchen table. He leaned back in his chair, one arm slung over the backrest while the other stretched across the table. In his hand was a sweaty tumbler filled with ice and bourbon. Clear blue eyes stared at her, unwavering. He looked the most like their mother in these moments, wearing a look of exasperation Parker was all too familiar with.

She didn't answer right away and focused on Tyson's frenetic scribbling, assisting as best she could in morphing the dog into the dinosaur he had decided to go with instead. Besides, Rob had damn well heard her the first time.

"It's really not that big of a deal." Parker frowned as she worked on the hybrid creature's tail. "Just some kids fu—screwing around." She glanced down at Tyson, who was too involved in his monstrous creation to care about the bad word she'd almost used.

Rob sipped his cocktail. "What did they make off with? Anything valuable?"

"That was the worst part!" Parker threw up her hands, nearly losing grip of the crayon. "They didn't even know what to look for. All they did was trash my store and steal some Air Force Ones you can get at the mall. Damn kids."

"Not the Coopers?" Rob still eyed her.

"No. Thank God." The deceptively nondescript sneakers were tucked away in the far back corner of her stockroom. She took a sip of her own drink and shuddered. Rob made great cocktails, but they were always a hair too strong for her.

Rob rolled another crayon in her direction. "I guess you dodged a bullet, then. Insurance will cover the damages to the window, right?"

Parker stiffened and picked up the crayon. The dog-slash-dinosaur grotesquery needed deep red eyes.

She'd really hoped to avoid this part. For the briefest of moments, she thought she had a shot at getting a new pane of glass installed before the end of the weekend and wouldn't have to mention it at all, but the rep from the company she called to get an estimate said they needed to special order a replacement. Shortly after that, Rob invited her over for cocktails and a Hong Kong action movie marathon. She was sore and exhausted from cleaning up the store all day but couldn't refuse a night of drinking Rob's expensive bourbon and Michelle Yeoh kicking the shit out of people.

Plus, it would also distract her from thinking about Cate.

Her entire body still felt like it was buzzing. The sharp turn of events had left her reeling, but she realized that it had more to do with Cate than the store. Parker couldn't quite get a read on her. Every time Parker thought they'd made a connection at the bar, Cate had pulled away, yet she jumped in to stop the robbery and helped clean up without a second thought. Parker kept returning to that quiet moment in the back room where they sat and talked, and when Cate had reached out with sure, gentle fingers and plucked the glass from her hair, Parker was positive something shifted between them.

Last night, wrapped up in Cate's jacket, she'd taken a long ride around the lake to clear her head, telling herself it was nothing. When she got home, though, she almost couldn't take the jacket off. It just smelled too damn good. The richness of the leather mingled with a mellow spice was an unfair combination on its own, but beneath those layers was an intoxicating hint of smoke. Parker was relieved that Rob gave her a reason to leave her apartment, otherwise she would've spent all night wondering if that was what Cate's skin smelled like and how it would feel to bury her face in Cate's neck and find out.

She turned her attention back to Rob, who was staring at her expectantly. Dealing with his reaction sounded a lot better than trying to unravel what had happened between herself and Cate. Rob was a known quantity. Cate was elusive. Rushing headlong into something was a complete recipe for disaster—at least, that had always been the result in Parker's experience. The mess with Sophia was proof enough of that.

"No, insurance isn't covering any of it. There's been, um, a delay in setting up coverage."

This time, instead of sipping, Rob knocked back a mouthful of liquor that would have made Parker choke. "So, you don't have insurance. At all." Rob leaned back in his chair and pinched the bridge of his nose. "Parker…"

"It's fine. I got it."

"How is it fine—"

"Hey, no fighting." Tyson twisted around in Parker's lap to look up at her, then over at his dad. Parker hugged his tiny waist and kissed his cheek.

"You're right, squirt. No fighting." Parker shot Rob a look over the top of Tyson's head. He glared right back. Parker loved her nephew dearly, but she also wasn't above weaponizing his presence if it defused an argument.

Rob looked at Tyson. "Five more minutes, bud, and then off to bed. Okay?"

Tyson nodded and handed Parker a different colored crayon. "Can you make the teeth bigger?"

"Sure." Parker didn't know of any dogs or dinosaurs that had purple teeth, but she went with it anyway, drawing a pair of elaborate fangs as she continued, "I ran into an issue with my fire inspection. There are a few things that need fixed before my retail permit is approved. Which I need for my insurance. I already got someone out today to give me an estimate on the damage. So, it's fine."

Rob scratched the stubble on his chin, like he hadn't expected such a measured response. "And how are you going to pay for a new window?"

"I'm not asking Dad, if that's what you mean."

Rob's eyes softened, a wounded look crossing his face. "That's not what I meant."

Parker stopped coloring long enough to take another sip of her drink. "I'm sorry. I'm just upset." She sighed. "I sold off a pair from my personal collection."

"Which ones?"

"The Red Octobers."

"Ouch."

Parker sighed again. The Red Octobers were one of her first rare finds. Nothing compared to the high she'd gotten when she snagged the Coopers, but laying her hands on those beautiful Octobers came pretty damn close. A limited, onetime collaboration between Nike's top designer and a prominent Tokyo street artist, they were notoriously hard to find. Parting with them was a hard choice, but Parker knew she could find a buyer quickly and get a decent price for them. New York Manni had brokered the deal within twenty minutes of receiving her text. First thing tomorrow she'd pack them up and drop them at the post office to ship to Montana, of all places. If they ended up smeared in horse shit, she was going to be very upset.

Rob was quiet for a moment. Parker could tell he was surprised at how promptly she had handled everything, as opposed to her usual foolproof strategy of ignoring the problem until it festered and then asking him how to clean up the mess. A small burst of pride filled her chest. It was almost worth selling off one of her best pairs.

"Do you need any help cleaning up the store, then?" Rob asked.

"Maybe later this week? I can't figure out how to put together those stupid clothing racks. And the register stand has a huge crack in it now. I might need to buy a new one."

"That's it?"

Parker opened her palm, and Tyson swapped out her purple crayon for a green one. "Yeah. A bunch of firefighters helped me with the worst of it last night. I took care of the rest today."

"Firefighters?" Rob sat up in his chair. "You mean that group you and Josie were out with?"

A sudden jolt went through Tyson's little body, and he nearly vibrated off Parker's lap. "Did you go into the fire station?" He swung around and gaped up at Parker with big brown eyes.

Parker hauled him back. "No, squirt, it was late. The fire station was closed." She looked at Rob. "They're all really cool. They all jumped in to help without a second thought. I had a fun time at the bar, too."

Her eyes darted to the amber liquid of her drink. The image of Cate standing next to a ragged barstool, hands on her hips, wearing that low-cut Henley flooded her brain.

Rob's expression shifted, and he looked at her with almost comically furrowed brows. It was the same face he made when they were younger, when he was determined to overcome whatever video game boss Parker had gotten stuck on. Being on the other end of that look unnerved her.

It felt like he was putting together pieces in his head he had no right to even have in the first place.

Rob leaned forward. "What's with you?"

"Nothing." Parker took a quick drink as Tyson began blabbering on about his field trip to the fire station, and how he slid down the pole and tried on a helmet and saw all the hoses and the axes and wanted to sit in the driver's seat of the ladder truck but his teacher wouldn't *let him.*

"You're blushing."

"I am not."

"Your ears are all red. And you have the same dopey look on your face you had back when you were ten and told me and Mom that you were in love with Jennifer Cunningham from homeroom."

"We'd gotten married during recess. It was a big deal."

Still in the throes of his firefighter-induced delirium, Tyson swept aside his dog-slash-dinosaur monster and came up with a fresh sheet of paper. He shoved a bright-red crayon into Parker's hand. "Can you draw the fire truck?" he asked breathlessly.

"Yep." Parker pursed her lips together. Now the image in her mind shifted to Cate stepping off the truck, hot and sweaty, a dusting of soot across her cheekbone, stripping off her gear and—

Rob slammed his tumbler onto the table and let out a triumphant shout. "You have a crush."

"I do not!"

"Tell me *everything.*" Rob leaned forward. "Who is it? Where'd you meet her?" His mouth dropped open. "It's a firefighter, isn't it? You totally have a crush on one of those firefighters."

"What's a crush?" Tyson looked between Rob and Parker. "Is that like when something falls on you?"

Rob laughed, eyes gleaming. "More or less."

Grumbling, Parker shifted Tyson on her lap and finished shading in the fire truck, telling herself to Stop. Thinking. About. Cate. She was only moderately successful. "Who cares? It's not like it means anything. I'm never dating again."

When the shiny MFD fire truck was done, she slid the paper over to Tyson, who giggled and started adding stick-figure firefighters.

Rob's eyes went soft again. "Come on, Park. Sophia sucked, but you know that doesn't mean you should shut yourself off forever."

"Yeah, but..." Parker raked a hand through her hair. "I've got too much going on. I need to focus on the store. See it through, remember?"

"You're right, you're right. I'm glad to hear you say that. But, as your brother, I reserve the right to tease you mercilessly about it."

"Ugh, fine. Whatever." Parker let Tyson finish the oblong helmet on his third firefighter and eased him off her lap. "Time for bed."

Rob stood and scooped up Tyson, ignoring his protests. "We'll do three stories, then your aunt and I are going to watch a movie, okay?"

Parker watched them both head up the stairs. Her eyes trailed down to the bright-red fire truck she'd drawn. She tapped her fingers against the picture, focusing on the waxy texture of the crayon under her fingertips instead of the flutter in her chest.

* * *

On Saturday morning, Parker shuffled west on Tomlinson, overloaded with two boxes full of muffins and scones, a tray of coffees, and a bagged egg sandwich jammed in her back pocket, all from Sweetcakes, the bakery down the street. Cate's leather jacket was tossed over her shoulder.

She cut across the street, nearly spilling the coffees in her haste to avoid traffic, and jammed her elbow into the bell next to the bright-red door. Freddie answered, his massive frame looming in the doorway.

"What's all this?" Gentle brown eyes lit up at the haul of pastries headed in his direction. Parker was beginning to really, really like him.

"I just wanted to drop these off for you guys, as a thank-you for the other night. And return Cate's jacket." Parker carefully lifted her chin from the top of the coffee tray. "I hope you guys like scones. And muffins. And croissants."

Freddie took the boxes, balancing them in one hand, the coffees in the other. "Hell yes, if it's a carb, we'll eat it. Thank you. Wanna come in?"

"Oh, no, I'm good—"

But Freddie was already yelling for Alex and Cate, and Parker had no choice but to follow him in. She took Cate's jacket off her shoulder, the leather soft under her palm.

They walked through the garage bay that housed the gleaming, spotless fire truck with a massive extendable ladder that had *MAYVILLE FIRE* painted along its side. Parked next to it was the ambulance, dwarfed by the size of the truck but equally pristine. The bay opened up to a large common area, oddly cozy given the size of the room. Several worn leather easy chairs were lined up like soldiers in front of a TV mounted on the exposed brick wall. A row of lockers ran across the opposite wall, ending at a large whiteboard, scribbled with what Parker assumed was a duty schedule. A few round tables were scattered in the center of the room, met by ragged chairs that looked as if they belonged in the collection at Crystal's. And of course, next to a staircase leading up to the second story, was the shiny brass fire pole that Tyson couldn't stop talking about. She had to admit, it was pretty cool.

Freddie slid the boxes and coffees onto the closest table, swatting away two other firefighters who had appeared out of nowhere and were nosing around the muffins. He clicked his tongue. "Wait your turn."

A tall, lanky guy with shaggy hair adopted an exaggerated pout. "What'd you do to deserve all this love? You know how I feel about baked goods."

"By being exemplary public servants," Freddie said.

Parker offered a friendly smile, rubbing the back of her neck. She tried not to look for Cate.

Alex elbowed his way in. "Hear that, Salt? 'Exemplary.' You may need to look up the definition. I doubt that word has ever been used in your presence." He punctuated the statement by shoving half of a muffin into his mouth right in front of Salt's face.

Parker couldn't help but snicker. Salt waved his middle finger at his assorted coworkers and turned to Parker.

"Now look at what you started. If Rutherford's head gets any bigger, he won't be able to fit in the rig's driver seat." He stuck out his hand with a warm smile, his irritation with his colleagues obviously feigned. "I'm James."

Parker introduced herself. "Parker. Where'd Salt come from?"

Freddie jumped in. "We usually go by last names. It's easier to distinguish between everyone when we're in a burning structure. Salt just happens to have a mouthful of a name that no one can be expected to pronounce in normal circumstances, let alone an emergency."

Salt's reply was almost apologetic. "Saltalamacchia."

Parker let out a low whistle. "Brutal."

"Tell me about it."

Alex jammed the rest of the muffin into his mouth. "I think you know Morgan. Syed's cleaning upstairs, and Wilds and Omar are already working on lunch. The captain is in her office. We can give you the full tour if you'd like." Parker had no idea how he got that out without choking.

Salt finally snatched a scone out from under Freddie's nose. "Not until I hear about how these guys are 'exemplary public servants.'"

Parker described the robbery and how the group from the firehouse had helped in the aftermath. She left out the part about Cate almost running down the perpetrators—and the exact details of how she ended up with Cate's jacket. Just as she finished, a now familiar voice came from the back of the fire station.

"Parker?"

Cate leaned against the doorway to the kitchen, arms crossed, a towel tossed over her shoulder. She wore that tight MFD T-shirt again, exposing the corded muscles of her forearms. Dark eyes captured Parker from across the common room, hard and flinty like usual, but Parker was sure the gold flecks in Cate's irises were glittering.

Parker remembered her conversation with Rob, annoyed that he had been able to call out her attraction to Cate so easily. Okay, yes, it was a crush. A big one. But she could handle it. Blessedly, she managed to respond, even though it felt like her brain had detached itself from her spinal cord. "Hi. I just wanted to drop by to say thank you. And return your jacket." Great. A perfectly reasonable, articulate reply. But then her mouth kept going. "Can I try your pole?"

Cate raised an eyebrow.

Parker almost crawled under the table. "I mean—the pole. Not that, like, you own it or anything. Not that there's anything wrong with owning a pole, I suppose."

Muffled laughter came from over her shoulder. She tried to ignore it, along with the multiple scenarios implied by pole ownership now running through her mind.

Oh my fucking God, I'm an idiot.

Cate rolled her eyes. Another firefighter wearing an apron squeezed past Cate and darted over to the table.

"No, you may not try the pole." Cate's face darkened. "You didn't have to do this."

Parker scrubbed the back of her neck again. She gripped Cate's jacket so tightly her hand started aching. "It's the least I could do. You all really saved my ass the other night."

Cate shifted her weight from one hip to the other, pushing herself off the doorframe, and walked over to examine the spread. She eschewed the parade of carbs in front of her and went for the coffee instead.

"At least you brought the only coffee in this neighborhood worth a damn." The corner of Cate's mouth twitched. She peeled off the top of the cup and took a sip, eyes fluttering closed for the briefest of moments. A low murmur of contentment rumbled from the back of her throat.

A flutter rippled up through Parker's chest, which almost immediately turned into a frantic drumbeat. She held up the jacket. "Wanted to give this back to you, too."

"Thanks." Cate stepped forward and took her jacket from Parker's hand. Cate's knuckles brushed against her own.

"No problem." The words caught in Parker's throat.

"I caught that knock against my coffee, Wilds." Alex shot Cate a look over his second muffin.

Cate's face twisted into a scowl. "If I wanted to drink an oil slick, I would."

The impromptu congregation was interrupted when another firefighter, wearing a MFD ball cap and a severe expression, barreled out of the office. Parker recognized her as the woman hunched over the pool table at Crystal's. "All right, everyone—kitchen, five minutes. Department-wide announcement incoming." She captured Parker's hand in a crushing grip that rivaled Freddie's. "You're the new neighbor from across the street, right? I'm Captain Jamie Cordell. Sorry to hear about the break-in. If there's anything else we can do for you, let us know. And you're welcome over here any time."

Parker's spine straightened under the captain's intense gaze. "Thank you…ma'am."

Cordell chuckled. Out of the corner of her eye, Parker saw Cate shake her head.

The assorted firefighters all grabbed one last piece of bakery and bombarded Parker with goodbyes as they disappeared into the kitchen. The last holdout, Syed, zoomed down the pole, grabbed a croissant, winked at her, then jogged into the kitchen. Just before Parker turned to leave, Cate handed her a business card that displayed Station Two's address and contact information. On the back, written in precise, careful lettering, was a phone number.

"That's my cell. Let me know when you're ready for that follow-up inspection. Even if I'm not on the schedule, I can make sure someone gets over there."

Parker held the card between her first two fingers and gave it a flick with her thumb. "I will."

As she walked back to her store, Parker turned the card over in her hand, examining the handwriting, and slid it into her unoccupied back pocket, suddenly aware that the grease from her egg sandwich was now seeping through the bag and probably staining her favorite jeans. Normally that would have bothered her. Instead, she couldn't stop smiling.

* * *

Parker surveyed the cans of spray paint at her feet, still deciding where to start. She glanced over at the reference drawing she'd sketched last night, anchored to the sidewalk by two small rocks. She had plenty of work to do in the store, but since she wasn't going to get very far without a new window and still needed her reinspection, she decided to fix something that had been nagging at her. That drab plywood was depressing as hell.

She put on her headphones, tightened the dust mask around her face, and reached for the bright-red can. The moment the first broad swath of color hit the plywood, she was instantly lighter. The tension in her chest uncoiled, and Parker allowed herself to sink into the process. Dynamic swirls and sharp edges of bold color soon covered the plywood, coming together to form the graffiti-style image of a sneaker underneath stylized lettering that read *Remix Footwear*.

"That's super cool!"

Parker almost jumped out of her paint-flecked Air Force Ones. She whipped around to find a perky woman standing next to her. Parker slid off her headphones and pulled down her mask, wiping her nose. The woman looked vaguely familiar. "Thanks. Do I know you?"

"Sarah DeWitt, *Mayville Reader*." She held out her hand, the other gripping a take-out coffee from down the block. "You might've seen me around. I interviewed one of the firefighters from Station Two last week."

"Oh. Cool." Parker shifted her weight from one foot to the other, glancing over to the station. The garage door was shut.

"Do you mind if I ask what happened? We ran a feature last month on a rash of vandalism in the neighborhood, mostly due to a lot of vacant storefronts."

"I wish it was just vandalism." Parker spun the paint can around on her palm while she spoke. She relayed the story again, like she did earlier at the fire station, explaining how she'd recently moved to town and her plans for the store, except this time she included the details of Cate's intervention. As she went on, Parker realized she was probably embellishing those details a bit too much, but she continued anyway. Something compelled her to make it clear how much she appreciated what Cate had done.

Sarah's eyes lit up when Parker finished, and she took a step forward. "Cate Wildman was the firefighter I interviewed the other day. We're doing a feature on her for this month's issue. This would be a perfect addition to the story. Would you be willing to do an interview together?"

Parker swallowed. "Together?"

Sarah's reply came in a flurry, which matched the uptick in Parker's heart rate. "I'd have to ask Cate, of course, but yes. These types of profiles aren't usually my thing, but Cate's reputation is impeccable. You remember that bus accident last winter—no, I guess you weren't living here then. Anyway, I can assure you our readership would eat it up."

The unspoken hint in Sarah's pitch was not lost on her. Parker couldn't turn down an opportunity to plug the store, even if it seemed a bit cynical to use the break-in to garner sympathy. Honestly, though, the chance to spend time with Cate appealed to her more than anything. The business card with Cate's number was still in her back pocket, burning a hole like a brand.

"I'm in."

"Great! Let me get your info, and I'll follow up."

After Sarah left, Parker turned back to the mural, still spinning the paint can around in her palm. She cocked her head at the picture, then looked down at the can. A glittering gold outline surrounded the black-and-red sneaker, different than what she had originally planned. She'd been so engrossed in the painting that she hadn't even realized she'd deviated from her design. It matched the shimmer of Cate's eyes.

CHAPTER EIGHT

Three days after Parker's conversation with Sarah, Cate stood in the middle of the store, signing off on the last piece of the now-successful inspection. This time, instead of following Cate as she went into the stockroom, Parker planted herself on the floor in the front of the store, scowling at the pile of hardware at her feet. She'd been trying—and failing—to assemble four sets of clothing racks for what seemed like weeks. At least the project kept Parker from staring at Cate while she walked around the store, or from sliding into that narrow alcove after Cate and pressing her up against the wall.

"Finished," Cate announced.

Parker looked up from the screws scattered around her feet. So far, she'd managed to attach one wobbly arm to what she kind of thought was the base. "No snakes?"

"No snakes. That electrical box looks good, and the back room is immaculate. Nice job."

Parker flushed at the compliment. "Thanks. I measured the distance from the top of the ceiling exactly. And anchored those shelves."

"I saw." Cate's mouth twitched.

Parker had seen that gesture a lot, both at the bar and when she'd dropped off the pastries and coffee at the fire station. She'd also seen it when Cate had arrived for the inspection, clutching the tablet to her chest. At first Parker thought the little twitch was Cate trying to hide a smile, but now it seemed the tight expression looked more like she was holding herself back, as if there was something simmering beneath the surface. Parker couldn't help wondering what it took to get Cate to let go, and what she'd have to do to witness it.

Shoving the thought aside, Parker scrambled to her feet and scribbled her name onto the tablet, a trembling hand making her signature even more illegible. "Now all I need is a damn window, and I'll have a real business."

"You have a new one coming, right?"

"Soon, hopefully. They had to special order it."

"Ah. Well." Cate glanced around the store, like she was more interested in examining all four walls than looking Parker in the eyes. "I like the painting outside. Did you do that?"

"Yep. Finally putting that art school education to use."

"You went to art school?"

"For a bit. I studied contemporary illustration. Then I went back to business school."

"Back?"

Parker rocked back on her heels and jammed her hands into her pockets. She was in jeans and a T-shirt, as usual, but this morning she chose a pair without holes, on the off chance Cate noticed such things. "I tried USC first, then an art and design college, then I ended up at Cal State LA. College really wasn't for me. I barely graduated."

Barely graduated didn't do justice to the herculean effort required over her last three semesters to squeak by with an accounting degree. Although drawing and painting had always been her favorite hobby, she'd never given thought to a career as an illustrator until she realized how much she didn't like studying business. But then art school turned out to be a poor fit, too, and her disinterest in school combined with the allure of Los Angeles had resulted in an unproductive several years, despite her best intentions. Rob was the only one who exhibited any real concern for her education—their mother being too wrapped up in her own anger and resentment around the divorce to notice her kids, and her dad just blindly paying the tuition bills without question. Parker supposed she was lucky her aimlessness hadn't resulted in a chunk of student loan debt, but the older she got it just made her feel embarrassed.

She'd spent most of her life oscillating between trying to be more like her brother or forging her own path, and failing at both. The only thing she'd really been good at was running her sneaker business on the side. Admitting to Cate her spotty academic background brought up familiar feelings of inadequacy. She doubted Cate had ever experienced such uncertainty. Cate couldn't be that much older than her, and already a lieutenant? Clearly, she'd known exactly what she wanted to do with her life.

Cate looked at her, not appearing judgmental in the slightest. The gold in her eyes stood out more than ever. "You didn't like art school?"

"For a while, sure. Until it became obvious I didn't have the talent."

"I don't think many schools are in the habit of admitting students without talent." Cate's voice turned soft.

Parker's face grew warm at the unexpected kindness in Cate's tone. She ran a hand through her hair, which she also made a point of actually styling that day. "Thanks."

"It's true." Cate gestured at the plain white wall that would eventually display rows of sneakers. "You should paint something there, too."

"Really?"

Cate looked away. Her voice was still soft. Shy, almost. "Not that my opinion matters. I really don't have an eye for that."

"Of course your opinion matters."

The words came out before Parker could temper them, and she fought the urge to make up an excuse to disappear into the stockroom. Just because she'd admitted to having a crush on Cate didn't mean she needed to drop goddamn hints about it all the time. Parker still hadn't recovered from asking to try Cate's pole.

Cate's mouth did that same twitch again. The right corner of her mouth always pulled a little more than her left, resulting in a lopsided effect that stood out in contrast to her fierce demeanor. The flintiness in her eyes had melted away. Bright gold shone through like the sun had split into a million little pieces and landed in her irises.

"I suppose you're right." Cate waved the tablet. "I haven't submitted your inspection results yet. I could always change my mind."

Parker clutched her chest, staggering backward. "But Lieutenant, I'm just a humble small-business owner. Surely you wouldn't do that to the backbone of this country's economy."

Cate laughed. "Sure. Real humble."

Parker grinned. She decided then and there she'd do anything to hear that laugh again. "You're right, I should check myself. I'm talking to someone who runs into burning buildings for a living."

"What can I say? It's a gift."

Parker's grin widened. Underneath Cate's crusty exterior was a delightful sense of humor, and it made Parker want her even more.

"Born a superhero. I knew it. You've probably wanted to be a firefighter ever since you were a kid."

"I wouldn't put it like that." Clouds settled in Cate's eyes, and just like that, the sun was gone.

The change in Cate's demeanor was so abrupt Parker almost jumped backward. "Something wrong?"

Cate turned her head, jaw tense. "No. It's just a long story."

Whatever Cate was holding back seemed primed to break through. Parker swallowed her curiosity, overwhelmed by a desire to dismantle those walls and learn every inch about the woman behind them. "I bet it's worth telling."

Cate's expression softened. "Maybe." She hugged the tablet into her chest again. "I'll finish up the report and you'll be good to go."

Parker bit back a sigh. The rhythm of their interactions was difficult to anticipate. Every time she felt they were getting closer, she did or said something to make Cate stiffen up again. While Parker intended to stick with her plan—stupid crush notwithstanding—she didn't want to keep making Cate uncomfortable, especially since she was about to ask for another favor on top of the fire inspection.

"I didn't mean to upset you." Parker looked up at Cate earnestly.

"It's fine. I get too sensitive about things."

Sensitive wasn't exactly the first word that came to mind when Parker thought of Cate, but she saw the truth behind it. A subject change was the best course of action, even though she'd be pushing her luck.

"Before you go, I was hoping I could ask you for something else." Parker scrunched up her nose. At Cate's curious look, she went on. "I know Sarah from the *Mayville Reader* reached out about doing a follow-up for her profile. You know, to talk about the robbery and all that."

"She did."

"I was hoping you'd do it."

"Why?"

Parker spoke quickly. "The publicity would be good for the store. Stopping the robbery is a really cool story. And I've never been interviewed with a real-life action hero."

Cate snorted. "Now you're just flattering me."

"Goddamn right I am."

Cate's mouth twitched again. This time, it definitely looked like Cate was hiding a smile. Parker took it as a sign her earlier misstep had at least been partially forgiven. "I really hate doing that type of stuff. I don't like talking about myself, Parker."

"Sure, I get that." Parker ignored the way her stomach flipped at the sound of Cate saying her name. "Is there any way I could change your mind? I'll bring you coffee from Sweetcakes every day for a week. No, two weeks."

Cate pinched the bridge of her nose. "Parker…"

"A month? Two months? Three?" Her stomach did another flip.

"You're relentless."

"I'm going to take that as a compliment. When do you work next?"

Still holding the tablet, Cate crossed her arms and eyed her skeptically. "I'm picking up an extra shift on Thursday. I'm at the firehouse by six thirty."

Parker's body rebelled at the thought of getting up before nine. "Done."

"Sometimes it's closer to six fifteen."

"Even better."

Cate's eyes narrowed. "This is not a yes."

"I know."

Captured by that dark gaze, Parker didn't dare move while Cate looked her up and down, as if waiting for her to back out or admit she was joking. Parker smiled. Eventually, Cate shook her head in defeat and headed toward the door.

"I drink a lot of coffee." Cate fired the parting shot over her shoulder.

"So do I," Parker yelled after Cate. Then, once certain that no one would see, she jumped up and pumped her fist into the air.

* * *

"You're quiet."

Cate's head snapped over to look at Cordell. The sun was just beginning to rise, the neighborhood slowly rousing in the first light of dawn as they walked to the firehouse together.

"I don't know what you're talking about." Cate glared at Cordell. The denial came swiftly, even though she didn't remember the last thing she'd said. Or if she'd spoken at all, really. The only thought in her mind was whether Parker would be waiting at the firehouse when they arrived.

Not that Cate would admit that.

Cordell let out a quiet sigh. "Right. Every time we walk together, you're either bitching about someone not pulling their weight on the line or trying to come up with a more efficient training schedule." Cordell shifted the duffel bag slung over her shoulder, ice-blue eyes looking straight ahead. "What's your deal?"

Their morning routine had started a few years ago, right after Cate bought her townhouse near Station Two. Cordell lived a few blocks over, and when their schedules lined up, they would often walk to work together, cutting through the shaded, tree-lined neighborhoods that ran along the lake before turning to pick up Tomlinson Street. Eventually their camaraderie developed into a solid friendship, and Cate often used their walks as an opportunity to pick her superior's brain. This morning, apparently, was different.

"Probably just tired," Cate said. The air was brisk against her face. Her cheeks were still flushed from the shower. At least, that's what she told herself.

Now it was Cordell's turn to unleash a look, one that was much more withering, and Cate deflated slightly under the scrutiny. "You're working too much. I shouldn't have let you pick up this shift."

"I'm fine, Jamie. Really. I didn't sleep all that well last night. That's all."

That part was true. An image of soft gray eyes and a bright smile had kept her up later than usual, along with a strange tightness in her chest at the thought of seeing Parker again. It was the wrong thing to say to her captain, though.

Cordell stopped and looked Cate up and down. "You're running yourself ragged. Between the extra shifts you're pulling and planning for that damn party, you're lucky to still be on your feet." She shook her head. "You're taking the weekend off."

"I don't want the weekend off."

"I don't give a shit what you want. You're no good to anyone if you're overworked. Take the time."

Jaw twitching, Cate bit back her protest. Cordell was aggravating when she was right, and she was a damn fine captain, which meant she was right more often than not. Beneath her bluntness was a keen insight into the crew working for her and their individual needs. It was true that Cate had been grabbing extra shifts, on top of spending most of her free time either at Butler Center or fundraising for the ball, mindlessly stretching herself thin without realizing it. That had always been an easy thing for her to do this time of year.

The anniversary of the accident always loomed at the change of the seasons, an annual rite she had to endure before spring gave way to summer. Usually, Cate commemorated the event by keeping busy enough at the firehouse that she didn't think about any of it until the actual day arrived. If she was lucky, she could throw herself into every call and find every reason in the book to stay well past the shift changeover.

If she wasn't working, she drank half a bottle of whiskey and avoided her parents' phone calls. Cate preferred the former. The opportunity to save a life on the day her brother had died always held a bit of poetry to her.

Except this year, she had the added worry about the rec center and the ball, and her usual work habits were now untenable. There was also the nagging feeling she couldn't shake since meeting Parker. She already had enough going on, and worrying about whether or not Parker would make good on her promise of coffee was not making things any easier. It didn't matter one way or another. It was just another distraction. She could get her own damn coffee, thank you very much.

They started walking again, and the moment they turned down Tomlinson Street, Cate's pulse quickened. Down the block, sitting on the curb in front of the firehouse, was a small figure wearing an oversized sweatshirt, ripped jeans, and blazing red sneakers. Next to her on the sidewalk were two white to-go cups. Parker let out a massive yawn and scrubbed her face with open palms.

Cordell made a small noise of surprise. "Is this for you?"

"I guess so." Cate bit down on the inside of her cheek to keep from smiling. Out of the corner of her eye, she caught Cordell's confused look.

"That's the kid from the other day, right? With the store?"

"Um. Yeah."

"Why would—oh." Cordell smiled and jabbed Cate with her elbow. "Looks like you have a not-so-secret admirer." Cate kept her eyes downcast and started fiddling with the strap of her G-Shock watch.

"Hey! Morning!" Parker scrambled to her feet, nearly tripping over herself in the process. She thrust out one of the coffees as Cate and Cordell approached, wearing a lopsided grin that grew even more crooked as she tried to stifle another yawn. Her short hair stuck out at uneven angles, reminding Cate of an animated character that had just stuck a fork into a light socket. An urge to reach out and smooth down the thick, wild hair came over Cate so suddenly she had to ball her hands into fists.

Cordell didn't miss a beat, sweeping in and grabbing the offered cup before either Cate or Parker could stop her. "Morning, kid. Thanks." She tapped the coffee against the brim of her ball cap in a salute and walked into the station, giving Cate a quick wink before disappearing behind the red door.

Parker blinked and stared at her empty hand, like she had no idea what the hell had just happened. Defeated, she surrendered the second coffee to Cate with bleary eyes. She obviously had just rolled out of bed and dashed down to Sweetcakes at the last minute, and her crestfallen expression at the lost caffeine was one of the cutest things Cate had ever seen.

"Thanks." Cate took a sip, feeling slightly guilty. "Not a morning person?"

Parker yawned again. "I love mornings. Mornings are great."

Cate rolled her eyes. "You really didn't have to do this."

"I said I would." Parker's reply made it seem like it was the simplest thing in the whole world. She ran a hand over the crown of her head, which just messed her hair up more.

"I didn't think that would mean sleeping at your store."

"I didn't sleep at the store. I just set, like, four alarms to get here on time."

"I'm honored."

"You should be. I never get up this early."

"I can see that." Cate took another triumphant sip, meeting Parker's jealous gaze over the rim of her cup. The open longing on Parker's face was almost enough to make her relinquish the coffee. Almost.

"So, same time tomorrow?" Eagerness brightened Parker's eyes, chasing the sleep away.

"Yes." The answer sprang from Cate's mouth without a second's hesitation, her brain throwing out the word before she could stop herself. Parker's grin widened, and her hand went to the back of her head again, still trying to smooth out her hair. For a moment, that smile drove all thought from Cate's mind, and it took her several breaths before remembering Cordell's orders.

"Actually, no. Sorry. I'm off tomorrow."

Parker's grin stumbled. "Next week, then."

"You really don't have to keep doing this."

"We had a deal, right?"

"We don't. I haven't said yes, remember?"

"Shit. Right." Parker screwed up her face and scratched her chin in an exaggerated thinking gesture. "I need to sweeten the pot, then."

"And how do you plan on doing that?"

"I was thinking…you said Butler had an after-school basketball program, right?"

"Yeah."

"Could I donate some shoes for the kids? I can get a really good deal on a bulk order."

Cate almost dropped her coffee. "Are you serious?"

"Absolutely. What do you think?"

"I mean—yes, of course. That's incredibly generous of you. You haven't even fixed your window yet." She'd need to talk to Jameel about league enrollment and the regular open gym attendees, but off the top of her head she could think of at least ten kids who would appreciate the gift. Even if they wouldn't be playing at Butler much longer. Her heart twisted at the thought.

"Don't worry about the window. It's a fair trade. So, two dozen pairs? Three?" Parker whipped out her phone. "I'm texting New York Manni now. I just need an idea of the size runs."

Cate's mouth opened and closed several times before she could reply. "That's worth more than a silly interview."

"Not to me. Plus, the rec center's important to you." Parker's head snapped up, eyes wide. "I-I mean, it's important for the whole neighborhood, not just you. Not that it shouldn't be important to you! I just…it's, um, cool."

By the time Parker managed to finish her tortured sentence, her ears were as red as the firehouse's door. She looked away, squinting directly into the rising sun with a pained expression. Cate was going to chalk up Parker's inarticulateness to the fact that Cordell had stolen her coffee, but this was hardly the first time Parker had done that in front of her. It was painfully adorable. The flush returned to Cate's cheeks, and this time she couldn't blame the reaction on a shower.

"I should get going." Cate gestured at the firehouse.

"Of course. Totally." Parker hopped to one side of the sidewalk, clearing the way for Cate. "Sorry to keep you."

"You didn't." Cate brushed past Parker, catching a faint scent she couldn't quite place, something crisp and bright that reminded her of summer. She'd never been to the ocean but imagined that was what it smelled like. "You'll coordinate with Sarah about scheduling the interview?"

"I will." The cheerful smile was back, the earlier display of tortured syntax already forgotten. Parker hitched a thumb over her shoulder to her darkened store. "You go be a hero. I'm gonna take a nap."

Cate paused, hand hovering above the door. Parker stood on the sidewalk, smile widening, framed by the morning sun's glow. All Cate could do was just shake her head as she gratefully disappeared into the safety of the firehouse.

CHAPTER NINE

For the second time in as many weeks, Cate found herself sitting across from Sarah DeWitt. The journalist was pleasant enough, but the apologetic look on her face was getting irritating. Cate checked her watch again and swallowed an impatient sigh.

Thursday had been busy; she was assigned to Medic Two with a veteran C-Shifter named Ally and caught several calls in a row that took up most of the day. When she got back to the house and checked her phone, a text from Parker was waiting for her listing potential interview times, all on Saturday and Sunday. Which she had off. Cate's thumb had lingered over the display, debating the exact wording of her reply for longer than she cared to admit, before agreeing to meet at the park near her townhouse on Saturday afternoon. Her phone was practically still vibrating from the enthusiasm in Parker's response.

The same enthusiasm with which she promised she was five minutes away. Fifteen minutes ago.

Cate drummed her fingers against her coffee cup. Tardiness was one of her pet peeves, but something told her that her agitation was related more to Parker's dangerously charming smile, not her promptness. Or lack thereof. Flimsy cardboard creaked under her hand.

"What's that?" Sarah looked up from her phone, appearing on the cusp of apologizing once more, even though it wasn't her fault.

"Nothing," Cate answered quickly, unsure what she had even muttered under her breath. Her eyes swept the park once more. Finally, Parker bounded into view, cutting through the playground with a to-go tray of coffees in one hand and a paper bag from Sweetcakes dangling from her mouth. Cate's heart thumped against her ribs, hard.

"Sorry, sorry!" Parker spoke through clenched teeth, the coffees tipping precariously as she stepped over a muddy patch near the picnic table. Today's sneaker choice was a pair of low-cut orange things so bright Cate was certain they could be seen from space, contrasting with the rest of her notably understated outfit of a plain black long-sleeved T-shirt and dark, tight jeans. Parker slid in next to her and took the bag out of her mouth. "I was on a call and lost track of time. Thanks for waiting—oh, you already got coffee."

Parker's cheeks were flushed, and she seemed a bit winded. The slight gasp in her voice triggered something deep within Cate that could only be described as primal.

"It's no problem." Cate tore her attention away from the sound of Parker's breathing and grabbed a fresh coffee, ripping off the top and adding it to her current drink. What she really needed was a stiff whiskey.

"Everything okay?" Sarah asked.

"What? Oh, everything's fine." Parker tore open the bag and slid three fresh scones across the table. "I was just talking to my sneaker hookup in New York. They think they can score me a few pairs of an exclusive release. I got a little excited and lost track of time." Parker gave Cate a shy look and nudged the scones. "Is blueberry okay? I took a guess. Sorry again to keep you waiting."

Cate broke the nearest pastry in half. "Blueberry's my favorite."

"Really?" Parker lit up like she had won a prize at the fair, leveling a broad, cockeyed smile at Cate. In that instant, any residual annoyance Cate felt at her tardiness vanished.

"Everything at Sweetcakes is amazing. Cora has a gift." Sarah pulled a notebook from her bag and set her iPhone in front of Cate and Parker. "Do you mind if I record this?"

Parker waggled her eyebrows. "This seems extra official."

Sarah chuckled, leaning in conspiratorially. "It is. I take human interest stories *very* seriously."

Cate watched the interaction with a bemused look, hiding a smile behind her coffee cup. Parker seemed to charm everyone she met.

Sarah tapped her phone. "Parker, why don't we get some background on how you ended up in Mayville? Then we can talk more about your business and the robbery."

"Sure thing."

For a while, Cate forgot she was supposed to be giving another interview and was content to observe Parker at a distance. She was an odd mix of hyperactivity and intense focus, bouncing one knee and spinning her phone around in her hand as she fielded Sarah's questions, yet every answer she gave was thorough and genuine. Parker talked about the origin of her sneaker obsession, how she had coveted her older brother's Nikes and tried to wear them to school even though they were at least three sizes too large. Naturally, her interest evolved into a side gig buying and selling sneakers while still in high school, inspired by her father's own success in business. She skimmed over the details of what exactly led her to Mayville, subtly deflecting the question with a controversial opinion on the town's Thai take-out options.

The conversation pivoted to the break-in, and Parker continued to shoulder the brunt of the storytelling duties. Cate only had to interject once or twice when the details became a little too embellished, but it was hard to be irritated by Parker's enthusiasm.

"A hero all around," Sarah said with a laugh after Parker insisted she'd never seen anyone run so fast in her entire life when Cate had taken off after the thieves. Cate didn't realize Parker had come out in time to see her chase them away.

"Just lucky, really. Right place, right time." Cate washed down more of the scone with the last of her coffee, struck by an urge to get up and move her body. It probably had more to do with her excess caffeine intake than her proximity to Parker. Probably.

"You seem to make a habit of that." Sarah snapped up her phone, shutting off the recording app. "I think that's everything I need. This is going to be a really great piece. How about a picture for the article?"

"Totally." Parker pocketed her phone and sat up straighter, folding her hands on the table. Cate did the same, pushing the scones and coffee out of frame. Sarah backed away as she lined up the shot.

"Can you two get a little closer? I'm trying to frame the tree in the background."

Parker let out a little cough, then inched over until their legs were touching. Her hands remained planted on the table, fingers laced together. Sitting this close together, Cate could no longer mimic the same pose without looking horribly awkward. She took her left hand off the table and, before she thought too much about it, wrapped her arm around Parker's shoulder. Parker shifted and leaned into her. Cate caught the same scent from yesterday morning again, wondering if it was Parker's cologne. It made Cate's entire body hum.

"Just a few more." Sara tapped her phone screen, adjusting the camera settings. Cate couldn't resist a quick glance over at Parker, whose winning smile had yet to falter. Cate gave Parker's shoulder a squeeze. Gray eyes immediately flicked over to hers, then glanced down at her lips.

"Look at the camera, ladies," Sarah admonished.

After a few more excruciating moments, they were finished. Cate let her hand fall away from Parker's shoulder, unsure if she was angry or relieved. For her part, Parker also seemed reluctant to move away.

They stood—Cate's legs shakier than she cared to admit—and shook hands with Sarah, who doled out a few more reassurances about the article. When she disappeared from view, Cate turned to Parker, who had jammed both hands into her pockets and was rocking back and forth on her heels. Even though a breeze was drifting in from the lake, the air between them was warm.

Cate had no other plans for the day, and suddenly she didn't want to spend it alone.

"Would you like to grab lunch?"

Parker beamed. "I'd love to."

* * *

The pizzeria was a few blocks away, farther down the west end of Tomlinson away from Parker's store. It was a beautiful day, bright and sunny, and the neighborhood buzzed with palpable anticipation of the warmer months to come. Groups of people milled about on the street, coming in and out of the small boutiques and shops lining Tomlinson. A family passed by, the moms wrangling a stroller and two other small children as they navigated their brood toward the park.

Parker was buoyed by the foot traffic. Josie's predictions about the Tomlinson area seemed to be proving accurate, and she felt a sense of relief despite Remix's rocky beginning.

Everything was going to work out. The interview had gone well, the sun was warm on her neck, and she was going out to lunch with an absolute stunner of a woman. This was the best she'd felt since moving to town.

Parker and Cate walked side by side, falling into an unexpectedly easy rhythm given their height difference. They stepped aside in unison to let a man and his dog pass, both of which looked vaguely familiar. Parker's eyes went to his feet. He wasn't wearing shoes. Parker shook her head.

"You said your dad runs his own business?" Cate asked.

"He founded an investment firm, actually. He bought himself out of his prior firm and set out on his own. It was a huge gamble, but he pulled it off. And then some."

"That's impressive."

"It is. He's a hard worker. Just not on his marriage."

Out of the corner of her eye, Parker saw Cate wince. "Your parents are divorced?"

"Yeah." Parker paused. This was a topic she usually avoided, but Cate's presence made it easier to talk about. "I was twelve. It was pretty brutal. My mom's still bitter about it. Rob tried to protect me as best he could, but he was already in college by then. He got me out of the house when he could. We spent a lot of time at his girlfriend's place. Well, she was his girlfriend back then. They got married after he graduated law school."

"Wow. That sounds awful."

"It sucked. Dad left us for his assistant, who's like twenty years younger." Parker let out a long breath. "Successful career man, absentee father, shitty husband—the trifecta of cliched divorces. Guess you really can have it all."

Something softened around Cate's eyes. "Sounds like you and your brother are really close."

"We are. I owe him a lot. He's almost ten years older than me, but it's never really felt like that. Probably due to his distinct lack of maturity." Cate chuckled, and Parker gave her a grin. "What about you? Parents? Siblings?"

"My parents live just outside of town. Dad is an English teacher, Mom's a civil engineer."

"No brothers or sisters?"

A muscle in Cate's jaw twitched. "No."

They stepped aside to allow another group of pedestrians to pass. Parker moved closer to Cate, their hands almost brushing. Parker wished Cate's arm was wrapped around her shoulder again.

"I noticed you didn't really answer when Sarah asked why you moved to town." Hazel eyes looked right at Parker, clear and direct.

Parker chewed her lip. She'd been getting used to Cate's straightforward manner of communication, and it was apparent Cate wasn't someone who opened up easily. Neither of those traits bothered

Parker, except that Cate had homed in on a sore spot. Although, as she thought about the way her mouth had gone dry when Cate touched her at the park, she should probably be thankful for the reminder yet again of the danger of diving into something too quickly.

"I went through a rough breakup. I had to move out of my ex-girlfriend's place on short notice and didn't really have anywhere else to go. Rob and Meagan live here, so I thought, why not?" Parker swiped a lock of hair off her forehead. "I needed a change, honestly."

Cate made a small noise, like she was noting something of interest. "Ouch."

"Yep. Dumped me over text, too."

Cate stopped dead in her tracks. "You're kidding."

The offense in her tone on Parker's behalf was completely unexpected. Parker didn't know how to react, so she tried to laugh it off. It was her default reaction whenever the conversation veered toward Sophia. "Wish I was."

"I'm really sorry to hear that."

The sun caught Cate's eyes, and Parker was awash in glittering gold. She cleared her throat and looked away. The fact that Cate seemed to care about her, even though they'd just met, was too dangerous to entertain seriously. They started walking again, still in perfect stride, and Parker wished Cate would pull her closer, like she had when they'd taken the picture. She scolded herself. *Too. Dangerous.*

Nero's Pizza was at the intersection of Tomlinson and Clark, in a small, two-story house converted into a restaurant, complete with a wood-burning stove. The seating area was cozy and compact, with only enough space for a smattering of two- and four-tops. They took a small table near the bay window that looked out over the street. A server with purple hair and creative facial piercings dropped off two menus and promised to return shortly to take their order.

Parker skimmed the pizza offerings, grateful for something else to hold her attention other than the perfect line of Cate's jaw. Or the thought of Cate touching her. Or fantasizing about Cate moving underneath her, long legs wrapped around—

Fucking hell, stop it!

"You all right?" Cate was looking at her over the top of her menu.

Parker adopted an exaggerated look of concentration, frowning at the options. "I think we ran into our first problem."

"What's that?"

"Pineapple on pizza: yes or no?"

"Since you're a Californian, I can venture where you stand."

Parker raised a finger, not looking up from the greasy laminated pages. "Technically, I only moved there when I was sixteen. I was mostly raised in Chicago. So my opinions on pizza are wild."

Cate cocked her head. "I didn't realize that. I assumed that's where you were from."

"My dad moved to Costa Mesa after the divorce, and I stayed with my mom in Chicago. I moved in with him after I came out during my sophomore year."

"Your mom didn't approve?"

Parker shrugged nonchalantly. "Not really. She didn't love the fact that I dated women, and I didn't love the fact that she was dating an unemployed wannabe novelist named Ron. It was just easier." Parker squirmed in her chair a little. The relationship hadn't lasted long and her mom had gotten over it quickly, but by then Parker had no interest in coming back to Chicago. It wasn't like Elizabeth had been begging her to return, anyway.

"Where's your mom now?"

"Jamaica. On an extended vacation, trying to get her groove back." Parker chuckled to herself. It was one of her and Rob's favorite jokes about the whole situation. She glanced up, hoping to find a hint of a smile on Cate's face, but was instead met with serious dark eyes.

"It seems like you moved around a lot."

Parker swallowed thickly. Cate's intense look pierced her to the core. It'd been a while since someone had paid attention to her so thoroughly. "I did, but I've been luckier than most. Everything usually works out in the end." Parker squirmed in her seat. "What about the English teacher and the civil engineer? Are they cool with the whole gay thing?"

"What makes you think I'm gay?"

The color immediately drained from Parker's face. "Shit, I'm sorry, I didn't mean—"

"Gotcha." Cate nudged the toe of Parker's bright-orange Jordan Four Retro Flyknit. "I'm kidding. They're fine with it. So supportive it's annoying, actually."

Parker shook her head, relieved she hadn't accidentally offended Cate and impressed once again at Cate's sneaky humor. "That was mean."

Cate gave a little shrug, mouth twitching. She looked pleased with herself. "Maybe. And yes, I do like pineapple on pizza."

"I knew you had good taste. In more ways than one."

Cate's eyes widened and she disappeared behind her menu, but not before Parker spied the obvious blush rising in her cheeks. Parker's heartbeat quickened in response.

The server returned a moment later, and they decided to split a pizza and a pitcher of the seasonal ale on tap. As he left with their order, Parker's phone buzzed with a message from New York Manni about the bulk order.

"You're a popular one."

"It's my livelihood." Parker tapped out a reply. "Manni can get me thirty pairs next week. Just need the size runs."

"That quickly?"

"They have connections everywhere. It's what they do."

"They sound like a drug dealer." Cate's eyes flashed. The barely there smile Parker had been searching for finally made an appearance.

Parker grinned and gestured with her hands, palms open. "Just another entrepreneur, like myself."

"Right. The backbone of our economy. I forgot."

The beer arrived, and Cate filled both glasses precisely to the top without foaming over. Parker wasn't even surprised. Everything Cate did radiated competence. Another buzz, and Parker went back to her phone, scrolling through a news release about a new collaboration she was keeping an eye on.

"I have to admit, I still don't get the shoe thing." Cate sipped her beer.

Parker tapped through to another pricing notification. "What don't you get about it?"

"I just can't believe how involved it is."

"It's an investment commodity." At Cate's skeptical eyebrow, Parker pulled up her trading app and leaned forward. The display showed a list of models, graphs of pricing history, and scrolling ticker. "This is one of the apps I use to forecast pricing trends. It's how I figure out how much I can flip a pair for and what my margin will be."

Cate leaned over the table, nearly brushing their foreheads together. The scent of spice and vanilla and smoke rose from her tan skin, reminding Parker of riding home in the cool night, warm and safe in Cate's jacket. Parker imagined pressing her mouth against the pulse point of Cate's neck and breathing her in. Parker clutched her phone harder, as if the device would somehow ground her.

"It's like a stock exchange." Cate's brow furrowed as she watched the ticker.

"Yeah, except it's not made up. These are tangible items, not bullshit instruments created to keep rich people richer."

Cate snorted. "No shit."

Dark eyes met her own, Cate's face inscrutable. A lump formed in Parker's throat, making it very hard to swallow. Or breathe. Cate slid back into her seat, and Parker did the same, aware of those eyes following her every move. As she moved backward, Cate's hand shot out and grabbed Parker's full pint glass right before she knocked it with her elbow.

"Thanks."

"No problem."

A moment later the pizza arrived, the smell of sweet and salty hitting Parker harder than she anticipated. Her stomach rumbled. She'd skipped breakfast again, and the scone had done little to hold her over.

By some blessed intervention of the universe, Parker managed to eat and drink and talk at the same time without completely embarrassing herself. The pizza and beer gave her hands something to do and her brain something to focus on, even as Cate's intense gaze barely wavered.

The conversation moved fluidly as they dove into the usual noncontroversial topics: movies, music, books. The longer they talked, the more Cate seemed to unwind, as if she were physically unfurling from an armored shell. The line of her jaw relaxed, her eyes sparkled, the smile hinting at the corner of her mouth began to emerge completely. Parker was delighted to discover that her instincts had been correct; once she started opening up, Cate was kind and gentle and dryly funny. She was also a voracious reader, consuming all manner of genres at a rate that put Parker to shame. Her enthusiasm was infectious as she described the plot of the queer sci-fi series she was reading—something wild involving gay necromancers in space that Parker couldn't begin to follow. Cate leaned forward, all broad shoulders and coiled muscle, the strong grace in her movements obvious even while confined to the small two-top. Parker imagined Cate navigating an obstacle course with just as much ease as breaking down a door with an axe.

"Wow, it's late," Cate said a while later, checking her watch.

Parker blinked, tearing her eyes away from the flexing muscles in Cate's forearm. A second pitcher sat empty on the table, their pint glasses also drained. Parker's phone was face down, and she realized she hadn't touched it all afternoon. An avalanche of unread notifications lit up her home screen, along with the time. They'd been at the pizzeria for nearly three hours.

They split the bill, exchanging sheepish looks as their server returned their cards with a huff. As they stepped out onto Tomlinson, a rush of energy overtook Parker, her head buzzing from both the beer and the company, and she had to stop herself from grabbing Cate's hand.

An ear-shattering siren ripped through the neighborhood, and Parker jumped back in surprise. Two blocks ahead, the gleaming fire truck from Station Two pulled out of the station, followed by the ambulance. The two vehicles tore down the street toward them urgently, yet also with a clear mindfulness of their surroundings. Alex was at the wheel of the fire truck, brows knitted in concentration, Cordell next to him and talking into a radio.

Cate's entire body tensed, followed by what sounded like a sigh of defeat. For the first time that afternoon, Cate reached for her phone. After a burst of scrolling, she shoved it back into her pocket with a huff.

"Do you need to go?"

Cate shook her head. "No, I'm not on call or anything. They'll be fine."

Parker had seen plenty of mediocre movies depicting firefighters and other first responders as adrenaline junkies with hero complexes, but she didn't get any of that from Cate. Still, she seemed bothered as the fire truck carrying her colleagues roared past.

"It must be hard missing out."

"Yeah, it is." They resumed walking. "I don't like them rearranging the schedule on my account."

"Why are you off, anyway?"

"Cordell thinks I've been working too much." Cate wrinkled her nose. "She said if I showed my face at the house before Monday morning, she'd furlough me for two weeks."

Parker couldn't resist giving Cate a nudge. "So…are you?"

"Am I what?"

"Working too much."

Cate sighed. "Probably. I've been picking up extra shifts on top of running fundraising. And it's—" Cate bit off her thought midsentence.

"What?"

Cate's shoulders tensed. She looked straight ahead, like she was staring far down the block at a ghost Parker couldn't see. Piece by piece, the armor slid back into place. "It's just a difficult time of year for me."

Parker opened her mouth to ask what she meant but decided to back off. At least now she knew she was right. Something simmered beneath the surface when it came to Cate. Maybe one day Parker would get to the bottom of it all.

They were almost at the store before Parker noticed the figure leaning up against the front door. Rob looked up when they approached, already grumbling to himself. He was dressed in his usual weekend uniform of slim dark-washed jeans, black T-shirt, and scuffed Stan Smiths.

"Dude. I've been waiting twenty minutes for you." He frowned in Parker's direction. "Didn't you want help putting together those clothing racks?"

"Sorry, I lost track of time." She must have missed his texts while they were at lunch.

Cate stepped forward, extending a hand. "It's my fault. I kept her late. Cate Wildman."

"Rob Mandli. I'm Parker's brother." Rob gripped Cate's hand. They stood eye to eye, and Rob looked her up and down. Parker groaned inwardly. Rob was not in the habit of acting like a bro-y, overprotective douchebag, which was Parker's favorite thing about him, but that side of his personality did come out on occasion. She shot him a look.

If you embarrass me, I swear to God…

Cate nodded. "Of course. Heard a lot about you."

"Really?" Rob glanced at Parker. "Don't believe anything she says."

"Don't worry. I didn't."

Rob laughed. Parker started panicking. Oh no. No no no. They were hitting it off. That was even worse.

"Actually," Cate continued. "I think I saw you the other day at the firehouse. Your son was on a field trip, I think?"

"Ah, yeah. Tyson. He's been obsessed with firefighters ever since he could talk. Loves the trucks." Rob's grin turned wicked. "Were you one of the firefighters that helped out after the break-in? Park can't stop talking about you."

Cate's eyebrow arched in curiosity. She looked at Parker. "Is that so?"

Parker fumbled for her keys to the store, no less than eight different plots to murder her brother quickly springing to mind. "Well, this was nice! Rob, why don't you go—"

Rob, as usual, wasn't listening to her. "You're a basketball fan, right? Who do you like out of the East?"

"Milwaukee. Giannis and Dame are killing it. I like college more, though."

"Cool. Do you follow men's or women's or—"

"Oh my God, Rob, she doesn't want to talk sports with you." Parker jammed her key into the lock and started fighting with the door, which, inexplicably, was refusing to open.

"Okay, okay. You're right." Rob held up his hands in defeat. "I'm sure you have other places to be."

Parker looked over her shoulder. Cate was pressing her lips together so hard they were turning white, trying with all her might to hold back a smile. "I should get going. Sorry to make you late."

"Don't apologize." Parker stopped fidgeting with the door. "You'll let me know about the sizes?"

"Definitely. We'll be in touch. Nice to meet you, Rob." Cate turned to leave, but something stopped her. She pointed at Parker's bright-red bike, parked on the street, and spoke to Rob. "She wears a helmet when she rides that thing, right?"

"It's the only rule she follows." Rob smiled at her.

Cate's eyes trailed over Parker, still biting back her smile. "Good." She walked off down the block without looking back, allowing a full view of her ass in tight jeans. Parker tried as hard as she could not to stare. She failed.

Rob laughed as he took the keys from her and unlocked the door with ease. "Holy shit, I've never seen you that twitterpated over a woman before."

"Stuff it, dickhead." Parker shoved past him and flipped on the lights.

"Come on, Park. You have nothing to worry about."

Parker stopped and looked back. "What do you mean?"

Still laughing, Rob slapped her on the back. "She's totally out of your league."

CHAPTER TEN

The newspaper hit the table with a loud slap. Cate looked up from her laptop. She was sitting in Station Two's common room, scowling her way through another donation request email. Cordell stood over her, wearing a pleased look.

"Nice job." A copy of the *Mayville Reader* now sat at Cate's elbow. "I owe you a bottle of whiskey. Something nice, too, not that swill you usually drink." Cordell's blue eyes twinkled.

"Not everyone makes a captain's salary." Cate peered around her computer at the paper's front page. The headlining article was the profile of Parker's store and the break-in, and dead center was the picture of the two of them in the park. Cate swallowed and returned to her computer screen.

Cordell clapped her on the shoulder. "You'll be earning a captain's salary soon enough. Thanks again." She shot Cate a wink, then disappeared into her office.

Cate pushed the paper away. She glared at the half-finished email, trying to recover her train of thought. Salesmanship was the least of her skills, and she always struggled to find the right words. Every time Alex read one of her drafts, he had to explain that "threatening" was not the same as "persuasive."

It didn't help that the picture of Parker was right there, her smile radiating up from the page. They looked good together, too, leaning into each other with an obvious ease that belied the fact that they'd spoken only a handful of times. The lake breeze had tousled Parker's hair, and once again Cate found herself wondering what it would feel like to run her fingers through it.

Without warning, Alex slid into the chair across from her and snapped up the paper. "Look at you, single-handedly saving the department from budget cuts."

The interruption saved Cate from slipping deeper into a daydream involving other pieces of Parker's anatomy, but she ignored Alex and began stabbing at the keyboard with her index fingers. On top of everything else, she also couldn't type worth a damn.

Alex continued, "Good picture, too. Seriously."

Cate's eyes flicked up to glare over the top of her computer. Alex leaned back in his chair, his face a picture of pure innocence. "What's that supposed to mean?"

"Just that it's a good picture." He grinned. "She's cute as hell, you know."

"Hadn't noticed," Cate grumbled.

"Right. Sure."

Just then Freddie appeared out of nowhere, looming over Alex's shoulder. Last time Cate saw him he'd been on the other side of the house, checking on the rig. She would never understand how such a large man moved so quietly.

"Nice picture," Freddie said. "She's cute."

"Wilds claims she hasn't noticed," Alex said.

"Wilds is full of shit."

Cate started massaging her temples. Sometimes she wondered if those two shared the same brain cell. "Don't you assholes have anything better to do?"

Alex and Freddie looked at each other, then back at Cate.

"No," they said in unison.

"It's just a picture. It doesn't mean anything."

Alex leaned forward and steepled his fingers. "So you agree. You do think she's cute."

"I didn't agree."

"But you didn't *disagree*."

Cate threw up her hands. "Fine. Parker is cute. Happy now?"

"No," Freddie said. "When are you going to ask her out again? Didn't you say you had lunch after the interview?"

"You asked her out?" Alex's voice shot up an octave.

Cate groaned. It'd been a mistake to mention that to Freddie. She'd only said something in passing when he asked what she'd done on her weekend off. She should've known better. They were the only ones who could get away with teasing her, and they damn well knew it.

"I didn't ask her out. We just both happened to be free." The excuse sounded weak before Cate even finished speaking.

"Sounds like a date to me," Alex said.

"I hardly know her."

Freddie's dark brows furrowed. "Correct me if I'm wrong, but isn't that the entire point of dating? To get to know someone better?"

"And make out. A lot," Alex added, ever so helpfully.

Cate abandoned her tortured typing attempts and shoved the laptop away.

She did know some things about Parker. Aside from the obvious— the constant fidgeting, the shoe obsession, her penchant for ripped jeans—she was thoughtful and attentive, and curious about damn near everything, in a way that was endearing rather than annoying. She was adorable in the early morning, was a gifted artist, and rode a bright-red motorcycle too fast, which bothered Cate far more than it had any right to.

She'd also taken up residence in Cate's head to an alarming degree. They hadn't spoken since that lunch a week ago, but Cate found herself checking her phone constantly hoping for a text, or scrolling through Instagram over and over, looking for Parker's updates. She sat outside the firehouse every opportunity she could to catch a wave and a smile as Parker bustled around across the street.

Cate raked her fingers through her hair and begrudgingly agreed with Freddie. "I guess. She's donating a bunch of shoes to Butler Center, so I'll see her again soon. That doesn't mean anything, though," she added quickly.

Freddie's brows went from furrowed to nearly touching his hairline. "That's generous of her."

"I think she likes you," Alex added. Very unhelpfully. Again.

Cate's heart thumped an extra beat at his words, and she forced out a long breath. The cool, cynical part of her issued a reminder: no matter how well you knew someone, people changed. It was inevitable. And if they didn't change, they were taken from you.

"She's perfectly nice. But I don't have time for that right now." Cate pushed the laptop toward Alex. "Here, help me with this."

Alex and Freddie exchanged glances, and through the same magic with which he'd appeared, Freddie was gone again.

Alex scooted closer to read Cate's email draft, getting the hint to drop the subjects of *Parker* and *dating*. "Good opening, but let's see if we can make the overall tone slightly less menacing, yeah?"

* * *

Friday, Cate pulled up outside Remix Footwear at exactly five, parking her Jeep behind Parker's red motorcycle. She took a deep breath before killing the engine and getting out. The bold colors of Parker's mural were still eye-catching. She wondered what would happen to it once the window was replaced.

"Hey!" Parker burst out of the stockroom when Cate entered the store, hopping on one foot and trying to shake off a piece of Bubble Wrap tangled around her ankle. Cate guessed that Parker's earlier attempts at organizing the back room were only temporary, but decided she didn't even want to ask.

"Hey, yourself." Cate pointed to a pile of shoeboxes stacked in the middle of the equally disorganized sales floor. "Are these the shoes? I can start loading them up."

Parker nodded enthusiastically, her smile bright. "Yep. Thirty pairs. I hope that's okay?"

"It's more than okay." Cate looked into her eyes. "Thank you."

"I'm happy to do it. Really." Parker dislodged the Bubble Wrap from her foot. "I'll be ready in just a second. Finishing something up."

"No problem."

Parker disappeared, skipping over the offending piece of Bubble Wrap. A cheerful whistle drifted out from the stockroom, followed by the crashing of cardboard boxes. Again, Cate decided not to ask. Shaking her head, she gathered up armfuls of boxes and started to load them into the back of her Jeep, admiring both the mural on the display wall and the one outside as she walked back and forth. She didn't have an artistic bone in her body, but the shared color palette between the two pieces was obvious. Bright slashes of gold cut through them both and seemed to unite them around a common theme. Honestly, the painting outside looked so good that Parker could probably get away without having a front window for a bit longer.

"Holy shit, is this your ride?"

Cate looked up from packing the last of the shoes. Parker was gawking wide-eyed at the Jeep, her keys clutched in her hand.

Cate gave her a small grin. "Yep."

She'd wanted a Wrangler ever since she was a kid. After about a year of working a second job bartending at Crystal's, she'd saved up enough so the car loan would be manageable. Upgrading to the Unlimited Rubicon trim level was a splurge, but she'd worked hard to afford it. And the dealership had thrown in a deal on the window tinting and custom rims package. It was flashy but earned.

Parker's eyes looked like they were going to fall out of her head and start rolling down the sidewalk. "That's hot as hell."

Cate swung the tailgate closed. "I've been known to indulge myself. From time to time."

She clamped her mouth shut. She hadn't meant for that to sound so suggestive, but the slow, lopsided smile spreading across Parker's face told Cate that it wasn't unwelcome.

"I'd like to see that."

Heat filled Cate's face and her pulse started racing. She turned away and climbed into the driver's seat, calling over her shoulder, "I bet you would."

Parker clambered into the passenger seat. "Can I drive on the way back?"

"Can you drive stick?"

"Of course."

Cate glanced over out of the corner of her eye. "No."

Parker was undeterred, smile growing and clearly enjoying herself. "Can I pick the music?"

"No."

Parker clicked her tongue. "You're no fun, Lieutenant."

Cate put on her oversized aviators, grateful to conceal at least part of her face, and threw the Jeep into gear. She'd spent an inordinate amount of time debating between the radio or one of her own playlists when she left her house, eventually giving up and driving over in silence, and Parker was grinning like she knew it. Cate huffed and flipped on the radio, turning to a Top 40 station.

Parker twisted around in her seat, looking at the boxes in back, then held up her phone and contorted her wrist at an uncomfortable angle.

"What are you doing?"

"Getting a picture for the store's Instagram page." Parker stuck out her tongue and flashed a peace sign. "Do you want to take one?"

"Okay." Cate downshifted as they approached a red light. She leaned across the console, aviators firmly in place, easing into frame while Parker lined up the picture. The bright, crisp, tantalizing scent filled her senses again. Parker pressed into Cate and made another face, slightly less ridiculous this time, and snapped the picture while Cate tried not to think about how easy it would be to turn her head and brush her lips against Parker's.

The light changed and Cate slid away. Her right hand gripped the gearshift so tightly her knuckles were white.

"Do you have Instagram? I'll tag you."

"Yeah, but I'm never on it." *Except for every day this week*, Cate reminded herself.

"That's okay. I'll post the link for the charity ball, too."

Cate swallowed thickly. "Thanks."

Parker scooted down in her seat, tapping her phone against the top of her thigh and bobbing her head to the R&B song that just came on.

"That was a pretty good article, don't you think?" Parker asked. Her voice sounded a little strained, but Cate couldn't be certain.

"I do." The corner of Cate's mouth twitched. "I liked your rant about Dragonfly. It is overrated, but no one admits it."

Parker laughed. "I didn't think she would use that quote."

"She told you it was on the record."

"I didn't know she meant *on the record*."

Cate turned onto the main avenue that led to the south side of town, smoothly shifting gears. She shot Parker a look. "That doesn't make any sense."

Parker shrugged. "Too late now, I guess. I hope no one breaks into my store again because of my opinion on this town's Thai food."

"You should try Red Curry House. It's a few blocks off Tomlinson."

Parker squirmed in her seat and went back to her phone. "I will. Sure."

Cate didn't say anything else, and by the time she realized she should've asked Parker if she wanted to go the restaurant together, they were pulling up to Butler Center's back entrance. Jameel and another volunteer were already waiting, greeting them with cheerful waves.

"Cate. Wonderful to see you." Jameel shifted his weight and held out his hand as Cate approached. Although his grip was firm, he appeared frailer than usual, even though only a week had passed since they'd last seen each other. Cate frowned, but Jameel turned to Parker before she could say anything. "And this is our generous benefactor?"

Parker took Jameel's hand with a shy smile. "Nice to meet you, sir."

"Likewise. These will be much appreciated," Jameel said. The volunteer started unloading shoes from the back of the Jeep. Cate jumped in to help, and Jameel turned stiffly to address them both. "Cate,

Michael—we can coordinate distribution next week at the Wednesday games."

"Sounds good," Cate said.

"I hope there's enough." Parker rocked back and forth on her heels. "I got as many sizes as I could. They're all Dame Certifieds, in a bunch of different colorways. They're supposed to be pretty durable and should hold up on both indoor and outdoor courts."

Cate paused, holding a stack of shoeboxes in her arms. "Dame?"

Parker shrugged. "Some of those kids have to be Bucks fans, right?"

Cate resumed unloading, handing off the boxes to Michael and hoping he didn't notice how her face was suddenly burning. She never told Parker directly that she was a Bucks fan, and she must have gleaned that information from the brief conversation with Rob outside the store—which meant that Parker paid closer attention to details than Cate originally gave her credit for.

Both of Jameel's hands went to the top of his cane as he leaned forward, giving Parker a closer look. "Cate tells me you run your own shoe store?"

"Trying to. I hope to open in a few weeks."

"You'll have to tell us when you do. I'm sure many of the kids here would be very interested, especially after a gift like this."

"I'll be sure to do that, sir."

"Call me Jameel, please." Jameel turned to Cate, who'd just finished unloading the last of the shoes. His brown eyes were mischievous. "You should bring your friends around more often."

"We'll see." Cate glanced at Parker, whose ears were turning a bright shade of red. Parker rubbed at the back of her neck and looked away.

After the shoes were unloaded, they followed Jameel inside, who proceeded to pepper Parker with questions as he gave a tour of the center. In between asking about when Parker had moved to town and exactly what type of law her brother practiced, Jameel laid out his plans for a hoped-for renovation and expanded program offerings. Cate lingered behind them. She'd heard this pitch countless times before, and each version became harder and harder to hear as Butler's dire financial situation became more apparent. Parker took it all in with a wide-eyed enthusiasm, nodding eagerly at the idea of a new computer lab and expanded after-school tutoring. Initially, Cate thought Parker was indulging Jameel for her benefit, but when Parker glanced back at her with a broad smile, she realized the reactions were nothing but genuine.

The sounds of shouting and sneakers on hardwood greeted them when they entered the gym. An enthusiastic pickup game took up the entire court, and another volunteer stood in the far corner, arms crossed, whistle between his teeth. The usual group of teens congregated at the top of the bleachers, alternating between yelling at the players and giggling at each other's phones.

"So this is where you spend your time when you're not being a hero." Parker sauntered up beside her. Her ears were still ridiculously red. Was she nervous about something? Cate couldn't tell.

"Yep." Cate jammed her hands into the pockets of her leather jacket, thinking about how good Parker had looked wearing it.

"Do you still play?"

"Occasionally. Nothing serious, though." She nodded down at her left leg. "Two knee surgeries kind of slowed me down."

"ACL?"

"And a partially torn meniscus."

Parker's eyes softened. "I'm sorry. That must have hurt."

"Not really." Cate paused. The corner of her mouth twitched. "It hurt the girl I fell on more."

Parker laughed. Cate had heard that bright, cheerful sound almost a dozen times by now, yet it still managed to catch her off guard. "Which time? When you tore your ACL or meniscus?"

"Both, actually. She played for our biggest conference rival. We didn't get along very well," Cate said dryly. She almost matched Parker's smile.

"Oh, you had a nemesis! Exciting. Always wanted one of those." Parker nudged her playfully.

Heat bloomed across her arm, like their skin had actually touched. Cate cleared her throat and focused her attention on the pickup game dominating the gym. But she didn't step away.

Jameel slid in next to them, a surprisingly dexterous move considering the cane he was working with. "Cate is a natural shooter. And one hell of a defender, too," he said. The mischievous glint in his eye had not dissipated; in fact, he was glowing in a way that Cate hadn't seen before and was making her quite nervous. He leaned over to speak to Parker as if Cate wasn't also standing right next to them. "She's been running our summer skills camp for the past five years. She's a great coach. The kids love her. We've even had a few of our players earn college scholarships."

"That's really cool." Parker's gaze lingered on Cate.

"Indeed," Jameel agreed.

Cate looked down at her boots. She supposed Jameel's curiosity could be forgiven. In all the years they'd known each other, she'd never brought a friend with her to Butler. Only her parents had come around a handful of times. Granted, she didn't have many friends outside of the firehouse, and even her previous girlfriends hadn't earned any invites. This was a part of her life that she just didn't share easily. Frankly, she didn't share most things easily. The sight of Parker standing there, fidgeting as usual, wearing an easy smile and drawing a laugh out of Jameel, suddenly seemed as natural as anything Cate had ever imagined.

A sharp whistle interrupted her thoughts. Play had stopped and everyone was grudgingly moving into place alongside the key. The ball rolled toward them, stopping at Cate's feet. They were standing behind the backboard, off to the left of the baseline that ran near the gym's entrance. From this angle, the hoop was completely hidden. Without thinking, Cate scooped it up and, with one snap of her wrist, let it fly. The ball soared over the backboard and fell through the net with a perfect swish.

The gym erupted. Thundering cheers and stomping shook the bleachers. Several of the kids waiting on the key collapsed to the hardwood in exaggerated gestures of dropping dead. Colin, the ref, just shook his head and went to hand the ball to the lanky white kid at the foul line, who was doubled over and laughing at his teammates' antics.

"Showing off?" Jameel asked.

Cate shrugged. "Maybe a little."

Parker's eyebrows shot to her hairline, and she looked from the backboard, to Cate, then to the backboard again as if she were trying to work out the geometry in her head and failing.

"Miss Cate!"

Tasha and her crew bounded down from the bleachers and surrounded them, careening between talking excitedly about the shot and providing a rapid update about some gossip Cate had lost track of weeks ago. She indulged the pack of teens, nodding intently even though she couldn't follow half of what they were saying.

"Hey, where'd you get those?" Parker pointed at Tasha's shoes, a pair of elaborate yellow-and-purple high-tops.

"My brother got them for me." Tasha eyed Parker skeptically.

"Nice. That's a limited-edition colorway. I tried to cop a pair myself but had to take the L."

"You know sneakers?"

Parker shrugged, but her excitement was palpable. At least, to Cate it was. "You could say that." Parker produced a palmful of shiny business cards from her back pocket. "I'm opening a store on Tomlinson, across the street from the fire station. Check out my website. You and your brother should come through when it opens." At Cate's raised eyebrow, she quickly added, "With a parent or other adult, of course."

Tasha's skepticism vanished when she took the card. The pack immediately shifted their attention to Parker, peppering her with questions about different shoe brands and colors and whether she could get this one or that one or if she had heard about the latest release. A few more kids came over from the bleachers to check out what was going on.

Tasha stepped back from the crowd gathering around Parker. She leaned closer to Cate, eyebrows waggling, the look on her face suggesting both genuine curiosity and joy at the possibility of fresh gossip.

"Who's that, Miss Cate? Is that your girl?" Tasha nodded in Parker's direction, making only the barest attempt at lowering her voice.

Cate's eyes flicked over to Parker. One of the older high schoolers took a business card and gave Parker a dap. Jameel remained in the same spot, leaning on his cane with a pleased expression.

"Just a friend, T."

Tasha looked like she didn't believe a word Cate just said. Cate silently agreed.

* * *

They left Butler an hour later, walking through a light drizzle back to Cate's Jeep. Cate didn't even feel the rain. Parker practically floated through the parking lot, fresh out of business cards and her grin threatening to split her face. Cate couldn't stop herself from watching Parker's every move as she settled into the passenger seat and whipped out her phone, flipping through the pictures she'd taken with a few kids to post to Instagram. She'd moved through the rec center so easily, like she'd been going there for years. It had been like that at Crystal's, too. And the firehouse. Everywhere Parker went, she breezed in with effortless confidence and just seemed to fit. Cate was helpless against that magnetism, but that wasn't what worried her. What worried her were the depths below that shiny, outgoing surface, and the fact that there was more to Parker than bright shoes and stylish clothes.

Cate threw the Jeep into gear, grateful for the physical demands of a manual transmission. It gave her something to focus on. "Jameel liked you."

Parker pocketed her phone and started drumming her fingers on the top of her knee. "I liked him, too. He's really nice." The reflection from the passing streetlights cast Parker's face in a flattering glow. Cate's eyes trailed over the curve of Parker's lips before snapping back to the road. "I can't believe the board completely dropped the ball like that when he got sick. What bullshit," Parker continued.

"You're telling me." Cate sighed. "It's a mess."

"Jameel said he asked you to run for a board seat next year."

"He told you that?"

"Yep." Parker's fingers kept up their beat. "Are you going to do it?"

"Thinking about it."

"You should. You obviously care about the place."

"Thanks."

The song changed, and with it the rhythm of Parker's fingers. Cate stared straight ahead.

"How did you end up volunteering there?" Parker asked.

Cate let out a long breath. "I needed some community service credits during my junior year of college. I was rehabbing my knee anyway, so I thought it'd be a good way to stay close to the game. Jameel and I hit it off. And I liked coaching the kids. I kind of never left." She meant to stop there, but the next piece just tumbled out without her even realizing until it was too late. "A lot of them remind me of my brother."

The drumming stopped. "I didn't know you had a brother. What's he like?"

"He died."

Just like that, all the air rushed out of the Jeep. Cate could practically feel Parker's eyes widen, but she didn't dare glance over. That gaze would be too open, too soft and sweet and gentle for her to manage right now.

"Oh, shit. I'm so sorry, Cate. What happened? No, wait, you don't have to tell me." Parker went back to tapping her thigh, only more rapidly. "Sorry, that was rude."

"I'm not upset."

Cate paused, taking a moment to gather her thoughts while she downshifted onto a side street. The rain was still just a ghost of a drizzle, but she was comforted by the sturdiness of her Jeep. It was part of why she had always wanted this car: it was reliable, steady. Safe. She started talking.

"My family was in a car accident. We were rear-ended at a stop light and then hit by another car. My parents and I were hurt, but we made it. Anthony didn't. He was fifteen. I was twelve."

The words sounded clipped, distant. Like they belonged to someone else. She couldn't remember the last time she'd told anyone about the accident. Even her closest friends through high school and college, who'd been to her parents' house and seen pictures of Anthony frozen in time, never learned exactly how he had died. Neither did the handful of women she'd dated over the years.

A nineties dance song came on the radio, one that Cate found personally grating and did not fit the tone of the conversation. As if reading her mind, Parker leaned forward and jabbed at the radio. The station landed on a droning NPR market report. The host's monotone eased Cate's suddenly frayed nerves.

Parker spoke a moment later, voice somber. "That must have been terrible. I can't even imagine it."

"Yeah. Pretty much." Cate sighed. "Anthony loved basketball, though. He was already six-three when he hit eighth grade. He was convinced he was going to get a D1 scholarship and be a lottery pick in the NBA draft." She let out a sharp, dry laugh. "He got me into basketball, actually. I was more into soccer until he joined a team. And after he died, something in me flipped, and it was all I wanted to do."

Anthony had been her best friend, champion, protector. And in one terrifying instant, he was gone.

A lump formed in the base of her throat. Neither of them spoke. Cate glanced over at the passenger seat. Parker's hands were folded tightly in her lap. She met Cate's eyes. Cate quickly looked back to the road.

"Thank you for telling me," Parker said.

Cate's fingers tightened around the gearshift like a death grip. The lump in her throat grew. The Jeep felt too small. She'd been hoping for a joke, or for Parker to change the subject. Not heart-wrenching sincerity.

A few moments later, as they pulled up to Parker's store, the sky ripped open. Rain thundered against the Jeep's hardtop. Parker looked out at her already drenched motorcycle and sighed. "I didn't know it was supposed to rain today."

The forecast had shown rain for most of the week, but Cate kept that to herself. She frowned at the bike in distaste. She'd never understood the appeal, and her career as a paramedic had illustrated in grisly detail how dangerous they could be. While Cate had no say in Parker's personal decisions, it was far too easy to imagine the back wheel of her bike slipping on wet pavement and Parker's head cracking against the ground. Cate was already shaking her head. "I'll take you home."

Parker turned toward her. "You wouldn't mind?"

"No way you're riding in this. It's too dangerous."

"I'm not about to argue. I never ride in the rain." That infectious, dangerous grin appeared again. "Just give me a minute to put my bike inside."

Cate unbuckled her seat belt. "Let me—"

Parker was out the door before Cate even finished her sentence, flipping up the hood of her sweatshirt over her head with a jaunty air. She moved with a deftness Cate didn't know she was capable of, muscling the motorcycle over the curb and to the overhang protecting the front door. Within seconds, the motorcycle was secured inside. It reinforced Cate's observation that Parker was capable of moving at only one speed, but it was also an impressive display of strength and coordination. Parker was stronger than she looked. Much stronger.

Parker darted through the rain and jumped back into the passenger seat, shaking off her hood and wiping the toes of her black-and-blue sneakers. A ripple shot through Cate's body like she'd just touched an exposed wire. She bit her lip to distract herself from the rush of sudden need. What the hell had gotten into her? First she was rambling on about Anthony, and now all she wanted was Parker's hands digging into her thighs. She began rationalizing the reaction—wasn't there something about the emotions surrounding grief leading to sex? Cate was certain she'd read that somewhere. It was perfectly reasonable. This was already a difficult time of year, coupled with the stress of the charity ball, and if she were being honest, it had been far too long since she'd slept with someone. This was nothing more than a sharp reminder of a basic, fundamental need. All the more reason to stay away. If a woman she barely even knew brought this out of her, what else could Parker do to her? What else could she take?

And why couldn't Cate stop herself?

"You okay?"

Parker was giving her a bemused look, waiting for Cate to start driving again.

"Your mural," Cate croaked. She pointed a shaky finger at Parker's store.

"What? Oh." Parker whipped around. The wind had kicked up, and a sheet of rain battered the plywood. The crisp edges of the mural were starting to bleed together. Parker waved a hand over her shoulder and settled back into the seat. "It's okay. I'll just do it again when it dries."

"Just like that?" Cate asked skeptically.

"Just like that." Parker's smile was just short of cocky. Cate wanted to kiss it off her face.

"So, um, where do you live?"

Parker gave her address, and Cate threw the Jeep back into gear, white-knuckling the gearshift again. She stared ahead at the road, trying not to focus on how the temperature inside her Jeep was starting to creep higher, or how she never really noticed how broad Parker's shoulders were.

After an excruciating ten minutes, Cate pulled up outside Mayville Lofts, a renovated warehouse converted into trendy loft apartments just south of the small downtown square. Cate shifted into neutral and set the parking brake. The rain continued to drum against the hardtop. Even in the dim light offered by the nearby streetlamp, she could see Parker's ears were turning that unnatural shade of red.

"Thanks for the ride. And for taking me to Butler. I had a lot of fun." Parker looked over at Cate from under her long eyelashes.

"It's literally the least I could do. You really didn't have to donate all those shoes." Cate had released her grip on the gearshift but still needed something to hold on to. The steering wheel creaked under her fingers.

"Like I said, I was happy to. Those kids deserve it." All the bravado drained from Parker's body. "And I like spending time with you."

"Me too," Cate said softly.

Parker started dragging her palms across the top of her thighs, like she was drying her hands. "I hope you don't think I donated the shoes just to get close to you, though."

"That didn't cross my mind for a second."

"Good." Parker stopped rubbing her hands on her jeans. She looked directly into Cate's face, her expression as serious as Cate had ever seen her. "Can I take you out for dinner sometime? Whenever you're free. I know you've got a lot going on."

This invitation was far weightier than when Cate asked Parker to lunch just days ago. Cate had told herself it was a matter of convenience, and sharing a pizza with someone didn't necessarily mean anything. But with how Parker was looking at her, there was no way to misinterpret the meaning, and despite her brain urging caution, Cate was speaking before she could catch herself. Something about this woman made her want to plunge ahead without reason or thought.

"I would really like that."

Parker's grin could have lit the entire street. Her hand went toward the door. "I'll call you."

For the first time ever, Cate regretted purchasing a manual transmission. It would take nothing to lean over and close the gap between them, twist her hand in the front of Parker's sweatshirt and pull her in, to breathe in that fresh, crisp cologne and finally taste Parker's lips. And, God help her, she would do it, too, if she wasn't mortified at the thought of accidentally jamming the gearshift into Parker's ribs. Instead, she sat frozen in place, only able to offer a tight nod as Parker slipped out of the Jeep and darted through the rain to the front entrance of her building. Once Parker was safely inside, Cate's head fell back against the headrest with a dull thud.

She should have just kissed her.

CHAPTER ELEVEN

What a shitty day.

Parker rummaged through the mess that had, despite her best efforts, accumulated yet again in her stockroom. The chaos was more localized this time, restricted to the back corner near the fire exit, where she was currently searching for a pair of Jordan Twelves in a size nine that her stupid new inventory program said she had in stock but couldn't find. It probably would be a little more accurate if she actually reorganized the stockroom, which she'd been planning to do that day, but that was before her online sales platform (also new, also stupid) decided it no longer wanted to work. Figuring out exactly why had eaten up her entire afternoon, topped off by a phone call from the window company telling her the piece they ordered was delayed several more days.

All this would have been manageable if she hadn't also been up until two in the morning trying (and failing) to snag an exclusive sneaker drop that New York Manni warned her about weeks ago but had completely slipped her mind. By the time she logged on to the online portal the bots had scooped them up, and she was forced to scramble to other secondary market sites and resellers to try and grab at least one pair that wasn't marked up astronomically. No luck.

That irritated her the most out of everything. She'd spent years crafting a reputation for reliability and fairness within her tight circle of customers and other resellers. It was one of the reasons New York Manni trusted her with their intel. Not only did she have the hottest, most desirable releases, she also had a sharp eye for the smaller, more niche designers and collaborations that eventually developed their own dedicated followings. When everyone else was sold out, Parker Mandli always came through. She wasn't used to taking a loss.

It felt like she'd taken a lot of losses lately.

After a few more minutes of searching, she finally found the Twelves jammed behind two completely unrelated pairs. She packaged them up and slapped a UPS sticker on the side of the shipping box, then grabbed a Sharpie and drew Remix Footwear's logo next to the label. She added the shoes to the growing pile that would be shipped out the next day and checked her phone. Just a few news notifications and a couple of Instagram messages from prospective buyers.

Nothing from Cate.

Parker sat cross-legged on the floor, surrounded by a mess of shoeboxes and packaging materials, and pulled her computer onto her lap. She had a few more online orders to process. She looked at her phone again. Still nothing.

Dinner with Cate had yet to materialize, though it wasn't from lack of trying. Memorial Day had been last weekend, and Cate had worked the entire holiday and had several last-minute meetings about the charity ball, which was set for this upcoming Saturday. They'd tentatively scheduled something for Wednesday, but Cate canceled almost as soon as Parker suggested it because Cordell needed her to cover a shift at another fire station at the last minute. And this was on top of her usual volunteer hours at Butler. Parker hadn't even seen her sitting outside of the fire station. She had no idea how Cate did it all without collapsing into an exhausted heap.

Now it was Thursday night, and with the ball coming up in two days, Parker doubted they'd get a moment alone together before that. They were texting regularly, though. Or as regularly as Cate's alleged disdain for texting allowed, which Parker was beginning to think was a bit exaggerated. To Parker's ongoing delight, she was just as dryly funny over text as she was in person, especially when responding to a firefighting meme or describing Alex and Freddie's latest antics around the station.

Unable to stop herself, Parker went to her dormant phone and scrolled through her texts to find their last exchange. Earlier that morning, Cate had sent a picture of Alex and Freddie screaming at two pieces of what looked like lunch meat stuck to Station Two's whiteboard. One appeared to be sliding down more than the other. Cate's caption read: *I'm not paid enough to deal with this.* Parker had no idea what the hell was supposed to be happening, but it was the funniest shit she'd seen in days. She replied with a string of LOL emojis and hadn't heard anything since.

Sighing, Parker closed her computer with a slap and flopped onto her back in defeat. Bright fluorescent light shone in her face. She couldn't stop thinking about the curve of Cate's lips, or the subtle amusement in her eyes even as her coworkers annoyed her. Parker's gaze flicked to the calendar hanging above her desk, and she resisted the urge to get up and shamelessly flip it over to November. Abs like that ought to be illegal.

She wondered what it would be like to feel those abs flexing under her mouth.

Christ. She was down bad.

Parker had meant it when she said she'd wait until Cate was free, but now she was second-guessing even asking Cate out. Looking back, after Cate's revelation about the accident and how that so clearly tied to her dedication to Butler Center, it was probably a little inappropriate to act on any sort of romantic intentions. Yet she had, blurting out the invitation in the passenger seat of Cate's Jeep like a goddamn idiot. Sure, Cate had said yes, but still.

Parker chewed at her bottom lip, staring at an oblong water stain on the ceiling. She was doing it again, wasn't she? Being impulsive and thoughtless and rushing into something without thinking of the consequences. Or collateral damage. She'd seen the cracks in Cate's armor while they toured the rec center, that wry, not-quite-smile on her face, the effortless grace in how she carried herself, the patience she displayed when talking to the pack of excitable teenagers, the barely concealed pain in her voice when she spoke about her brother. Beneath that armor was a fragility that Parker hadn't expected. Parker wasn't good at fragile. She was clumsy, inattentive. She dropped things and they shattered at her feet. Cate deserved better than that. She deserved to be cared for.

Parker was almost too afraid to try. What if she messed this up, too?

What a shitty fucking day.

A flash in the corner of Parker's eye caught her attention, and she sat up. Red and white lights reflected through the stockroom door's small window. She sat up, brushed off her jeans, and went to the front of her store.

Ladder Two was slowly backing into the station garage, lights spinning. Medic Two pulled up a moment later. Parker couldn't see anyone in the engine's cab, but her recent lessons in basic firefighting told her that Alex was driving and Cordell was in the passenger seat. Cate, Freddie, and the rest were in the back. Syed and Omar were on the bus this shift.

The spot between Parker's shoulder blades began to unwind. She rubbed the back of her neck. She hadn't even realized she'd been nervous. The sirens had gone off a while ago, right when she was in the middle of her ongoing battle with her inventory program, and she'd stopped cursing at her computer long enough to watch the engine and ambulance tear down the street. She checked her phone again, finally registering the time—just after eleven at night. They'd been gone for hours. Parker hoped it hadn't been a bad call. Cate had hinted at that, once or twice, never going into details, but Parker gleaned enough to know that some calls were worse than others. Cate didn't talk about those.

Once both vehicles were safely inside the garage, Parker turned away with a renewed focus. She would pack up a few more online orders, respond to those Instagram messages, and head home. The ride would clear her head. Hopefully. Her motorcycle hadn't offered its usual reprieve as of late. Somehow, it made her think of Cate even more.

After she finished boxing up the last order, her back pocket buzzed. Parker's heart jumped into her throat. It was Cate.

Are you still working?

Parker ignored the trembling in her hands as she tapped out a reply. *Yeahhhhhhhh.*

She paused, then added a few crying emojis for maximum drama. Mere seconds after the message was sent, her phone went off.

"I simply must know who is buying sneakers at 11:32 on a Thursday night." Cate's voice was warm in her ear, and Parker could picture that half-smile so clearly it was like they were standing in the same room. Her irritation at the inventory program that had kept her there so late— her brilliant, fantastic, innovative inventory program—vanished.

Parker grinned. "Supply and demand. The world never stops spinning, y'know?"

"So you're the backbone of the global economy now."

"Yep."

"You're ridiculous."

"The word you're looking for is 'dedicated.'"

Cate snorted. The sound of someone talking in the background came over the line. "Hang on."

Parker went to the front of the store. Across the street, Station Two was still, the brick building lit only by a single floodlight in the driveway. She wondered what Cate was doing right then.

"Sorry." Cate's voice came back. "Morgan needed something."

"How'd it go? You were gone for a while."

"We caught two calls back-to-back. It was fine."

Parker's eyes narrowed. She wasn't fluent enough in Cate's language to determine if "fine" meant its usual definition, or if Cate was avoiding the subject. She didn't have any evidence for the latter, but the thought was still there. "Is everyone okay?"

"Yes, we're good. Thanks." The call became muffled again, and it sounded like Cate was walking somewhere. The station door opened. A tall, dark figure stepped outside and was lit up by the floodlight, one hand in her pocket, the other holding her phone to her ear.

Parker peered through the glass door, breath catching. "Hey there, Lieutenant."

"Hi." Cate took a few steps toward the sidewalk, dipping in and out of the circle of light cast by the floodlight, as if teasing the distance between them. Parker watched every movement.

Cate's voice grew soft. "Why don't you come over here?"

"Why don't *you* come over *here*?"

"I'm supposed to be working."

"So am I."

Cate huffed. She took her hand out of her pocket and placed it on her hip indignantly. "You enjoy being difficult, don't you?"

Parker felt her stare from across the street. "Very much so."

"I came out here to talk to you, but if you're too busy…"

"On my way!"

Parker slipped her phone into her back pocket and pushed open the door. The night was pleasantly warm for the first week of June. Tomlinson was deserted and eerily quiet at the late hour. The surrounding homes and businesses were all dark, save for Parker's shop. Parker broke into a slight jog as she stepped off the curb, cutting across the darkness until she was standing in front of Cate.

Even under unflattering, orange-tinged light, Cate was gorgeous. Her face was only half lit, and shadows played across the strong line of her jaw and full lips. Her bangs fell across her forehead, damp from the shower. Cate's gaze was steady, as always, but Parker sensed the urgent energy coursing through her. She seemed to be breathing a little harder than usual.

"Are you all right?" Parker asked.

"I'm fine. Why?"

There was that word again. *Fine.* "You're shaking." Parker eased forward, catching the scent of crisp, slightly floral soap. She touched the back of Cate's hand. The night was so quiet and still it felt like they were the only two people in the entire town.

"Oh. Yeah." Cate flexed her fingers. "It's just adrenaline. It will wear off."

Parker was intensely curious about what had triggered that adrenaline surge but assumed Cate wouldn't want to discuss it. Plus, as she tried not to stare so blatantly at Cate's chest in that too-tight MFD T-shirt, she was too busy thinking about what she could do to elicit that reaction herself. Did Cate deliberately wear a size too small to torture her? It sure as hell felt that way.

"I wanted to apologize for all the back-and-forth this week. My schedule gets really intense sometimes." Cate raked both hands through her hair, a few more jet-black curls flopping onto her forehead. Parker liked how wavy it was when it was damp.

"I get it, Cate. I didn't take it personally."

"I also didn't want you to get the wrong impression."

Oh.

There it was.

Parker took a step back. Cate had made it very clear from the beginning everything she was juggling, and that was even before she'd told Parker about Anthony. It made sense that she didn't have the time or space for dating, and certainly not with someone like Parker, who barely had her own shit together. Not too long ago, she would've just brushed it off and suggested they hook up anyway for some fun, no strings attached, but the thought of reducing Cate to a meaningless fling made Parker's insides twist. Cate was more than that. It was probably better this way, honestly. Best to end it before she fucked it up.

"It's okay. I get that, too." Parker looked down at her shoes, face burning in embarrassment. Her lucky Jordan One Retros were failing at the moment.

"You…do?"

When Parker looked back up, Cate's brow was furrowed in such befuddlement it was comical. And undeniably adorable. Parker shoved that last thought away. "You're busy, I'm busy. You're dealing with a lot, I'm trying to open a business. It's just bad timing."

Cate was frowning now. "Yes, I suppose that's true—"

"It's not a big deal. Really. We can still be friends." Parker wanted to kick herself. She should've known better. "I'm not going anywhere."

Except she was. She was *going* to march back over to her store, dig a hole in the back lot, and not leave for a month. Rob would bring her food and water. She could run things from a cozy little hole with that goddamn inventory program and online sales portal and eventually emerge when this blew over and the awkwardness was forgotten.

She was about to turn and make her glorious retreat across the street, wondering where she could find a shovel at this hour, when Cate's voice stopped her.

"I don't think—that's not what I meant."

"What?" Now it was Parker's turn to be confused, mimicking Cate's expression from earlier.

Cate let out a frustrated huff. "Dammit, I've never been good at this." Her mouth opened and closed several times, and she grimaced like trying to form words was causing her physical pain. With every attempt Parker got more and more confused, until Cate finally reached forward, took Parker's face in her hands, and kissed her.

Parker froze. Cate's lips were soft, her kiss gentle and tentative like she expected Parker to pull away. Her thumb traced the line of Parker's jaw, tilting her head up. She parted Parker's mouth with her own and stopped just short of brushing her tongue over Parker's bottom lip.

Parker's brain kicked back on, and she sank into Cate, wrapping her arms around her waist and digging her fingers into the small of Cate's back, scratching at the thin MFD T-shirt. She inhaled deeply, breathing in the scent of Cate's soap mixed with the smell of smoke that clung to Cate's skin. Cate trailed her hand up the back of Parker's neck and buried it in her hair. A soft, breaking noise slipped past Cate's lips, almost like she was sighing in relief. It was the sexiest thing Parker had ever heard. Parker grabbed Cate's hips and walked her backward out of the light until she was pressed against the brick exterior of the station. Cate's knees buckled, bringing her down to Parker's height, and Parker slipped her thigh between Cate's legs at the same time she grazed Cate's bottom lip with her teeth.

Parker expected Cate to push her away, to use her obvious size and strength advantage to change their positions, but that didn't happen. Rock-hard muscle yielded underneath Parker's hands as Cate let out another small gasp. It was so incongruous with the stoic firefighter's demeanor that Parker almost stopped in absolute wonder, but the contrast spurred her on. She rocked her thigh a little harder, gripped

Cate's hips tighter, and kissed the line of Cate's jaw, down to the soft skin of her neck. She bit gently at Cate's throat. A shudder racked Cate's entire frame and she choked back another noise, one lower and deeper and richer than the one she'd made before.

Actually, *that* was the sexiest thing Parker had ever heard.

Parker found Cate's lips again, but it wasn't enough. She was already losing herself. She wanted to feel those warm, taut muscles straining underneath her, hear all the noises Cate was capable of making, learn where to touch her and taste her to draw each one of them out in turn.

Cate's hand fell to Parker's forearm, the blunt of her nails digging into Parker's skin. "Parker…"

Jesus fucking Christ, she only wanted to hear her name in Cate's voice from now on.

"I…I have to get back." Cate tugged at the back of Parker's head, pulling her away. Dark eyes met her own, blown wide, and Parker hoped the reluctance on Cate's face wasn't some trick of the shadows.

"Sorry." Dazed, she released Cate and stepped back. She was lightheaded and couldn't catch her breath. She smoothed down the back of her hair where Cate had been holding on for dear life.

Cate let out a strained chuckle. "Why are you apologizing? I started this." She pushed herself away from the wall, legs not quite steady, and led them back into the light. Parker looked around. The street was still quiet. The odds that anyone had seen them appeared low, although she wouldn't have cared if they did.

Parker found Cate's hand, their fingers lacing together. "I'm not sure what impression you'd think I'd get, but that definitely cleared things up."

Cate squeezed Parker's hand then let it drop. "Can I call you tomorrow?"

"After that? You damn well better."

Casting one last look over her shoulder, Cate disappeared back into the station. Parker managed a wave, then stood in the driveway, blinking at Station Two's bright-red door in disbelief. Cate had ducked back in so quickly she wondered if it had all been a particularly vivid hallucination, but the sting where Cate had dug into her arm and the lingering taste of smoke told her it was real.

Parker staggered back across the street. She stumbled through the front of the store to the stockroom, pressed her back against the wall, and slid down, legs sticking straight out in front of her. Her face ached from smiling so hard. She stretched forward and slapped the toes of her sneakers in glee.

"Lucky shoes!"

* * *

Cate placed both palms on the door and let her head fall forward, keeping her back to the rest of the firehouse. Her heart thundered in her chest, and she felt like the ground was about to fall away from under her feet. And, God help her, she was smiling. Luckily, the ladder truck kept her hidden from view.

She didn't know what the hell had possessed her to kiss Parker right outside the firehouse. No, that wasn't right—she knew *exactly* what had possessed her, and it was the feeling she'd been unable to shake for weeks that had steadily grown until it was impossible to ignore: the fact that she'd wanted to kiss Parker ever since the night of the break-in. If anything, Cate should be considering what the hell took her so long, because in that brief, breathless moment, Parker had annihilated the memory of every other kiss that came before.

Setting her shoulders, Cate headed back toward the common area, forcing her smile away. Freddie and Alex were checking their gear, and Omar and Syed were restocking the bus. A loud bang came from the kitchen, which Cate assumed came from Salt trying to round up a midnight snack. Morgan was probably off in the showers. Cate exhaled slowly. No one had noticed that she had snuck out for a few moments, and if anyone asked, she would easily brush it off and say she needed to grab some fresh air. She nodded at Alex and Freddie.

"Wilds? You okay?" Cordell appeared out of nowhere, sharp blue eyes stopping Cate dead in her tracks.

"I'm fine." Cate hitched a thumb over her shoulder, readying her excuse. "I just needed—"

"The probie said she saw something fall on you. What happened?" Cordell's gaze swept over Cate, scanning for injuries. Cate's hand flew to the side of her neck, still feeling the ghosting of Parker's teeth across her skin. She hoped there wasn't a mark.

Her captain's piercing look snapped Cate back to the present. "A piece of a support beam from the ceiling caught me as we were pulling out," she said. "It wasn't anything serious."

Cordell's eyes flashed. "I still want Syed to look at you. You should have said something."

Cate didn't argue when Cordell ordered her to take a seat at the nearest table and waved Syed over. The adrenaline and exhilaration were wearing off, and a dull ache took root between her shoulder blades.

The call had been a vacant apartment building. When they arrived, flames were already shooting out of the bottom-story window. Apparently, a couple of squatters started a fire to cook something or keep warm—whatever the reason, it got out of hand quickly. She, Freddie, and Morgan led the interior attack, taking a line into the inner rooms on the first-floor apartment. They'd knocked down the fire pretty quickly and found the two squatters unconscious. As Cate was hauling one of them out, a piece of the ceiling came crashing down, catching her across the shoulder and barely missing her air tank. She hadn't even realized it happened until they were all outside, when Morgan asked if she was okay.

Syed finished looking her over. No burns or other obvious injuries; she would most likely be sore for a day or so. Cate nodded at his prognosis and accepted his offer of ibuprofen and a water bottle, Cordell still eyeing her warily. Cate slammed the water in one go and headed upstairs. She passed her bunker gear hanging outside her locker, boots already inside her pants so all she had to do was step into them. The gear beckoned for another call, but she wouldn't mind if the rest of her shift was uneventful.

Each step she took felt heavier and heavier, and it was clear the last few weeks were finally catching up to her. She was tired and sore and hurting, and no matter how many shifts she covered or calls she went on, she wasn't going to escape the inevitable anniversary of Anthony's death. Her chest tightened uncomfortably. The whole idea that "time healed all wounds" was bullshit; the grief was just as sharp as the day it happened. Every year she hoped the pain would dull, but it never did. The weight was exhausting, but she had taught herself how to carry it.

Cate stripped to a tank top and shorts, but instead of collapsing into her bunk she padded past a snoring Morgan to the window across the room that looked out over Tomlinson Street. Remix's lights shut off and Parker stepped out onto the sidewalk, helmet dangling from two fingers while she locked up the store. She walked over to her bike, casually tossing her helmet in the air a few times and with an added spring to her step that made it look like she was dancing. She spun around and threw a leg over the motorcycle, kick-starting it all in one motion. Before driving away, she slipped on her helmet and turned in the direction of the firehouse. Then the engine revved and she was gone.

Cate realized that her hand was raised, her fingertips grazing the windowpane. Parker's hair had felt so soft tangled in her fingers. Just like she knew it would. She smiled to herself, feeling just a little bit lighter.

CHAPTER TWELVE

Cate trudged down the stairs of her townhouse, fighting both a throbbing headache and pain shooting through her back. She shuffled into the kitchen and pulled a bottle of water out of the fridge. The microwave clock told her it was just before six p.m. She let out a groan. She hadn't meant to sleep that long.

The rest of her shift, unfortunately, had not been as uneventful as hoped. She should've known better; even just *thinking* that would surely jinx them. After only an hour in her bunk, the tone had gone off, the dispatcher ordering them to respond to another structure fire near downtown. Turned out that it was merely a drunk undergrad who'd passed out with a frozen pizza in the oven, which mostly resulted in a lot of smoke damage. Immediately after that, they caught another call, this one for a car accident on the south side. Luckily, the two drivers involved would be okay, but they had to extricate the one in a Volvo SUV, a make that was a bitch and a half to cut through. Cate and her crew didn't return to the firehouse until just after dawn. By then, she was hopped up on caffeine and adrenaline and it was too late to get any sleep. She ended up staying late to help with the shift changeover and morning briefing to cover for the B Shift lieutenant whose kid had gotten sick. It was nearly ten when she got home and almost noon before she was able to fall asleep. Usually she limited her naps to only a few hours, or else she would wreck her normal sleep schedule, but if there was any day to sleep through, it was this one.

Cate sighed and surveyed the fridge again. Well-stocked, but everything she had for a proper meal required assembly, and she just didn't have it in her. Pizza was an option, but the act of actually ordering it seemed exhausting. She downed the water and grabbed a tumbler from the cupboard. Whiskey on an empty stomach wasn't the healthiest choice either, but she'd damned well earned it. After pouring a generous slug, she grabbed her phone off the charger and sat down on the couch, grimacing at the twinge in her back.

Three notifications stared up at her: a text from Parker, and a text and missed call from her dad. Cate started with Parker's message, which was so uncharacteristically reserved and sweet she wasn't sure how to reply.

Hey there, hope the rest of your shift went well. Can't wait to see you again.

No jokes or innuendo, or even a mention of the blazing kiss they'd shared yesterday. Cate thought that was odd at first, but then realized that Parker was probably giving her space and not trying to push anything, which just made her even more attractive. Desire lanced through Cate, momentarily drowning out fatigue and grief. Cate took a sip of whiskey, feeling the echo of Parker's hands digging into her hips. She had a good idea of what else those hands were capable of.

Thanks, Cate texted back. *Long night. Can I call you soon?*

Barely a second went by before the response came through. *Absolutely.*

Cate's mouth twitched. How Parker managed to cut through her sour moods remained a mystery, but one that Cate wasn't going to question. Especially tonight. She looked at the message from her dad. His text was nothing but a simple heart emoji. She didn't check the voice mail.

After another sip she brought the phone to her ear, dreading the call and then feeling guilty about dreading the call and then dreading the call all over again. Nothing like a Catholic upbringing rearing its head.

"Hey, kid." Jack Wildman's voice was warm and only a little somber.

"Hi, Dad. Sorry I missed you."

"No problem. I figured you were working. Busy day?"

Cate rubbed her forehead. "All night, actually. My shift was ridiculous."

"Yeah, you sound tired," Jack agreed. "Everything okay?"

"Nothing I can't handle."

"I wouldn't expect otherwise."

Silence stretched over the line. Another wave of guilt struck Cate. She knew her parents were wonderful people—kind, generous, supportive. The fact that they weren't very close was not the result of anything her parents had done. Cate knew where the fault lay.

Anthony's death hadn't torn them apart, like such losses often did. Within weeks of the accident, the three of them were in family therapy sessions, in addition to one-on-one appointments they mandated she attend. With the benefit of hindsight, she realized it most likely saved her parents' marriage. But after a year or so it became tedious, and she told them both she no longer wanted to go. Grudgingly, they'd agreed. Cate never went back. Soon after, she'd started high school and threw herself into sports and classes and friends. And with each passing year, she'd slowly pulled away from them.

Maybe one day she could make them understand. They hadn't been in the back seat with her, witnessing the life drain from Anthony's eyes. They hadn't frozen at the sight, unable to offer help or comfort in those final moments. No amount of therapy could change that.

Cate cleared her throat. "What's Mom up to?"

"Over at Nonna's. She wanted me to tell you again that we're sorry to miss the fundraiser tomorrow."

An errant thread poked out from the seam on her faded basketball shorts. They were a relic from high school, the Lady Bulldogs logo now practically invisible. Her attention focused on the thread like a laser, and she began plucking it with a sudden intensity. "I know. Jameel got your donation, though. That was really generous of you both, thank you."

"Happy to. How are you doing?" he asked. Cate pictured her father's broad, easy smile and salt-and-pepper stubble. The gentleness in his voice grated on her. The thread was almost freed from the seam, opening up an even larger hole in the ancient shorts.

"I'm fine. It's just a shitty day."

"I understand." Jack paused. "We worry about you, you know."

"I said I was fine, Dad."

"I know you are, it's—"

"Why do you insist on doing this every year?" Cate stiffened, her hand balling into a fist on top of her thigh.

"Because none of it was your fault."

Her anger receded. She was too tired to maintain anything more than a brief flare. "I know that," she said weakly.

Her father's voice became even gentler. "Maybe one day you'll believe it." More silence. More whiskey. When Jack spoke again, he steered the conversation toward safer waters: the *Dune* movies, the WNBA season.

Cate did her best to indulge him, forcing herself to give more than one-word answers and not act like a sullen teenager, but as hard as she tried, she couldn't muster any enthusiasm. Eventually, her father relented.

"Well, I'll let you go. I'm sure you have other plans tonight."

Parker's smile came to mind far too quickly, softening the hard edges of Cate's mood. "No, not really. Just going to call a friend."

"Ah, one of those fellows from the station?"

"No. She's new. We, um, just met."

"Oh really?" A slightly choked sound came over the line, like Jack was about to say something and thought better of it. His next question was cautious. "Does she have a name?"

"Her name is Parker. She's…" *Adorable. Charming. An incredible kisser.* "Really nice."

"Indeed." Jack's tone was teasing, but only ever so slightly. Cate had always been fiercely private, even as a child and well before Anthony's death, and he knew better than to pry further. Hell, she hadn't even introduced them to Melissa until they'd practically already moved in. Her dad's curiosity bristled over the line, but she didn't say anything. Cate didn't want to jinx…whatever was happening between her and Parker. Or whatever was about to happen.

Jack let out a theatrical sigh, finally unleashing the tendencies of a man who'd taught English and theatre for the better part of twenty-five years. "Your mother and I shall await a further dispatch with bated breath, dear Catherine. Also, we beseech you to call your Nonna. She's quite tired of reading about your exploits in the paper."

"Yes, I will. I promise."

"And we wouldn't mind hearing from you more often, either."

Cate stared at the fresh hole in her shorts. Now she *was* acting like a sullen teenager. "Yeah."

"Love you, Cate. Have a good night."

"Love you too, Dad."

Cate leaned back into the cushion and heaved a sigh. That wasn't terrible. In past years, that call had consisted mostly of awkward silences sandwiched between angry outbursts. If her mother, Anna, was on, it would be more of the latter, topped off with a nice lecture about how Cate couldn't just keep herself closed off like this forever. And how worried they were about her. And maybe she could just give Melissa a call, because, really, why hadn't they been able to work it out? She had just been so nice, *dear*. Never mind the fact that Melissa was probably married by now. Her mother wielded terms of endearment like a paring knife.

The glass of whiskey was nearly gone by the time she hit Parker's number. The call picked up after the first ring.

"Why is this town obsessed with Dragonfly? I swear I don't get it."

Apparently Parker didn't believe in standard phone etiquette, though that was hardly surprising. She was like that with her texts, too, picking up in the middle of a conversation Cate didn't know they were having. "Told you." Cate's mouth quirked into a half-smile.

"There was a ninety-minute wait on a Tuesday. A Tuesday! Make it make sense!"

"I can't explain it, either. Alex loves that place. He orders it every week. When I told him Red Curry House was better, he acted like I had insulted his mother."

Parker laughed. "They must be slipping some kind of psychedelic into that mediocre fish sauce. Or the owner is blackmailing someone."

"Blackmail. Definitely."

Parker laughed again and Cate's smile grew in spite of herself. The ache in her back receded. She imagined Parker's hands on her skin, finding all the sources of tension in her body and massaging them toward release. Cate's mouth went dry at the thought.

"I know you had a long shift." Parker sounded hesitant. "But do you want to go get a drink or something?"

Want and exhaustion warred within her. The pull in her chest demanded that she accept the invitation, but the rational part of her brain took over. She needed food and sleep, otherwise she would be absolutely worthless tomorrow evening during the charity ball, where she was expected to at least say a word or two about Butler Center— which she already wasn't looking forward to and would be excruciating if she wasn't well-rested. The heaviness was there, too, as it always was, coupled with an annoying stab of guilt at the idea of going out and enjoying herself tonight, of all nights.

"I'd love to, I really would…" Cate's eyes drifted back down to the hole in her shorts.

"But?"

A flimsy excuse, born out of reflex, was ready on her lips. Cate stopped. Parker deserved more than that. And just like the ride home from the center, safely ensconced in the cab of her Jeep, Cate wanted to tell her. "You remember what I told you the other day? About the accident?"

"Yeah…?"

"Today's the anniversary."

Parker inhaled sharply. "I'm so sorry, Cate."

"It's fine. How could you know?" The shorts that had somehow survived the past decade were now in danger of becoming completely unwearable. "I really appreciate the invitation, and frankly, if it were any other day, I would already be out the door." *And a flaming support beam almost fell on my head. I should probably mention that at some point.*

"I won't lie to you, that's the nicest way anyone has ever turned me down for a date."

"I can't imagine that happens very often."

Parker paused for half a breath, and Cate pictured her ears turning bright red at the compliment. "More often than you'd think. But I'm really not interested in asking anyone else out." Parker cleared her throat. "Just, um, to be clear."

Cate bit her bottom lip. Although Parker had made her interest obvious, it felt good to hear it stated so plainly, especially since Cate had technically turned her down twice now. Despite her discordant texts, Parker was rather straightforward. Cate really, really liked that about her.

"Likewise. Just to be clear." She echoed Parker's words to make her own point.

"Good." The reply came in a low, raspy register that Cate had never heard in Parker's voice before. She shivered. "Is there anything I can do for you?"

You have no idea. "I don't think so. I think I just need to eat and go to bed."

Parker paused again. "I could bring some food over, if you want."

"You don't have to do that."

"I know I don't have to, I *want* to." Parker started talking faster. "I went a little crazy when I ordered lunch today. I have a ton left over in the fridge here, and I'm just finishing up at the store. I can run it over in a few minutes. It's really no trouble at all."

"It's not from Dragonfly, is it?"

"Blech. God no." Parker's voice turned smug. "Red Curry House."

Cate hesitated, but her growling stomach overrode any further objection. "Okay, yes. That would be amazing. Thank you."

"Perfect. Text me your address and I'll be over soon."

After sending the message, Cate tossed her phone aside and drummed her fingers on the tops of her thighs, an undeniable thrill fluttering in her chest. She looked down. The shorts were even rattier than she thought, complemented by an equally worn-out MFD Fire Academy T-shirt with matching holes in the armpits.

Cate shot off the couch, ignoring the ache in her back, and took the stairs up to her bedroom two at a time. She wrenched open her dresser drawer and frantically began searching for something else to wear. Jeans were too formal. Right? In her right hand she held up her favorite pair. They made her ass look spectacular, which she knew for a fact because Freddie had announced it to everyone at Crystal's the first time she'd worn them out. She'd also caught Parker staring a not-insignificant number of times.

In her other hand was a pair of fleece sweatpants. Comfortable, but shapeless. It also wasn't the middle of winter. She threw them both down and unearthed a pair of yoga pants she'd worn maybe twice. She kicked off the basketball shorts and slipped them on. Tight, but not too tight. Or were they?

To hell with it. Cate pulled on a plain white T-shirt with intact armpits and raked her fingers through her hair, which wasn't as grimy as she feared. Sometimes after structure fires it took multiple showers to get clean. She darted into the bathroom to brush her teeth and made it back downstairs just as the doorbell rang.

Parker's face was flushed, her grin crooked, hair even wilder than usual. She was in tight, ripped black jeans and a short-sleeved Nike hoodie. A battered leather backpack hung from her shoulder. In one hand was her helmet, in the other, a plastic bag brimming with take-out boxes. Parker handed over the food with a half bow, her backpack almost falling off her shoulder.

"At your service, Lieutenant. There's pad thai, red curry, crab rangoons, and a couple of spring rolls. And some mango sticky rice."

"These are your leftovers?" Cate grabbed the bottom of the bag, not wanting to test its load-bearing capacity any further. There had to be at least ten pounds' worth of food in it.

Parker gave a little shrug. "I was hungry."

"I don't mean to take all of this."

"It's my pleasure. I still plan on taking you out to dinner, though." Parker's gaze dropped to the yoga pants, then quickly shot back up to focus on a point just over Cate's shoulder. Before she looked away, Cate caught a glimpse of sheer heat behind Parker's soft gray eyes. Cate's cheeks flushed, even as she silently praised the long-forgotten yoga class she'd been dragged to.

"I'm looking forward to that." Cate's stomach reminded her that she barely had enough energy to stand, let alone entertain fantasies of Parker peeling those pants off her, yet once again her mouth was overriding her common sense. "Would you like to come in?"

Parker's eyes widened. "Are you sure? I understand if you just want to be alone tonight."

Boundaries, Catherine. Grief settled in Cate's chest again, tempering her earlier enthusiasm but not extinguishing it completely. "I'm not up for much, honestly, but some company would be nice."

"I can do that."

Cate stepped aside and Parker kicked off her shoes at the door, an understated pair of black-and-dark-gray high-tops. Cate led her through the foyer and into the kitchen, depositing the overflowing bag on the breakfast island. She pulled out several plates and another glass, watching out of the corner of her eye as Parker wandered over to the packed bookcase in the corner of the living room. Cate wasn't much of a decorator. Her townhouse was very sparse, with only the basic pieces of furniture and a few pictures on the wall, and she was religious about keeping it clean. The only area of chaos was the bookcases, which she allowed to overflow with no real rhyme or reason. Parker cocked her head to the side like a child would, as if that made reading the titles easier. Cate smiled at the sight.

"I need to read more," Parker said wistfully.

"What do you like?"

Parker grimaced over her shoulder. "*The Hunger Games?*"

"Those are good. I can make a couple of suggestions, if you'd like."

"I'd love that."

Cate busied herself with the take-out boxes. "Can I get you something to drink? Tea, water, beer?"

Parker walked over to the island and slid onto a stool across from Cate, pointing at the half-empty tumbler. "I'll have one of those. Lots of ice."

Cate poured Parker a drink and freshened her own. Neither of them spoke. She kept her head down, focusing on dishing out the food, even as she felt Parker's eyes following her every movement. Cate couldn't quite bring herself to look up. She knew what she would see: a cheerful smile, bright eyes. Parker perched easily on the stool as if she'd always been there, as if Cate couldn't imagine being with anyone else right now.

"Do you want to talk about it?"

Cate heard the clink of ice against glass. "About what?" She frowned at the uncooperative pad thai congealed into the bottom of the box. She dumped it all into a bowl and tossed it in the microwave.

"Any of it."

She finally met Parker's gaze. Parker was bouncing her foot on the rung of the stool, head cocked, fingers wrapped around her glass. She wasn't giving her a look of overwrought sympathy like so many people had after Anthony died. Even her parents used to look at her that way. Sometimes they still did. Cate had grown to hate that look. There was none of that in Parker's eyes. No judgment, no expectations. Just earnest curiosity. A willingness to receive whatever Cate had to give, and nothing more.

Cate looked back down at the food, turning her attention to the curry and rice. "I keep getting told I should talk about it more. Helps with the trauma, I guess."

Parker sipped her drink. "You don't have to. But I'm happy to listen."

Cate took a breath in and exhaled slowly through her nose. "The funniest part of it all is that I don't remember what we were doing that day. I remember everything else so clearly, but I couldn't tell you where we were going or why." She sighed. "Anthony and I were arguing in the back seat. He'd made plans to go to the movies with his friends that night, and our mom was making him take me. The last thing he wanted was his little sister tagging along."

Cate spooned the curry into another bowl. Her hands weren't shaking as much as she thought they would be. "We were rear-ended as we pulled up to a red light. To this day, I still know nothing about that driver. Not that I want to. We were pushed into the intersection and immediately T-boned by a pickup truck. We had a sedan at the time. It didn't stand much of a chance." Cate's eyes flicked up. A small furrow appeared in Parker's brow, but aside from that her patient expression hadn't changed. The microwave beeped and Cate spun around. The pad thai needed a few more minutes. She gave it a stir and jabbed at the microwave's buttons. "The truck hit us on the driver's side. Dad was driving, and Anthony was behind him. Both my parents screamed, almost at the same time. Then they were quiet. Anthony never made a noise. The worst part was—" Cate stopped and nearly laughed out loud at herself. Like any of it could be categorized in some order of terribleness.

"Was what?" Parker asked softly.

"Both my parents lost consciousness, but I never did. So I saw it all. The make and color of the truck. The damn license plate. I heard the horns of all the other cars around us, like that was going to do anything. The passenger-side window shattered on impact, and a piece of metal or something from the truck came through the window and caught Anthony in the neck." Cate shuddered. "He couldn't talk. But he was looking at me the whole time. His lips were moving, asking me for help. I froze. I watched my brother die."

A sharp inhale came from across the island. Cate turned back. Parker's jaw was clenched, like she was fighting back tears. Cate placed both palms on the cool granite surface and hung her head. God, what a mood-killer. And what mood had she been trying to set tonight, anyway? Why had she even invited Parker inside? Why had she even started talking? This was all just a bad idea—

Parker reached across the bar and curled her hand over Cate's. Parker's grip was warm and strong. She didn't say anything, keeping her hand on Cate's until she spoke again. "I'm sorry. I'm sure you didn't want to hear that. Only my parents know how it happened."

Parker squeezed the top of her hand. "Don't apologize. I said I would listen, and I meant it."

Cate shook her head, eyes downcast. She turned her hand over so her palm was facing up and watched Parker's fingers slowly tangle around hers. "I should have done more, though. I just sat there. I didn't even try to help him."

"You were a kid, Cate. What else could you do?"

"You're going to tell me I'm wrong?" Cate's head snapped up, eyes flashing. She'd heard this many times, too, almost as often as she'd gotten that damn sympathetic look from people who didn't know any better. But she didn't release Parker's hand.

"No." Parker shook her head. "I would never tell you how to feel about any of it. I just think you could be a little kinder to yourself. For what it's worth."

Parker brushed her thumb across the top of Cate's knuckles, tracing a thin scar from a cut she'd gotten during a training exercise. The motion was oddly soothing. The heaviness lifted from her shoulders, and the painful tightness in her chest receded. Cate didn't know how or why, but Parker made everything brighter, chasing away the shadow that so often accompanied her. She couldn't explain it.

"Thank you," she muttered.

"Anytime." Parker raised her index finger from Cate's hand, subtly pointing to the microwave behind her. "I think the pad thai is done."

Incessant beeping finally grabbed Cate's attention. Reluctantly, Cate dropped Parker's hand and returned to the meal. She warmed up the curry and split everything in half, plating a serving of each in two shallow bowls, topped off with the rangoons and spring rolls. Cate's stomach rumbled again, grateful that Parker ordered takeout with the same enthusiasm she did everything else. It was quite charming, really.

"Want to watch a movie or something? Might take your mind off things." Parker accepted the bowl slid in her direction.

Cate nodded. "Yeah."

They moved into the sparse living area. Her couch was almost demure compared to the chaotic bookshelves in opposite corners of the room. Parker put her drink on the dark-wood coffee table and leapt onto the couch cushion, crossing her legs in midair without spilling a drop of food. Cate settled in next to her, shaking her head, and turned on the TV.

A moment later, her mistake was clear.

The only reason she even had one of those damn smart TVs was because she couldn't find any other models. She hated it at first, but it eventually grew on her through its intuitiveness and how it clearly laid out her streaming apps. Of which, she had only two: Netflix and…the Hallmark Channel.

Parker nearly choked on a crab rangoon. "No way. No fucking way."

"Don't judge my entertainment choices." Cate fumbled with the remote, which at that moment had decided to stop working. She stabbed at the buttons, but instead of scrolling away from the app, Cate watched in horror as the opening credits to one of Hallmark's patented, formulaic Christmas movies started playing across the screen. It was as if all the electronic devices in her vicinity had joined forces to betray her. She wasn't about to apologize for enjoying some harmless fluff, considering how difficult her job was, but she hadn't intended on letting Parker in on that little secret tonight. She'd already confessed enough. "Oh, goddammit," Cate hissed.

"Leave it on. We're totally doing this." Parker shoved the rest of the rangoon into her mouth.

"Seriously?"

"Absolutely." Parker grinned around the mouthful of rangoon, blissfully unashamed. "No judgment."

Cate eyed her suspiciously, then put the remote down and began eating. The movie was one of the releases from last year's "Christmas in July," a typically formulaic tale involving a big-city real estate developer returning to her hometown to close a business deal, only to fall in love with the hunky butch baker she was supposed to convince to sell her business. The usual supporting cast of precocious kids and meddling family members. Lots of chunky knits. She'd already seen it twice.

Cate's hunger distracted her from her embarrassment as the movie's opening scene played, set in some small New England town that had been poorly approximated on a Vancouver soundstage. Cate glanced at Parker out of the corner of her eye. She was watching like she was studying for a film course, leaning forward with a furrowed brow and only looking away long enough to load her fork with pad thai. No snarky remarks. No disbelieving sighs.

It was so right. So easy. Of course, they'd be sitting next to each other, eating takeout and watching a mediocre movie after Cate had just talked about the worst day of her life. And it didn't scare her nearly as much as it should.

"What?" Parker caught Cate looking and gave her a shy smile.

"Nothing. I'm just glad you're here."

Parker's smile widened. "Me too."

Cate smiled back.

* * *

Cate came awake suddenly, blinking in confusion. Her torso was on the couch, but her legs were stretched out at an angle and her ankles were crossed on the coffee table. The back of her head was lying against the arm rest. All of the lights were still on, and Netflix was paused on an episode of *Arrested Development*, helpfully asking if Cate was still watching. A weight pressed into her chest, and she heard soft, gentle breathing in her ear.

Parker was curled up on top of her, face buried in Cate's neck and a hand closed around the collar of Cate's shirt. Cate's arm wrapped tightly around Parker's shoulders. Cate had no memory of nodding off, or switching from a movie to a TV show, nor did she remember Parker tucking herself into her side. Not that Cate was complaining.

She trailed her hand over Parker's shoulder and up the back of her neck, burying her fingers in thick, wild hair that was just as soft as when Parker had pressed her up against the firehouse. Cate's body stirred, both at the memory and the feel of Parker on top of her. That night Parker had been strong and assertive in a way that made Cate's knees go weak, but now, in Cate's arms, Parker seemed smaller. More vulnerable. The surge of protectiveness that had come over Cate on the night of the store break-in returned with such intensity it stole her breath away.

Cate allowed herself a moment of indulgence. She lightly stroked Parker's hair, breathing in her bright cologne intermingled with the herbal scent of her hair product. Cate's own heart beat in time to the rise and fall of Parker's chest. She pressed her lips to Parker's hair. What was the harm in staying just like this until morning?

Her back answered a moment later. A jolt of pain shot through her spine all the way to her tailbone, and she had to stifle a groan. As with most indulgences, this was to be short-lived.

She gave Parker's shoulder a shake. Nothing happened. She tried again with no luck. Apparently, nothing short of a bomb was going to rouse her. The pain in her back became more insistent, and Cate lifted Parker's head from her shoulder and maneuvered her way off the couch.

Cate scooped up their empty dishes and deposited them in the sink, then swiftly cleaned up the rest of the kitchen. When she returned to the couch, Parker's face was pressed into the couch cushion, a lock of hair spilling onto her forehead. She regretted having to wake Parker but didn't want to leave her on the couch alone. Another twinge in her back reminded Cate that returning to the couch herself wasn't an option.

"Hey." Cate knelt down in front of Parker and shook her again with a little more force. It still took several tries before Parker bolted awake, sitting straight up and blinking in confusion.

"Wha—? What time is it?"

"Almost one."

Parker rubbed her eyes and looked around. After blinking a few more times, she muttered, "I should get going." She tried standing, but when she attempted to gather her legs under her, she just slumped back onto the cushion. Parker rubbed her eyes again. Cate doubted Parker could recall her own name, much less operate a motorcycle, which was dangerous enough in broad daylight, let alone the middle of the night.

Cate squeezed the top of Parker's knee. "You can stay here." Want and anticipation surged through her, blocking out the ache in her back, so she quickly added, "I have a guest room." It was more for her benefit than Parker's.

Parker's brows furrowed, eyes still glazed over with sleep. Cate wanted to reach out and smooth the crease between Parker's eyebrows.

"You sure?"

Cate almost laughed as Parker stifled the biggest yawn she'd ever seen. "Yes, I'm sure." Cate took her hand and pulled her to her feet. Lacing their fingers together, Cate silently led Parker out of the living room and to the stairs leading to the second floor, hitting the light switch as they went. As she climbed the stairs, she felt a tug and looked over her shoulder. Parker's other hand was twisted in the hem of her T-shirt.

Cate opened the door to the modest guest room and steered Parker toward the bed, where she promptly flopped down on top of the covers and curled up on her side. Cate pulled a blanket out of the closet and draped it over Parker.

The hall light spilled into the small room, allowing Cate a full view of Parker's profile, flushed cheeks, and full, red lips. The same lock of hair had fallen onto her face. Cate bent down to brush it away, fingertips pausing for a breath on Parker's brow. The only sound was Parker's gentle, steady breathing. Every fabric of Cate's being wanted to lie down next to her and pull her close, feeling each rise and fall of her chest, just like when they'd been on the couch. Instead, she dropped a kiss onto Parker's temple and quietly shut the door behind her.

CHAPTER THIRTEEN

Parker woke slowly. Morning light filtered through the window, bringing into focus a room she didn't recognize. A framed picture of a wooded landscape hung on the far wall. It looked like something that came from Target or Home Goods but was still tasteful. On a shelf across from that were several framed medals and plaques, and a photo of Cate in a formal uniform, flanked by a man and a woman. On the floor near the foot of the bed was a weight bench, a stack of dumbbells, and a foam roller.

Parker's cheeks flushed. She was at Cate's, but not in Cate's bed, and she wasn't sure if she was relieved or disappointed. Vague memories floated to the surface: a pair of strong arms around her, being led up the stairs, the whisper of a touch across her brow. She decided she was disappointed. Definitely disappointed. Parker's hand curled around the soft blanket tucked against her, bringing it to her face. The scent of smoke layered under the fresh detergent filled her senses, and she smiled to herself. She was beginning to really like that smell. Stretching her arms overhead, she yawned and rolled over, feeling something crinkle under her cheek.

The note was lying on her pillow, folded in half, small, precise lettering at the top of the page.

Went to the coffee shop. Back soon. Make yourself at home. –C
Underneath that, a postscript: *FYI—it's 7 a.m.*
Parker pulled her phone out of her front pocket, wincing at the soreness from the device digging into her thigh. It was almost nine. She tossed it aside, ignoring her usual bevy of notifications, and read the note again, taking in the sharp angles of Cate's handwriting. The fact that Cate had left an honest-to-God note instead of just texting her was both perfectly in line with her character and adorably quaint. Carefully, she folded it into quarters and slipped it into her pocket. Parker rolled off the bed, scrubbing her face with open palms. She folded the blanket and placed it on the corner of the bed, then went over to examine the shelf with the awards and picture.

Several ribbons and medals were displayed in a shadow box, the largest of which was marked as a Distinguished Service medal. The medal also featured in the picture of Cate with the two people Parker assumed were her parents. Cate was dressed in a formal blue uniform with gold trim, holding the medal in one hand and the accompanying plaque in the other. She looked directly into the camera, unsmiling. It was a similar expression to the one in her professional headshot that Parker had seen in the paper, and just like before, Parker was drawn to those intense dark eyes. Cate looked damn good in that uniform, too.

Parker's focus turned to Cate's parents, who were both wearing the exact opposite expression from their daughter. They beamed happily at the photographer, Cate's mother's arm resting around Cate's waist while her father's was around her shoulder. She studied their features, noting how Cate was a perfect combination of both: her father's chin, her mother's nose. Dark hair and eyes from her mother, but when Cate smiled—or when that fleeting hint of a smile crossed her face—she looked the most like her dad. Pride radiated off them both, and there was no hint of the tragedy they'd experienced. They were perfectly happy, perfectly normal, and really proud of their kid. Parker smiled at the picture. She couldn't remember the last time her parents had been in the same room together.

Shaking off that last thought, Parker poked her head out of the room, finding the bathroom just down the hall. It was pristine, which wasn't surprising, and waiting for her on the flawless sink was a brand-new toothbrush, still in its packaging. For perhaps the first time ever, Parker took care not to squeeze the toothpaste tube from the middle.

Cate was sitting at the kitchen island when Parker bounded down the stairs, dressed in a casual white button-down shirt with the sleeves pushed to her elbows and loose jeans rolled up just past her ankles. Her dark, wavy air was messy, like she'd just ran her hands through it once or twice and let it be. She was writing something, head down, scowling at the page, but the muscles in her neck and shoulders seemed less tense than they had last night. Not that Parker would ever take credit for that, but it was still nice to see.

Tossing her pen aside, Cate looked up. The scowl vanished. "Good morning."

"Morning." Parker slid onto the barstool next to Cate, heart flip-flopping at Cate's gentle tone. "Thanks for the toothbrush. And the note."

"You're welcome. I didn't want to wake you. As I recall, you're not much of a morning person."

"What are you talking about? I love mornings."

Cate snorted, concealing a smile, and slid off her stool. Parker's eyes followed Cate as she went to the microwave, admiring the drape of the shirt across Cate's shoulder blades. A few moments later, Cate returned to the island with a hot breakfast sandwich. "I wasn't sure what you liked, so I took a guess. Egg and cheese?" Cate slid over a plate, then poured a cup from the French press without being asked.

"That's perfect. Thank you." Both the sandwich and the fresh coffee smelled amazing, and for a moment Parker didn't know what to start with.

Cate pushed the coffee mug closer with a gentle chuckle. "So I know your breakfast order, but how do you take your coffee?"

Parker wrapped her hand around the steaming mug. "Just an exorbitant amount of sugar."

"Do I even want to witness this?" Cate passed over a glass dish and a spoon.

"No, this is my own unholy ritual." Parker twisted away and hunched her shoulder, hiding her mug as she shoveled in the sugar. When she turned back, Cate was shaking her head with a bemused look on her face. "What are you writing?"

The scowl flashed across Cate's face briefly, followed by a sigh. "I'm supposed to speak about Butler Center at the ball tonight, and I have no idea what to say. I hate public speaking."

"Can't imagine that." Parker nudged her with a smile. "Anything I can help with?"

Cate shook her head, looking incredibly put-upon by the whole thing. It was very cute. "No, thank you. I'll think of something." Her hand drifted down to graze along the inside of Parker's forearm. "Thanks for coming over last night. I had a good time."

Parker suppressed a shudder, but just barely. "Me too. Sorry I fell asleep."

"So did I."

Parker looked down at Cate's hand on her arm and bit her lip. "Yeah, you were out pretty much the second you got done eating."

"God, that's embarrassing."

"Not in the slightest. I hope it's okay that I stayed. I finished the movie and flipped on Netflix to wait until you woke up. It didn't feel right to just leave, and I knew you were tired. I just didn't think I'd fall asleep, too." Parker chuckled. "I even liked the movie."

Cate rolled her eyes. "You don't have to humor me. They're all ridiculous."

"It was cute. Don't apologize for what you like. You pull people out of burning buildings for a living—it makes sense that you prefer the low-stakes story of a handsome baker with a real estate dispute."

Cate's mouth opened, then closed again. After a moment she said, "I suppose that's true. Don't tell anyone at the firehouse, though. I'll never hear the end of it."

"Your secret's safe with me, Lieutenant."

Cate rolled her eyes and looked away, but her hand tightened around Parker's arm. When she glanced back, her expression was almost shy, her voice a near whisper as if she were confessing something. "I'm glad you stayed."

The walls of Parker's throat closed in. She was already hoping to stay over again in the very near future, hopefully after an evening much more graphic than anything Hallmark would air, but she didn't say that. Ever since that kiss in front of the fire station, Parker had thought of nothing but getting Cate in bed, but last night her motives had been pure. Yesterday was clearly difficult for Cate, and Parker was content to just be here, listening to Cate talk and offering what little comfort she could. Making a move would've not only been inappropriate but disrespectful, no matter how badly she wanted Cate's body pressed against her own.

This morning, Parker was still in limbo. The sharp, strong lines of Cate's face were relaxed, the fierceness gone from her gaze. In her casual outfit, Cate looked soft and vulnerable in a way Parker hadn't yet seen. Her shirt was unbuttoned just enough to tantalize, exposing the curve of her shoulder and neck. Although she was imagining tearing that shirt off Cate, Parker kept herself glued to the stool. She wasn't sure where Cate stood emotionally, and she didn't want to crush the fragile trust newly established between them. Cate had made the first overture, had kissed her first, and Parker was resigned that Cate would have to do it again.

"Me too." Parker's reply was nothing more than a croak.

As if recognizing the question on Parker's face, Cate looked her up and down. Hazel eyes darkened with desire. She clutched Parker's arm and pulled.

In one motion, Parker was off the stool, pressing their lips together. Cate remained seated, which put them at nearly the same height, and she shifted just enough so that Parker could step between her legs. Parker tasted coffee and sweet pastry, the remnants of a berry scone still on Cate's tongue. Parker's hands went to Cate's waist, digging into her jeans, almost dragging her off the seat. Cate grabbed a fistful of Parker's hair and deepened the kiss, hooking her heel around the back of Parker's calf to draw her in closer. Blood thundered in Parker's ears. She was dizzy with need. Her body craved more, a hunger that she didn't know existed unleashed from a previously undiscovered place within her. Parker had desired women before, but not like this. Not in a way that threatened to consume all thought and control. Not in a way that made her want Cate to shatter underneath her, over and over again, and then pick up the pieces afterward.

Parker's hand was already at the button of Cate's jeans before she stopped herself. Christ, was she seriously considering fucking this woman on a barstool, in the middle of her own damn kitchen, before she'd even finished her coffee?

A soft, broken moan slipped past Cate's lips.

Yes. Yes, she was.

Her back pocket started to buzz. She ignored it, teasing at Cate's jeans. The buzzing grew louder. Parker muttered a curse and fumbled with her phone, trying to shut the ringer off and keep kissing Cate at the same time. Cate pulled back with a low chuckle, eyes shining.

"Better get that."

Parker answered the call with trembling hands, nearly dropping it in the process. "Yeah?"

The voice on the other end was both too chipper and too apologetic, but the combination made it difficult for Parker to muster true irritation. Especially with Cate's arms wrapped around her. "Hello, Parker Mandli? This is Stu down at Apex Windows. I wanted to tell you that your window is ready. I'm sorry it took so long, but if you're available today we can get it installed for you right away…"

Cate nipped at Parker's neck. Stu's voice evaporated completely, and Parker found herself stammering an incoherent reply at whatever was being asked. Cate's lips curled into a smile, breath tickling Parker's skin.

She caught Parker's earlobe between her teeth. Parker's knees almost buckled.

"Great! So we'll be there in about twenty minutes. I have a crew ready right now," Stu paused. "Um, you still there?"

"Yep!" Parker's voice rose an octave as Cate breathed into her ear and slipped a hand under her sweatshirt. Nails grazed along her stomach. "See you then!" Parker jammed her phone in her pocket and leaned back in for another kiss, only to be stopped by a firm hand on her chest.

"And what was that about?" Cate was looking very pleased with herself.

It took Parker a moment to piece together the conversation. She'd been too distracted by Cate's lips to process exactly what she had agreed to. "I'm getting my new front window installed. I think."

"I see." Cate's fingertips skimmed the top of Parker's jeans, dipping low to tease at the waistband of her boxer briefs. "Seems important. You should probably get going."

"I have twenty minutes."

"That's not much time."

"You'd be surprised at what I can accomplish in twenty minutes."

Cate pulled her close and pressed her forehead to Parker's. "That may be, but I want more than twenty minutes with you."

At the emphasis on the word *more*, a thrill rocketed through Parker. She felt drunk and tripped over her own feet when she reluctantly stepped out of Cate's arms. Only Cate's bright laugh saved her from any lasting embarrassment. Cate swiftly wrapped up Parker's sandwich and poured her coffee into an MFD travel mug and walked her to the door.

"I'll see you tonight?" Parker asked, shoving her coffee and sandwich into her backpack.

Cate nodded, lowering her head to drop a chaste kiss on Parker's cheek. "Looking forward to it." A rasp had creeped into the edges of her voice. She handed Parker her helmet. "Don't forget this. Please."

"Never do." Parker gave her one last grin, backing up slowly and not breaking eye contact until Cate closed the door.

She spun around on her heel and breathed in, taking in the fresh morning air. Still smiling, Parker bounded off the porch and skipped over to her bike. A cyclone of energy churned in her stomach, begging for release. She couldn't remember the last time she was this excited.

* * *

"We're done."

Parker looked up from her computer, where instead of processing orders she'd spent the last forty minutes daydreaming about Cate. "Huh?"

A man dressed in dark-blue coveralls and a grimy baseball cap had poked his head into the back room. He hitched a thumb toward the front. "I said we're done. You're all set."

"Oh. Thanks." Parker pushed her chair away from the desk, the piles of unopened mail and paperwork less mountainous than usual, and went to sign off on the invoice. She'd zoomed straight over to the store from Cate's house, arriving about ten minutes before the crew got there, and spent the rest of the morning vibrating in her chair, thinking of Cate in that shirt, buttons undone. And nothing else.

Her phone went off the moment after the installers left. She was almost disappointed that it was New York Manni and not Cate. She walked over to the new window as she answered, admiring the way the sun now filled the store. Just like the day she had first looked at the property with Josie. It looked even better now, with the bright mural on the display wall and new rows of shelving. Smelled better, too. Finally.

"I've been trying to get ahold of you all morning. The fuck you've been?"

The sound of loud crunching assaulted Parker's ears, along with the drone of traffic in the background. If she had to guess, Manni was eating a bag of chips while walking to the subway and was more than happy to subject her to both.

"Sorry. Had a busy morning."

"All good." Another loud crunch. "How's the store coming along?"

Pride surged through Parker. "It's looking good. Really good."

When she'd told New York Manni about the break-in, they were even more upset about it than Parker was and threatened the perpetrators with a stream of obscenities that went on for so long Parker had been tempted to time it. With the new window and her steady work on the rest of the setup, it felt like everything was coming together. That she was actually going to pull this off, and she hoped to show it to her friend soon.

"Awesome. I can't wait to come out and see it." The chewing finally stopped and the background noise became muffled, like Manni had stepped off the street. Their voice lowered. "I got something for you. It's huge. Super exclusive. It'll make the Coopers look like New Balance dad shoes."

Parker froze. The world stopped spinning. "The fuck you talking about?"

"A new Vincent Clark collab. It's a previously unknown design. They think he was working on it before he died but didn't tell anyone."

"Holy shit."

Vincent Clark was one of the most influential and respected fashion designers of his generation. He'd started a line of luxury streetwear clothing and eventually became CEO of his own fashion house based out of Milan. His design aesthetic was nothing less than transformative, and he'd been widely considered an icon until his untimely death from cancer. Anything he'd touched would be the grail to end all grails. It didn't matter the construction details or the colorway—whoever got ahold of the very last sneakers designed by Vincent Clark would be the envy of anyone with the slightest knowledge of the industry. The price was incalculable, but the cachet was even more valuable. Jake, especially, would be frothing at the mouth with jealousy. Parker had to remind herself to breathe.

"When? Where?"

"Tonight, which is why you need to answer my texts. How soon can you get to Chicago?"

"What part of town?"

"The West Loop. A pop-up shop off Randolph is going to host it. I have an in with the owner. The owner's sister, actually." Manni paused. "Well, I guess it's more like the owner's sister's current girlfriend, but that's beside the point. Can you get here by five? That's when they're going to bring them out. I can have a spot saved for you."

Oh hell *yes*. It was almost eleven. Chicago was about two hours away, on a good day with no traffic. She could grab another coffee, head home for a shower, and hit the city before three, well before the store would open. More than enough time. She could stick it to Jake, who she still hadn't forgiven for being so shitty about the Bumblebee mids, and take herself out for a celebratory dinner afterward. She could already imagine the color draining from his stupid, smarmy face when she posted on her socials that Remix Footwear was in possession of the hottest drop in *years*—

Except.

Except the charity ball started at six.

The hell am I thinking?

"Sorry, I can't make it." Parker couldn't believe the words even as they left her mouth. Judging by the long silence on the other end of the line, Manni couldn't believe it either.

"What."

"I can't come. I have something to be at tonight."

"Park, what could possibly be more important than the biggest sneaker drop of the past five years?" The background noise started up again. Manni had moved back out to the street, probably waving their arms in wild indignation.

Parker bit her lower lip. She didn't answer.

"Holy shit. It's a girl. You're missing this for a girl."

A small flare of indignation bloomed within her, but the promise in Cate's kiss tempered her reaction. "Look, it's just—"

"Oh my God. Oh my *God*," Manni's voice rose an octave, harmonizing with the surrounding din of the city. "What's her name? Is she hot? I bet she's hot. I swear, it better be the best sex of your entire goddamn life if you aren't on your way down here right now."

Parker's face burned. "We're not sleeping together." *Yet*. "There's a big benefit tonight that she helped plan. I want to be there."

"Useless! You are a fucking useless lesbian, my friend." A loud clank reverberated through the phone, followed by a burst of static. Manni was probably getting on the subway. Another long pause filled the connection, and Parker wondered if the call had been dropped. Manni's voice came back on the line, sounding thoughtful. "It's serious, isn't it?"

"It's not serious," Parker said quickly. "I mean—it's not *not* serious. I think? I don't know yet."

"Do you want it to be serious?"

Parker sighed. She rubbed at her forehead, feeling the onset of a headache. She needed more coffee before dealing with that loaded and direct of a question. Cate's smile came to mind, gentle and fleeting, and how Parker was seeing it more and more often. Her laugh, too, which was even rarer yet.

"Yeah," she admitted softly. "I do."

Manni let out a low whistle. "Obviously, or you wouldn't hang me out to dry. I called in a couple of favors to get this spot for you."

"How the hell was I supposed to know that?"

"I know, Park. I'm just surprised. What's her name?"

"Cate." Parker bit back a smile. Even saying Cate's name was enough to make her giddy.

"Hold up, is this that woman you tagged on your Instagram the other day? That you got the shoes for?"

"Yeah."

Manni whooped. Parker could clearly imagine them standing on the subway platform, pumping their fist in the air. "Not to be totally shallow, but way to punch above your weight class. So what's her deal? Is she cool? Nice? Smart? The exact opposite of Sophia in every possible way?"

God, Sophia. The sting lessened each time Parker thought about her—which, she just now realized, hadn't happened in quite some time. Although mentioning her ex wasn't helping her headache. "Sophia was smart."

"Okay, fine, she was smart. She also invited you to move in with her while neglecting to mention the fact that she was still married. And then dumped you over text." The uncharacteristic venom in Manni's tone filled Parker with affection. The whole situation had been a mess, and Parker shouldered a fair share of the blame, but Manni had always been nothing but steadfast in their support.

"Cate's not like that at all. First off, she's not married. Second, she hates texting. I have those basics out of the way this time."

Manni laughed. "Glad you're finally learning something." A rumble started to build in the background. "Shit, here's my train. I'll call you later. Have fun tonight."

"I will. Thanks for the offer, Manni. You know I appreciate it."

"I got you next time."

Parker pocketed her phone and raked both hands through her hair. She looked around the fledgling store. Had she made a mistake? She had already missed the last exclusive release Manni had told her about, and that still gnawed at her. And now she had just turned down what could be the biggest score of her career. For what?

The answer was already there, before she was even done asking the question. There was something more important than driving hours away at a moment's notice or dropping everything to fly to New York or even aggravating Jake. And it was waiting for her.

Her instincts had led her astray before. This time, though, it would be different. She couldn't explain it, but she knew it to be true.

But first, she needed another coffee.

CHAPTER FOURTEEN

People were just starting to trickle in when Cate arrived at the Mayville Concourse Hotel, the nicest hotel in the city, located just off the downtown square. Cate nodded at several officers from Station Ten milling about the front desk, then followed the signs to the Main Ballroom. A poster board set on an easel advertised the Mayville Fire Department Annual Fundraising Gala, the bottom half of which prominently displayed Butler Center's logo and proclaimed that all proceeds raised would go directly to the center. Her lips pursed together in a thin smile. She and a few other volunteers from Butler had stopped by earlier that day to help with the setup, and Cate had a moment where she became irrationally fixated on the size of the signage. Clearly she'd been overreacting. The look on the event coordinator's face should have been enough to tell her that.

Cate paused at the entrance to the ballroom. A bar station was positioned in each corner, a stage and DJ station set up in front of a dance floor. Round banquet tables were set up throughout the room. At the far side was the silent auction table, displaying at least two dozen items to bid on. Projected on a screen behind the DJ was a presentation about Butler, showing pictures of kids playing basketball and other activities, along with quotes and brief testimonials about what the rec center meant to them. It had taken Cate months to pull those together. Next to that was another screen with a thermometer graphic displaying the amount raised for Butler so far and their goal of $80,000.

She decided she wouldn't focus on that one quite yet.

Smoothing down the front of her vest, she looked around the room. Two other Butler volunteers were also in attendance tonight; she spotted one of them at the auction table but didn't see the other. Jameel had been planning to come but woke up that morning not feeling well, and Cate told him in no uncertain terms to stay at home. She snapped a picture of the growing crowd and sent it to him with a thumbs-up emoji. It was just past six. Parker had said she'd be there no later than six thirty.

Freddie was by one of the bar stations, standing nearly a head taller than everyone else around him. He waved her over and stepped aside when she approached, revealing both Alex and David. Alex greeted her first, smile wide, and passed her a drink.

"Hot damn, Wilds. You're already shaming everyone in the calendar this year. Stop making us look bad."

Cate tugged at her vest again. She'd thought her outfit was dressy but still simple: black vest over a white dress shirt, with matching cropped trousers. Although right before she left, she did undo one more button on her shirt. "Is it too much?"

David jumped in. "Absolutely not. You look like you stepped off the set of a lesbian reboot of *Peaky Blinders*."

"That's a good thing?"

"Yes. And those boots! Stunning. Well done."

Cate looked down. The ankle-high, cap-toe dress boots sported a loud red, blue, and gold paisley pattern. They were a last-minute addition, even though she thought the embellishments were a bit much.

"Thanks." Cate took a sip of her drink and almost gagged. "The hell is this?"

Alex matched her grimace. "Jameson and ginger ale. Mixed drinks only. Nothing straight, and no shots."

Cate opened her mouth to complain further but decided against it. That was probably wise on the venue's part, considering what the MFD had been capable of in previous years. People still talked about the 2017 gala with equal parts disbelief and admiration.

She took another sip as Alex and Freddie exchanged looks. Cate braced herself. The shared brain cell, back at work.

"So." Freddie sipped at his own drink with a far too innocent look. "Is Parker still coming?"

Cate sighed inwardly. Might as well get it over with. "Yes."

"Who's Parker?" David whirled on her again, in typically dramatic fashion. He shot a look at Freddie, who shrugged and smiled over the rim of his glass, then whipped back to her. "Lieutenant Cate Wildman, do you have a date?"

I hate you, Cate mouthed at Freddie. Freddie was notoriously closed-lipped, eschewing all forms of station gossip, but wasn't above enlisting his husband's flair for theatrics to bust her chops a little bit. No matter. At the end of the day, Freddie and Alex and Cordell and everyone else at the firehouse were family, for better or worse, and she wasn't going to escape the evening without some amount of teasing. It was expected, considering it'd been some time since she'd met anyone worth more than a passing mention, let alone an invite to the department's biggest event of the year. The novelty would wear off eventually.

But that suggested Parker would continue to be around, a thought that made Cate's pulse stutter. "She's on her way."

David swatted at Freddie's massive arm straining under the dress shirt. "Why didn't you tell me?" He turned back to Cate. "What's she like? How'd you meet? Is she cute?"

Alex leaned in, answering helpfully. "*Very* cute. She's opening a new store across the street from the firehouse."

"Where that pet shop used to be? I heard that guy used to sell illegally imported animals out of there."

Alex gave Cate a nudge. "I heard that too."

"I never thought that place would get rented. Did Josie perform her usual witchcraft?" David asked.

"I did indeed."

Josie appeared out of nowhere, sidling up beside David and looking flawless in an elegant emerald dress, her megawatt smile matching the headshot on the Beaumont Real Estate Group's gold-level sponsorship signage throughout the ballroom. She also appeared to be the only one in the room holding a martini. The group acknowledged her with a robust greeting—apart from David, who regarded her a little coolly, and Cate was reminded of their not-so-subtle professional rivalry. David Prince Realty was a silver-level sponsor, and his signs were notably smaller.

The conversation turned into a debate over Mayville's black-market demand for exotic pets. Cate's attention turned to the ballroom entrance. A steady stream of people passed through the doors, but there was no sign of Parker yet. Her growing anticipation wasn't quite enough to distract her from her nervousness about the fundraising goal and her impending speech. She looked down at the sweaty tumbler in her hand and realized her drink was already empty.

"Relax, Wilds." Alex pried the glass out of her fingers and replaced it with a fresh one. If he saw the tremor in her hand, he didn't mention it. "Everything looks great. This is going to be huge, trust me."

Cate sighed. "We've barely raised eight grand."

"Yeah, but the silent auction just opened, and donations always trickle in a few days after the party. Don't be so quick to write it off."

"I know, I know." She took a drink. Goddamn, she needed something stiffer.

"It'll be okay," Alex said.

From anyone else it would have come off as condescending, but Alex was nothing if not sincere. She nodded and looked back at the door.

Parker walked through a moment later.

Cate nearly dropped her glass.

Her phone was out, as usual, but with a flick of her wrist the device vanished and she straightened to survey the room, seeming almost taller as she did so. Parker's wild hair had been corralled and styled into a precise side-part like a dapper schoolboy. She wore a tuxedo jacket perfectly cut for her frame, just tight enough across the chest to accent the broadness of her shoulders in a way that Cate found particularly unfair. Underneath the tux was a simple black T-shirt. Matching black pants and shiny Chelsea boots completed the outfit. She looked completely different than the bold, bright, casual dresser Cate was used to, yet the outfit was immaculate and had a flair that was undeniably Parker's.

Their eyes met across the ballroom, and Cate's heart stopped. Parker glanced at her feet, smoothing both hands over the back of her neck with a shy smile and made her way over, weaving through the growing crowd. Cate watched each step. The low din of the crowd and the music playing over the sound system melted away. Her anxiety was forgotten. In that breath, all that mattered was the smile playing on Parker's lips and those soft gray eyes and that perfectly dashing suit.

"Hey." Parker stood in front of her and reached out to graze the back of Cate's hand. "You look incredible."

A shiver went through Cate at the gentle touch. Up close, Cate saw that Parker's jacket wasn't black but a dark-blue velvet. She was struck by an overwhelming urge to run her palms over Parker's shoulders, grab her by the lapels, drag her into a secluded corner, and pick up where they left off this morning. Instead, she just said, "You too."

Parker's gaze raked her up and down, lingering on the open collar of Cate's shirt, which for her was conveniently at eye level. "I like your boots."

"I'd hoped so," Cate admitted.

Parker's grin grew wicked, and another thrill shot through her.

She was in trouble.

Alex inched in next to them. "Hey, Parker. Good to see you again. Grab you a drink?"

Parker jumped like she'd just broken out of a spell. "Yeah, thanks. Whatever you're having, lots of ice." She greeted Josie and Freddie, the former eyeing her suit in clear appreciation.

Alex headed off toward the bar, muttering about the quality of the drinks. Freddie slung his arm around David's shoulders. "Have you met David, my husband?"

Parker extended her hand, smiling broadly. "Don't think so."

"That suit is excellent. Hugo Boss?" David asked.

"Ah, no." Parker's smile turned a little sheepish, eyes darting over to Cate.

Josie interjected before Parker spoke again, tipping her martini in Parker's direction. "Ermenegildo Zegna?"

"Yeah."

David's eyes flicked over to Josie, but he ignored her correct guess. "I've been trying to get this guy in a more modern cut, but to no avail." He nudged Freddie, who just shrugged. Freddie's simple button-down and trousers were plain but perfectly flattering, although they didn't have the flair of David's dark-red suit, black turtleneck, and matching loafers. Imagining Freddie's large frame in such an outfit almost made Cate laugh. She found Parker's gaze again, and she could tell they were sharing the same thought. Parker gave Cate a wink and inched closer to her. She was wearing a different cologne tonight; instead of the bright summery scent Cate had come to associate with Parker, a rich, woody fragrance struck her. Cate brushed her fingers against the small of Parker's back, then let them fall away. The suit material was soft and sleek under her hand.

David watched them with obvious interest but was less giddy about the whole situation than Alex and Freddie. He asked Parker about her store, and soon they were deep in a detailed discussion about streetwear fashion that she couldn't even pretend to follow. Freddie smiled at her warmly and nodded, which Cate took as a sign of approval, then went to help Alex with the drinks. Josie excused herself to go prowl the room.

After the next round had been passed out, Parker suddenly pulled out her phone like she'd forgotten something. She scanned the QR code on the donation projection and began tapping. "I invited Rob and Meagan, but they couldn't make it. They made a donation on the website, though. The silent auction's open, right?"

"Yes," Cate answered. She ignored the pointed looks she was getting as Parker tucked herself in closer to Cate's side and flipped through the bidding app at an inhuman speed. "Are you bidding on something?"

"I'm setting auto bids on all the items. Trying to drive prices up."

Cate frowned. "What happens if no one outbids you?"

"RIP my credit card balance, I guess." Parker pocketed her phone with one hand. "I'm not going too crazy. Just enough to keep things interesting."

"Clever. And slightly devious." David raised his drink. "I approve."

Parker mimicked his gesture. "All I'm saying is that if Anonymous Bidder 16 really wants that wine and cheese basket, they gotta go through me first. Besides." She looked at Cate. "It all goes to Butler Center, right? These fancy people can afford it."

Were they anywhere else, Cate would have taken Parker's face in both hands and kissed her square on the mouth. She turned her head to look away from Parker but immediately regretted it when pain shot up her neck. She grimaced and rolled her shoulder, still aching from when she and Parker had fallen asleep on the couch last night.

Alex eyed her. "You okay?"

"Just sore."

"Still?"

"Slept on it funny. That's all."

Parker's brow furrowed. "What happened?"

"You didn't tell her?" Alex asked.

"Didn't tell me what?"

Cate sighed and gestured at Alex. "By all means."

"The call we caught on Thursday night was at a vacant apartment complex," Alex said. "A couple of squatters had started a fire to keep warm and it got away from them. Wilds and Freddie took a line into the bottom apartment to knock it down and hauled them out. Wilds got nailed by part of a support beam. They got the squatters out before they were really hurt, though."

David squeezed Freddie's arm and gave him a wink.

Parker met Cate's eyes. "You didn't tell me that."

"It wasn't that big of a deal," Cate muttered into her drink. She tensed involuntarily. While she hadn't intended to deceive or hide anything from Parker, her minor injury also hadn't come up last night, giving her a perfect opportunity to avoid the subject entirely. This was something she always loathed getting into, either with her parents or whoever she was dating. Ultimately it came down to the fact that, yes, her job was dangerous at times. It was also nonnegotiable. She didn't know how Parker felt about that, and part of her didn't want to know yet.

Parker's face darkened for a split second, but then she grinned so brightly Cate wondered if she was seeing things. "Isn't it boring being a total badass all the time?"

The group laughed. Cate shook her head but reached her arm around Parker and let her hand linger on Parker's hip. The corner of Parker's mouth turned up, the bright grin becoming more playful over the rim of her glass. Cate wanted to sink her teeth into that full bottom lip like a ripe fruit.

"So, should we work the room?"

Cate blinked, lost in a fantasy of kissing Parker until they both couldn't breathe. "What?"

Parker gestured with her drink. "Walk around. Talk to people. Hype up the rec center."

Cate's eyes swept the room. The crowd was even bigger than she realized, and a steady line of people was weaving through the tables displaying the silent auction items. She couldn't see the other two volunteers from Butler. Her back pocket buzzed. Jameel had texted back a heart emoji.

Parker's arrival in her unfairly perfect suit had kept Cate's anxiety at bay, but now it came rushing back in full force. She drained her cocktail, casting a look over to the total donation amount. The number was growing, but slowly. She sighed and looked back at her crew. Alex, Freddie, and David were wrapped up in an argument over the latest NFL preseason power rankings. She felt Parker's fingers tangle in her own.

"You know." Parker's smile never wavered. "For someone who's dedicated themselves to public service, you sure don't like people."

"I like helping people, I just don't like talking to them. I never know what to say."

"It's easy." Parker tugged at her hand, pulling her toward the silent auction table. "All you have to do is start with a compliment. Say you like something they're wearing, then just keep asking questions."

Cate's hand tightened around Parker's as they maneuvered through the crowd together. "You want me to interrogate a stranger?"

Parker laughed. "No, not interrogate. Be curious. People love talking about themselves."

"Is that what you did with me?" Cate lowered her head to speak into Parker's ear and was rewarded when she heard Parker's breath hitch.

"No." Parker's voice strained. "I saw you across the street, then bought that stupid calendar and completely embarrassed myself."

"You didn't embarrass yourself. It was charming."

Parker stopped and raised a brow. "You think I'm charming?"

"Very."

Parker's ears flushed red. Cate smiled to herself.

A sophisticated-looking woman hovered over one of the silent auction items, glancing between the sign on the table and her phone. Her blond waves were styled in a trendy shag cut, and she wore a sleek black cocktail dress that didn't quite scream wealth so much as attention to detail. Parker dropped Cate's hand and gave her a wink, then sidled up next to the woman. Mere seconds later, the woman was smiling, and Parker was pulling Cate over to be introduced. The woman's green eyes widened when she shook Cate's hand.

"You were in the paper, weren't you? You saved that family from a house fire a few months ago," the woman said urgently.

"Yes, ma'am."

"That was three doors down from us. Our kids are in the same grade." A slight tremble reverberated through her voice. "Thank God you were there."

Cate shifted her weight from one foot to the other, eyes darting away from the women's suddenly earnest and expressive face. Her chest and neck turned hot, and she tried to articulate a reply but stumbled over her words. This was why she didn't talk to people. She was too damn bad at it, even if they were being appreciative.

"It's not just her, of course." Parker eased closer to Cate, like she was shielding her from further interaction. "There's a whole crew, and they all work really closely together. If Cate hadn't been on duty, then someone else would've jumped right in there. Without a doubt."

The woman cocked her head, looking amused. "You must be the department's PR."

"No, just passionate about community service." Parker gestured at the slideshow.

The woman raised her phone, showing the silent auction app on her screen. "So am I."

"You won't get that weekend cabin getaway without a fight."

"We'll see."

Parker tipped her drink in acknowledgment and slipped her hand into Cate's just as the woman seemed a little too intrigued by Parker's challenge. They headed to the other end of the table.

"How did you do that?" Cate muttered in disbelief. Another donation to Butler Center lit up the display, pushing the total amount just a little further.

Parker shrugged. "What can I say? It's a gift." She handed her empty glass to Cate. "Want to grab us another round? I'm going to work on that couple by the wine and cheese basket. I think I found Anonymous Bidder 16." Without another word, she was gone like a flash, swerving through the crowd on a mission. Cate shook her head.

A moment later, just as the bartender finished pouring her Jameson and gingers—one with a heaping mound of ice almost spilling over the rim of the glass—a hand clamped down on her shoulder.

"She's really cool, you know." Alex slid his empty glass across the bar. The bartender scooped it up without a word.

"Who?"

Alex scoffed, pointing at the whiskey snow cone sitting in front of Cate. "Oh, please."

Cate sighed in defeat. "I know."

Alex rolled his hand, gesturing for her to go on. "Okay…so?"

"So?"

"So why the hell are you being so weird about it?"

Cate squirmed under his gaze. "I'm not being weird."

"Knock that shit off, Wilds. We know each other too well for that."

"Fine." Cate turned, leaning an elbow on the bar. This was hardly the topic for a public conversation, but Alex was right—they knew each other too well. And she knew he could be just as stubborn as her. She scanned the crowd, but Parker was nowhere to be found. "She's great, okay? She's kind and funny and sweet and completely ridiculous and I—" Cate stopped, rubbing her forehead, not anticipating how good it felt to finally say all that out loud, to give voice to everything she had been pressing down inside herself, desperate to keep locked away out of a habit she almost didn't understand anymore.

Alex smiled brightly at her. "That's fantastic! Seriously. I'm thrilled for you. Stop acting like you're going to throw up."

She took a sip of her drink. Honestly, she did feel a little nauseous. "Yeah, but…"

"But what?"

"What if she can't handle it? The job, I mean." Cate flexed her hands. Her palms were sweating. "What if the same thing happens, like with Melissa?"

What if I wake up one morning and she's gone?

"Why would you think that?"

"Why wouldn't I? Remember everything Freddie and David went through? And Syed and Mitch?" Each couple had gone through multiple stretches where divorce appeared to loom on the horizon. Syed had been candid about the hard work both he and Mitch did to save their marriage.

Alex pursed his lips. "Can I be honest with you?"

"Of course."

"I think the job can be a convenient excuse when you want it to be. And I think you used that excuse with Melissa."

Cate recoiled. "You never told me that."

Alex trailed a finger along the white linen covering the bar, tracing some imaginary design. "I'm not trying to be a dick. It's not like you were miserable with Melissa, but I don't think you were happy, either. And when you qualified for the lieutenant's exam, it became real easy to spend all your free time studying. We all saw it." He looked up. "Am I wrong?"

Cate was just about to say that, yes, he was *absolutely* wrong, but the words died away in the wake of Alex's steadfast gaze. "No. You're not."

"It's Parker's decision to make. Don't shut her out before she's had a chance to make it. It'd be a shame if you did. After all." Alex raised his glass. "You sure as hell didn't look at Melissa the way you do at her."

Cate grumbled under her breath. Alex grinned at her and let the subject drop.

Had she really been so obvious with Melissa? Did she really use her job to push her away? She'd always chalked up their breakup to the hours she worked, mixed with a fair amount of incompatibility. It really hadn't been either of their faults, right? Or had Cate always kept her at arm's length, hiding behind a firefighter's shield and a sense of duty that overrode all else?

She was so lost in thought she didn't see Parker enter her field of view. She was chatting with someone completely different now and ended the conversation with a fist bump as she approached the bar. A slight flush painted her cheeks and her gray eyes shone, but there wasn't a hair out of place. Alex clapped her shoulder again and melted away into the crowd.

"How are you doing? Thanks for the drink."

Cate felt hot again, like she had when Parker first entered the ballroom. Cate watched Parker reach for her drink, lean fingers wrapping around the glass. The heat building within her was suddenly unbearable. "I'm okay. I just hope everything goes well tonight."

"It will. Don't worry." Parker's easy smile was full of reassurance, her face nothing but sincere. Cate looked down. Slowly, she reached out and tangled their fingers together, letting out a long breath. Parker squeezed her hand. She nodded. Cate decided not to question how easy it was to believe Parker's words.

She tightened her grip. "Yeah, it will."

CHAPTER FIFTEEN

The program was more interesting than Parker thought it would be. A round of old, stately officers in full uniforms took turns giving speeches and introducing presentations, but each one was an engaging speaker, and even though she didn't understand a couple of the references or inside jokes, the delivery was entertaining. And the stories, too, were incredible—not just recognizing the acts of heroism, but also the Mayville Fire Department's dedication to service in the community. From smaller charity fundraisers to school programs to safety demonstrations, the MFD firefighters were clearly proud of their involvement. By the time a Captain (Or maybe it was a Major? Or a Battalion Something?) finished presenting an award to a group from Station Five who had participated in the state-wide AIDS Ride, Parker was clapping harder than anyone.

She and the crew from Station Two took up one of the banquet tables, and they all seemed to be enjoying the program as much as she was, with one notable exception. Next to her, Cate clapped mechanically, face hardly changing expression. Parker looked over at Cate as the last presentation ended. The line of Cate's jaw had been gradually tightening all evening, and now the muscle below her earlobe was spasming. It must be close to when she was supposed to speak. Cate reached into her back pocket with a shaky hand and pulled out a thin stack of index cards.

Parker leaned over, resisting the boyish urge to look down Cate's shirt. Goddamn, she looked incredible. All it took was locking eyes once across the ballroom, and Parker had forgotten all about New York Manni's exclusive sneaker drop. She needed all her previously untapped reserves of decorum not to stare at Cate all evening. "Don't worry. You're going to be great," Parker whispered.

Cate's eyes were wide. Her hands curled around the index cards, crunching them in half. "You think so?"

"Absolutely," Parker replied without hesitation. "Just remember to breathe. And take your time."

She stopped. It wasn't her place to give advice on stressful situations to a trained first responder, especially one as experienced as Cate, but if she was out of line, Cate didn't say so. She inhaled deeply through her nose and exhaled through her mouth, broad shoulders relaxing ever so slightly. Parker tried not to think about tearing that vest off her.

"Good advice. Thank you," Cate said.

The officer on stage (now this one was a Battalion Something, Parker was sure of it) briefly introduced Captain Cordell, who walked purposefully toward the stage amid another round of cheering, noticeably louder than anyone else that evening. Freddie let out the sharpest whistle she'd ever heard a human being make.

Cordell held up both hands and the applause died down. "Thank you. It's great to see you all here tonight. Especially since we're not only celebrating the entire Mayville community as a whole, but raising money for a very worthy cause. To tell you all a little more about that, I'd like to bring someone else to the stage."

Cate's fingers tightened, and the index cards folded like an accordion. Parker hoped they were still legible.

"This is someone who, really, needs no introduction," Cordell continued, a wry smile on her face. "And I know you've all heard that phrase before, but this time it's not bullshit." Laughter washed over the crowd, and Cordell had to wait for it to die down before she could go on. "I'm serious. In my time with the MFD, I can honestly say I have never met anyone more dedicated to the mission of the department, or who better exemplifies our ideals. I can tell you all, it has been a privilege to serve with her." Cordell paused and licked her lips. "Please welcome to the stage Lieutenant Cate Wildman."

Cate stood solemnly, giving her vest a tug, and walked to the stage. Freddie whistled again, even louder than before, and Alex and Morgan and Syed and the rest of the firefighters from Station Two whooped and cheered. A few scattered cries of "Ms. November!" echoed through the ballroom. Parker forced herself to stay seated, but she clapped until her hands stung.

When Cate got to the podium, Cordell gave her an encouraging slap on the back and stepped away. Slowly, Cate's hands unfurled around the notecards and she methodically smoothed them out in front of her. She took a breath and gently raised the arm of the mic.

"Thank you very much," she began. "I've been asked to tell you all a little bit about Butler Center." She exhaled again and looked out over the crowd. Parker sat up straighter, trying to catch Cate's attention, and when Cate's eyes swept in her direction, she flashed a quick thumbs-up.

Cate started hesitantly, focusing too much on her notes and not the audience, but she loosened up as she spoke. Her shoulders relaxed and she raised her head to address the entire room, a warm timbre filling her voice. She talked about her history of volunteering at Butler, and how she'd witnessed firsthand the impact the rec center's programs had on hundreds of kids throughout Mayville's south side. Eyes bright, and even with the hint of a smile on her face, Cate emphasized the real-life skills the kids developed—leadership, problem-solving, interpersonal communication—and how crucial they were to personal and professional success. When Cate nailed her closing line, calling to action everyone in attendance, Parker couldn't contain herself anymore and bolted to her feet. The rest of the table followed. Cate stepped back from the podium, visibly relieved. She found Parker's gaze again, and her smile broadened for the briefest of moments. Before she could make her escape, though, Cordell intercepted her.

"Hang on a second, Wilds." Cordell leaned into the mic. "I know you hate surprises, but this was the only way we were gonna get you up here."

Cate froze. The smile evaporated. Parker heard Alex's barely suppressed giggle, and she turned to find Freddie wriggling in excitement in his seat.

"What's going on?"

"You'll see," Alex said.

Just as Alex spoke, an older woman appeared from behind the stage. She was also wearing a full dress uniform, but her sleeves were decorated with thick gold stripes and an array of stars that Parker hadn't seen on anyone else's jacket. The woman was carrying a plaque.

This looked important. Really important.

"Oh, shit," Parker muttered.

Cate was standing very still, eyeing the woman as she stepped up to the mic. Cordell was next to her, keeping a hand on Cate's arm as if she were about to bolt.

"As you all know, each year we honor a single paramedic or firefighter with our most prestigious award: the Mayville Firefighter of the Year," the woman began. "The recipient is chosen by a committee of peers and officers, and commemorates outstanding acts of heroism and bravery, as well as community service. And as department chief, it is a privilege for me to present this award to someone who truly embodies our core values of service, professionalism, integrity, respect, and trust."

Cate clasped her hands in front of her, the color rapidly draining from her face. The chief continued, "I would add one more trait to that list: humility. In fact, she's so humble that we had to keep this all a secret, because we knew that if she found out in advance, she'd refuse to show up."

Laughter filled the ballroom. Cate rolled her eyes, and Cordell grinned wickedly, nudging her with an elbow. The chief matched Cordell's smile. "This year, once the nominations closed, it became clear who the winner would be. And as much as Lieutenant Wildman loathes the attention, I'm going to ask her to endure this for a few minutes longer while I tell a brief story.

"This winter, as you recall, was one of the worst in recent memory, both in terms of snowfall and unpredictability. In February, a massive blizzard caused a multiple-car pileup on the interstate, which included a school bus of students from Jefferson Elementary on their way back from a field trip. Lieutenant Wildman was the first officer on the scene. She took charge immediately, and through her calm, steady command, oversaw the successful rescue of the children, all of whom survived. Through sheer determination and grit, Lieutenant Wildman clawed order out of a horrific scene. In my career as a first responder, I've never seen such a showing of bravery and leadership. And this is only one example of the many I could give over her ten years of service with the department, not counting her fierce dedication to Butler Center and its community initiatives."

The chief hefted the plaque. "Truly, I can't think of anyone more deserving of this award. It is my sincere honor and privilege to present this year's Firefighter of the Year award to Lieutenant Cate Wildman from Station Two."

Thunderous applause rolled through the ballroom. Wearing a dumbfounded look, Cate accepted the plaque stiffly, like her limbs weren't quite working properly. The crowd started chanting for a speech. Cordell steered her toward the mic. Cate took a breath, then leaned in.

"I have the best damn job in the world. Thank you."

It felt like the entire hotel was shaking. Cheers rattled the entire room, down to the floorboards, and Parker felt the vibration in her teeth. She cupped her hands to her mouth, enthusiastically adding to the chorus. Beside her, the crew from Station Two were practically screaming their heads off, including David, who apparently could match his husband's ear-piercing whistle.

"She's gonna be so pissed at you guys," Parker said to Freddie.

He giggled. "Yep."

The program closed after that, the stage lights shifting to the DJ station and officially announcing the opening of the dance floor. Cate lingered off to the side of the stage, still talking to Cordell and the fire chief. A crowd sprang up around them, along with several photographers. Parker recognized Sarah DeWitt in the fray, snapping some photos and sneaking in with her phone to snag a few quotes from Cate. Josie even managed to slide in, giving Cate a huge hug and grabbing a quick selfie with her. Eventually, Cate extracted herself from the group and returned to the table, clutching the plaque in a white-knuckled grip. Her scowl had returned, and she leveled a glare at all of them.

"You knew, didn't you?"

"Nope," Alex said.

"No idea what you're talking about," added Freddie.

Morgan shrugged. "How would we know?"

Cate sighed, defeated. "I hate all of you."

That apparently was the permission the crew was waiting for. They descended on her in a bout of playful grappling, pounding her back and shooting jabs at her shoulder. Freddie lunged forward, wrapped her up in his huge arms, and lifted her straight into the air. Cate yelped and pretended to bash the plaque over his head. Parker stood off to the side, laughing at the scene and feeling a little envious at the camaraderie among the group. Never in her whole life had she ever had friends like that. Not in LA, Costa Mesa, Chicago. She and New York Manni were close, but they only got to see each other once or twice a year. Maybe she'd find something like that here, in Mayville. She was starting to wish she'd moved here earlier, a feeling that got stronger as Cate freed herself from the crew's clutches and came to her, the edge in her eyes softening.

"Congratulations," Parker said, self-conscious at her earlier excitement, like she hadn't earned the right yet to be so enthusiastic. Or proud. She hoped she hadn't embarrassed Cate. "You were great."

"Thanks. Your advice was really helpful." Cate placed the plaque on the table and smoothed down her hair, which Alex had ruffled mercilessly in the attack.

Parker waved her off, laughing nervously. "It's just something Rob told me ages ago. Not like it was earth-shattering or anything." She glanced up at the donation total displayed behind the DJ. Although they were only halfway to their goal, the number was growing steadily. Parker pointed at the screen. "Look, it's going up."

Cate didn't look. She moved closer and took Parker's hand. "I'm glad you're here. Thank you for coming."

Parker bit her lip. "There's nowhere else I'd rather be."

* * *

The next hour consisted of more cocktails and enthusiastic—if not especially skilled—dancing. David had cornered Parker at the bar and dragged her out to the dance floor, ignoring her protests and helpless glances in Cate's direction, who seemed more amused than anything. Soon Parker had shed her suit jacket and, cocktail in hand, was trying to keep up with Freddie and David and Morgan as they salsa danced to Bad Bunny. She was overmatched but didn't care. Alex was also unbothered, jumping up and down and throwing his hands up to his own beat, whether or not it followed the song. Josie kept close to him, matching his enthusiasm but with far more rhythm. Cate remained at the bar, talking to Cordell and fielding more well-wishers, but every time Parker looked in her direction, she felt Cate's eyes following her.

Parker found her later, leaning against the wall in a secluded corner of the ballroom. "Having fun?" Cate asked as Parker approached, sweaty and breathing hard from dancing. She handed Parker a water.

"Yeah. Your friends are great." Parker downed the water gratefully. She tugged her T-shirt away from her chest, trying to cool off.

"They like you." Cate's gaze trailed over her. She inched closer so their thighs almost touched and reached out to run her fingers along the hem of Parker's shirt. Parker swallowed, her throat dry despite the water she'd just drunk. She wondered how much it would cost to get a room in the hotel, and if anyone would miss them.

"How does it feel to be the Firefighter of the Year?" Parker asked, hoping to distract herself from the fantasy of Cate's hand slipping farther up her shirt.

Cate shook her head. "Surreal. I never thought I'd even be nominated for something like that, much less win."

"Which is exactly why you won."

Cate chuckled in response, shaking her head. Booming music surrounded them, the beat shifting as the DJ skillfully mashed up Nicki

Minaj and Doja Cat. Freddie and Alex went appropriately apeshit, bounding around the floor wildly. Parker couldn't help but laugh. Cate snorted into her drink.

"Dorks."

"Total dorks," Parker agreed. Without realizing it, they'd moved even closer while talking, and Parker felt the warmth radiating from Cate's skin. "I have a question I've been wanting to ask you."

"Okay."

"You don't have to answer if you don't want to."

Cate cocked her head. "Hit me."

"Why'd you become a firefighter?"

Cate's hand tightened around her drink, and she looked down at her feet. Parker waited, watching the emotions flash across Cate's face. The signs were subtle, but they were there: the slight quirk of her lips, a small crinkle around her eyes. What was once inscrutable to Parker now appeared as plain as day—you just needed to know where and how to look. Parker wondered how many other people had figured that out about Cate.

"Honestly, um." Cate frowned in that way Parker had seen her do when she was searching for the right words. "It was the accident."

"Really?"

Cate kept her eyes downcast. "Like I told you, I didn't lose consciousness, but some parts are a blur. But one of the clearest images in my mind is the responding firefighters running to our car. I remember the bright yellow of their turnout gear. The shiny badges on their helmets." Cate shuddered. Her voice dipped low, and Parker angled her ear toward Cate's mouth to hear. "They had to cut us out of the car. The tools were so loud, and they smelled like burning when the saw cut through the frame. But they were all so kind. And calm. They made me feel safe. I knew that's what I wanted to do with my life. I wanted..." Cate trailed off, still staring fiercely at the ground.

"You wanted to help people the same way they helped you," Parker gently finished for her.

Cate raised her head. Her mouth curled into the smallest of smiles. "Yes. Exactly."

The music changed again, the echo of a booming drum followed by a warbling keyboard filling the ballroom, a distinct shift from the R&B that'd just been playing. Cate shot Parker a questioning look.

Parker ran her thumb along the side of her empty water glass. "I can never remember if this is the song from *Top Gun* or *Pretty Woman*. But I thought you'd rather hear this version than the guy at karaoke."

"You requested this?"

"I had to Venmo the DJ twenty bucks, but yeah."

"You're not serious."

Parker kept her shrug casual but couldn't hold back a shit-eating grin. "I'm not above using some light bribery to get my way. Don't worry. I'm not going to ask you to dance."

Cate's face changed. The furrow in her brow melted away, that sliver of a smile following soon after. Her gaze became dark, piercing Parker with a searing intensity that she felt along her entire body. The tendons in Cate's neck tightened as she swallowed several times. Then the glass was gone from Parker's hand and she was being pulled out onto the dance floor.

Cate turned, eyes locking on Parker's face. Heart hammering, Parker stepped in and slid both hands around Cate's waist, settling into the small of her back. Cate draped a wrist over Parker's shoulder, her other hand coming to rest on Parker's chest. The movement felt so natural, so easy, that their height difference didn't matter in the slightest.

"*Top Gun*," Cate said thickly.

"Huh?" Parker was already lost in fierce hazel eyes.

"This is the song from *Top Gun*."

"I'll remember that for next time."

"I like the one from *Pretty Woman* better."

Parker groaned and bumped her forehead into Cate's shoulder. "I just can't win with you."

"You're doing a pretty good job so far."

"Only pretty good?"

Cate's mouth twitched, that small smile making another rare appearance. Her fingers trailed along the back of Parker's neck. "Don't get cocky. I'm dancing with you, aren't I?"

Parker tightened her arms around Cate's waist, pulling her closer, reveling in the hitch in Cate's breath that followed. "You're not too bad at it, either."

"Neither are you."

Parker bit her lip. She was aware of the rest of the dance floor, felt the stares from Cate's crew, but Cate no longer seemed to care about the attention. Like she had suddenly decided to be bold. Fearless.

"Why didn't you tell me you got hurt the other day?" Parker asked.

"It wasn't that big of a deal." Cate glanced away. "I really didn't think of it."

Parker laughed. "A flaming chunk of building fell on you, and you didn't think it was a big deal?"

Cate's eyes snapped back to Parker's face. "It's the job."

The air chilled between them. Cate's lips pressed together in a thin line, her fingers stilling on Parker's neck. The armor that Parker thought she'd eased her way through was now slipping back into place. She didn't know why her question triggered that reaction, but she wasn't going down without a fight. Maybe she didn't run into burning buildings for a living, but she could be fearless, too.

"I know it's the job. That doesn't mean you can't talk to me about it." Parker looked up at her earnestly. "I'm not afraid of it. I'm not."

Cate's face softened for the briefest of moments. She looked almost sad. "You say that now."

Understanding dawned over Parker. "Someone's told you that before, haven't they?"

Cate didn't answer. The music changed, and the soft ballad drifted away, replaced by a midtempo R&B track. It was still upbeat enough that they could keep dancing without appearing completely out of place.

Parker leaned in, pressed herself closer to Cate as if to keep her from escaping. "Look, I'm going to worry because I care about you, but I get it's who you are. I don't want to change that."

Cate's fingertips dipped below Parker's shirt collar, tracing the line of her collarbone. Her voice was so soft Parker strained to hear her over the music. "Are you sure?"

"I've never been more sure of anything in my life."

Cate's gaze flicked down to Parker's lips, then back up. Parker met the hazel eyes steadily. The moment stretched out before them, and Parker no longer heard the thrumming bass of the music or the laughter from the crowded ballroom. The only things that mattered were the muscles in Cate's back, tense underneath her palm, and the line of Cate's jaw as she clenched her teeth. Parker didn't let her go.

"So, what *are* you afraid of?" Cate's voice was still soft, yet hoarser somehow.

Parker answered quickly. "Being lied to."

"I won't lie to you."

"I know." As Parker said the words, she felt the truth in them, as sure as she knew her own name.

"Okay." Cate nodded, licking her lips. Her back unwound under Parker's touch.

"Okay." Parker broke into a grin. She lifted her head and brushed her lips ever so slightly over Cate's neck. "So, am I going home with the Firefighter of the Year, or what?"

Cate ran her fingers up the back of Parker's head and lowered her mouth to Parker's ear. "What did I tell you about getting cocky?"

CHAPTER SIXTEEN

By the time the Uber pulled up in front of her townhouse, Cate's hands were shaking so much she couldn't get her key in the lock. As soon as she managed to open the door, Parker's hands dug into her hips, spinning her around and pinning her against the wall of the entryway. An instant later, Parker's mouth was on hers. Cate melted against Parker's firm body as if on command, just as she had done when they first kissed outside the fire station, barely finding the presence of mind to put her plaque down on the table next to the door. Her keys slipped out of her hand and fell onto the floor.

Cate cupped Parker's face in her hands, breathing in rich layers of Parker's cologne, tasting the hint of whiskey lingering on Parker's lips. The combination made her head spin. Giddiness bubbled up through her chest, an effervescent sensation she didn't know what to do with. She was still reeling from the award she'd received, the unexpected recognition from her peers, and the amount they'd raised for Butler Center. When they'd left, the total was edging toward fifty thousand, with more coming in. And, of course, Parker had been perfect, fitting in with Station Two's crew like they'd all been lifelong friends. How this gorgeous, charming, ridiculous person had shown up out of nowhere and slid into her life with such ease, Cate would never understand.

She tugged Parker's tuxedo jacket off her shoulders and dropped it on the floor. Parker's mouth curled into a smile. One breath later, Cate's vest was off and nimble fingers were working over the buttons of her shirt, exposing her flushed skin to the cool air. Parker kissed along the line of her jaw, over the pulse point of her neck, to her collarbone. Teeth grazed her shoulder, and she gasped.

Parker pulled back. "Sorry, too fast?" Gray eyes looked at her, wide with concern. Parker's lips and cheeks were bright cherry red, her hands settling back on Cate's waist as if stopping them from wandering further. "I didn't mean—"

Cate quickly kissed her, rushing to offer reassurance as her body rebelled at the suggestion of stopping. "Upstairs," she managed to rasp.

Parker held herself in place. She took a gulp of air and leveled her gaze directly into Cate's. "Are you sure?" she whispered.

Cate kissed her again, harder this time. "God, yes."

Finally using her size and strength advantage, Cate grabbed Parker's hand and hauled her up the stairs and to the bedroom. Parker let out a small noise of surprise and followed, and the second they entered the room, her hands were back on Cate's waist, urging her to spin around. Cate's shirt slipped off her shoulder with a whisper. Her bra followed. Parker walked her backward, and when the back of Cate's knees hit the bed, Parker sank down on top of her and slipped a thigh between her legs.

Another gasp filled the room, a high-pitched noise she didn't recognize as her own. Parker smiled against her neck, breath tickling her skin, and didn't say a word. She rolled her hips deliberately, slowly, pressing right into Cate exactly where she wanted pressure most.

Cate clutched at the back of Parker's head with one hand, pulling her away from her neck. She caught Parker's bottom lip between her teeth and bit down. Her other hand fisted the collar of Parker's soft, outrageously well-fitting black T-shirt.

"Why are you still wearing this?" Cate growled.

"I like this shirt." Parker's bravado didn't conceal the shiver that ran through her when Cate's tongue swiped across her lip.

Cate huffed. "Apparently I have to do everything around here."

In one powerful motion, she sat up, catching Parker's wrists and pulling her into her lap. She yanked Parker's shirt over her head and undid her bra. Parker's skin was hot to the touch, her nipples hard against Cate's own as she arched into her, clutching Cate's face with both hands. Cate ran her hands over Parker's back, reveling at the smooth, hard muscle under her fingers. Each movement and flex of Parker's body sent a thrill through Cate, giving proof to her theory that Parker was stronger than her slight frame suggested. Her center pulsed at the thought.

After another searing kiss, Parker broke away, breathless, and pressed her forehead to Cate's. She was shaking, and her smile had faded.

"What?" Cate asked.

"You're absolutely incredible, you know that?" Parker brushed her thumb along Cate's jaw.

Cate looked away, digging her nails into Parker's back. The words washed over her. She'd never been spoken to with such reverence. Such awe. It matched the way Parker had been looking at her all night, how Parker held her while dancing, the sincerity with which Parker told her that she wasn't afraid of being with a firefighter.

She'd heard that one before, too, but this time she believed it. A wall she'd never intended to build was being disassembled, brick by brick. And she didn't have it in her to fight.

Parker's lips brushed the corner of her mouth. "Did I say something wrong? We can stop if you want."

"I don't want to stop." Cate took a breath, forcing out the next words. Her cheeks burned. "I want you to fuck me."

A slow, easy smile spread across Parker's face. "How?"

"Your hand."

Thankfully, Parker didn't need further elaboration. She ran her thumb across Cate's lower lip, down her neck, then splayed her hand across Cate's sternum and shoved her backward. The moment Cate's head hit the pillow, Parker was on top of her, kissing the column of her throat while deftly undoing Cate's belt with one hand. She propped herself up on her elbow, bowing her head to bite at Cate's collarbone, and slid her hand down the front of Cate's pants.

A jolt ran through Cate's spine. Fingers moved over her in slow, unhurried circles, spreading wetness with each stroke. Cate clutched at the back of Parker's head, hips rocking, wordlessly begging for deeper contact. Parker dipped toward her entrance but didn't venture any further. Cate bit back a frustrated growl. Of course Parker would pick now of all moments to exercise some restraint. She probably should have expected that.

Parker's breath was hot against the shell of her ear, lips curling into a grin. With each roll of Cate's hips she pulled her hand back, reducing her touch to a light ghosting. Every one of Cate's nerve endings screamed in desperation. She hated it and loved it and somehow knew that Parker could tell—and that knowledge just made it all the more arousing.

Parker nipped at her earlobe. "I want to taste you first. Then I'm going to fuck you."

Cate almost told her to get the hell on with it, but her words dissolved into a near whimper as Parker's hand disappeared from between her legs and all she could do was nod. Parker ran the tip of her tongue over the hollow of Cate's throat, then dragged her mouth over to her breasts, teasing each of her nipples in turn. She kept that same maddeningly slow pace as she kissed her way down Cate's trembling stomach. A low, pleased hum reverberated deep in Parker's throat when she traced the furrows of Cate's abs with her tongue. By the time Parker's teeth grazed the top of her underwear, Cate had never wanted someone inside her so much in her entire life. With a shift in her hips and a quick pull, Cate's pants were finally gone. Parker settled between her legs. Cate's heart was in her throat.

At the first swipe of Parker's tongue, Cate threw her head back and cried out. She reached out blindly and tangled her fingers in Parker's thick, wild hair, yanking her head closer and shamelessly grinding against her mouth. Need raged through her. In the back of her mind, insecurity reared up, a brief notion that she should be embarrassed at her body's reaction, at how quickly and thoroughly she was undone, at how long it had been since she'd slept with someone. Then Parker shifted and pushed two fingers inside.

All coherent thought was obliterated.

Parker pumped her hand firmly, hitting that spot deep inside so precisely Cate almost wept. Her tongue circled Cate's clit with a perfect amount of pressure, as if she knew instinctively just when to back off without being told.

God, she was good at this. Really, *really* good at this.

"Tell me what you want." Parker's mouth hovered just above Cate's clit. Her voice dropped an octave, issuing the order in a harsh rasp Cate didn't know she was capable of. A new flood of wetness surged between her legs.

"Faster."

Parker increased her pace. With her left hand she grabbed Cate's thigh, pushing her open farther to run her tongue along the inner crease. She found the throbbing pulse point and bit down. Cate's hips jerked involuntarily, and she nearly came. Parker chuckled.

"What else?" Parker's breath ghosted over tender skin as she spoke in that same low, firm voice. She soothed the bite with a soft kiss.

"More."

"More what?" Parker's fingers stopped, still buried inside her. She lowered her head and took Cate's clit in her mouth, sucking gently. Cate's entire body seized.

Gentleness was the last thing Cate wanted right now. She pulsed helplessly against Parker's hand and clawed at soft brown hair, trying to urge Parker in deeper, harder, but Parker remained unmoved. She would have to ask for what she needed. Cate's chest flushed, face hot. Her breath came out in desperate, racking gasps. Her right hand fisted the sheet underneath her. It began to tear.

"More fingers." She didn't recognize the aching keen in her own voice. "Please."

Parker slid out, adding a third finger, then back in again. Hard.

Stars exploded behind Cate's eyelids. The heat coiled at the base of her spine finally reached a breaking point, and her release cascaded over her like a wave. Parker rose to meet her, lifting herself up on one hand to ride out Cate's pleasure together. She kept an easy, steady rhythm, and before Cate had a chance to register what was happening, she was coming a second time.

When the room came back into focus, Parker was lying next to her, topless, stretched out with her head propped up on her hand. She had drawn the sheets up over Cate and was tracing an idle pattern over the fabric covering her stomach.

"Oh my God." Her throat was dry and scratchy; Lord knew how loud she'd been. She ran a hand through her sweat-soaked hair and turned to face Parker.

Cate expected to be met with a cocky grin and sly remark, but instead Parker gazed at her softly. Her lips were wet and parted ever so slightly. Without breaking eye contact, she brought Cate's hand to her mouth and gently kissed her palm. "Are you okay?"

The earnest look on Parker's face almost cleaved Cate's heart in two. "I'm perfect." She caught Parker's jaw with her hand. "You're perfect."

Parker glanced away sheepishly, a stark contrast to the confidence she had wielded only moments before. It was utterly endearing. An emotion that Cate didn't want to name simmered dangerously close to the surface.

"I was a little nervous," Parker admitted with a laugh.

"You didn't seem nervous."

"Yeah, but I'm all talk."

Cate pulled her in, tasting herself on Parker's lips. Heat bloomed again between her thighs. She pressed the length of her body into Parker, tangling their legs together between the sheet. She rolled her hips slowly, earning a moan from Parker as she rocked into her. Something hard pushed into Cate's stomach. It was Parker's belt buckle.

"You're still wearing pants?" Cate sucked gently on Parker's bottom lip.

"I was…distracted."

Cate pushed Parker onto her back and sat up. Her eyes raked over Parker, laid out in front of her, admiring the curve of her shoulders, her firm breasts, the trim stomach giving way to the slight swell of her hips. Cate dragged her nails over Parker's skin, watching the muscles twitch and flex under her touch. She reached Parker's waist and started unbuckling her belt. Gray eyes stared up at her with undisguised eagerness.

"You're about to be even *more* distracted."

* * *

Parker's eyes fluttered open. Sunlight spilled into the room. A soft breeze drifted in from the cracked window next to the bed, ruffling the hair spilling onto her forehead. She stretched out slowly, still lying on her side, and suppressed a groan. She was sore all over, but in the best possible way. She was certain that bruises dappled her hips and thighs, not to mention the marks that surely covered her collarbone. The memory of Cate underneath her, gripping her tightly, desperate and asking for more, sent a pleased hum through Parker's body.

The mattress dipped behind her. A strong arm slipped over her waist and a gentle sigh brushed her ear. "Good morning." Cate's lips grazed the back of her neck.

"Hey." Their fingers laced together over Parker's stomach. "What time is it?"

Cate's mouth found the sensitive spot behind Parker's ear. "Almost nine."

"It's too early."

"You *really* don't like mornings, do you?"

"I like them with you." Parker rolled over, burrowing her face into the crook of Cate's neck, breathing in the mingled scents of sweat and sex and smoke. She was pretty sure it had been well past midnight when they finally fell asleep, boneless and sated. Cate shifted and pulled Parker in closer, resting her chin on the top of Parker's head and threading her fingers through Parker's hair. Parker let out a sigh, reveling in the sensation of Cate's fingertips along her scalp.

She'd never been good at morning afters. Too many times, no matter how much fun she had the night before, when the light of day broke she'd be filled with anxiety. Whether it was the disorientation of waking up somewhere else, or the surge of regret at having one too many drinks, or the awkwardness that came with mismatched expectations, Parker was always keen to escape. To run. Even at Sophia's she never felt completely comfortable, probably because part of her knew it was never going to work.

Honestly, there was never a time where she wasn't anxious or worried, wondering what she would wake up to in the morning. Whether it was one of her parent's explosive fights, or shuffling between their homes, hoping to feel like something more than just a nuisance—so many days of her life started with a dreadful unsettling feeling. Like she wasn't quite welcome anywhere. Even while crashing at Rob's when she first got into town and being explicitly told she could stay as long as she needed to, Parker couldn't escape the feeling that she was just in the way.

She didn't experience any of that with Cate. All Parker wanted was to sink deeper into Cate's arms and never leave.

Maybe everything that had happened was supposed to bring her here, to Mayville, to Cate's bed. Maybe she actually had been given a map but just didn't realize it. The walls of her throat closed in at the thought, and she huddled closer to Cate.

"You okay?" Cate's voice was still thick with sleep. Parker wanted to wrap herself up in that sound.

"More than okay." Suddenly, Parker was grateful Cate couldn't see her face.

They lay together quietly for a little while longer, Parker almost falling back asleep while Cate's fingers played in her hair. When Cate spoke next, her voice was clearer, and Parker felt her body come awake.

"Coffee?" Cate asked.

"Constantly."

Cate chuckled, her fingers now trailing over Parker's shoulder blades. "I'll make breakfast, too."

"Holy hell, is there anything you can't do?"

"My mom's side is Italian. Learning to cook was pretty much mandatory." Cate's mouth curled into a smile against Parker's forehead. "What do you like?"

"What do you have?"

"The usual. Eggs, bacon, French toast, pancakes—"

"I fucking love French toast."

Cate chuckled again. "I bet you do."

Parker pulled away, blinking. "What's that supposed to mean?"

Cate's eyes were heavy and half closed, a satisfied smile playing across her lips. Her hair was messy against the pillow, the short waves of her usually tame pixie cut splayed out in all directions. She was beautiful. Parker had to remind herself to breathe. "It means you don't half-ass things. I like that about you."

Parker bit back a laugh. "Oh, I half-ass *plenty* of things."

Cate raised her chin, her dark gaze sharpening. She gave Parker that same appraising look she had when they first met, but now Parker read the playfulness behind her eyes. The tips of her fingers grazed over Parker's lips. "No, I don't think you do."

Parker wanted to argue the point, but the way Cate was looking at her left her unable to find words, like she was seeing all the way down to Parker's core. Blushing, Parker turned away, trying to hide her face in the pillow, but Cate caught her chin and kissed her. Parker marveled at the softness of Cate's lips, at how gentle she could be, and how this kiss somehow held more potential and promise than any they'd shared last night.

A buzzing sound came from somewhere around the bed. Parker tried to ignore it, but a part of her brain she couldn't turn off latched on to the noise. She pulled away from Cate and flopped onto her stomach, scooting over to the edge of the bed. A discontented growl followed. "You have got to be kidding."

"Let me just check it real quick." Parker fumbled around the pile of clothes near the bed, finally coming up with her suit pants. Her phone was lit up like a Christmas tree, as if the device was offended that it had been ignored all evening. She flipped through the usual noise—auction updates, Discord notifications, texts from Manni and Rob, typical bullshit from Jake—to find the most recent notification. It was a text from Josie, asking how the rest of the night had gone, accompanied by a string of suggestive emojis. Parker rolled onto her back.

"What?" Cate slid her arm over Parker's stomach.

"It's Josie. Looks like our ghosting last night did not go unnoticed." Parker frowned at her phone and shimmied closer to Cate. It had only taken two songs after Parker's request before they slipped out of the ballroom without saying goodbye.

Cate let out a gentle snort, the puff of warm air near Parker's ear sending a shiver down the length of her body. "Of course not. I'm sure she and Alex were speculating wildly all night. I'm sorry, the crew loves gossip." She kissed Parker's temple. "I'll tell them to knock it off."

Parker hesitated, thumbs poised over the keyboard. "Does it bother you?"

"No." Cate brushed her nose against Parker's cheek. "But I'll still tell them to cut that shit out."

"Okay." Relief filled her. She hadn't even realized she'd been nervous about that, even though it had been obvious they were going to leave together. "I'll just let her know we're alive. And that the sex was mind-blowing." Cate jerked back, and Parker laughed at the questioning brow arched in her direction. "Kidding. I'm kidding."

"Ah. I get it. So you don't think it was mind-blowing?" Cate frowned at her but was doing a poor job of hiding her amusement.

"Nope." Parker hit send and turned her head to kiss the corner of Cate's mouth. "It was *earth-shattering*."

"Earth-shattering," Cate repeated as she leaned into the kiss. "I like that." She eased over to slide on top of Parker. Still holding her phone, Parker looped her arms around Cate's neck, welcoming hard muscle and soft skin pressing into her. Slowly, she raised her thigh, finding Cate's hot, wet center. Cate's breath hitched in her mouth and Parker rolled her hips, urging Cate to move.

Another buzz interrupted them. Parker flicked her thumb across the display, reading the notification over Cate's shoulder. It was Josie again, with another trail of emojis.

Cate planted both hands on either side of Parker's head and pushed herself up, still rocking against Parker's leg. "I swear, I am going to throw that damn thing into the lake." The last part of the threat came out as a gasp.

Parker grinned. "What do you care? I thought you were going to make coffee and French toast." She held her phone out with one hand and grabbed Cate's hip with the other, keeping them pressed together as she increased the pace. Wetness painted Parker's thigh. Dark eyes looked down at her, half closed with desire, and Cate bit her lip before dipping her head for a kiss that blew away all thoughts of food.

Then her phone was gone and Cate was above her, hips stilled, triumphantly tossing the device over her shoulder. It landed somewhere near the door with a *thump*. "Still want breakfast?" Heat was still behind those dark eyes, but now she favored Parker with a smile that could almost be described as cocky.

Parker reached up and took Cate's face in her hands. She shook her head, and although she gave Cate a cocky smile right back, her words came out softer than she expected. "No. I want you."

CHAPTER SEVENTEEN

Cate stood with her hands on her hips, eyeing the weight rack. After a moment's consideration, she added five more pounds to each side of the bar. She hadn't expected to go for a PR today, but screw it. A lot of things had happened over the last few weeks she hadn't expected.

She took a sip from her water bottle, steadying herself before the next set, and surveyed the room. Chevy's Gym was a run-down, hole-in-the-wall garage on the same side of town as Station Two that looked like a cross between a prison gym yard and a set piece from *Rocky IV*. Ancient metal machines lined the walls near the free weights, some of them so old Cate didn't know what muscles they were supposed to work, and next to them was a row of dusty treadmills that she doubted had ever been used. A boxing ring was set up in the corner; next to that was an array of heavy bags and speed bags for drills. Along the wall near the window was an honest-to-God set of Atlas stones from a Strongman competition.

People came to Chevy's for two reasons: to lift heavy and punch things. They also minded their own business. Cate loved it. She did most of her workouts at the firehouse, even on her off days, but when she didn't feel like dealing with anyone, she went to Chevy's.

At five thirty on a Sunday night, the place was nearly deserted, and since there were plenty of open benches and racks, Cate wasn't in a hurry. The bubbling sensation that'd been in her chest since last night had yet to disappear, and no matter how much she benched it still felt like her heart was about to jump out of her throat. By the time she and Parker had managed to pull themselves away from the bed, it was long past a reasonable hour for breakfast or even brunch. Only the need for caffeine spurred them from the tangled sheets, and after coffee and a quick snack, they tumbled back into bed together—after a brief detour to the couch, where Parker's mouth had once again left her shattered and gasping for air.

Cate still couldn't believe it. She'd had good sex before, but this was something else entirely. She hadn't wanted it to end, and when Parker finally had to leave to make it to her brother's house for dinner, Cate's body was alive and humming in a way she didn't know was possible.

She lay down and settled herself under the bar, reining in her spinning mind to focus on the lift. Dropping the bar on her head would definitely put a damper on any future encounters with Parker. Just before Cate eased the bar up, a pair of blinding neon-pink gym shorts appeared behind her head. Alex peeked over the bar.

"Need a spot?" He grinned down at her.

Cate scrunched up her nose. "Those shorts are too small to be that close to my face."

"Skies out, thighs out, baby." Alex stepped up on the back of the bench and guided the bar into Cate's hands. She ripped off five clean reps, paused, and with Alex's encouragement, did three more.

"Show-off." Alex set the bar back with a clang. Cate sat up and shrugged, avoiding his eyes as she took another sip of water.

"What are you doing here?" she asked.

Alex laughed and started throwing weights onto the empty rack next to her. Those shorts were ridiculous, but he was pulling them off. Alex was religious about leg day. "The same reason everyone else is, Wilds." He paused, his grin widening dangerously. "So, how was your night?"

"Fine."

"Only fine?"

Cate bit the inside of her cheek so hard she almost drew blood. Alex immediately saw through her attempt to remain stoic.

"Hell yeah!" Alex held up his hand. Sighing, Cate gave him a high five. "Was it good? Did you enjoy yourself? Did you go all night and fall asleep in each other's arms?"

Cate regretted confirming that, in her experience, the data about lesbians orgasming more often than straight women was accurate. It certainly had been true last night. Her face flushed. "Something like that."

"I am fucking thrilled. You're always so much nicer after you get laid."

In one blinding motion, Cate snatched the sweaty towel off her bench and snapped it right at Alex's ass and those too-tight shorts. He yelped and leapt backward. "Take it back, dickhead."

"Jesus, okay." Alex rubbed the bright-red spot on his thigh. "I'm just glad you thought about what I said."

Cate twisted the towel between her hands to keep them from trembling. "I didn't do much thinking last night, honestly." *Or this morning. And afternoon.*

"You should try that more often. Not thinking. Looks good on you."

Cate's eyes darted to the dirty gym floor and the worn pair of Converse she always lifted in. When she looked back up at him, she didn't try to hide her smile. "Yeah. Maybe." She dropped the towel, stood up, and started throwing more plates onto Alex's bar. "Come on, I'll spot you."

Alex looked at the plates and hesitated, then slid under the bar. "This is bullying. You're bullying me."

"Those shorts are bullying *me*." Cate stepped up behind him. "Give me ten, Rutherford."

* * *

Forty-five minutes later, Cate said goodbye to Alex at Chevy's dented bicycle rack, unable to hold back a chuckle as he rode off in his absurd shorts. She climbed into her Jeep, hand hovering over the ignition. Instead of starting the car, she went for her gym bag and came up with her phone.

A text from Parker was waiting, informing her that promptly upon Parker's arrival at her brother's house, Tyson had stuck a crayon up his nose and Parker wanted to know exactly how far up it needed to be before worrying. A second text followed shortly after, telling her to never mind and that Tyson had managed to get it out himself. A half dozen angry emojis filled the display. Cate shook her head and tapped on Parker's number.

Parker answered on the second ring, all breathless, unbridled enthusiasm. "Hi! How are you?" The exuberant greeting was followed by a *thunk* and a loud curse.

"Are you okay?" Cate asked.

"Yeah, I just stepped on one of Tyson's Hot Wheels." Parker's voice lowered to a grumble, and Cate's heart thumped as she pictured the adorably annoyed look on Parker's face. "That kid is a goddamn menace."

"Sounds like it. Has he recovered from the crayon incident?"

Parker heaved a sigh. "He's fine. He got it out on his own. I was supposed to be watching him while Meagan was grilling. I swear he does stuff like that just to mess with me."

The idea of the wild little boy that had visited the firehouse deliberately antagonizing Parker brought a smile to Cate's face. Even though she hadn't spent any time with Tyson, it was clear that Parker doted on him. It was also clear, based on his antics, that he took after his aunt.

"I wouldn't worry too much. He really has to jam it up there to do any lasting damage."

Parker huffed. "Thanks. I just got nervous. Sorry to bother you."

"You're not a bother."

"Good."

Parker's confident reply sent a ripple through her core. Cate ran her fingers over the gearshift and realized she was nervous—which seemed ridiculous. After the night they had and spending the entire day together, how could she doubt what was going on between them? Yet something held her back. Alex's advice to stop thinking echoed through her mind, but all that did was make her think more. She traced her thumb over the grooves in the shifter knob, trying to figure out what to say next. This was why she sucked at dating. There were always moments like this, where there was the emotionally intelligent thing to say or do, and she always missed it.

Was this even dating? Somehow, it felt like more than that.

Electricity crackled over the line, giving weight to the silence. It was Parker who spoke again, in that same confident tone that made Cate want to melt into her seat.

"When can I see you again?"

It took a remarkable amount of willpower not to invite Parker over that night. "I work tomorrow. And Tuesday I'm at the rec center in the afternoon."

"So Tuesday night when you're done at Butler? If you're not too tired?" Parker's voice brimmed with hope. "I still owe you dinner."

"And I still owe you breakfast." Cate smiled into the phone.

Parker's voice dropped an octave. "Is that a promise?"

"Absolutely." Without looking, Cate knew her smile had turned lopsided. She didn't mind at all.

* * *

Pocketing her phone, Parker bounded back into Rob's kitchen, already silently counting down the hours until Tuesday night. She slid into her seat at the kitchen table and resumed chopping cucumber. It was mid-June, and summer was finally making an appearance. The last several days had been warm, and dinner that night was simple grilled chicken and a quinoa salad Parker had seen trending on TikTok. Showing up with the ingredients for the side dish saved her from questions about her being late, or why she looked more frazzled than usual. She barely had time to shower and change after leaving Cate's and had slapped her helmet on over damp hair as she raced out the door.

Parker felt Rob's eyes on her while she chopped. She bit her lip, staring intently at the vegetables.

"Who was that?" Rob pushed a beer in her direction. He was still on a Mexican beer kick, and today it was Pacifico.

Parker kept her head down. Each piece of cucumber was precisely uniform. "Cate."

Rob let out a noise she'd never heard before, like he'd suddenly morphed into a middle schooler. "Oooohhh! Last night must have gone well."

Parker's ears started burning. Before she was forced to reply, Meagan swept into the kitchen with a plateful of chicken, yelling over her shoulder for Tyson to go wash up. She looked from Rob to Parker to the half-cut cucumber. "You still haven't finished that?"

Rob took the plate out of Meagan's hands and placed it on the counter. "I think someone is still a little distracted by their date last night."

"Really? With that hot firefighter?"

Parker looked up, exasperated. "You told her?"

"Of course I did." Rob leaned back against the counter and smugly sipped his beer.

"Personally, I thought he was exaggerating when he told me how pretty she was, but then I Googled her, and goddamn," Meagan said. Brown eyes flashed playfully at Parker, always a bit more perceptive than her brother's. She shouldn't be surprised Meagan knew about Cate. Meagan and Rob had met in their sophomore year of high school and dated on and off all through college, finally settling down after Meagan was accepted to grad school and Rob followed her to the same city. Parker had been only seven when she met Meagan, and she'd been a more reliable presence in Parker's life than most of her other family members. Meagan had also, early on, seen right through her.

Parker returned to the cucumber, her chopping more erratic. "I had fun. It was a good night."

"The sex was that good, huh?"

"Meg!" Parker felt like her entire face was on fire. Rob choked on his beer. "I didn't say anything about having sex."

Meagan pointed at her. "How'd you get that hickey on your neck, then?"

"What? Where?" Parker leapt to her feet, sending the kitchen chair scraping across the floor. She swiped at her neck, twisting her head around to find the mark even though it was physically impossible without snapping her own spine.

"Nowhere." Meagan plucked a piece of cucumber off the cutting board, popped it into her mouth, and dumped the rest into the bowl sitting on the table. "But you just proved me right, so thanks."

Parker sank into her chair. Meagan took over assembling the salad, adding quinoa and chickpeas in the bowl with a splash of olive oil and lemon juice. "You really like her," she announced, jabbing the air with the wooden spoon in her hand. Parker hated that tone. Meagan always sounded like that when she was right. Which, more often than not, she was.

"Why would you say that?"

"Because every other time you've gotten laid, you bounced off the walls like a giddy high school boy."

"That's not true."

"Sure it is." Meagan held up a hand, fingers splayed, looking dangerously close to ticking off a list of Parker's prior conquests. "What about—"

"Can we please stop discussing my sister's sex life?" Rob let out a dramatic groan and pulled another beer from the fridge.

"Fine. But I'm right."

Meagan joined Rob by the counter and began plating the chicken. Parker stood to assemble the remainder of the salad, head down. Her next words came out so quietly she didn't recognize her own voice. "Yeah. You are."

"Really?" Rob dropped into the chair across from her, throwing an arm over the back. His disinterest was forgotten. Apparently, so long as she didn't go into details, Rob was more than eager to hear about her romantic escapades. She remembered his earlier promise to tease her mercilessly about Cate but couldn't bring herself to care.

"She's…" Parker looked up, unable to hide her smile. "Breathtaking."

Rob and Meagan exchanged glances. Rob looked genuinely surprised. "I've never heard you talk about a woman like that before."

"It's true. She's smart and strong and kind. And funny—like the kind of funny where you don't realize it until after you walk away. And yeah, she's gorgeous, but it's so much more than that." Parker stopped, realizing she was teetering on the edge of a full-on ramble. Or reciting a sonnet.

It was so easy to do, though. She'd never been good at exercising restraint, often letting her feelings pour over and out of her with little regard for the future consequences. With Cate, everything was different. It didn't feel like she was rushing into something again. Each moment with Cate felt deliberate, every step carefully considered, every interaction resonating through them both. She didn't know exactly how to explain it to Rob and Meagan, other than saying she'd never felt something like this before.

"And we're meeting her…when?" Meagan took the seat next to Rob. She crossed her legs and leaned forward, propping her chin on her fist.

Parker resumed stirring the salad. "Yeah, right. Like I'm about to subject her to the Inquisition."

Rob opened his arms wide, feigning innocence. "Why are you including me in that statement? She's the one you have to worry about." He nudged Meagan, who swiped the beer from his hand and took a swallow.

"Watch yourself, Counselor." Meagan gripped the neck of the bottle between her first two fingers, letting it dangle within reach of Rob. He made no move to take it back. Parker had always appreciated the easy way Rob and Meagan interacted, but now the obvious affection they had for each other struck a chord.

"Mom, my show turned off." Tyson appeared around the corner, waving his iPad.

"Boy, you were supposed to be cleaning up." Meagan sighed. "No more screens. Go wash your hands."

After Tyson whined all the way to the bathroom and all the way back, they finally sat down for dinner. The conversation turned away from Cate but landed on a subject that also tied Parker's stomach in knots.

"Still on track for Friday?" Rob asked her, helping Tyson spoon salad onto his plate.

Friday. Right.

Parker exhaled, blowing a wayward strand of hair off her forehead. "Yep. Good to go."

Cate and the ball hadn't exactly been a distraction from getting her store ready to open, but Parker's momentum had slowed over the past week or so. Now, with her back room fully stocked and the assembled clothes racks and a brand-new window, there was no reason to push the soft opening out any further. As the day loomed closer, though, Parker's anxiety grew. What if she fell flat on her face? This time she couldn't just pivot to something new; Rob and Meagan were tied up in the store, both personally and financially. This didn't just affect her, and the thought terrified Parker.

Parker watched as Rob plated Tyson's food, laughing at a joke Meagan made but that Parker didn't have the context to understand. She nudged the chicken with her fork, her appetite gone.

CHAPTER EIGHTEEN

On Tuesday evening Cate swerved into her driveway just after six p.m., killed the Jeep's engine, and hopped out with barely a look back at her place. She headed in the familiar direction toward Tomlinson Street, cutting through the park and crossing over to the next block with only the faintest glance for oncoming cars. Soon the top of the firehouse came into view, then Parker's store. As if on cue, that bubbly feeling rose in her chest again. She hadn't seen Parker since Sunday, and days apart had somehow felt like a week. No matter how hard she tried, Cate couldn't temper her enthusiasm. She couldn't remember the last time she was so excited about someone. The cynical part of her brain piped up with a helpful reminder that her excitement was in no small part due to the ridiculously good sex and the notable drought she'd been in before meeting Parker. Cate pushed the thought away. Yes, sex was no doubt contributing to the spring in her step, but it wasn't the only factor. She shoved that thought away, too.

Her pace slowed as she approached Remix, the figure sitting on the floor of the store visible through the new window. Parker sat cross-legged next to a box of T-shirts and appeared to be in the process of unpacking and folding them, although the project looked like it had been abandoned. Or derailed. A pile of folded shirts had toppled over at

Parker's feet, and a few more were crumpled up in her lap. Her elbows were propped up on her knees, her head in both hands. Suddenly she stood up, spilling more shirts onto the floor, and aimed a kick at the box. The outburst alone was cause for concern, but the fact that Parker didn't seem to care if she scuffed her gray-and-lime shoes was even more alarming.

Cate knocked twice and pushed the door open. "Hey there."

Parker jumped and spun around. The ever-present smile was there, although it came off as a bit forced. "Hi! How was the rec center?"

"Good. Hardly any arguments today." Cate cocked her head. That darling face was just too expressive, and no matter how hard Parker was trying, Cate recognized that something was clearly bothering her. In two strides she crossed the floor and stood in front of Parker, reaching for her hand.

"What's wrong?"

"Nothing."

Parker's grin widened, but Cate didn't buy it. She traced the curves of Parker's knuckles with her thumb. "You sure about that?"

Parker looked away, rubbing the back of her neck, but didn't drop Cate's hand. The smile finally evaporated. When she began talking, her words rushed out like a waterfall.

"The screen-printing company fucked up the size runs on my T-shirt order, so now I have fifteen XXL shirts, instead of ten larges and five XLs. The hell am I going to do with *fifteen* XXLs? And earlier today I thought I going to score at least three pairs of a new release but I didn't get any, and my stupid inventory program is acting up again and I—" Parker puffed out her cheeks, looking at the new window. "Maybe I should push the opening back. By like a week or two."

Cate glanced around the store. Aside from the mess of shirts at her feet, everything seemed in order. The clothing racks Parker had been battling for weeks were all assembled and standing in a perfect, crisp line. The display wall was full of shoes, each one placed strategically in relation to the painting behind them, the particular color of the shoe complementing the pattern of the mural and making each one pop. Behind her, which Cate had noticed as soon as she walked in, was the cash wrap stand, gleaming in all white with an iPad plugged in and ready to go. Parker had even set up a low couch and glass coffee table in the corner opposite the entrance with sneaker magazines artfully splayed across the surface. Chaotic T-shirt explosion notwithstanding, the store looked as prepared as Cate had ever seen it. She guessed that even the back room was cleaned up and organized, too.

The hell was going on? Sure, maybe Parker was prone to the occasional theatrics, but postponing the opening because of an order mishap was a bit extreme. It was only Tuesday and the soft opening wasn't until Thursday—more than enough time for any last-minute preparations.

"Are you sure? The place looks great."

"Yeah, but I can't..."

"Can't what?"

"I can't do this." Parker pulled away from Cate's grasp and started pacing, raking both hands through her hair. It was an almost identical scene as the night of the break-in, except now Parker seemed gripped by a different kind of panic. She stopped, almost tripping over her own feet, and planted herself in front of the display wall. "What was I thinking? If I mess this up..." Her voice was distant. A shudder racked her small frame.

Cate shifted her weight from one foot to the other. She didn't know what brought this on and wanted to say something to comfort Parker, but she hadn't the slightest idea of where to start. Each time the beginning of a sentence formed in her head it came off as too trite or condescending, and she immediately tossed it aside. She sidled up next to Parker, balling her hands in her jacket pockets, and looked at the kaleidoscope display in front of her. How Parker could be so talented and not realize it was beyond her.

"I don't understand why you're upset," Cate admitted softly.

Parker sighed. Her shoulders slumped forward like the weight of the entire world had landed across her back. Cate felt like she was looming over her. "I've never really had an idea of what I wanted to do with my life. Like, not even the slightest clue. I suppose that doesn't make me different from a lot of people, but compared to everyone else in my family I think I've always felt a little lost." Parker glanced down at her lime-tinged shoes, then back up at the wall. "For a while, I did whatever I wanted. If something wasn't working out, I'd just bounce. It didn't matter who I left hanging. And I guess as long as my dad paid my bills, there weren't any consequences."

"But now there are." Cate took her hand out of her pocket and touched the small of Parker's back, feeling a small tremor under her fingertips.

Parker took a deep breath. "Rob and Meagan cosigned on the loan I needed to open this place. I couldn't get approved by myself, and I didn't want to ask my dad. If I fuck this up, I'll be screwing them over, too."

"You're being too hard on yourself. Look at this place. Look at what you built. It's incredible. Who cares about a bunch of shirts?" Cate leaned over and kissed Parker's temple. "You even got the gerbil smell out."

"Ferrets."

"Whatever."

Parker laughed. Cate slipped behind Parker, wrapping her arms around her waist and hugging her from behind. Parker leaned back against Cate's chest, the back of her head falling to Cate's shoulder. "It's funny. Now that I finally know what I want to do, I've never been more terrified."

Cate hummed thoughtfully against Parker's temple. "Rob and Meagan have faith in you. I'm sure they wouldn't have cosigned that loan if they didn't think you'd be successful."

"Probably."

"And." Cate lowered her voice. "I think you can do it, too."

Parker slid her hand over Cate's and laced their fingers together. She kept her eyes straight ahead, looking at the display wall. "You do?"

"Of course I do. I've worked in this neighborhood for over ten years, and I've seen a lot of things come and go. There's nothing like this on Tomlinson, let alone the rest of town. It's a niche thing, sure, but you have something special here. Something really unique."

"What's that?"

Now, for a reason she didn't understand, the words she'd been searching for earlier came to her. "It's you. People won't just come because of whatever ultra-exclusive, super-hyped, wild-ass shoe you're selling that week. They'll come because of you." She paused, meaning to stop there, but she couldn't hold herself back. "You're genuine and kind and funny, and people love you. I don't get how you can't see that."

Parker stiffened in her arms, her chest hitching. Cate hugged her closer but kept staring straight ahead. Parker kept her own gaze locked forward, too, like they both couldn't quite bring themselves to look at each other. Softly, Parker cleared her throat.

"You really mean all that?"

"Yes."

A long moment passed before Parker spoke again. "I think I've found something else I really want. And it scares me, too."

Cate inhaled. Her heart thundered against her ribs so sharply she was sure it echoed through Parker's own chest. Again the words came easily, so easily she didn't believe she was the one saying them.

"You have nothing to be scared of."

Parker's hand clamped down tightly. Another shudder went through her, although to Cate it felt like a shattering deep in her own core. She didn't know why, but the air was shifting between them, adding a solemn weight to an interaction that had started so casually. Maybe that was part of why she was drawn so inexorably into Parker's orbit—the warm, playful exterior that glossed over an unexpected depth. Cate knew it the night of the break-in, she now realized. The eloquent way Parker had spoken about her sneaker business had caught Cate off guard. She also realized, with the delayed benefit of hindsight, that she'd wanted to kiss Parker ever since that night. Now there was no reason to hold back.

Cate unclasped their hands and trailed her fingers over Parker's hip, turning her slowly. She caught Parker's chin with a finger, raising her head so their eyes met. Raw emotions flashed across Parker's open face so quickly Cate couldn't track them all: excitement, fear, arousal. Something else was there, too. A look hinting at the feeling hovering just below the surface, the precursor to a word Cate was closer to saying than she wanted to admit. The reason why she'd been so excited on her way over to the store, the reason why that sparkling, frothy feeling in her chest had yet to dissipate.

She touched their lips together, and on contact the kiss deepened immediately. Parker sighed, a low sound of relief that filled Cate to the brim. She pulled Parker closer while Parker wrapped her hands in the lapels of her jacket, clutching so tightly Cate wondered if Parker was afraid she'd disappear into thin air. When they broke apart, it was only by mere centimeters, their lips still hovering close as Cate pressed her forehead to Parker's.

"Why don't I help you clean up here and then we go back to my place? I'll make dinner."

"Isn't it my turn to come up with a meal?"

"I like to cook. Let me make you something. Do you like carbonara?"

"I fucking love carbonara."

Cate laughed, the sound resonating deep in her chest. "How did I know you were going to say that?" She kissed Parker's forehead.

"Shit. I'm too predictable already."

"No." Cate cupped Parker's face, swiping her thumb over the curve of Parker's jaw as she repeated her words from Saturday night. They were still true, even if the truth of them should have scared her. "You're perfect."

Parker's skin flushed under her hand. Cate didn't let her turn away, leaning in before Parker could deflect the compliment with a joke or a laugh, or squirm away from Cate's touch. Something told her Parker needed to hear that. Another slow, easy kiss drove the sentiment home further. At least, she hoped it did.

When they pulled back, Parker's bright eyes and brighter smile was back, as if she hadn't been upset at all. She returned to the pile of shirts and examined the mess with a thoughtful look.

"This isn't that bad. Right?" Parker held up one of the shirts, comically wide when juxtaposed against her small frame. The black fabric was high-quality and the design on the chest shone like a beacon: a swirling, multicolored interpretation of the store's graffiti-style logo that complemented the bright display wall mural. The shirts were lovely, but Cate could understand Parker's frustration at having to deal with almost a dozen of them that she didn't expect to receive.

"They do look great." Cate picked up the one nearest to her feet. "The design is fantastic."

"Thanks." Parker sighed and dropped her arms, but the gesture didn't feel like one of defeat. She surveyed the pile, chewing on her bottom lip. "I can figure this out."

"Don't you always?"

With a flick of her wrist, Parker threw the shirt across her shoulder and flashed Cate a cocky grin. "I will now."

* * *

"Your mother is gonna kill me." The put-upon father pinched the bridge of his nose in the universal gesture of an exasperated parent.

His daughter was unrelenting. In a tightly cinched ponytail, wide jeans, and a blocky, dropped-shoulder T-shirt, she looked every inch the trendy high schooler. The well-worn Yeezys on her feet confirmed Parker's assessment.

"Dad, I have the money. You and Mom know I've been saving for a car since forever. I can totally afford these." The teenager pointed once again to the cool gray Jordan Eleven Retros she'd been eyeing, which Parker thought were priced very reasonably considering how popular that release had been. She admired both the girl's taste and her tenacity. They continued to go back and forth about the Elevens, and Parker stepped back, sensing that the father's resolve was close to crumbling. She took the opportunity to take a quick lap around the store.

Rob was working the cash register, just finishing bagging up a customer who'd bought a pair of low Panda Dunks for his girlfriend. Meagan was greeting a preteen boy and his mother who'd just walked in, leading them to the part of the display wall that held the latest Air

Maxes. Tyson sat on the floor, cross-legged, coloring at the low glass coffee table and smearing fingerprints all over the surface. The back issues of *Sneakerheadz Magazine* Parker had carefully fanned out that morning now resided on the floor. A couple out for their morning coffee was hovering near the clothing racks, flipping through the Remix shirts, vintage sports tees, and old school Starter jackets. They'd been getting a steady stream of Saturday-morning foot traffic into the store, and even if it didn't translate directly to sales, Parker was happy to see that at least people seemed interested.

Parker's eyes swept to the corner farthest from the front door to the drink station offering free beer, wine, and soda. She'd wanted to serve potential customers herself and use it as an opportunity to chat them up, but the temporary alcohol permit required a licensed bartender to serve the drinks. The bartender in question was a mop-topped, inattentive twenty-something named Samuel, and while Parker wished he was a little more outgoing, he'd also agreed to work both Saturday and Sunday in exchange for a pair of the J Balvin Jordan Ones as payment. The shoes were easy enough to track down, but Parker still wasn't sure if she was getting ripped off or not.

Samuel looked up from his phone and caught Parker glaring at him. He literally jumped up like he'd been called to attention and swept over to the woman Meagan was still talking to, presenting her with a glass of chardonnay and a Coke for her son, who was staring at Meagan in hormone-addled distress. For good measure, Samuel went over to the couple too and brought them two Amstel Lights. Parker sighed. He must really want those shoes.

Speaking of shoes, she looped back to the teenager and her father she'd been talking to earlier. They were still arguing, but clearly the teenager was winning. When there was a break in the conversation, Parker took the opportunity to jump in.

"If it helps, I offer a layaway program. Twenty-five percent down now, pay the balance in four weeks." Technically, she'd only been *thinking* about offering a layaway program, but they didn't need to know that. Parker's eyes flicked from father to daughter. The former ran a hand down his long, bearded face.

"Okay." Defeat rang through his tone. "Do you want to do layaway or take them now?"

"Now, please!" the teenager chirped in Parker's direction, then turned back to her father. "Thanks, Dad."

"Excellent choice, young'un." Parker winked at her. "Want to wear them out?"

The teenager gasped. "Seriously? Without waterproofing them first? Or crease protectors?"

Parker's heart swelled. "I got crease protectors up front and can treat them real quick in the back before you go. For an extra twenty-five bucks, I can clean your Yeezys, too."

"For real?" The teenager looked down at her shoes.

"Absolutely. What's the point of buying these things if you can't show them off, right? Come back in a week and I'll have them looking fresh out of the box."

The girl's eyes widened, a smile of pure joy spreading across her face. Parker recognized the look; it was that unbridled enthusiasm that swelled within you when you were talking to someone else who just *got it*. "Shit yeah! That'd be awesome."

"Stacey. Come on." Her father groaned.

"Right. Sorry, Dad." Stacey leaned forward and lowered her voice to a whisper, even though it didn't seem like she was really trying. "I'm not supposed to swear so goddamn much."

Parker laughed. "I didn't hear a fucking thing. I'll meet y'all at the register. Don't mind my brother's grumpy-ass face. He's actually pretty cool."

Parker grabbed a pair of crease protectors from a small rack, then shoved through the double doors and plucked a box of size eight Eleven Retros off the shelf. She unpacked the sneakers, laced them up, slid a pair of crease protectors into each toe, and methodically sprayed them down with leather treatment. She walked back out with the Elevens perched on top of the box, holding them out on splayed fingers like a waiter at a French restaurant. After paying, the teenager flipped off her Yeezys and slid into the new Elevens with palpable glee. Parker handed her a receipt and business card and told her the Yeezys would be done next Saturday. They slapped hands, and Stacey practically skipped out of the store, father in tow.

Rob made a note on his phone. "Nice job. That's your third sale this hour."

"Thanks. How are we looking?" Parker packed the Yeezys into the box the Elevens had come in.

"Not bad, really." Rob rocked back and forth on his stool and skimmed his phone. "Ten sales since opening overall, which considering your prices and specific market, isn't that bad. And that doesn't include any online sales from the website. You're doing great, Park." He looked up at her, the ridiculously large Remix T-shirt swallowing his broad frame. All three of them were wearing the XXL shirts, with various alterations to make them fit. Parker had cropped the hem and rolled up the sleeves, while Meagan cut away the collar and sleeves and tied it in the back to turn it into a tank top. Rob had the least work to do; he only hacked off half of the sleeves and tucked it into the front of his dark jeans.

Parker's eyes flicked to her new, shiny front window and the fire station across the street. Station Two had been quiet all morning. She forced her attention back to her brother. "You really think so, Bobby?"

"Yes, I do." Rob reached up and ruffled the back of her head.

Parker spun away with a loud huff and smoothed down her hair. She'd gotten it cut for the occasion, and she had styled it into a perfect pompadour that accented the layered zigzags shaved into the sides and back. She'd brought Tyson along to her appointment and they'd gotten matching designs.

On Thursday night, she'd held a soft opening from four until nine, just to make sure her payment apps and goddamn inventory program were working. It had rained that whole night, and her only customer was a runner who got caught in the deluge and was looking for a rain jacket. All Parker had to offer was an oversized T-shirt and a towel. The runner politely declined. She decided not to take it as an omen.

Friday was another soft open, but the weather was still shitty and foot traffic was minimal. Only two or three people popped in during breaks in the rain, but none seemed interested in purchasing anything. Just before she'd closed, the same guy she'd seen walking his dog around Tomlinson stopped in. Barefoot. It was a solid ten minutes before he understood she sold only sneakers and not Birkenstocks.

Panic had gripped her that night as she lay in bed staring up at the ceiling, but she told herself it was the weather. Not that she was about to make the biggest mistake of her life. Thankfully, Saturday morning was beautiful, a complete one-eighty from the past two days. The sun had shone through the windows and lit up Parker's small loft. She woke with a renewed excitement and practically skipped down to her motorcycle, arriving at the store nearly two hours before her official grand opening. The event turned out to be a family affair—Rob, Meagan, and Tyson were all waiting for her when she arrived, which she hadn't expected at all. Her heart had swelled at the sight, and when she'd dismounted her bike she was choking back tears. In her heart she'd known that Rob and his family would show up for her, but part of her hadn't quite believed it.

All that was missing was Cate.

Parker left Rob at the cash register and went into the back to drop off the Yeezys on her desk. When she came back, her eyes went to the fire station again, the mute brick of the building somehow gleaming in the sun. Her hand hovered over her back pocket, but she stopped herself from pulling out her phone. Parker swallowed hard, spun on her heel, and went back through the double doors. She fumbled for the volume on the stereo system, turning up her early 2000s R&B playlist. Missy Elliott thrummed through the store, providing a helpful distraction.

As soon as she reappeared, Rob asked, "Is Cate coming?"

"Probably. She worked yesterday, so maybe not until later." This time, she couldn't stop herself from checking her phone. No texts. She put it away, keeping her face neutral.

Despite their schedules, she and Cate had seen each other most of the week, and Cate promised she'd be at the grand opening. Cate was scheduled to work Friday, which meant she wouldn't be off her twenty-four-hour shift until seven on Saturday morning. If it had been slow and Cate got enough sleep, Parker would've expected to see her by now. Since she hadn't appeared yet, Parker assumed that Cate was still at home, napping. But even then, Cate only allowed herself to sleep for two or three hours at the most. As the morning dragged on with no word, Parker became more and more agitated. The obvious explanations were that Cate was recovering from a long, eventful shift, or that she'd caught a last-minute job and stayed late, but Parker couldn't stop her head from snapping around every time the door opened, hoping to see Cate walk in. Parker wanted to share this with Cate, but more than that, she wanted to feel that steady, calming presence next to her and the reassurance of Cate's hand resting on her shoulder.

She'll call. Or text. She always has so far.

Parker thought back to the firefighter's ball, how they'd danced together and the way Cate flinched when Parker asked about her getting hurt. The wall that went up immediately after seemed to erect out of Cate's instinct more than anything. Parker had meant every word during that conversation. She wasn't afraid of Cate's job, and that night she'd learned it was important to prove that. But, goddamn, it'd just be nice to hear from her.

Another thought crept into the back of her mind: What if something serious happened this time? What if instead of a wooden beam sliding off Cate's shoulder, one landed on her head, or pinned her underneath? How would Parker know? Who would even think to call her? And what right did she have to assume that *anyone* would call? They hadn't even talked yet about how serious this was getting—a topic Parker was, until very recently, determined to avoid. Now it was all she could think about.

The mother and her son eventually left without buying anything, despite Meagan's charms. The couple followed soon after, also empty-handed. It was almost one o'clock.

"Dude, did you see this?"

Parker turned. Rob was holding up his phone, beckoning her to come over. Something in his tone made the hair on the back of her neck stand up.

The local news station was streaming a live report. A reporter stood in front of the camera, calmly describing the scene behind her. Fleets of fire trucks and ambulances and SUVs circled around a massive warehouse. Roaring flames shot out from broken, jagged windows and rolled across the roof. Dark, impenetrable smoke billowed high into the air, casting a shadow on the firefighters positioning themselves around the blaze. Each engine had multiple crews manning the hoses, but the barrage of water seemed to have no effect. On the side of the building, away from the larger bursts of flame, a ladder company was hacking away at a window at least four stories up.

"Shit," Parker whispered.

Rob turned up the volume on his phone.

"…truly an incredible scene, Jerry." The reporter pressed a hand to her earpiece, her severe blond bob blowing around in the wind. A bright rain jacket indicated she was from Channel 12 News, and she was disheveled enough to appear like the news crew had leapt into action to cover the breaking story. "I'm being told that this is one of the largest responses in the entire history of the Mayville Fire Department. Crews have been on site since four a.m. battling the blaze."

Meagan appeared over Parker's shoulder. "That's the cold storage warehouse on the outside of town. Uncle Marvin used to work overnights there."

"Fuck me," Rob muttered.

The newscast continued, cutting back to the anchor in the studio. "Any word on the cause of the fire, Marty?" the anchor asked, a middle-aged white man with salt-and-pepper hair, genetically engineered to exude the gravitas necessary for local news.

"Not yet, Jerry. Preliminary reports suggest that it was caused by some kind of electrical malfunction, but, again, the MFD has not confirmed anything." Marty paused. "We have received word that several employees were trapped inside when the fire began and were successfully rescued by the first MFD companies on the scene. They've been taken to St. Mary's with only minor injuries."

Jerry's brow furrowed in a practiced look of concern. "That's certainly good news. Have there been any reports of injured firefighters?"

"A few, yes, Jerry." Marty nodded gravely. "Initial reports indicate two firefighters were also taken to St. Mary's, and they are in stable condition."

Parker let out a long, slow breath, staring grimly at Rob's phone. The reporter and her camera operator were set up a safe distance away from the blaze, and it was too far for Parker to make out the numbers of all the engine and ladder companies on the scene. The two firefighters on the ladder successfully broke open the window and darted through the opening, throwing themselves into a belching cloud of smoke.

"Is Cate there?" Meagan asked.

"It looks like the whole damn department is there," Parker said tightly. "There's nowhere else she'd be."

Rob silently exited out of the app, cutting off Jerry midsentence. The syncopated beat of an Aaliyah song filled the store. Tyson continued coloring at the table, bopping his head to the music. No one spoke.

"I'm sure she's fine." Rob placed his phone face down on the counter.

"Yeah, totally." Meagan looked over at Rob. "She's probably just—"

"I'm okay." Parker held up both of her hands. "Really."

Meagan raised her brow. "Are you sure?"

Parker couldn't explain it. A nervous flutter beat in her chest, yet at the same time an odd calm descended over her. Now that she at least had an explanation for why Cate hadn't contacted her, she felt better. Relieved, actually—which was a strange reaction, considering Cate was probably one of the firefighters she'd just watch launch themselves into a burning building. On an intellectual level Parker was very much aware of the danger Cate put herself in, yet she wasn't panicked. Or overwhelmed. It was simply the job that Cate did. And Cate did it very, very well. She wanted to help people. It was the core of her identity. To ask Cate to do anything else was almost blasphemous.

"It's what she does," Parker said softly.

"It doesn't bother you?" Rob asked.

Parker rubbed the back of her neck. She thought about her first night at Cate's place, the halting, cracked tone in Cate's voice as she told Parker about her brother. Parker imagined a young Cate in the back seat of a crunched sedan, watching in paralyzed horror as her brother died. It was clear now that Cate dedicated her adult life to not only atone for a guilt she didn't need to carry around, but to also prevent the same tragedy from happening to anyone else.

"Maybe a little," Parker admitted. "But I think she was meant to do this. I would never take that away from her."

Rob nodded solemnly. "I get that. She looks really hot in those firefighting pants."

Meagan slapped his shoulder. "Robert!"

"It's true!" Rob looked at Parker for confirmation. Parker whacked him across his other shoulder. Rob curled into himself as if trying to disappear into the ballooning T-shirt. "Oh, come on, like you both wouldn't—"

The door opened, and Rob clamped his mouth shut. A herd of teenagers seemingly appeared out of nowhere, filing into the store in a cloud of disinterest and skepticism. They broke off into groups, a chunk of them making a beeline to the display wall and letting out excited whoops at the models for sale, while the others scattered to opposite corners of the store, glued to their phones like they had been dragged outside and were already bored. Samuel jumped a foot in the air and started pulling sodas from the cooler.

"Hey, you're Parker, right?" A young Black girl wearing a Chicago Sky Candace Parker jersey and a pair of Jordan Fours in the pastel university blue colorway emerged from the crowd. Parker recognized her immediately.

"That's me." Parker walked out from behind the register and slapped hands with the teenager. "Tasha? From Butler?"

Tasha flashed the business card Parker had left a few weeks ago. "You're the one who donated those shoes, yeah? My friend's sister got a pair. Really needed them."

"Happy to help out."

Tasha nodded, looking around the store. "Miss Cate said y'all were opening this weekend. Thought I'd come check it out, bring my people through."

Parker grinned. "I appreciate that. Looking for something in particular?"

Tasha tugged on her Yankees cap, which was the same shade of blue as her sneakers. "You have the new Fours in the red cement?"

"Hell yes, I do." Parker's grin grew wider. She pushed away her residual anxiety about Cate and focused on the kid in front of her. They were both exactly where they needed to be. "What size?"

CHAPTER NINETEEN

"…this is a massive complex that has been completely destroyed. Veteran firefighters have told me they've never seen anything like it. Losses are expected to be in the tens of millions of dollars."

Parker perched on the edge of her couch, clutching her phone in both hands and watching the live stream of Channel 12's Saturday night newscast. She was dressed in a pair of red-and-white checkered boxers and a Nirvana T-shirt, her hair damp from the shower and spilling onto her forehead. At her feet was a tumbler with a splash of Jameson, long forgotten, that now contained mostly melted ice.

The newscast continued. Compared to that afternoon's reporters, the evening anchor looked barely older than Parker herself and was far too chipper in delivering his update. He should take notes from the afternoon guy. "Workers report that the fire started around 3:45 this morning when a forklift battery malfunctioned, causing the machine to explode. Twelve employees were inside the warehouse at the time, and all got out safely thanks to the swift response of the Mayville Fire Department."

Parker leaned forward, nearly pitching herself off the couch. The report switched to footage from the fire scene, the anchor's voice continuing over images of flames and thick black clouds. The massive building had been reduced to a flaming carcass, and most, if not all, of the interior had to have been completely destroyed. Parker watched as the fire wrapped around the frame of the warehouse, chunks of material falling away like charred meat off bone. Soon the entire structure started to buckle, and a moment later the back half of the warehouse collapsed in an orange fireball. A great plume of smoke and debris burst forth from the wreckage. The camera panned back, revealing a group of spectators lined up by the fire trucks, gaping in horror and astonishment. Parker had never seen anything like it, either.

And Cate threw herself into that without hesitation. Parker's stomach twisted. She glanced down at the tumbler but didn't pick it up.

"So complex was the layout of the warehouse, with multiple rows of refrigerators and freezers, that a blueprint was needed to map out the firefighting battle plans," the anchor's voiceover continued. The footage cut to a group of firefighters crowded around a laptop, iPads, and stacks of paper plans spread out on the hood of an MFD SUV. Parker thought she recognized Cordell in the mix, but the camera cut away too quickly for her to be sure. The anchor pivoted now to the injured firefighters, cheerily providing an update as their headshots appeared on screen. They wore matching dress uniforms and stoic expressions. The one on the left was from Engine Five on the north side of town, the right from Ladder Eight near the far west side. They'd been clearing a back office, the anchor chirped, when part of the ceiling collapsed, trapping them both for a short while. They were both hospitalized with mild concussions and symptoms of smoke inhalation.

"Stay tuned for more updates as we—"

Parker closed the app and threw her phone onto the cushion next to her. She got up and dumped her drink down the sink.

The day had gone better than Parker expected; at closing the final tally was eleven sales, including two pairs purchased from members of Tasha's crew. Her online orders were double that amount, and she was already well on her way to recouping the cost of the window. At the end of the night, Rob and Meagan wanted to stay and help close up, but she shoved all three of them out the door at promptly six o'clock. Tyson, who'd been announcing he was bored every five minutes since at least three that afternoon, was especially grateful to be released.

It wasn't like Parker was unappreciative of their offer, but she suspected they also wanted to keep an eye on her, like she was going to do something crazy while waiting for Cate to call. Something about that rankled her more than anything. Although, after reconciling the sales and straightening everything and turning off the lights, she'd stood outside for a long while, looking up and down Tomlinson and willing the lights of Ladder Two to appear.

Sighing, Parker padded through the studio to her bed, hidden from the rest of the open floor by a privacy screen. She grabbed a pillow and a blanket and headed back to the couch. Her phone was quiet, the usual volcanic eruption of notifications dormant. She flopped down and turned on the TV mounted on the exposed brick wall. Might as well try to find something to watch. She doubted she'd be able to sleep.

Her gut twisted again, unable to ignore the images of the injured firefighters. Their headshots were exactly like the one of Cate she'd seen in the newspaper months ago. That time, the story had celebrated her heroism. What if next time the ending was different? Yet every churn of her stomach was accompanied by another feeling: pride. God, no wonder Cate was weird about dating. It was enough to drive anyone nuts.

After flipping through Netflix aimlessly, she gave in and queued up *The Old Guard* for the bazillionth time. Just after Charlize Theron finished wiping the floor with some unfortunate mercenaries, her phone buzzed. Parker almost fell off the couch.

"Hey." Cate's voice was thick with exhaustion and muffled through the phone. Despite that, the unmistakable warmth was still there, and it sent a shiver down Parker's spine.

"Oh, hey," Parker answered casually, flopping onto her back and tossing an arm over her head. "I bet you had an interesting day."

Cate's raspy chuckle made Parker sink deeper into the couch. "Understatement of the year. I just got home. You've been watching?"

"All day. I couldn't believe it." Parker smiled into the phone, the last of her churning anxiety dissipating. "I sat through a local newscast for the first time in my life because of you."

Cate made a noise like she was stifling a yawn. "How bad was it?"

"The coverage? Or the evening anchor's suit?"

"Either. Both."

Parker thought for a moment. "Dramatic and ill-fitting."

Cate let out a full laugh, right from her chest. Parker knew that reaction was rare, and she couldn't help but note she'd been earning a laugh from Cate more and more often. God, what she wouldn't do to hear it every day.

"You're ridiculous."

"I thought I was charming."

"Yes. That, too." Cate's voice dropped an octave. Another shiver went through Parker. The response was practically automatic at this point, but Parker didn't feel any shame in it. A weighty pause filled the line. "I didn't have time to call," Cate said eventually, her tone shifting into defensiveness. Clearly her guard was up, waiting for a challenge.

"You were busy. I was worried when I hadn't heard from you, but once I found out about the warehouse fire, I was okay. It's your job."

"You aren't upset?" Defensiveness was replaced by skepticism.

"Not at all. I don't expect you to drop everything and text me every time you leave the station. That's painfully uncool." Parker laughed gently.

Cate still sounded unconvinced. "Yeah."

Parker sat up. She thought she'd made herself clear, put it all on the table the night of the ball, but apparently Cate still didn't believe her. Parker was done holding back, done doubting the instincts that told her to run headlong into the incredible chemistry she felt with Cate. Who cared if last time it all exploded spectacularly? This was different. Cate was different. And more than being afraid of messing it all up, Parker was afraid of missing out on something amazing.

"Look, Cate." Parker licked her lips. "I meant what I said. I wouldn't change a single thing about who you are or what you do. And I promise I won't freak out on you because of your job. Just give me a chance to prove it. Please."

Cate's voice turned urgent. "I know, but I've seen what other couples have gone through. It's a lot to ask of someone. I don't want you to be scared or worried all the time."

Parker smiled. "I thought I had nothing to be scared of."

Cate hesitated. "Right. I did say that." She took a breath. "Okay."

"Okay," Parker repeated. "So can we be done with this conversation, at least for now? I'm in. All in. Everything. Bring it."

"You're going to regret saying that." Warmth seeped back into Cate's tone.

"No, I don't think so." Parker's smile widened. "I really like you, Cate."

"I really like you, too."

Parker flopped onto her back, chest fluttering, tugging the blanket closer. She let Cate's words wash over her, reveling in the victory. If only they were having this conversation in person. The charged energy between them was palpable, even over the phone. "Good. So how are you doing? That was the longest day ever."

"Fine." Cate's answer came too quickly. "How was the opening? I'm sorry I missed it."

"Don't change the subject. You should have seen the obnoxious pinstriped suit I had to suffer through. I want details." An edge had creeped into her tone, and Parker stopped herself before it became more pronounced. Cate's job and schedule didn't bother her. This did. "What I mean is, you don't have to be *fine* all the time. It's okay if you're not."

A muffled noise came over the line. For a split second, Parker thought the call had been dropped, but then Parker heard a grumble and what sounded like a car door closing. Cate must have gone outside.

"It was…intense. I've never seen anything like that before." Cate's voice quivered for a second.

Parker sat up again, pushing her back against the arm of the couch. She tucked her knees into her chest. "Wow. Were you scared?"

"Maybe a little?" Cate sounded confused, like she'd never considered the question before, and Parker pictured the little crease between Cate's brows that appeared whenever she was trying to find the words. "You don't really get afraid. Not like it takes over or anything. You have to think about how to approach it safely. How you're going to knock it down. You learn to respect fire."

"Do you know the guys that got hurt?"

"Yes."

"The news said they'll be okay. Just minor injuries."

"Yeah, I heard." Cate paused. "Freddie and I were the ones who pulled them out."

That burst of pride reverberated through her again. Combined with the relief from hearing Cate's voice and the importance of their conversation, the swell of emotion was too much, and Parker failed to bite back a laugh.

"Are you *laughing*?" Cate was incredulous, and Parker swiftly composed herself.

"No, I'm not, it's just like—" Parker shook her head. "There you go, being a total badass again. I bet you tossed the biggest one over your shoulder and marched out in slow motion, like an action movie."

"It was hardly that dramatic. I didn't have time to hire someone to play electric guitar in the background."

"I'm going to learn to play and follow you around from job to job."

"Please don't. I catch enough shit from the crew as it is."

"Poor Ms. November."

Cate let out a huff, but it didn't sound like she was truly upset. "Do I get to hear about the store, or what?"

Parker gave a quick summary of her day, describing her struggles with the inattentive bartender, apathetic window shoppers, and Tyson's various made-up games to keep himself entertained. She ended on a high note, totaling her overall sales, including the pairs she'd sold to Tasha's friends.

"Do you think you might come by tomorrow?" she asked, then made sure to add: "If you're too tired, I understand."

"Parker. Of course I will. You're home, right?" The rumble of a passing car sounded in the background. Cate was outside, then, most likely taking a walk around the block before going to bed. Parker knew she did that sometimes after long shifts to burn away the residual adrenaline.

"Yeah, but I'll probably be up for a while yet. Are you out for a walk?"

"Um." Cate inhaled. "You might say that."

"What do you mean?"

The door buzzer went off.

"Can I come in?"

Parker would have flown to the front door if she could. She rolled backward, uncrossing her legs and kicking her feet in the air to get out from under the blanket, a haphazard technique that only resulted in it twisting around her ankles even more, and she ended up slipping off the couch and flopping around the floor like a sentient, hapless burrito. Wriggling free, she clambered to her feet, darted for the panel by her door, and jammed the entry button so hard her knuckle cracked. A few breaths later, Cate was standing in her apartment and Parker was in her arms.

Parker buried her face in Cate's neck. Cate smelled crisp and clean, fresh from a shower, but no amount of soap could wash away that darkly enticing smoke that clung to Cate's skin. Cate's hands ran up Parker's spine, over her neck, to the back of her head. She peeled Parker's face away from her shoulder, cupped her jaw with both hands, and kissed her like she was coming up for air after too long under water. Parker's knees became weak, and she nearly dissolved into a puddle on the floor.

"I needed to see you. I hope that's okay." Cate's voice was a desperate rasp, a dazed look across her face. Parker tilted her head to take her in. Cate was dressed simply but impeccably in a black V-neck T-shirt that showed off the line of her collarbones, and tight, perfect jeans. Her pupils were already blown wide, her dark eyes almost bottomless.

"Are you kidding? I fucking love surprises." Parker circled Cate's belt, hands coming to rest at the front of her jeans, fingertips tugging lightly at the buckle. "Will you stay?"

Cate's hand slid down Parker's spine and plucked at the waistband of her boxers, letting them snap back against her waist. "Who could resist these?"

Parker leaned forward, lips hovering near Cate's mouth. "You should see what else I have in my dresser."

Cate swallowed a groan. "What else do you have in your dresser?" she asked, breathless, eyes suddenly hooded and a little shy.

Parker didn't answer. Leather creaked beneath her palms as she grabbed Cate's belt and slowly pushed her backward. Cate gasped when her back met the door, a small, light sound that broke over her lips and sent a bloom of warmth through Parker's abdomen. Releasing Cate's belt, she placed both hands on either side of Cate's ribs and pressed herself against Cate's firm body. It wasn't enough to keep Cate in place by any means; the strong, tall firefighter could easily slip away or change their positions, but she didn't. Parker leaned in and, ever so slowly, took Cate's bottom lip between her teeth. Cate yielded with a whimper, melting between Parker and the door. Cate tangled her fingers in Parker's hair, holding on like it was the only thing keeping her upright, and she rolled her hips forward, seeking contact with Parker's thigh.

Desire raged through her. They wouldn't last long upright like this, staggered against the door. Parker wanted Cate underneath her just as they had been after the ball, open and wet and desperate, but this time she wasn't going to tease. She was going to give Cate everything she needed, everything she could possibly ask for, and she didn't want to wait.

Parker kissed the line of Cate's jaw and down her neck. Cate's head fell back against the door, exposing her throat, and Parker grazed her teeth over the sensitive skin. Cate's pulse jumped under her mouth. Smiling, she pulled back and in one motion dropped to her knees.

"Oh, *Christ*," Cate gasped.

With a flick of Parker's wrist, Cate's belt and jeans were undone. Her tongue teased along the waistband of Cate's underwear, groaning at the sweet, heady scent filling her senses. She reached up under the hem of Cate's shirt to feel the taut abs flexing and straining under her hand. Slowly, Parker worked her way downward, kissing Cate through the fabric and earning another gasp. Cate clutched the back of Parker's head, nails scraping against her scalp. Parker yanked Cate's underwear down over the swell of her hips and tipped her head back at just the right angle to find Cate's clit.

"Oh my God—Parker..." Cate's hips jerked forward, knocking Parker's head away. Not to be deterred, Parker reached up and cupped Cate's ass, pulling her closer to her mouth. She delved back in, holding Cate in place as she took her clit in her mouth and sucked. Cate fumbled for the door handle, searching for something to grab to hold herself up, her moans dissolving into breathy whimpers. Her thighs started trembling. Parker increased her pace, determined to wring every last drop of pleasure from Cate that she could.

Fingers tightened over the crown of her head, which Parker interpreted as the beginnings of Cate's orgasm, but instead she was yanked to her feet by her hair. Cate met her with a kiss, wet and sloppy and unguarded.

"I'm about to fall over," Cate rasped. "Where's your bed?"

Unable to form words, Parker took Cate's hand and pulled her away from the door, leading her across the living room. Parker's bed was tucked up against the exposed brick wall. Cate sank down onto the top sheet, tugging Parker on top of her. Long, lean legs immediately wrapped around Parker's waist as they rocked together. The friction of Cate's jeans against the thin material of her boxers sent jolts down Parker's spine. Cate twisted her fist around the collar of Parker's T-shirt, tugging her close. Parker was desperate to feel Cate's skin against her own, yet breaking contact to undress seemed unbearable. She slipped her hand down Cate's jeans and dug into her hip, setting the pace and rhythm of their motion. Cate let out a whimper and immediately followed Parker's direction, arching up to meet each practiced thrust of Parker's hips. The thought of driving into Cate overcame her, and Parker knew she would never be able to shake that image.

"Hey." Parker propped herself up on one elbow. She brushed her mouth against Cate's, keeping her voice gentle. "If you want, I have a—"

"Yes." Cate nodded, eyes closed. She swallowed thickly. When her eyes opened again, Parker saw rich molten heat.

Parker rolled away, stripping off her shirt and boxers, and fumbled for her nightstand. Hands shaking, she pulled out the drawstring bag that held her harness and toy and managed to slip them on without falling over. She made sure the toy sat at the correct angle so it pressed against her comfortably, with just enough pressure on her clit. She thumbed open a small bottle of lube and squirted some into her palm. Her hand ran over the toy in a familiar motion even as she was struck by a sudden uncertainty. It hadn't been *that* long since she'd had this kind of sex, but the weight this moment carried cut through the haze of arousal. She wanted to be good for Cate. Not just good, but to do anything she wanted, however she wanted it, bring her as high as she wanted to go and fall with her on the way back down.

When Parker turned back, she almost fainted.

Cate was stretched out on her bed, gloriously naked, her incredible physique on full display. Parker's eyes roved hungrily over the sight, savoring Cate's powerful thighs, taut abs, full breasts, and the tight sinew through her arms and shoulders. Cate glanced away shyly like she had no idea how stunning she was. Parker was certain that in all her life, she'd never seen anything so beautiful.

She crawled back over to Cate wordlessly, heart lodged in her throat. When she slid inside, a broken sob echoed through the room, and Parker wasn't sure if it came from her or Cate.

"Okay?" Parker's voice cracked. She swore she felt Cate pulse around her, even through the silicone.

Cate arched into Parker. "Yes. More." Parker watched her throat muscles work as she swallowed again, breath ragged, and she dipped her head to bite at the soft skin of Cate's neck. Cate's hips bucked and Parker rocked into her harder, earning another broken gasp. Her own orgasm started to build deep inside her. It felt like she could come just like this, from listening to Cate's gasps and sighs and moving with her like it was the only thing Parker had been put on Earth to do.

"D-don't stop…"

Parker almost laughed. There was no way in hell she was going to stop. Not now, not ever. Cate's nails dug into the back of Parker's neck, her other hand clamped on Parker's thigh, almost certainly leaving bruises. The thought spurred Parker on even more. Parker loved the idea of Cate losing control so much that she left marks on Parker's skin. She would wear them like medals.

Parker slowed her hips, pulling away, and for a breath, earning a frustrated growl. Reaching around, she gathered both of Cate's hands in her own and pinned them above her head. At the same time, she thrust into Cate as hard as she could.

Cate cried out. Parker clasped Cate's wrists and brought her entire weight down to keep Cate's hands in place but didn't break rhythm. Bowing her back, she bent her head and kissed Cate, swiping her tongue across red, swollen lips.

Wonder filled her. Cate could shake her off with a flick of her hand, yet with each thrust Parker felt them sink further into each other, muscles straining and then relaxing beneath her. Never before had such power yielded to her. Never before had she felt so trusted. Dark hazel eyes drew her in deeper, and in them she saw a million shards of gold converging to form a single point of light. A light that Parker would follow anywhere.

Cate's back arched up from the mattress as she came, almost breaking Parker's grip on her wrists, her entire body shuddering. Parker watched her cheeks flush red and felt her cry echo through them both.

And then Parker followed.

She collapsed against Cate, forehead falling onto Cate's shoulder, chest heaving. Her hands slipped from Cate's wrists. Tasting salt on her lips, she ran her mouth over the curve of Cate's collarbone, not quite able to raise her head to find Cate's eyes and lose herself in them again. The clarity of the moment struck her. She'd been hopelessly lost since the day Cate first stepped into her store. There was nothing she would not do for this woman.

Before Parker had a chance to grapple with the consequence of that thought, Cate shifted, and suddenly Parker was on her back. Strong, rough hands stripped the harness off her and tossed it aside. Cate stretched out on top of her, stealing Parker's breath with a fiery kiss and slipping her fingers between Parker's thighs. Parker squeezed her eyes shut, nearly crying in relief. She heard Cate say her name again, this time a plea. Parker opened her eyes. Cate's searing gaze fixed on her, not leaving Parker's face while she pumped her hand between Parker's legs, like she was trying to commit it all to memory. It felt like Cate was looking all the way through her, past layers Parker hadn't realized even existed and down to the very marrow of her bones.

Parker came again, her cry swallowed by Cate's lips on her mouth.

They clung to each other for a few moments after, Parker burying her face against Cate's neck. Eventually, Cate rolled off her and Parker followed, her head coming to rest on Cate's chest. Instantly Cate's breathing slipped into the deep, steady rhythm that signaled sleep. Parker lay there, legs tangled around Cate's, listening to the cadence of Cate's heartbeat. When the sweat cooled enough to prompt a shiver, she reached for the sheet and pulled it over them both, then returned to her spot on Cate's shoulder.

Just as she was about to drift off, a small, delicate noise slipped from Cate's lips. Her fingers threaded through Parker's hair, and she muttered against the top of Parker's head, voice muffled but still audible. Barely.

"Don't leave me."

Something in Parker's chest broke, and for a second she couldn't breathe. Just as it happened, though, a rush of warmth filled her, soothing the ache. She reached her arm over Cate's waist, holding her tight, and whispered into the darkness.

"Never."

CHAPTER TWENTY

When Cate's eyes opened, she was instantly met by a wave of exhaustion and soreness that settled all the way into her bones. Groaning, she rolled onto her side, her body protesting, and as she shifted a different kind of ache throbbed between her legs. She smiled to herself through the haze of discomfort and buried her face into the pillow. It smelled of Parker's hair. She closed her eyes and started to doze off.

Hurried footsteps thumped through the apartment, echoing off the high walls and exposed brick. The thumping drew closer, until a weight landed on the mattress next to her. Cate cracked a heavy eyelid to find Parker kneeling in front of her, elbows pressing into the bed. She was dressed for the day, wearing the oversized T-shirt splashed with Remix Footwear's logo with the sleeves rolled up. Her hair was swept up in a neat pompadour, and if it wasn't for the lines shaved into the sides, Cate would've thought she looked almost like a fifties greaser, although she was pretty sure whatever shoes Parker had on would shatter that illusion.

"Morning." Parker's grin was as bright as the sun.

"Hi." Cate reached out with a clumsy hand to stroke Parker's cheek. "I like your haircut. Sorry I didn't notice it yesterday."

Parker kissed Cate's palm, eyes sparkling and direct, looking at Cate without shyness or shame. "You were pretty distracted."

"That's one way of putting it."

Parker squeezed her hand. "I'm sorry, but I gotta go. I have to be at the store in ten minutes."

Cate dropped Parker's face and fumbled for the sheets, limbs not cooperating. She tried to sit up. "Shit, I'll—"

"No, no, no." Parker eased her back down and drew the sheet over her, fingers ghosting along Cate's hip. "Stay as long as you want. There's a fresh towel in the bathroom, and I put out some coffee stuff on the kitchen counter. Help yourself to whatever you want. Just lock the door when you leave." Wrinkling her nose, she quickly added, "Um, stay away from the take-out containers in the fridge, though."

Cate sank back into the bed, grateful beyond measure that she didn't have to move yet. "Containers? As in, multiple?"

"You know what? Maybe just avoid the fridge entirely."

"Gross." She tried to playfully shove Parker's face away, but Parker caught her hand and turned it over to nip at the inside of her wrist.

"Hey, I wasn't expecting company last night. I didn't have time to clean." Parker's smile turned wicked, and Cate leaned in closer, smelling the fresh, crisp cologne that had first caught her attention. Cate felt her senses come alive. "I'm so glad you came over."

"Me too." Cate was fully awake now, her exhaustion from the previous day chased away by Parker's sunny presence and replaced by a sharp, sudden need. Her fingers twisted through Parker's shirt collar, wishing she could pull her back into bed for the rest of the day. Instead, Cate settled for a fierce kiss, and Parker's eager moan suggested that she was equally disappointed to be leaving. When they pulled apart, Parker was breathless and officially late for work.

"Will I see you later?" Parker asked.

"Absolutely."

"Good."

Parker popped to her feet and smoothed the collar of her shirt. After another too-short kiss, she was gone. Cate drew the covers over her shoulder and fell into a deep, dreamless sleep.

A few hours later, she woke to a violent jackhammering in her skull. She scrubbed her face with open palms and managed to sit up, swinging her legs over the side of the bed. On the nightstand was a glass of water and a bottle of Advil; propped up against the glass was a small greeting card with a bright geometric design. Inside was a cartoon sketch in pen of a firefighter in full turnout gear pointing a hose at a burning building. A group of firefighters stood around cheering, their little arms raised in the air in triumph. Labels dotted the picture, with small arrows helpfully pointing to the object being described: *warehouse fire, water, hose, Alex, Freddie, Freddie's bicep, Freddie's other bicep.* Below was the caption: *Lieutenant Cate Wildman. Firefighter of the Year. Ms. November. Total Badass.*

Cate rolled her eyes even as she traced the perfect, clean lettering of her name with the tip of a finger. Carefully, she placed the card next to her on the bunched-up sheets and reached for the water and Advil. She polished off the entire glass and put it back with a trembling hand, hoping the medicine would quickly counter the raging drumbeat of her headache and the throbbing soreness radiating down her neck and back.

Yesterday had been a very, very long day.

Not trusting herself to stand quite yet, Cate rubbed her face again and looked around, finally taking in the details of Parker's apartment. The industrial loft was an open floor plan, with high ceilings and tall windows, and late-morning light spilled into the entire apartment. A privacy screen sequestered the bedroom from the living area, which held a small gray couch and matching chair. Mounted on the exposed red brick wall was a flat-screen TV. Lining the walls near the TV were stacks of shoeboxes, arranged in crisp columns that clearly held a meaning Cate couldn't decipher. She wondered if they all were backstock for Parker's store or part of her personal collection, either of which wouldn't have surprised her.

Cate rubbed the back of her neck and twisted to her right side, trying to stretch out her upper back. Her eyes drifted up. Above the bed hung a framed painting, a striking abstract pattern full of bold colors. Cate winced at the bright display, her head still pounding, then caught the artist's signature in the bottom corner: *PM.* Thinking about Parker sent a ripple of warmth through her, and the pain in her skull eased for the slightest of moments.

Cate decided to take up Parker's offer of a shower. The groan she let out when the steaming water hit her aching shoulders was obscene. She placed her palms flat on the tile wall and hung her head, letting the water run down her neck and back. Gradually the tight knots in her muscles unwound, and she thought back to last night.

They'd been the third station to arrive at the scene, and the first of MFD's ladder companies. Her mouth had gone dry the moment she'd leapt out of the rig. She'd never seen a structure fire like that before, half of the building already engulfed in wild flames that made it clear this one was going to be a real bitch to knock down. Her entire crew froze at the sight, taking it all in with a wild cocktail of awe, excitement, and fear. Even Cordell was rendered speechless, jaw twitching, until she ran off to meet with the battalion chief to figure out the interior attack.

She and Freddie had been ordered to stretch a hose line through the southeast corridor, the section of the warehouse comprised of freezer units that housed dairy products. As they'd tried to knock down the flames, the heat caused everything to start melting. Ice cream and milk and butter had oozed out into the corridor, mixing with the water to create slick puddles that turned the floor into a damn Slip 'N Slide. They kept losing their grip on the line as their gloves became caked with goo, and they'd been struggling to move deeper into the structure when the call came through that the office ceiling had collapsed, trapping two firefighters inside. Cate and Freddie had been the closest ones.

Cate only knew them vaguely. Harris was from Engine Five, and she'd met Johanssen from Ladder Eight at the calendar photoshoot. A large chunk of ceiling had fallen across Harris's leg, pinning him completely. He was still conscious and talking into his radio. He gestured deeper into the room, where Johanssen had fallen. While Freddie had set to work on freeing Harris, Cate dropped to her hands and knees, barely able to see through the billowing smoke and flames. She'd felt along the ground until she found Johanssen's boot. He was dazed and bleeding from his scalp, his helmet knocked away and his mask half off. Pipes and paneling and pieces of debris had been scattered around his head. Cate checked his air line, tightened his mask around his face, and hauled him up to his feet. They'd all staggered out together, Johanssen sagged against her, Freddie and Harris right behind them. They'd made it back through the hallway and the river of melted butter and cream, and out to one of the main staging areas, where they were met by paramedics and other firefighters. After a quick debrief and an even quicker drink of water, Cate had been thrown back into the inferno.

By the end of her shift, she never wanted anything to do with ice cream ever again.

The pulsing water chased away the remains of her headache. She turned off the shower, toweled herself dry, and got dressed, making sure to grab the card Parker had drawn for her. She jammed her underwear into her back pocket with a grimace—how *cliched*—and headed into the small kitchen, bracing herself for Parker's definition of "coffee stuff." She sighed in relief when she found a stovetop espresso maker waiting for her on the burner and a bag of beans set out next to the grinder. The tag was still on the espresso maker.

After she started the coffee, her eyes flicked over to the refrigerator. Chuckling to herself, she opened the door and was met by no less than half a dozen white take-out containers, a few of which looked to have been there for quite some time. The only other items were a jar of peanut butter, strawberry jelly, a half-eaten loaf of bread, and some oat milk. Cate shook her head and closed the door. Well. Parker did tell her to stay out of the fridge.

Cate leaned against the counter as she sipped her coffee. The first item on the agenda was to get Parker a burr grinder; that would be absolutely critical, as she refused to lower her coffee standards for anyone, no matter how good the sex was. Second, she would kindly suggest that maybe fresh fruits and vegetables were not a bad thing to have around the house. Not that Parker couldn't take care of herself, but some variety in her diet couldn't hurt. How she'd fallen for someone who apparently only subsisted on Thai takeout and peanut butter and jelly sandwiches was beyond her—

The coffee mug froze halfway to Cate's mouth. Her breath caught in her throat as she rewound the thought.

Fallen for.

The truth had been hovering on the edge of her lips for weeks now, probably longer than she even realized. Cate didn't know how or when it happened, but despite her reservations, there it was. Parker was never far from her thoughts, whether it was during the most mundane moments or while she was fighting a five-alarm blaze. Even last night, in the midst of the largest response of Cate's career, she'd wished Parker was there. Not to show off or brag, but to explain the strategies and approaches used during a structure fire, how and when to ventilate, the specific water pressure and flow rate on the 2020 Pierce Ascendent ladder truck. That Station Two wasn't reckless or full of adrenaline junkies.

That she would always come back.

She'd never wanted to share that part of her before. Doing so meant that she would have to explain why she had the job that she did, why she put herself in harm's way for others, and why it was so important to her. Things that, before Parker, had been difficult if not impossible to articulate.

Cate looked around Parker's apartment, gripping the coffee mug with a white-knuckled fist. Nerves twisted her stomach. Despite the tall ceiling and exposed walls, the loft was warm and inviting, Parker's presence filling the space as if she were right next to Cate, sitting on the counter, legs swinging and sipping a coffee, hair still mussed from bed. The place was tidy but dotted with little pockets of chaos: a stack of unread mail on an end table by the door, a small pile of clothes in the bedroom corner. It was so much like Parker—a wrecking ball of energy, charm, and bright sneakers that broke down Cate's walls without her realizing it.

Is this what I want?
Cate swirled the rich black coffee in her mug.
Of course it is.

* * *

The rhythmic thumping of R&B met Cate the moment she passed through Remix Footwear's door. The small space was full of customers, mostly young adults, grouped around the display wall and browsing the three racks of clothes. Behind the small table in the corner was a gangly bartender distributing soda and beer and pointing at his bright red-and-white patterned shoes every chance he got. Cate scanned the crowd. Working the cash register was Rob, but there was no sign of Parker.

"Hi, can I help you?"

A striking Black woman walked up to her with a friendly smile. She was wearing the same oversized T-shirt as Parker's but had cut the excess fabric from the neck and sides and tied it in the back to make it more formfitting. The look was complemented by black flowing pants and multicolored running shoes.

"I just came by to see the opening." Cate shifted her weight, suddenly feeling underdressed in her long-sleeved Henley, jeans, and scuffed boots. "Is Parker around?"

"She's running around like a chicken with her head cut off, as usual." The woman cocked her head, smile turning playful. "Are you Cate?"

"Yes?"

The woman held out her hand. "I'm Meagan, Parker's sister-in-law. I think you met Rob a few weeks ago. It's nice to finally meet you. We've heard a lot about you."

Blood rushed to Cate's cheeks. Of course. Parker had mentioned her immediate family was helping with the opening and spoke about Meagan with something akin to reverence. Now she really wished she had worn something else. "Yeah?"

Meagan's eyes shone. "All good things, though. Can we get you a beer?" She waved at the bartender, who scurried over with a sweaty Amstel Light. Cate accepted with a thanks and made sure to compliment him on his shoes. "Were you at the fire yesterday?" Meagan continued. "We were worried about you."

"I was, thanks." Cate sipped her beer. "It was a long day."

Meagan didn't say anything, instead appraising her up and down, one hand planted on her hip. Cate wondered if she had said something wrong. She took another swig of beer, hoping she didn't look as awkward as she felt.

Meagan wagged a finger. "Ah, I get it. You're the strong, silent type."

Before Cate could reply, Parker burst through the stockroom doors, arms loaded with shoeboxes, and began passing them around to several waiting customers, excitedly talking to each one. She caught Cate staring and gave her a shy smile before turning away to address someone who had impatiently jammed a display shoe into her face.

She arrived at Cate's side a moment later, holding the shoe. Her cheeks were flushed, and two locks of her hair had dislodged themselves from her perfect pomp to fall onto her forehead. Bristling with enthusiasm, she practically glowed. She was in her element and loving every second of it.

The revelation Cate had earlier that morning struck her again like a thunderbolt. Her mind emptied, and she wasn't sure how to greet Parker or what to do with her free hand. A roiling mix of nervousness and anticipation hit her all at once, and she almost excused herself to go outside and clear her head.

"You made it." Parker's smile was so wide her face nearly split in two. "You met Meagan?"

"I did," Cate said. Meagan watched their interaction eagerly, but Cate couldn't bring herself to be too annoyed at the scrutiny. Her attention was on Parker. "This is amazing."

"Yeah, right?" Parker let out a weak laugh, like she couldn't believe it herself. She looked over her shoulder at the crowd and ran a hand through her hair, more pieces spilling onto her forehead. Cate's hand tightened around her beer, resisting the urge to brush the hair away, which was almost excruciating now that she knew what those soft strands felt like tangled between her fingers.

The demanding customer who shoved the shoe at Parker was now staring at them and heaving aggrieved sighs in their direction. Parker rolled her eyes. "That guy's been the most difficult customer all day." She brushed her fingers against the back of Cate's hand. "I'll be back in a bit."

Parker offered the customer a placating smile, then paused at the cash register to look over Rob's shoulder. Cate wasn't sure what they were discussing, but the conversation abruptly devolved into an absurd slap fight, both swinging at each other with open, flapping hands before Parker scurried away. Rob turned to the person waiting to check out with a polished smile, like nothing had happened.

Meagan pinched the bridge of her nose and sighed with the weight of someone who'd endured years of such nonsense. "Goof asses. You already have my sympathies. You're coming to dinner tonight, right?"

Dinner? Cate's brow furrowed, but before she could get details, a teenager politely interjected to ask Meagan about something called an "Air Max 90." Meagan excused herself, and just as she did, a familiar voice boomed through the store. Cate turned and found herself next to Freddie and David.

"Nice!" Freddie exclaimed in delight. David stepped around him, phone pressed to his ear, having what looked to be a frustrating conversation. He planted himself in front of the display wall, crossed one arm across his chest, and began reading off shoes and prices. Freddie got a beer of his own, stifling a yawn.

"How are you doing?" she asked.

"Fuckin' exhausted." Freddie rolled his neck, releasing a series of pops and cracks that were audible over the music. Despite his enthusiastic entrance, his demeanor quickly shifted and Cate noticed the dark circles under his eyes. His clothes, usually bursting at the seams, appeared to hang a little looser, like he hadn't gotten enough to eat. In one gulp, Freddie polished off half the beer and looked Cate up and down. "You?"

"Same." While Cate's headache was gone and she couldn't deny the low-level vibration running through her at seeing Parker, her lower back was already twinging in protest from standing too long.

"That was a bad one," Freddie muttered. He kept his voice low as if mentioning yesterday's job would dampen the jovial atmosphere.

"Did you hear from Cordell?"

"Yeah. She said Johanssen and Harris are going to be okay. They should be out of the hospital tomorrow," Freddie said, then nudged her. She barely had time to brace herself. Sometimes the man truly didn't know how strong he was. It was like trying to roughhouse with a grizzly bear. "Looks like you'll be in line for another medal, Ms. November."

Cate snorted, rubbing her arm where Freddie elbowed her. "How's David?"

Freddie's mouth twitched. "He's fine. Slept through most of it. That's what he says, at least. I think he just puts it out of his mind now." He finished his beer and gave Cate a look. "What about Parker?"

"She's good. Was pretty calm about the whole thing, actually." Cate knocked back a mouthful of beer and changed the subject. "Who's David talking to?"

"Our nephew. He's thirteen and fucking impossible. Javy used to worship David when he was younger but now couldn't care less. I keep telling David it's just a phase, but he's really been taking it personally. I guess the kid nearly had an aneurysm when David mentioned we knew the owner of Remix, so I'm assuming they're negotiating the exact price of Javy's affections." Freddie waggled his eyebrows in amusement at his husband's efforts.

Cate let out a small laugh. "Here, let me show you those shirts I told you about." She led him to the rack holding the store logo shirts that had all come in the wrong size. Freddie grabbed one and held it up to his massive frame, tucking it under his chin.

"Holy shit, these actually fit. Good material, too. I'm getting three of them."

"You're welcome. I know how hard it is for you to find clothes sometimes."

"David appreciates your efforts, too." Freddie's brown eyes flicked over to his husband, who had just tipped his head back and groaned, still holding his phone against his ear. "Where's your girlfriend? I'm sorry her order got messed up, but I still feel like I should thank her."

"She's in the ba—" Cate froze. Something inside her made her pause, not quite ready to admit publicly that her crew had been right. They'd seen it from the beginning, yet she'd stubbornly held back. She took a long pull of beer.

Freddie looked at her in surprise. "Oh, you're just sleeping together? Not your style, but whatever makes you happy."

Cate bristled, mustering some mild offense to salvage her dignity. She was never going to hear the end of this. "I never said anything about us sleeping together."

"You don't have to. It's written all over your face." The clothing rack whined in protest as Freddie draped his forearm across it. "Generally speaking, you're always in a better mood when you're getting laid."

"What?"

Freddie shrugged. "It's true. The entire crew sees it."

"For fuck's sake, Freddie."

"We're thinking about sending Parker a gift basket. Something really tasteful. Does she like soft cheeses?"

Cate groaned. "Please don't."

"Fine. I'll tell them it's a bad idea." Freddie leveled a finger in her face with a cockeyed grin. "But you have to stop singing Belinda Carlisle to yourself during work. I can't protect you if you keep that up."

"I don't sing!"

Freddie's laugh rattled the store. Several customers turned to look at them, which only made Cate blush more fiercely. "I think 'Heaven Is a

Place on Earth' is a classic, too, but a person can only listen to that hook so many times. Especially when it's off-key."

Cate scowled. "You're supposed to be the nice one."

"Oh, come on, Wilds. You can't expect us not to bust your chops a little bit. Would you rather it be about this, or your upcoming centerfold?"

"I'd rather it be about neither."

Freddie held up his dinner-plate-sized palms. "We just want you to be happy. That's all." He grabbed a handful of hangers with the T-shirts still on them and walked over to David, dropping a kiss on the top of his head. David tried to shoo him away but was met by another booming, joyful laugh.

Cate finished her beer and grabbed one of the shirts. She wasn't creative enough to doctor it the way Meagan had, but she could at least wear it to bed or at the gym. As she approached the register, Parker appeared out of the stockroom.

"You brought Freddie and David?" she asked. More of her hair had fallen askew, which just continued to add to her charm. And how did she manage to make that boxy tee look so good?

"They wanted to support you. Everyone at the station does," Cate said.

Parker bit her lip and glanced away. When she looked back at Cate, her gray eyes were shining. "You told the kids at the rec center, too."

"I figured that was your key demographic." She stepped up and put the shirt on the counter, nodding at Rob.

Parker tried to wave her off. "No, no. You don't have to do that."

"I'm happy to."

Rob looked at them with the same eagerness Meagan displayed earlier. He scooped up the shirt and popped it into the bag. "Couple more protein shakes and you'll fit into it, right?" Rob ran her card and handed it back. "Coming to dinner?"

Cate looked to Parker, raising a brow.

"Sorry, I forgot to mention that. With the fire and all." Parker rubbed the back of her neck. "We're going out tonight to celebrate the store opening. Josie told us about a new place downtown. Meagan's mom is watching Tyson. Will you come? Unless you're too tired, of course."

Cate didn't hesitate. "I'd love to."

"Great! That's great." Parker did a little shimmy, wearing the smile that Cate was now certain would be the death of her, bright and sunny and full of unguarded cheer.

"Perfect. Just let me know the details." A quick glance at her watch told her it was just past one o'clock—enough time for a light lunch, another nap, and maybe even another shower. She was convinced a thin layer of film still coated her skin despite how hard she'd scrubbed herself.

The stockroom door swung open, and Tyson burst onto the sales floor in a huff. He marched over to his mother and planted himself at her hip, crossing his arms.

"Mom, I'm bored." Tyson stuck his bottom lip out in an exaggerated pout. Cate had seen a similar expression on Parker's face more than once.

Meagan looked down at him. "You're going to have to entertain yourself a bit longer. We're not going over to Granny's until later."

Tyson heaved a sigh that was far too large and dramatic for his size. Freddie and David sauntered up to the register, the former with an armful of shirts and the latter still arguing on the phone. Tyson's eyes widened at Freddie's arrival. Cate's eyes went from her crewmate to the firehouse across the street.

"I could show him the station, if he wants." Cate looked between Rob and Meagan.

"You wouldn't mind?" Meagan asked, clearly relieved.

"Not at all." Cate slapped Freddie's arm with the back of her hand and crouched down to Tyson's height. "I heard you really like fire trucks."

"Yeah…" Tyson answered suspiciously.

"Well, my name's Cate, and that's my friend Freddie. We work across the street at the firehouse. Do you want to go check it out?"

Tyson's squeal of joy ricocheted through the store. "Are you *firefighters*? Can I sit in the driver's seat? Can I go down the pole? Can I see the axes?"

"Sure thing." Cate stood and offered her hand for a high five. Tyson jumped and slapped his palm against hers.

"Seriously?" Freddie whispered.

"Just go with it," Cate muttered back.

Cate felt Parker's eyes on her the entire exchange, and when their gazes met, the broad smile had turned into something quieter—a tender mix of appreciation and affection. Cate just gave her a wink.

"Sorry to interrupt." David offered his phone to Parker, hand clamped over the mic. "Can you talk to this ungrateful child? He keeps telling me you don't have whatever it is he's looking for, and I'm not reading off all the display models again."

"Impossible. Give me the phone." Parker tossed a glance back at Cate, then put the phone to her ear. "Remix, this is Parker. How can I help you?" Parker frowned, listening intently, then burst out laughing.

"If I had a pair of Coopers, you'd think I'd tell you, young'un?" She mouthed to another customer to give her one moment, then headed to her stockroom. "Yeah, I can get those for you, but they aren't gonna be cheap…no, I don't have a lawn you can mow…"

Cate watched as the whirlwind of energy disappeared behind the swinging door, the store feeling emptier now that Parker was out of sight.

She looked down at Tyson. "Ready?"

"Yes!"

"Okay," Cate said, then to Meagan: "We won't be gone long."

"Girl, please. You can have him the rest of the afternoon if you want."

Rob finished ringing up Freddie's T-shirts and shoved them all into a bag. After Freddie told David he'd be right back, Cate led them out the door, Tyson slipping his hand into hers as they reached the curb.

"You really like her, huh?" Freddie's amused chuckle rumbled in Cate's ear.

Cate checked for traffic three times, then tightened her grip on Tyson and stepped into the street. "Oh, shut up."

CHAPTER TWENTY-ONE

As usual, Josie was right. The new gastropub downtown not only had some excellent microbrews, but the burger could legitimately lay claim as one of the best Parker ever had. In fact, the food was so good that the four of them were too busy eating to talk, which made Parker nervous at first, but it soon became clear that she had nothing to worry about. Once their plates were clear, conversation flowed easily. Too damn easily, actually, because now instead of being nervous, Parker was trying not to murder her brother.

"You promised not to tell anyone that, *Robert*."

Parker scowled. Next to her, Cate leaned back, draping her wrist over the back of her chair, her other arm stretching across the back of Parker's seat. A light touch ghosted across the nape of her neck, so subtle Parker thought she imagined it.

"I made no such promise. Besides, you can't have been the first lesbian to try to impress a girl by singing a Justin Bieber song." Rob looked at her smugly over his beer. "Or trying to sing, anyway."

"I was thirteen."

"Yeah, and you still look like him, too."

Parker grabbed the butter knife at her left elbow and waved it at her brother. "I'm gonna key your Audi."

"Touch my car and I'll personally throw your bike into the lake."

"If *you* touch *my*—"

"This is why we can't have nice things." Meagan reached across the table and yanked the butter knife out of Parker's hand. She turned to Cate. "Ignore them. They're idiots."

"So I've gathered." Cate tipped her pint glass in Meagan's direction. "I really only came to hang out with you."

Meagan laughed and clinked her own glass against Cate's. "I like you."

"Hey!" Parker and Rob exclaimed in unison. Meagan laughed. Cate just sipped her beer.

"This dinner is going rapidly downhill if you're already resorting to government names." Cate looked over at Parker, eyebrow raised.

"That's not even his full government name. It's actually Clayton Robert Mandli III." Parker leaned in like she was confessing a secret, but in reality it was just an excuse to move closer to Cate. "Call him Trip. He loves it."

Rob rolled his eyes. "You're the worst. Please, do not call me Trip."

Cate raised a hand, palm out. "Fair enough. I haven't answered to Catherine in years."

Even though Rob was smiling, Parker picked up on the muscle twitching in his jaw. He'd always hated that he'd been named after their father, which became more pronounced after their parents separated. They teased each other a lot, but she loved her brother dearly and knew he harbored more anger about their parents and the divorce than she did. Mostly she didn't think about it, which, considering the level of interest her parents exhibited in her life, wasn't that hard.

Honestly, thinking about her parents was more exhausting than upsetting. The success of this weekend bolstered her more. She didn't need her dad's inattentive bailouts anymore, or her mother's weak attempts at communication. They were all on different paths, and there was a time when that really bothered her. But now, that seemed…fine. For the first time in her adult life, she felt like she had a purpose, that her path was now clear, like the sun had finally broken through the clouds and illuminated everything in front of her. One weekend didn't guarantee anything, of course, but her confidence was sky-high, the doubt she'd felt mere days ago nonexistent. She could do this, and she would. And part of that confidence was in no small part because of the woman sitting next to her. She cast a quick glance in Cate's direction. Cate's fingers grazed the back of her neck again. Parker wished it were her lips instead.

"So what about you, Cate? Any aggravating younger siblings that insist on using your full name?" Rob asked.

Parker tensed. Her hand fell to Cate's thigh. "Um, Rob—"

"It's okay, Parker." Dark eyes met hers evenly, the flecks of gold glittering like small pinpricks of stars. Cate looked to Rob. "I had an older brother. He died several years ago. Car accident."

"Oh, damn." Rob's face fell. "I'm really sorry to hear that."

"Thank you." Cate frowned in that way that Parker had come to realize didn't mean confusion, but that she was searching for the right words to say. Cate lowered her arm and found Parker's hand on her thigh, clasping tightly. "I don't talk about it much. But I'm trying to."

"That's a start, right?" Meagan clinked their pint glasses together for the second time but didn't press further.

Cate sat up a little straighter, cocking her head. "I suppose so."

"To fresh starts, then. In more ways than one." Rob raised his glass, then knocked back the rest of his beer in one go.

"Fresh starts," Cate agreed, finishing her beer as well. The weight behind the gesture wasn't lost on Parker, and her ears started to burn.

"So. Tell us more about yourself, Cate." Meagan leaned forward and crossed her arms on the table.

Cate shrugged. "Sure. Where do you want to start?"

"How long have you been a firefighter? Do you like it? Are you now, or have you ever been, any of the following: married, an axe murderer, or a tax fraud?"

Parker buried her face in her hands, her hope that Rob and Meagan would behave woefully premature. It was one thing to detail her hapless middle school exploits; it was another to give Cate the third degree like a bad *Law and Order* episode. "I hate you both," she said, voice muffled against her palms as she contemplated sliding under the table and dissolving into a puddle of primordial goo.

Cate laughed, a bright, full, glorious sound. Parker lifted her head, watching the lopsided smile spread across Cate's face, the sharp angles she'd studied for weeks softening in delight.

Clearly entertained by Meagan's rapid-fire questions, Cate planted her elbow on the table and checked off her answers on her fingers, one by one. "Twelve years, I love it, no, definitely no, and not to my knowledge."

Rob shook his head. "I don't buy it. Too squeaky clean."

"Okay." Cate rubbed her chin in an exaggerated thinking pose. "When I was in college, I got drunk and made out with a girl from the gymnastics team right in front of her boyfriend. I snuck out once during my senior year of high school, but now that I think about it, I was already eighteen, so I guess that doesn't count. I did cheat on a spelling test in second grade, though."

Rob narrowed his eyes, trying to look suspicious but failing because he couldn't stop laughing at Cate's answer. "I'm pretty sure the statute of limitations has run out on spelling test violations, so you're probably okay. I was right about one thing, though—you're definitely out of Park's league. You're far too nice."

Parker wished she had the butter knife that was now resting at Meagan's elbow. "See, this is why I don't bring people around. You talk too much for someone who used to spend half his paycheck on Von Dutch trucker hats."

Meagan nodded solemnly. "It's true. There's boxes of them in the basement. Boxes."

"It was the style." Now it was Rob's turn to bury his face in his hands.

"If you ever want to get rid of those things, Meagan, let me know. I have experience with controlled burns." Cate's smile turned wicked.

Meagan whipped out her phone. "Let me get your number. I'll send you some pics of young Trip. Baby boy was going through it in the early 2000s."

Rob let out a low moan.

"How long have you two been together?" Cate asked.

"Twenty years, minus a few breaks here and there." Meagan was already scrolling through her photo gallery. "We met in high school. He had the skinniest little chicken legs you've ever seen."

"Like someone else I know." Cate cast a sidelong glance at Parker.

"I got pictures of her, too."

Rob raised his head and locked eyes with Parker. Cate and Meagan began tittering over Meagan's phone. At the same time, brother and sister gestured at the approaching server.

"Ma'am?" Parker asked weakly, resigned to her fate. "Can we please get another round?"

* * *

After two more rounds of beer, three desserts, and no less than two dozen humiliating pictures on Meagan's phone, they all finally left the pub. Parker was lightheaded and giddy, and not just from the beer and food. Her chest swelled with the rolling triumph of victory, amplified to an almost painful degree when Meagan pulled Cate into a hug and demanded that she come to Sunday dinner soon. Cate's eyes widened, looking almost frightened at Meagan's ferocity, and she stammered out a promise that she would. Rob watched the display with a knowing smile, then reached out and ruffled the back of Parker's head.

"I like her. A lot," he said in a low voice. "You're doing real good, Park."

Parker nodded, the sincerity on Rob's face almost bringing tears to her eyes.

A moment later, Rob and Meagan's Uber appeared and they hopped in, hand in hand, leaving Parker and Cate alone on the sidewalk. Parker turned to face Cate. Her cheeks were flushed from laughing, the broad line of her shoulders relaxed in a way that Parker was seeing more and more often, which, if she were being honest, she absolutely loved.

Loved.

The word started her heart thundering in her chest, but she didn't back away. Instead, she let her eyes rove over Cate, taking in the easy style of her loose striped button-down shirt and dark jeans. A sly, cocky grin spread over her face as she imagined undoing those buttons one by one.

"So, my place or—"

Before she even finished speaking, Cate's hand was around her wrist, tugging her away from the streetlights and into the side alley. Her back pressed into the brick wall of the restaurant, Cate's mouth on hers. Strong hands slid up her neck to cup her face. Parker whimpered, squirming helplessly between Cate's body and the wall, slipping her hands under the tail of Cate's shirt and digging her fingers into the small of Cate's back. Eventually, when all the breath had been stolen from Parker's lungs, Cate pulled back to whisper hoarsely against her lips.

"Whichever gets us in bed the quickest."

Voice breaking, Parker barely managed to reply. "My place. Definitely my place."

Cate stepped away, a smug look on her face as Parker gathered herself. She could hardly remember her own damn name, let alone her address. Wordlessly, Cate took her hand and led Parker out of the alley.

Parker's loft was just off Mayville's downtown square, a lively, if small, four-block radius that made up the heart of the town. Usually bustling with people running in and out of shops, restaurants, and bars, at this hour on a Sunday night, most establishments were closed up. They had the sidewalk to themselves as they walked back to Parker's, tracing the same route they'd taken to the pub. Cate had left her Jeep parked outside Parker's place after firmly turning down Parker's offer to drive them both to the restaurant on her bike. Just as they had earlier that evening, they fell into an easy pace walking side by side, something that amazed Parker considering how tall Cate was. Their fingers were loosely tangled together.

"Thanks for coming." Parker watched the shadows play across Cate's face as they walked past a streetlamp.

"You're welcome. I had a great time."

"Really? They came on kinda strong. I wouldn't be surprised if you didn't want to see me again after that."

Cate turned her head, still wearing that same smug expression. It looked good on her. Really good. "And miss more opportunities to see evidence of your My Chemical Romance phase?"

"That lasted like a week." Parker scrunched up her nose. "I can't believe Meagan has all those damn pics on her phone."

Cate made a soft clicking noise and cocked her head. "I don't know about that. Bangs like that don't happen overnight."

"Keep talking like that and I'll rescind your invite to Sunday dinner."

"Didn't think it was your invite to give."

Parker gave her a playful shove. Tried to, at least. Cate barely moved when Parker knocked into her and countered with a hip check that would have sent Parker sprawling if she hadn't squeezed Parker's hand at the very last second and kept her from falling. Cate's arm slipped around Parker's shoulders, and nothing in Parker's life up until that moment had ever felt so perfect.

"They're really protective of you," Cate said.

"Annoyingly so," Parker grumbled, even as she tucked herself closer to Cate. "They question my judgment."

"Is that what you believe?"

"Well…yeah. They're always second-guessing me."

"I think they don't want to see you hurt again."

Parker opened her mouth to reply, then just as swiftly shut it again. She hadn't thought about it from that angle before. "Maybe."

Cate's arm tightened around her. "Was it really that bad? If you don't mind me asking."

In that moment, Parker realized she hadn't thought about Sophia in what seemed like weeks. Everything felt like it had happened to a completely different person. Gingerly, Parker unearthed the wound, twisting and turning it around in her head. Whereas before she'd just been performing first aid, desperate to control the bleeding, now she was able to examine it with a clinical eye, like an archaeologist who'd uncovered the ruins of something long gone.

"I don't mind you asking at all." She paused, thinking of the best way to summarize her last relationship. "Yeah, it sucked. We were going too fast. I knew we were. But I was having fun, and I believed her when she told me it was what she wanted. That *I* was what she wanted. Rob will tell you I'm too impulsive, and that's probably true most of the time, but it didn't feel impulsive. I was still wrong, though. I suppose that's the thing about being impulsive—you don't recognize it at the time." Parker chuckled. "Honestly, it all feels like a lifetime ago."

"And she ended it all with only a text? Just like that?"

"Yep. Just like that. Can you believe it?"

Cate lowered her head. Her lips brushed against Parker's temple. "No. I can't."

Parker swallowed hard, the rasp in Cate's voice giving weight to her words in a way Parker hadn't heard before. From anyone.

They paused at the intersection, waiting as two slow-moving cars took their time easing through the light. Cate's arm dropped from Parker's shoulder, but her hand lightly dragged across the small of Parker's back before she pulled away completely. It wasn't a possessive gesture, and Cate wasn't trying to direct her or changed how she moved. It felt more like Cate was reluctant to let her go.

They crossed the street in silence, the renovated warehouse that held Parker's apartment gradually coming into view. A thought pinged the back of Parker's mind, something that occurred to her after Cate had met Rob at the store but she'd never revisited until now. It probably wasn't any of her business, but she wondered if it would somehow become an issue between them. She didn't want to kill the mood of a truly wonderful evening, but her mouth was moving before her brain had a chance to catch up.

"Can I ask you a question?"

"Sure."

Dammit. That was the last time she would let Rob order that high-gravity nonsense. Her head was swimming from the beer, but there was no choice but to plunge ahead. "Does it, um, bother you? My brother and I? I'm sorry he was being so nosy at dinner."

Cate's jaw twitched, but the line of her shoulders remained relaxed. She exhaled slowly. "You mean is it triggering?"

"Yes, I think that's what I'm asking," Parker said. Cate slid her hands into the front pockets of her jeans, and Parker took the opportunity to sneak her arm through the crook of Cate's elbow. "I'm not sure what the right vocabulary would be."

Cate nodded. She hugged her arm close to her body, keeping Parker near. "No, it's not triggering for me. Makes me jealous, maybe." She exhaled again, even slower this time, and her voice became quiet. "I miss him every day."

"What did you mean when you said you're trying to talk about it more? Like, the accident?"

"Not the accident. I…" Cate glanced down and shoved her hands deeper into her pockets. "As much as I think about Anthony, I never mention him. At all. I know it bothers my parents. Especially my mom. They talk about him all the time, always bringing up a funny story or joke, or something that reminded them of him. I know they just like to remember him, but I can't stand it. And I hate that I can't stand it." Cate kicked at a small pebble on the sidewalk, and it flew into a nearby patch of grass.

"That makes sense. It has to be hard." Parker squeezed her arm. "Do you want to give it a try?"

"Try what?"

"Talking about Anthony."

"You mean now?"

Parker wasn't sure if Cate was stalling or just adorably obtuse. Probably a combination of both. "Yeah, I mean now. Unless it's too much."

Cate raised her head, looking up at the stars. She was impossibly beautiful. Parker doubted she'd ever get tired of that profile. "He was funny. Really funny. A great athlete but also a total nerd. He'd kill me if I ever told anyone that. He read comic books all through high school. Loved Marvel. Wanted to play D1 basketball more than anything."

Parker smiled but didn't say anything, letting Cate continue.

"When I was five or six, I fell off the swings in our backyard and broke my arm. He calmed me down and carried me into the house. He sat with me in the back seat and made stupid faces to distract me while my dad drove us to the emergency room. I used to beg my parents to let me go to basketball practice with him. When I was old enough to join a league, he and I would spend all day in the summer running shooting drills in the driveway.

"I think a lot about what he would have done. What he had yet to do. Would he have played ball in college? Eventually gotten married? What would his partner be like? What if they had kids?" Her tone shifted abruptly, a sharpness edging into her words. "He was loyal and trustworthy and kind. He protected me. He was a good kid that would've grown up to be a good man. It's so unfair that he's gone." Her jaw spasmed, and the next thing she said came through clenched teeth. "I never want to lose someone that close to me ever again."

Parker slid her hand down Cate's bare forearm, chorded muscles tensing under her touch. "It is unfair. I'm really sorry."

The anger receded from Cate's voice, in its place a distant coldness. She kept her eyes focused straight ahead. "See. This is why I don't talk about him."

A lump formed in Parker's throat. That cool, detached monotone didn't suit Cate at all. It seemed like she was trying to cut something out of herself, or bury it so deep it would never see the light of day. Although she'd only seen glimpses of Cate's emotional depths, Parker knew she was capable of feeling so much, and she realized now that it was a part of herself that Cate simply denied.

They both fell silent, the only sound the occasional passing car and the scrape of their shoes on the sidewalk. Cate was in her lace-up boots, of course, and Parker had on her lucky Jordan Ones. They were almost at her place. "Can I ask you something else?"

"Yes."

"You told me you became a firefighter because of the accident, right?"

"That's right."

"And didn't you play basketball in college?"

Cate gave her a sidelong glance. "What's your point?"

"I think you're keeping Anthony alive in your own way, you know? You don't have to talk about him if you don't want to, and I don't think you should feel guilty about that. Everyone handles grief in their own way."

Cate stopped midstride, and Parker almost tripped over herself. Her dark eyes were inscrutable, and the flecks of gold Parker was usually able to find were absorbed by a thick shroud. Her lips were pressed together in a thin line, her shoulders tight. Parker was being examined again, like Cate had done when they first met, conducting the same silent appraisal that had ended with a quirk of her mouth and softening of the eyes. This time, there were no hints of amusement to be found.

Parker offered a smile, but it faltered instantly. The lump in Parker's throat settled into her stomach like a boulder. She'd fucked up, clearly overstepped and said the wrong thing. What the hell did she know of grief? Or of losing someone so traumatically? She had no right to speak on it. Parker's face burned, incensed at her own insensitivity, and she started stammering an apology, hoping that she hadn't torpedoed the rest of the night—

Cate reached out and caught Parker's jaw. Her thumb gently traced the line of Parker's bottom lip. A glossy sheen appeared in Cate's eyes.

She bent her head and kissed Parker, slower and deeper than she had behind the restaurant, but it was just as powerful, maybe even more so. Parker's breath was stolen from her once again, a need and desperation flaring between them both that was something more than mere lust.

The kiss lingered, and the fact that Cate didn't seem to care that they were standing on the sidewalk on full display made Parker dizzy. She gripped the collar of Cate's shirt to keep herself from swaying.

"I didn't mean to upset you." Parker's voice was hoarse when the kiss finally broke.

Cate kept her hand on Parker's face. "No, I just…" She swallowed. "You're very insightful sometimes. For someone who listens to Justin Bieber."

Parker wanted to know what Cate was going to say before she cut herself off, but she pushed it out of her mind. "I contain multitudes, baby. Plus, you can't deny, the man has made some bangers." To emphasize her point, she did a spin right there on the sidewalk and started singing shamelessly off-key.

Cate rolled her eyes. "Girls really fall for that?"

"You tell me." Parker shimmied down the sidewalk, spun again, and hopped up the stairs leading to the main entrance to her apartment, shaking her hips the entire time.

Cate stood on the step below her, looking up with a raised eyebrow. "You should stick to Madonna."

"I'll sing Madonna every night, if you want."

"Why would you threaten me like that?"

Parker kept dancing. "Fine, I won't sing, but only if you promise to tell me all about you and that gymnast from college."

"You should be so lucky." Suddenly, Cate surged forward, caught Parker's hand, and pulled her off the step. Parker yelped as Cate threw her onto her shoulder, legs dangling helplessly. Cate took the two remaining steps without breaking a sweat and carried Parker toward the front door. "Come on, I know a better way to burn off all that energy."

CHAPTER TWENTY-TWO

For reasons she didn't care to interrogate too closely, the physics of car wrecks had always fascinated Cate. The velocity of impact, the angles of the trajectory, the force generated by collisions—there was something remarkable and sobering about how little it took to damage a vehicle, and by extension, the people inside. That reflection never lasted long before her body propelled into action, training and experience narrowing her focus to the people she could save. But there was always a moment before she kicked into gear where she couldn't stop herself from wondering what the hell had happened.

Therefore, it meant that a deep part of Lieutenant Cate Wildman viscerally hated McChesney Road.

The old, black GMC Yukon was barely visible from the edge of the steep embankment when Ladder Two and Medic Two arrived on the scene. Across the twisty two-lane road was a Camry with the front end smashed in, the burnt tire marks in the road suggesting it had spun around no fewer than two times upon impact before ending up in the other lane and facing oncoming traffic. McChesney Road's notorious blind curves had struck once again. Cate's jaw twitched. She hopped out of Ladder Two's cab, turnout coat unbuttoned, into the stifling July humidity. Sweat prickled across the back of her neck as she jogged over to Cordell, bracing herself for what they were going to find inside the vehicles.

The captain stood at the front of the rig, talking into her radio. Alex and Freddie joined her, Morgan and Salt just behind them. Omar and Syed had thrown open the back doors of Medic Two. Sirens wailed in the distance, heralding the arrival of more teams.

"Engine Five and Medic Eight are en route." Cordell gestured with her radio antenna. "Wilds, Rutherford, and I will take the Yukon. Salt, Munoz—you and the probie get the Camry. Stabilize and assist Engine Five when they get here."

Cate ran over to the side of the road and peered down. The ditch that ran alongside the west side of the road dropped away suddenly to a steep, tree-lined gully with a pond at the bottom. The Yukon had rolled down the embankment, plowed through several bushes, and come to rest on its passenger side, leaning against a tree halfway down. Cate carefully walked down the muddy trail left by the SUV and looked through the windshield. A woman hung from her seat belt in the driver's seat, unmoving, face obscured by a curtain of dark hair. Blood trailed across her forehead and fell onto the vacant passenger seat in a steady drip. Behind the driver was a girl strapped into a car seat—four, maybe five years old at the most, utterly terrified. Wide, panic-blown eyes stared at Cate under a mop of curly brown hair. Huge tears rolled down the girl's face, spilling onto the car seat. With both hands she clung to a stuffed rabbit, miraculously unlost through the whole ordeal.

"You're going to be okay," Cate said, even though she knew her voice was muffled through the windshield. A plaintive wail answered her. She reached for her radio. "We got a female driver, unconscious with a head wound, and a kid in the back. We'll need the extrication tools." She looked back into the SUV, carefully placing her gloved hand on the windshield. "We'll get you out. I promise. I need you to stay still, though. Can you do that for me?"

The little girl nodded and clutched the rabbit tighter to her chest.

Seconds later, Cordell and Alex appeared at the top of the hill, carrying the cutter and spreader, along with a strut to stabilize the vehicle and several ratchet straps. Omar followed with his kit, backboard, and restraints.

They fanned out, working in efficient tandem. Alex immediately went to the undercarriage of the SUV and jammed the extendable strut against the frame to keep it stabilized. The end of the strut sank into the soft ground at first, then bit and held firmly. He attached a ratchet strap to the top of the frame, ran it down to the strut, and cinched it tight, then tied a longer strap to a nearby tree, ensuring the SUV wouldn't roll again. As Alex secured the vehicle, Cordell broke the back windshield with her rescue tool, allowing Omar to climb inside with two tarps. Cate heard him talking to the young girl, explaining that he was going to cover them to protect from glass. The girl kept silent. A fierce, resilient look settled over her tiny features before it disappeared behind Omar's tarp. Even though Cate had never met her before, she couldn't help but feel a small burst of pride at the little kid's toughness—and maybe a little bit of kinship, as well. She knew firsthand how terrifying it was to be trapped in the back of a wrecked car. She forced the thought away with a sharp shake of her head.

Cordell popped the hood open with her Halligan tool and clipped the battery wiring, then grabbed the saw and cut through the hood hinges. It fell off easily and she pushed it aside. Once Cordell was done, Cate nimbly climbed on top of the Yukon, waiting for Alex to hand up the spreading tool.

"Breaking glass!" Cordell announced, using her tool to pop the two door windows. Glass rained down on the tarp-covered forms. Cate saw the girl squirm in the back seat, but there was no sound.

Alex passed her the spreader, and Cate set to work on removing the Yukon's smashed front fender. She jammed the spreader between the frame and the panel. The fender folded under the pressure of the hydraulic jaws, crumpling like a wadded-up piece of paper. When the fender was dislodged enough, she used the spreader to pop the hinges of the driver's door. Alex cut out the windshield with the smaller reciprocating saw while Cordell hefted the cutting tool and began cutting through the frame posts. Within minutes, the roof was peeled back like a can of tuna and they could access both the driver and the little girl.

From her position on top of the Yukon, Cate watched Cordell and Alex slide in the backboard as close as possible to the driver while Omar held her neck to stabilize her spine. At Cordell's command, Cate slid over on her knees and pulled the door latch. The door came off completely, giving them enough room to gently pull the driver out, keeping her on her side. She appeared only vaguely conscious. Cordell called for assistance, and two paramedics from Medic Eight barreled down the hill carrying another backboard, mud slopping up the shins of their uniform pants. Omar and Alex carried the driver out of the ravine, Cordell following, while Cate hopped down to help the new paramedics extract the kid.

"All right, baby girl, we're going to pull you out onto this board, okay?" Cate pulled out her rescue tool, hand poised above the straps of the car seat. "Got your bunny?"

Sniffling, the little girl squeezed her stuffed animal and nodded. Cate cut the straps of the car seat, and they pulled her free.

"You did great." Up close, with those wide eyes and floppy hair, she bore a slight resemblance to Tyson. Cate almost allowed herself a smile, but the girl started fighting the paramedics stabilizing her on the backboard. Her head whipped around in panic. One of the paramedics—Jenny, maybe, Cate wasn't too sure of her name—tried to calm the girl before they carried her up the hill but was failing. The kid's panic mounted. Cate paused. Something in the kid's demeanor wasn't right. She was sobbing again, which was to be expected, but it also looked like she was trying to say something.

"Hold up." Cate grabbed the paramedic's shoulder and stepped closer. "What is it, honey?" The words kept catching in the girl's throat, but eventually Cate was able to parse through the racking, hiccupping gasps. "What are you saying? Are you saying the name 'Sam'?"

She nodded.

"Who's Sam?"

"M-my brother."

"Where is he?"

The girl didn't answer. Her head whipped around again, bottom lip quivering.

The hairs on the back of Cate's neck stood on end. Dread filled her. She was familiar with the feeling, the sinking sensation in her gut that always told her when something bad was about to happen. Not for the first time, she wished she wasn't always right about these things.

Cate looked into those big, wet eyes and spoke very clearly. "Was your brother in the car with you?"

An eternity seemed to pass before the girl gave a trembling, tiny nod.

Shit.

Cate slapped the radio mic on her shoulder. "Captain, I think we have another patient. The girl's saying her brother was in the car, too."

"Goddammit." Cordell's voice was strained. "All units, be advised. We have another person in the wreck. Apparently thrown from the SUV. Fan out and search the area."

Cate patted the top of the girl's head and forced a smile. "We'll find him." The girl didn't look hopeful. Cate found herself agreeing.

Leaving the girl to Medic Eight, Cate climbed back on top of the Yukon and scanned the area. Radio chatter filled her ear. Two people in the Camry, both injured but okay. Early guesses were that the driver of the Camry took the turn too fast, overcorrected, and hit the Yukon. Mayville PD had shut down both eastbound and westbound lanes; those officers not busy diverting traffic were looking for the third passenger in the Yukon. Omar came over the line and confirmed: yes, there had been someone else in the car—a ten-year-old boy. The voices faded away, replaced by the sound of her own ragged breathing.

Normally the bowl of the gully was nothing more than a glorified puddle, but it had been an unusually rainy summer. Instead of draining away, the gully had swollen to nearly three times its size, the surrounding brush and muck covered in standing water at least six inches deep. From her vantage point, looking over the bushes and weeds, Cate spied a flash of red. Basketball sneakers. Matching red shorts, slathered in mud. The boy was face down in the water. Not moving.

Cate launched herself off the Yukon, throwing off her helmet and tearing at the tabs of her bunker coat. Even as she barreled down the hill, she knew she was too late.

CHAPTER TWENTY-THREE

"Miss Cate!"

Cate blinked, the thud of balls bouncing on hardwood matching the pulsing ache in her head. Butler Center was bustling with the usual after-school crowds, and she'd hoped she would be able to sneak through the gym to the back office without being noticed. No such luck. Tasha stood by the bleachers with her usual crew, baggy shorts hanging to her knees and a ball tucked under her arm, glowing with effortless teenage cool. Cate nodded at the group and walked over, gripping the largest coffee she could find on her drive to Butler.

Tasha grimaced. "Damn, Miss Cate. You look like shit."

"Language." Cate narrowed her eyes.

The gaggle of girls that always seemed to be orbiting Tasha erupted in giggles. Tasha glanced down at her shoes—brand-new, Cate noticed—then regained her composure. Witnesses or no, Tasha was well aware that further attitude could potentially reduce her court time when Cate oversaw the open gym, or worse, garner straight-up wind sprints. Cate had done worse when other kids had gotten unruly.

"Sorry," Tasha apologized. "I just meant you looked tired."

That wasn't much better, but Cate would take it. "Had a long night."

"You okay?"

"I'm fine." Cate sipped her coffee as she lied. She was the farthest away from fine as someone could possibly be. In fact, she was so far past fine that she'd broken clear on through to the other side, to the strange, calm waters beyond that allowed her to slip a blank mask over her face when all she wanted to do was scream.

She hadn't been there in time. She'd been too slow to realize what had happened, and so she was the one to look into that boy's face when she rolled him over, unseeing, unbreathing. A small voice inside her said that it wasn't her crew's fault, that it wasn't obvious there'd been another passenger in the Yukon, let alone any evidence that he'd been ejected. That Cate had done her best. But the voice was tiny and weak and couldn't drown out the fact that her best just hadn't been good enough.

And now she was here to witness another failure.

It took a minute for Cate's sleep-deprived brain to realize that Tasha had changed subjects and was now talking excitedly about Parker's store. She took another sip of coffee. Christ, she wished she could administer it intravenously.

"…anyways, she was able to find a pair for my brother, too. They are so crispy, Miss Cate, you don't even know."

Cate forced a smile. "I really don't."

"That's all right. Park will hook you up." Tasha gave her a nudge, displaying a cocky smile. "So what's up? Y'all been dating, right?"

Another wave of giggles rose up behind Tasha. Cate bristled. Exhaustion had lowered her tolerance for teenage antics to subterranean levels, especially at the mention of Parker.

The remainder of her shift after the accident had been incredibly hectic and ran long, but when she tried to nap after she'd gotten home, she ended up lying in bed and staring blankly at the ceiling thinking about all the things she could have done differently. Eventually she gave up and went for a run, but she'd deliberately gone in the opposite direction of Parker's store. She'd also done the bare minimum in her responses to Parker's texts, even if they were as entertaining as usual. Even though they'd been seeing each other for nearly a month, right now she couldn't be in the presence of Parker's whirlwind energy and megawatt grin or look into those soft gray eyes. It was all too much to handle. And Cate definitely couldn't call and explain herself, because then Parker's voice would shift into that gentle tone and she would say that she understood, that it was totally fine, and that Cate should get some sleep and they would talk in the morning. It would be kind and perfect and everything Cate had ever wanted. Yet, somehow, that made her feel worse.

Cate eyed Tasha over her coffee cup. "Since when is that your business?"

Her tart reply earned a chorus of appreciative *oooooohs* from the teenagers. Tasha merely shrugged like she never cared in the first place. "Whatever. That store is dope, though."

"It is quite dope."

Tasha laughed. "You're a trip, Miss Cate. I'll see you around."

Cate crossed the gym and headed toward the back hallway, where Jameel's cramped office was located. The other volunteers were waiting for her, all five of them shoved into the tiny room with Jameel behind his overflowing desk. She was never late, which just added to her frustration, but that was soon displaced by a growing sense of dread.

Jameel was serene, a steady rock in the maelstrom of events that had led them to this moment. She loved and hated that aspect of his personality, now more than ever.

"Sorry I'm late." Cate took up position in the back, leaning against the wall.

"Of course." Jameel's calm smile never wavered. "I wanted to tell you all in person. Despite the funds raised by the MFD ball, the bank is not willing to negotiate. I've spoken to them multiple times, and they are adamant they will begin foreclosure proceedings. They said they've been more than generous in granting extensions."

Silence blanketed the tiny room, the implication of Jameel's words hanging in the air. Colin, the volunteer that ran the basketball program with Cate, sat up in his chair, gym pants rustling in agitation. A whistle swung from his neck. "Wait, what? How much do we still owe?"

"Twenty thousand."

The entire room deflated. Cate clenched her teeth and focused on a spot on the far wall, trying not to crush the to-go cup in her hand.

"So if we don't come up with twenty thousand that's…that's it?" Rakim, another volunteer, spoke up.

"Yes, unless someone buys it outright," Jameel said.

Rakim took off his Yankees hat and shook his head. "I thought those firefighters had it handled." He shot a look in Cate's direction. In the back of her mind, Cate knew not to take it personally, but it felt like she'd been stabbed in the gut. All the time and effort they'd put in for months trying to save Butler—the late nights, the brainstorming sessions, the pleading for money from any and every source they could think of—it'd all been for nothing.

It hadn't been good enough.

"What do we tell the kids?" Cate asked softly.

Jameel scratched at the gray stubble on his chin. "Let's not tell them anything until we know exactly what to say."

Cate scoffed. "What does that mean?"

"Miracles can still happen, yes?" Jameel opened his hands, palms skyward, as if invoking a higher power. His eyes were sad, yet hope resonated in his words. "The foreclosure process takes time, and there is a redemption period. We may still find the money. It's also possible that whoever ultimately purchases this space will keep it as a community center. Or perhaps we can rent space at a different location. Maybe even one of the high schools. We may lose the basketball program, but we can still offer after-school programs to the community. We won't give up on this neighborhood, or the families that have come to rely on us."

It was a good speech, Cate admitted. The atmosphere in the room lightened, the gathered volunteers all sitting up a bit straighter. Light chatter sprang up among the group as the volunteers floated tentative ideas of what the programs could look like if they did move. The Unitarian church just down the street often rented out its basement to local businesses and organizations, and someone knew of a café that had a large meeting space. It wasn't much, but enough to get started. After another lingering look at Cate, Rakim put his hat back on and started talking to Colin.

Jameel raised his chin and caught Cate's gaze in the back of the room. She knew she should be feeling a sense of pride at the resiliency of the group, and the dedication they all exhibited. The kids deserved this, and so much more, but she couldn't dredge herself out of her black mood. Silently, she shook her head and ducked out. In her experience, there was no such thing as miracles.

* * *

With a practiced flip of a wrist, Parker took out her phone and switched to the next song on her playlist. Rumbling bass filled the back room. She finished boxing up her last order, taping the box closed with a flourish, and added to the pile for UPS pickup in the morning. As she set the box down (a pair of Jordan Fives Retroes in the bright-yellow Michigan colorway, destined for an appreciative buyer in Ann Arbor), she spun around and threw a hand up when the beat dropped. Sure, it was a Justin Bieber song, but that didn't take away from the fact it had a killer chorus. She sang along, shamelessly off-key and not caring. In all honesty, her singing ability was fueled mostly by liquid courage, which made her well-suited for karaoke and not much else. She really only did it because it was guaranteed to draw a smile from Cate.

Parker plopped down in her chair, casting a quick glance at the MFD calendar hanging over her shoulder. July's centerfold was some guy from Station Five. November couldn't come fast enough. She scrolled through her online orders on her laptop, checking them off as fulfilled. Soon a cheesy grin threatened to split her face in half. She and Cate were supposed to join the crew at Crystal's for karaoke in about a half hour, and the thought of seeing Cate made her giddy, especially since they hadn't spoken much since Cate got off work that morning. Parker wasn't worried. Cate probably had a long shift and was tired. Over the last few weeks, Parker had gotten used to the stretches of silence that accompanied Cate's work shifts. It made it all the more thrilling when they finally connected again.

Just as she shut down her computer, the door opened. Parker paused the music and bounded out of the back room. Cate stood in the center of the store, looking perfect as always in a simple white V-neck T-shirt and tight jeans. Parker had silently cursed the summer weather that'd taken Cate's leather jacket from her, but she wasn't complaining at seeing Cate's muscular arms on display.

Cate's mouth twitched into a smile when she saw Parker, but there were dark rings under her eyes, and her cheeks looked more gaunt than usual. Parker stopped short. "Are you okay?"

Cate reached up and pinched her brow. "Long shift. I couldn't sleep when I got home. And…" Cate stopped and looked away.

Parker eased forward, her enthusiasm tempered. "And?"

"I just came from the rec center. The bank isn't negotiating anymore. They're going to foreclose."

"Oh, no." Parker ran a hand through her hair. "I'm really sorry."

"It is what it is." Cate gave a limp shrug.

"How much is still owed?"

"Twenty thousand."

Parker winced. "Ouch."

"Yeah." Cate started flexing her hand, and Parker swore she heard every single one of Cate's knuckles pop. "Jameel says that we might still be able to offer after-school programs even if we lose the building, but I don't know. Doesn't seem feasible to me."

Parker inched closer, sliding her foot along the floor until she could tap the toe of Cate's lace-up boot with her cherry-red Jordan Elevens. She was at a loss for words. Everything that came to mind sounded unhelpful. "We don't have to go out if you don't want to. We can just get food and watch something at my place. Or whatever you need."

Cate closed the distance between them, draping her arms over Parker's shoulders. "What I need is multiple shots of whiskey, the greasiest bar burger I can find, and you."

Parker flushed as Cate's arms tightened around her. "I can do that." She leaned forward and found Cate's lips. The kiss seemed to ease the stress in Cate's body—until her phone vibrated from her back pocket. Cate broke away.

"It's Jameel. I'm going to take this outside and then we can go, okay?"

"No problem."

Parker watched Cate leave and start pacing up and down the sidewalk outside the store, her shoulders slumped forward dejectedly. With each step her entire frame seemed to collapse in on herself, a startling physical transformation for someone so tall. Parker reeled at the sight.

A wild, crazed idea gripped her, and before she realized what she was doing, her phone was in her hand. New York Manni answered on the second ring.

"Parker! How you doing? Congrats on the store, it looks fucking amazing." The drone of New York City traffic in the background couldn't drown out their enthusiasm. "I'm going to come through soon, I promise."

"That'd be awesome. You just let me know." Her brow furrowed and she cleared her throat. "Listen, I need a favor. If I needed to move something fast, cash up front, do you think you could help?"

"Depends on the product, but yeah. Probably. What are you selling?"

Taking a deep breath, her eyes flicked over to her stockroom. The nondescript box was safely tucked away in a back corner. "You're not gonna believe this…"

* * *

Cate jerked awake, head snapping to the side on her sweat-soaked pillow. She stared up at the dark ceiling of her bedroom, blinking until the room came into focus. Soft breathing and the weight next to her brought her back to reality, and eventually her heart rate slowed to something close to normal. The display of her bedside alarm clock read just after four a.m.

Parker was curled up against her side, head on her shoulder, completely undisturbed by the motion of Cate's body. Not that Cate was surprised; she'd figured out quickly that Parker didn't so much fall asleep as crash into immediate unconsciousness once she wound down from whatever excitement had captured her attention that day. Short of a bomb going off in a fireworks factory, nothing would wake her, especially after a night at Crystal's.

Last night Parker had dedicated herself to improving Cate's mood, or at least distracting her enough so that she wouldn't think about Butler's imminent closing. Parker ordered shots and food as soon as they arrived and threw herself into yet another over-the-top karaoke performance that brought the house down and gave Cate the best laugh she'd had in days. And later, when they tumbled into bed together, Parker settled between her legs with a devious smile and didn't stop until Cate could no longer form sentences. Cate had never been with someone so enthusiastic and responsive, so attuned to her body that Parker knew what she needed before she could even ask for it, and yet those efforts hadn't been enough to ensure she'd get a full night's sleep.

Cate eased out from underneath Parker's arm. She hauled herself to her feet and walked down the hallway to the bathroom, flicking on the lights but ignoring her reflection until after she'd splashed cold water on her face. Her eyes were sunk in deeply, framed by dark circles, and her face was pale. Her cheekbones were hollow, bangs damp from the water and her own sweat. As much as she'd like to blame her ragged appearance on her bathroom's unforgiving lighting, that only got her so far. There was no denying she'd barely slept since that accident call two days ago. She leaned forward, peering closer into the mirror. Was that the start of a wrinkle at the corner of her eye? Only thirty-four, and getting crow's feet? Another injustice. Her hands dug into the lip of the sink, knuckles turning as white as the porcelain.

Between the accident and the news about Butler Center, she was spinning out of control. She was supposed to be the person who stopped these things. Who, without a moment's hesitation, plunged into dangerous situations, willing to sacrifice herself if that was what needed to be done. Who had virtually single-handedly convinced the MFD planning committee that Butler was worth saving, that those kids deserved someone looking out for them. And yet, she'd lost. She'd been so close, and it all had slipped through her fingers. If only she'd just reached out to a few more donors, made a few more calls.

If only she'd realized a few minutes earlier that the boy had also been in the car.

What other mistakes would she make?

Her thoughts drifted back to her bed and the person curled up under a mess of blankets, a wild tuft of hair on the corner of a pillow.

What else would she lose?

Cate's nails scraped against the sink. Her heart rate spiked again. She kept herself planted in place, stark naked in the bright light, and forced herself to take deep, calming breaths. The panic passed through her, but in its wake followed a surge of restlessness that couldn't be shaken.

Silently, she walked back to the bedroom and pulled out some running clothes from her dresser. She dressed in the dark. The mattress dipped when she sat on the edge to tie her shoes, but Parker didn't stir. Cate looked back at the mess of blankets. Her hand hovered in midair, as if to reach out to Parker, but she stopped. Instead, she stood and made her way downstairs. She slipped out and shut the door behind her.

CHAPTER TWENTY-FOUR

Parker twirled the crayon in her hand, frowning at the blazing red fire truck she'd just finished shading in. Tyson wiggled in her lap happily, working on his raging fire in the background, unconcerned with the fact that it appeared to spring up out of nowhere. His stick-figure firefighters were all posed around their truck, ready to jump into action. Tyson's obsession with all things firefighting showed no signs of stopping, especially after the private tour Cate had given him. He hadn't stopped talking about the turnout gear and SCBA masks and the various heavy tools, and how he'd *finally* gotten to sit in the driver's seat of the ladder truck. Parker sighed and started sketching a hose unfurling from the side of the truck.

"More water, Aunt Parker!" Tyson ordered, adding a red-and-orange arm of flame reaching for the firefighters.

"Copy, Captain." Parker grabbed the blue crayon and sent a burst of water toward the oncoming fire. Cate would've loved this. An unsettling feeling crept into the back of her mind. She shook her head, trying to force the feeling away, and started drawing another hose to defend against Tyson's pyromaniac onslaught.

"You all right, Park?"

Parker looked up. Rob had appeared in the kitchen and was checking the pot on the stove. This Sunday's dinner was a simple homemade chicken soup with a loaf of sourdough.

"I'm fine. Why?"

"You've been quiet all night." Rob pulled a beer from the fridge and set it down in front of her.

Parker shrugged. "Long day, I guess."

Rob opened his beer but didn't take a drink, still looking at her with a furrowed brow. "How's the store?"

"Good. Steady in the morning, but it dropped off after about two. Still trying to get a sense of it."

Rob nodded but apparently wasn't satisfied by what Parker thought had been a rather thorough, mature answer. "How are things with Cate?"

Tyson's head whipped around at Cate's name, who still held the mantle of Favorite Adult Ever. "Is Cate coming?"

Parker forced a smile. "No, bud. She has to work, remember?"

"Can we go see her? At the firehouse?"

"Maybe next time."

Tyson pulled away into a full-blown sulk, and Parker released him from her lap. He grabbed the picture and stomped away in a huff, presumably to call Station Two himself and demand to speak to Lieutenant Wildman.

Rob winked. "He's dramatic, like his aunt."

"Ha ha."

"You've made bigger scenes over a girl before."

Parker flipped him off.

"See? You're in a mood. What's going on?"

Parker ran a face over her hand. She pulled her beer bottle closer and started picking at the label with her thumb. "I don't know. Cate's been distant the past couple of days. Really distant. We've barely spoken." The unsettling feeling burrowed deeper into her brain, clinging stubbornly no matter how hard she tried to ignore it. "She's got a lot on her mind, though. Especially with Butler closing." Parker added the last part to remind herself more than anything. It didn't really work.

Thursday night was fun. Or so she thought. She'd kept Cate entertained with shots of Jameson and another Madonna performance, and when they returned to Cate's place, the sex had been nothing short of incredible. Despite that, the next morning everything felt off, and since Cate had to work on Saturday, communication over the weekend was reduced to nothing more than spotty texts. At Rob and Meagan's insistence Parker had even invited Cate over for dinner, but Cate had replied with a short message saying she and Freddie were staying over to help the next shift. Parker sent back a simple *k* even though it was universally acknowledged as the most passive-aggressive response in the history of humankind. She couldn't muster anything else.

This was a perfect example of the push-and-pull dynamic that, despite Parker's intentions, continued to plague their interactions. She thought they'd finally overcome that tension, but now she was afraid they'd taken two steps back again, yet she had no idea what she'd done. After she'd closed down the store and was about to leave for Rob's, she stood on the sidewalk and looked across Tomlinson at Station Two. Everything she wanted, everything she didn't even think she'd deserved, was just behind that solid brick exterior. So close, yet completely unattainable.

Clearly, Cate was upset about Butler, but there was something else going on as well—Parker was sure of it, and Cate's stoicism was becoming frustrating, if not downright irritating. They were close enough now that Parker deserved some kind of answer, right? They'd been seeing each other regularly for nearly a month, yet they hadn't discussed how serious things were getting. Cate certainly had broken down Parker's own walls, harder and faster than anyone ever before, but maybe the simple truth was that Cate didn't feel the same way. Maybe they just weren't on the same page.

It wouldn't be the first time she was wrong about that.

Rob cocked his head. "That sucks about the rec center. I can't believe the bank won't budge. Assholes."

Parker dragged her beer back and forth across the table, leaving trails of condensation on the surface. "You don't know anyone that could help, do you?"

"Not off the top of my head." Rob scratched the stubble on his chin. "I'll think on it some more tomorrow at work. Josie may have some ideas, too."

Parker nodded. She opened her mouth to say something but changed her mind and took a swallow of beer instead. New York Manni had flipped their shit after she called, and Parker was sure Rob would probably flip his as well. No need to get him worked up until she knew for sure that Manni would be able to come through with a reliable buyer. And more often than not, New York Manni came through. Still, it was probably a good idea to explore other options, just in case.

"I can't imagine some of the shit Cate sees." Rob started picking at the label of his own beer. "I have to be honest, I don't know how anyone is supposed to handle a job like that."

"She's had some pretty rough calls lately, I think," Parker said. "She doesn't talk about it at all."

"Probably easier not to."

"I think she's convinced she has to go through it all alone. It's like she completely shuts off a part of herself. I don't get it." Parker traced her finger along the condensation on the neck of the bottle. Rob had switched up his usual selections and was serving Sam Adams tonight. It was heavier than she preferred, and she was already close to losing her appetite. "I don't know. I'm just trying to give her space, I guess."

"She definitely strikes me as Not A Talker."

"Oh, she *sucks* at talking."

"I'm sure you talk enough for the both of you."

Parker balled up the soggy chunks of beer label and chucked the glob at Rob's face. "I don't even know why I come over here."

"Okay, okay." Rob laughed and held up his hands in surrender. "Yes, I'm being dickish. Look, space can be good. Even necessary. But eventually you've both got to come to the table."

Parker was scraping off the reminder of the label to manufacture more ammunition, but Rob's change in tone made her pause. "What do you mean?"

"Tell her."

"Tell her what?"

"That you're obviously twitterpated over her."

"Why do you keep using that word? That is a nonsense word."

"It's a wholly accurate description."

Abandoning her mess with the label, Parker screwed herself down on her seat and crossed her arms. She stared at the corner above the fridge, chewing her lip so hard she nearly drew blood. "I don't want to mess this up."

"So don't."

"It's that easy?"

Rob leaned close. "Yeah. It is."

Parker let out a sharp laugh. "I don't know if you've been paying attention for my entire life, but it is definitely not."

"That's not true. You try hard, and you deserve to be happy."

Parker's eyes flicked over to her brother skeptically but found nothing but warmth and sincerity. Groaning, she wrapped her arms around her stomach and pitched forward, her forehead landing on the table with a thud. "I really like her, Bobby," she said to the table.

A heavy hand landed on her back. "You're in love."

"You know nothing."

"Do you simultaneously feel like you can leap tall buildings in a single bound and that your guts are about to spill out of you at any moment?"

Parker paused. Her face pressed deeper into the table. "Maybe."

"Then you're in love. Congrats." Rob squeezed her shoulders. "I'm going to find my wife and kid, and then we can eat. Don't worry. It'll work out."

Parker sat back up as her brother left the room. She wished for all the world she believed him.

* * *

Dusk slipped into night as Parker zoomed down McChesney Road. A light drizzle had started up after she left Rob and Meagan's, just enough to be annoying. She swiped at her helmet visor with the palm of her hand, then flipped on her headlight, illuminating the sleek black surface in front of her. She slowed and downshifted, navigating one of the sharper turns with uncharacteristic caution.

The conversation with her brother turned round and round in Parker's head. The answer to his question was so obvious it might as well have smacked her in the face. Of course she was in love with Cate. She'd yet to say it out loud, or really admit it to herself, but the truth ran deep into her bones. How could she not love that woman? Cate was gorgeous, kind, strong, and dedicated to service in a way that rivaled anyone Parker had ever known. The absolute best, what made Parker go weak, were the moments when Cate opened up and displayed her soft, warm heart. Once Parker had seen that, she was done for.

The only problem was whether Cate felt the same.

The more Parker thought about it, the more her heart sank. Generally, Rob gave good advice, but she wasn't about to put anything on the line without being absolutely clear of the other person's intentions. The last time she'd done that, it had ended with her crashing on Rob's couch. If you'd asked her a week ago, Parker would've been confident that it was different with Cate. Now, she wasn't sure. Once again, her instincts had steered her wrong.

Fuck. When the hell was she going to get this *right*? How many more times was she going to let herself get swept up in something so obviously unattainable?

Parker sighed and revved the throttle, this time powering out of a turn instead of slowing. The rain picked up, splattering against her face shield, and she cursed under her breath. She hadn't realized it was supposed to rain. Parker briefly considered going back to Rob's, but she didn't want to turn around. An ache settled deep into her chest. She revved the throttle again and the Sportster surged forward, but it didn't drown out the feeling.

She'd just have to resign herself to the fact that this wasn't what she thought it was going to be. What she'd hoped it could be. That she'd fucked up again. Bitter, acidic disappointment filled her mouth. It was probably better this way. She should just let Cate off the hook and spare them both. Fuck it. She should pull over and do it now. No point in drawing it out. At least this time, she'd be the one sending the text instead of receiving it.

But…no. That didn't feel right, either. Parker couldn't bring herself to give up on Cate yet, even if that meant risking utter heartbreak. Heartbreak she had no idea how she'd ever heal from. Rob was right about one thing—she definitely felt like throwing up.

The turnoff that led to the secluded waterfront was just ahead. She needed to take her helmet off and just breathe for a minute. Parker clamped the hand brake and downshifted, just as she'd done dozens of times on her ride home from Rob and Meagan's, except the road was slicker than she realized. Instead of catching, her back wheel kept sliding out from under her. She hauled the bike upright, back onto its original line, just as a pair of headlights entered her field of vision. A car rounded the curve, going too fast. It drifted into her lane.

She yanked the handlebars in the opposite direction. Too hard. The bike wobbled. Black, wet asphalt rushed up to meet her. A car horn blared in her ears, followed by the crack of her own helmet against the ground.

* * *

"It's not a problem, sir. Have a nice day." Freddie closed the door and rolled his eyes. "Christ on a cracker, who the hell calls 911 because their hands are dry?"

Cate sighed as they walked down the modest bungalow's front stoop to Medic Two parked in the drive. That was the first call they'd had in hours, and she should have known something was up. She didn't recognize it until they pulled up in front of the house, when she realized she'd been to at least ten calls at that address. Frequent fliers usually didn't bother her, but she didn't have the patience today.

"What a joke," she muttered, climbing into the passenger seat and slamming the door behind her.

Freddie paused before turning the key. Cate felt his eyes on her. She didn't react. He'd been giving her looks all day but hadn't asked what was bothering her. At first, she'd appreciated that he wasn't prying. Now she wished he'd just bring it up and quit staring at her like that. Light raindrops misted the windshield.

"Are we going?" Cate asked.

Freddie backed the ambulance out of the driveway and turned toward Station Two. "Did you hear about the call C Shift got the other day? Someone got food poisoning, and when they arrived on scene, the poor bastard was doubled over the toilet and the entire bathroom floor was covered in—"

"I don't need details."

"I guess when they walked in, Stan slipped in a huge puddle of—"

"I will pay you not to finish that sentence."

"—puke and landed right on his back. Shirt and pants completely soaked through. Alex sent me a pic. I swear it is the funniest thing you've ever seen."

Cate's face twisted into a grimace, extremely grateful she hadn't been on that call. She swatted Freddie's arm with the back of her hand. "You're terrible."

Freddie grinned back wildly. He'd obviously just been trying to get a rise out of her, most likely to break her out of the sullen mood she'd been in the past few days. She appreciated the effort but couldn't bring herself to muster a smile.

Cate hadn't been very enthusiastic about staying over and helping the next shift, but Alex was the only other person available, and he chose that moment to call in a favor that Cate completely forgot she owed. That meant canceling dinner with Parker and her family. Technically, Parker had reassured her it was fine, but her short, curt texts said otherwise. Not that Cate could blame Parker; she'd been a shitty communicator herself lately. And the worst of it was that Cate *knew* she was screwing this up, knew how special and precious Parker was, yet she was letting it all slip through her fingers. Her stomach churned, full of roiling guilt that'd been plaguing her all day.

Cate pinched the bridge of her nose. Parker was amazing, yet Cate seemed determined to sabotage this. What the hell was she doing? She really needed to get her head on straight.

The radio suddenly came alive, and the dispatcher's voice cut through her thoughts. Cate grabbed the handset. "Medic Two, go ahead."

"MVA reported on McChesney Road. Motorcycle involved, one rider, status unknown. Nearest cross street is Harbor."

McChesney Road. Just what she needed to improve her mood. At least she had something to focus on. "Copy, dispatch. We're going to need help with traffic control."

"Copy, Medic Two. Mayville PD en route."

"Medic Two, responding."

Freddie tossed Cate a grim look and hit the siren.

Less than three minutes later, they reached the intersection of Harbor and McChesney, near the hidden turnoff that Cate knew led to a walking path along the lakeshore. It was right before one of McChesney's notorious blind turns. When Cate jumped out of the passenger seat and grabbed her bag, the story had already formed in her mind: someone had been going too fast and wasn't prepared for the sharpness of the turn. She'd seen it almost a dozen times by now.

Her eyes swept the scene, finding the motorcycle first.

Blazing red, lying on its side on the gravel shoulder of the road.

There were other red motorcycles around town. There had to be. It wasn't that uncommon of a color, was it? Parker said she never rode in the rain. Except that the red was so, so bright. A custom job. Almost as shiny and bright as Ladder Two. That color was impossible to miss, especially when it was parked across the street from the firehouse.

She saw the helmet next. Bright red, too. A matching color to the bike. Parker was sitting up on the side of the road, partially slumped over, blood smeared over the side of her face and neck.

Cate froze.

Her chest clenched. Her bag fell to the ground. Ice-cold fingers had reached into her rib cage, wrapped around her heart, and squeezed. The rest of the scene drained away like watercolors that were too wet. The gray of the clouds descended from the darkening sky, muddying her sight. The sound of other vehicles and sirens and her own radio became distant. She was transported to the back of her family's sedan, spun around the intersection like a deranged top, screaming and terrified and watching helplessly as blood ran down the neck of the person she loved most in the world.

It was happening again.

Cate didn't know what to do. Her feet were welded in place, her hands clenched at her sides. She willed her body to move forward, to take a step, to do anything, but she remained locked in position, unable to function. Her breath caught in her throat. Her skin was cold, clammy. The drizzle had evolved into proper raindrops, and the moisture seeped through the shoulders of her uniform shirt. A shudder racked her entire frame. She wasn't sure if she was going to sob, or throw up, or fall to her knees and cry out. All she knew was that her world was ending, again, and there was nothing she could do about it. After all her years of training, of dedicating herself to ensuring that she would always know what to do, that she would always be able to respond to any emergency—it was all for nothing. She was too late.

"Cate! Come on!"

It wasn't the urgency in Freddie's voice that finally broke through, or the look on his face, or the fact he called her by her first name. It was Parker's wide eyes. Glassy and disoriented, her gaze sharpened when she found Cate. A weak, shaky smile flashed across her face, and she sat up straighter. Finally, Cate's body snapped into action. She picked up her bag, slung it over her shoulder, and slapped on a pair of examination gloves, cheeks burning in embarrassment and relief.

"What the hell happened?" Cate hissed between clenched teeth. She knelt in front of Parker and shone her penlight in Parker's eyes. Her pupillary response was normal.

"I already checked her. She's okay," Freddie said.

Cate lowered the light and prodded at Parker's hairline. Despite the blood on her face, Cate couldn't find a wound. She looked toward Parker's helmet and saw the scratched paint along its side. Parker's shaky grin turned confident.

"Hey, babe. Come here often?"

A joke. Of course there was a joke. Cate's jaw started spasming. "What happened?" she demanded again.

The grin disappeared. "I-I'm not sure. I was trying to turn off, then a car came around the corner. I tried to avoid them and spilled."

"Where's that blood coming from?" Cate's glare darted from Parker to Freddie. Freddie gently raised Parker's trembling hand, displaying a fresh bandage.

"She's got a pretty deep cut on her hand," he answered, turning to Parker. "Must have been some broken glass on the road back there. I think you probably got blood all over you when you took your helmet off."

Parker's face was pale. She nodded gratefully at Freddie. "Yeah, okay. I don't remember doing that."

Cate put her hand on Parker's knee, looking away. The cops had arrived on scene and were redirecting traffic. A small line of cars eased past them, ferried by a bored-looking officer. A minivan was parked on the same side of the street, the driver was speaking to another officer. The opposite side of the street, where the oncoming traffic came from, was empty. No sign of the other car that ran Parker off the road.

It could have been much, much worse, but that knowledge brought little relief. Cate forced herself to take a breath. Her heart was pounding. Parker had come so close to being seriously injured, if not killed. If she hadn't picked up the extra shift today, they would be driving home together in her Jeep. Every decision she made seemed to be the wrong one.

She took her hand off Parker's knee. "You're going to the hospital."

"Cate, I'm okay. I swear."

"I don't care. You're going." Her tone made it clear there would be no argument.

Parker nodded, looking down at her bandaged hand. Freddie raised a brow but chose not to contradict her. He placed a hand on Parker's back. "I know a tow guy. I'll give him a call to come get your bike." His hand moved from Parker's back to under her arm, and he helped her to her feet. Parker's knees wobbled slightly at first, then steadied. "Let's get you into the bus. Wilds, do you want to ride—"

"I'm driving." Cate stood, yanking off her gloves with a loud snap and pointedly avoiding Parker's eyes. She grabbed her bag and marched to the bus without looking back. When she settled into the driver's seat, she gripped the wheel with both hands like it was a life buoy and she was drowning. Her head fell forward, and she let out a single, gasping sob.

CHAPTER TWENTY-FIVE

Cate hovered outside the hospital room, grateful that the St. Mary's observation unit had regular wooden doors rather than the glass see-through ones in the ER. She'd barely moved in the past twenty minutes, and every time she raised her hand and placed it on the door handle, something stopped her. Still clad in her MFD uniform, she'd been asked no less than three times by different nurses if she was there for a patient transfer, and after three curt replies she earned a wide berth from the rest of the staff and a nasty glare from the charge nurse.

She'd gotten off earlier than expected, about three hours after they'd dropped Parker off at the ER, and gone back to the hospital from the firehouse without stopping home to change. The rest of her shift had passed in a blur, with Cate spending most of her energy reminding herself that Parker was going to be fine. Freddie told her that, too, pulling her aside in the common room out of earshot from everyone else and speaking to her in a kind but urgent tone. She trusted him. Freddie was excellent at his job, and when he said that Parker was okay, she believed him. Same with the ER nurses who'd taken the handoff and seemed entirely unconcerned at Parker's stable condition.

But when she arrived outside Parker's room, the rational part of her brain switched off and all she could think of was the blood smeared down Parker's face.

She pushed the door open.

Parker was propped up in bed with the sheet across her waist, the TV droning in the background. She perked up immediately, pushing herself up higher on the mattress, her obvious wince covered quickly by an eager smile. The color had come back into her cheeks and her eyes were bright and alert, but it was clear from the ginger way she moved that she was sore. Under the flimsy hospital gown was certainly a patchwork of bruising and scrapes up Parker's torso.

Cate's heart wrenched. Parker looked so small and vulnerable under that thin sheet, and all Cate wanted was to wrap her up in her arms and pull her close, press her lips to her forehead, and bask in utter relief. Instead, Cate remained standing at the foot of the bed, hands in her pockets.

"Hi." Parker's smile fell away.

"Hey," Cate said. "How are you feeling?"

"Okay. Pretty sore, I guess." A sheepish look came over Parker's face, and she folded her hands in her lap. The gesture was surprisingly demure for someone so outgoing. "The doctor said it was just a mild concussion. They're keeping me overnight for observation, but I should be fine."

Cate nodded. Parker was fine. Just like Freddie said. She took one hand out of her pocket and dropped it onto the bed. She looked everywhere around the room but at Parker. Her fingers twisted in the sheet. "Any road rash?"

"No, not really. Pretty lucky in that regard." Parker chuckled. "My jeans took the worst of it. And my favorite jacket is trashed."

At that laugh, a sound that Cate now associated with pure joy, the frayed thread holding her together snapped. She whipped her head around to find that smile flashed at her again.

She understood that it was just Parker's way of coping, a tick of her personality like her constant fidgeting, but seeing it offered now so casually set off the spark of anger simmering below the surface. Cate snapped before she could stop herself.

"Really? You're worried about your *clothes*?"

Parker recoiled. Her mouth opened, then closed again. The moment hung between them, and it took her a second before she spoke again, voice subdued. "I didn't mean to scare you. I was—"

"You did scare me. You scared the hell out of me. Jesus, you could've been—" Cate stopped herself before she said the word. Both hands were balled into fists at her side. She changed the subject. "Have you heard from Rob?"

"He came by a little bit ago. He's going to pick me up tomorrow when I'm discharged." Parker's eyes darkened dangerously. "Don't worry. He's pissed at me, too."

"Good," Cate shot back without thinking. She was attacking her anguish at the source, which just so happened to be the person she cared about more than anything. No, no, no—she was handling this all wrong, but she couldn't stop it.

Parker threw up her hands. "What the hell do you want me to say, Cate? You and Rob both seem to think it was all my fault. I swear that car came out of nowhere, but details like that don't matter, do they? Fine. I fucked up. Happy?"

"You told me you never rode in the rain."

Parker's mouth clapped shut. She was silent for a moment before saying, "I didn't know it was supposed to rain."

"So you did fuck up."

"I guess so."

Cate exhaled very slowly, needing to regain control. This conversation was spiraling too fast. She bit the inside of her cheek. She had to make Parker understand. Cate couldn't handle losing someone again. Not like this. Not ever again. She forced out another breath, trying to remain calm, trying to tell herself that Parker was fine, to be grateful it hadn't been worse—because if only one variable had been different, it *would* have been worse. Parker could've been going faster, the road could've been slicker, the car could've drifted into her lane even more, or struck her head-on. Or, God forbid, she might have been on the highway, clipped by an inattentive semi changing lanes, and ended up—

"I can't do this."

The color left Parker's face, and the room became very, very still. "What…what did you say?"

What the hell was she doing? Despite the warning klaxons firing in her head, she plunged ahead, her mouth speaking before her brain could process what she was saying. "I said I can't do this." Somehow, Cate was able to speak despite the walls of her throat closing in.

"Us, you mean."

Cate looked away.

Parker looked down at her hands, then over to the window. "Not much else to say, then." She swiped roughly at her cheek.

Cate shifted her weight awkwardly. Every cell of her body was screaming for her to do something—*anything*—before it was too late. She already knew she was making the biggest mistake of her life. "Parker, I—"

"Get out."

The moment stretched out for too long, beyond the point of repair, but Cate waited, hoping that Parker would turn back toward her. She didn't. Parker was as still as Cate had ever seen her, eyes trained out the window and not acknowledging Cate's existence. Tears rolled slowly down her face.

What had happened? How had this gotten away from her? A piece of her brain must have malfunctioned, ran a calculus that Cate didn't intend, and her mouth had spit out an answer she didn't want. That had no bearing on reality or the truth. Her body rebelled against the lie she'd just spoken, but now it was out in the open and it was too late to take it back.

Silently, Cate left, hanging her head as she shut the door behind her.

She couldn't fix this.

She couldn't fix anything.

* * *

The buzzer went off for the third time. Parker's phone followed soon after. She sighed and hauled herself up from her spot on the floor where she'd been lying on her back staring up at the ceiling. Wincing, she limped over to the keypad and buzzed open the outer door. She hobbled back to the floor and flopped down, surrounded by the mess of shoeboxes and packing material strewn around her living room. She had no energy to attempt even a half-hearted cleanup, or even change the song she'd been listening to on repeat for most of the day.

Rob walked in a moment later, followed by Josie. They were both dressed like they came from work—Rob in a dark suit, crisp white dress suit with the collar unbuttoned, and Josie in a sleek pencil skirt, blouse, and heels. She held her purse in one hand and a six-pack in the other. Parker scratched her head from her spot on the floor. Their attire didn't make sense. It was only two in the afternoon or so. She was pretty sure it was still afternoon, at least. Or was it nighttime already? Parker realized she'd kept the shades drawn all day and had no real concept of what time it was. She hadn't bothered to check her phone after it went off. No point in finding out now.

"Hey, Park." Josie put the beers on the counter and pulled three from the pack.

Parker didn't raise her head. "Hey."

Rob cracked the beers with the opener on his key chain and brought them into the living room. Josie opened the fridge and immediately grimaced. She shoved the rest of the six-pack inside and swiftly shut the door.

"I came by the store after work today and saw that it was closed." Rob placed a beer on the floor by Parker's arm and sat down on the couch. Josie joined him.

Parker sighed and ran a hand over her face. "I needed a day off. I still fulfilled a bunch of online orders, though."

A week had passed since the accident, and Parker never thought that spilling her bike, cracking her head on the pavement, and ruining her favorite jeans wouldn't be the worst thing to happen to her that day. She was still sore and fighting a lingering headache, and the entire left side of her body was one big bruise, but her physical discomfort paled in comparison to the emptiness in her chest.

She remembered most of it. The cold rain, the slick pavement. Most vividly, she recalled the damn car appearing out of nowhere around the turn, seemingly headed right for her. Her tire slipped, and that was it. The sound of her helmet slamming to the ground ricocheted through her skull, rattling her teeth and jaw. A sharp pain in her side followed, like she had been stabbed right in her hip bone, then a tearing sensation as her jeans shredded themselves on the road. She'd probably panicked right after that, or maybe gone into some kind of shock. She didn't recall cutting her hand or taking off her helmet. What she did remember next was Cate kneeling beside her and the relief that coursed through her at the sight. Relief that was, unfortunately, short-lived once she realized the look Cate was giving her. At the hospital, Cate's icy demeanor was even worse, and when Cate turned and walked out with barely a word, the new, fragile world Parker magically found herself in had dissolved into ash.

Days later, Parker was still trying to figure out what the hell had happened. Sure, the accident had been scary—and she should be the one to know, goddammit—but it didn't make sense that that alone would be enough to send Cate running. That wasn't the Cate she knew. The Cate she'd fallen for. The version of Cate that showed up at the hospital was unrecognizable, a callous robot that had coldly reached into her chest and ripped her heart out of her rib cage. Every night since she'd lain awake in bed, unable to sleep, and replayed the moment over and over, trying to wrap her head around the fact that she'd messed up yet again. Maybe one day she'd learn how to see it coming and stop herself from giving her heart to women who would eventually punt it across the room. She'd always been a slow learner.

"How've you been?" Josie's voice was kind and not at all condescending, but Parker had to bite back a sarcastic reply. She was lying flat on the floor in a grimy T-shirt and joggers, unable to remember the last time she ate or showered, and listening to Taylor Swift on repeat. She was doing fucking great. Obviously.

"Okay." Parker muttered. She glanced up at the couch. Both Josie and Rob looked down at her wearing matching expressions of concern. Parker sighed and rolled over, almost knocking into her beer, and pawed for her phone. She flipped through her apps and brought up Remix's latest sales figures. She pushed herself up to sit cross-legged and held the display up for both of them to see.

"What's this?" Rob asked.

"Numbers from the past week. I meant to send them to you." Parker's eyes darted between them both. "Isn't that why you guys are here? To check on the store?"

Rob had a vested interest in Remix doing well, and Parker always assumed Josie had some kind of arrangement with Parker's landlord, which explained the good deal she'd gotten on the space, ferret smell notwithstanding. It probably didn't look good that she'd kept the store closed today, but when her alarm went off that morning it felt like her chest was caving in. The A Shift was on duty at the station, and the possibility of seeing Cate, or even Alex or Freddie, was too much to bear.

Rob and Josie exchanged looks. Josie cocked her head with a smile, leaning back and crossing her legs. Parker's eyes were immediately drawn to the red bottoms of her Louboutin stilettos. Josie always had excellent taste.

Rob chuckled and shook his head. "No, that's not why we're here. We're here because we love you and you don't need to go through this alone."

"Oh." Parker lowered her phone, hand falling to her lap. She reached around and found the beer, taking a long drink to conceal the tears welling in the corner of her eyes. She avoided her brother's gaze. The kindness in his expression would just make her cry harder.

Josie perked up. "Parker, are you listening to 'Cornelia Street' on repeat?" At Parker's pathetic nod, she immediately clicked her tongue. "Oh, honey, no. We're not doing that. Hand it over." She held out her palm. Parker dutifully unlocked her phone and slid it into her hand. Taylor was silenced midbridge, replaced by crunching, frenetic guitars and screaming vocals.

"Josie, what the hell is this?" Rob asked.

"It's my Swedish death metal playlist. We need to change the vibe in here, stat."

Parker let out a snort. Death metal matched the blackness of her mood over the past week, but her amusement was short-lived. She took another sip of beer and gazed at the far-off corner, tears threatening again.

"I was so stupid…I should've just…"

"None of this was your fault," Rob said fiercely. "The road was slick, and the other car clearly wasn't paying attention."

"Everyone in town knows how dangerous McChesney Road is," Josie added. "There's been several city council hearings about it. They've been talking for years about reworking the entire section where you crashed."

Parker shook her head sharply, once. "I mean Cate. I fucked it up with Cate. I knew I would." She doubted she would ever understand what happened, or what was going through Cate's mind. The only explanation she could come up with was that she'd done something wrong. Again.

"You didn't fuck anything up." The sharpness in Rob's tone almost made her sit up straighter. Parker wiped her nose, eyebrows raised. Rob continued, "This isn't on you. Cate has her own issues. Clearly. And if she decides to run away instead of working things out, that's not on you. You're better off."

Parker took a sip of beer. "Maybe."

Josie leaned forward, crossing her wrists over her knees. "For what it's worth, Alex said Cate's being an absolute terror at the station. Sounds like she's just as upset."

"She should've thought about that before being a total dickhead," Rob snapped.

Josie shot him an irritated look. "I'm not defending her, Rob. I'm just saying this is a complicated situation."

Parker resisted asking for more details about Cate's mood. The vehemence in Rob's voice acted as a lifeline, and she was able to grab hold and pull herself out of her misery for just a little bit, using the news that Cate was suffering to buoy herself. After all, wasn't there some petty joy to be taken at another's misery, especially when they broke your heart? Serves her right, Parker wanted to say, leaping from the floor in triumph, full of righteous, indignant anger. But she couldn't muster any of that. The lifeline slipped through her fingers, and she sank back down to the abyss.

Rob let out a breath. His voice softened. "If you want to wait for her, see if she figures things out on her own, you can always do that. Or you can move on. Either way, just know you did nothing wrong. Okay?"

Tears fell freely now, steady rivulets running down her cheeks and dripping onto the collar of her shirt. She wrapped an arm around herself. Her back was tight from sitting on the floor, her ribs hurt like hell, and a throbbing ache was building behind her eyes. The couch creaked, and then Rob was next to her on the floor, arm around her shoulder, quietly holding her while she trembled. When her tears finally stopped and the headache receded, she straightened and looked at her brother.

"Thank you."

Rob blinked, his own eyes glistening. He smiled wanly. "Anytime."

Josie gently cleared her throat, dabbing at the corner of her own eyes. "There is another reason we came by, though."

"What's that?"

"I recently discovered a hidden gem of a taco place on the east side of town, and we are taking you there immediately."

Parker's chest tightened. "Will Alex be there? Or any other guys from the station?"

"No. Just the three of us. And as many al pastor tacos I can shove into your face." Rob nudged her shoulder. "You need to eat. And take a shower."

Just the thought of dredging up the energy to peel herself off the floor was exhausting, but her stomach overrode her with a mighty growl—the first evidence of an appetite in days. She raised her arm and sniffed her shirt. A shower was definitely in order.

"Can I get a margarita?" she asked.

Josie laughed brightly, a stark contrast to the dark, raging metal vocals growling in the background. "Honey, you can get as many margaritas as you can handle."

Parker nodded. She pitched forward with a grimace and slowly began to stand. Rob slid a hand under her arm and helped her up the rest of the way. When she was steady with both feet under her, Rob gave her a wink. "There ya go. Need help getting ready?"

"I'm good. Just moving slowly."

"Take your time." Rob plopped himself next to Josie on the couch and dug between the cushions, coming up with Parker's Xbox remote. He took a long pull of beer and put his feet up on her coffee table with a *thunk*. "You got FIFA, right?"

Josie yanked the controller from Rob's hands. "Absolutely not. I'm playing." She kicked off her heels and leaned forward, intently focusing on the TV.

Parker shuffled off to the bathroom, smiling as Rob and Josie bickered over whether PSG or Man United was the better club to play.

Warmth filled her chest, and for the first time in days the gaping ache receded into the background, replaced by overwhelming affection for both of them. The unexpected visit was a welcome reminder of how much they cared for her. She hadn't realized how badly she'd needed that.

A spark ignited in her chest. It was barely noticeable, but still there. Maybe Cate would come back. Maybe she wouldn't. That was completely out of Parker's control. All she knew was that she was about to eat a shit-ton of tacos with two people she loved. And then maybe she'd be okay. For today, it was enough.

CHAPTER TWENTY-SIX

"Who the hell repacked this?"

Cate burst into the common room, holding up the trauma bag that lived in the right rear compartment of the ladder truck. One by one, the occupants of the brown easy chairs turned to look at her with matching bland expressions, none of them as remotely concerned as she was.

Morgan looked her up and down, then turned back to the basketball game on TV. "I did, Wilds," she said mildly.

"Well, it's a shit job." Cate shook the bag at her.

"It's perfectly fine." Morgan kept her eyes on the TV. "Freddie checked it. So did Alex."

Grateful for more targets, Cate locked on Freddie. He stifled a yawn behind his hand.

"It's perfectly fine," he echoed.

Cate's jaw tightened. She moved to Alex, arching a brow. He merely shrugged. "Fine. I'll fix it my goddamn self."

She stalked back to Ladder Two, crouched next to the storage compartment, and started tearing everything out and repacking it all over again. Sweet baby Jesus, did she have to do everything around here?

A pair of boots entered her vision, but she didn't acknowledge their presence until the owner sat next to her. Alex leaned back against the rig's tire and crossed his legs. Her hands stilled for a brief moment as she glanced over at him, then went back to her project. "What?"

"I have an idea. It's kind of out there, though, so hear me out."

"What?" Cate huffed.

"Maybe you could try not being a total dick for the rest of our shift?"

"I'm not being a dick."

Alex dropped the back of his head against the tire and let out a weary laugh. "Cate. Come on. You're my best friend. And as your friend, I owe it to you to be honest. You've been a fucking asshole for at least two weeks now, and you denying it is starting to piss people off."

Indignation flared within her and her face flushed with heat. She opened her mouth to fire off a retort but fell short. Alex was right. He was annoying that way. Anger bled away to exhaustion. She finished packing up the gear, less violently this time, then slumped onto her butt next to him, crossing her ankles and pulling her knees into her chest.

She'd been spending as much time as possible at the firehouse, working every extra shift she could, choking down viscous coffee, bitching about people using her creamer, and probably annoying the hell out of B and C Shift. She only left when Cordell yelled at her to get the fuck out of her station because she'd hit too much OT and was blowing up their payroll budget. She wouldn't go home, though. She'd go over to Chevy's and lift until she felt like puking, and if Chevy's was closed, she'd drive to the twenty-four-hour gym across town and do the same. Only after she punished herself physically did she return to a townhouse that was too dark and too still. And sometimes it still wasn't enough for her to find sleep.

"I'm sorry," Cate said.

"I'm not who you should apologize to."

"You're right."

"What's going on?"

Cate rocked backward, mimicking Alex's earlier move and letting the back of her head thump against the rig. Everything was too overwhelming, and she didn't know where to begin. She still couldn't believe how it had all gone so wrong so fast, but there was one ice-cold fact she couldn't escape. "I broke up with Parker."

To his credit, Alex didn't immediately jump to his feet and tell her that she was a complete and total fucking idiot. "Freddie and I were wondering about that. You haven't mentioned her for a while." He paused. "Fred told me about the accident. That must have been awful."

Cate nodded, clenching her teeth to fight back tears. So far, she'd managed not to cry at work, but it seemed like that streak was coming close to an end. "It was."

"I guessed something might have happened after that, but…shit. Why'd you end it?"

That was the question that had tortured her for weeks, the one that she couldn't answer fully. In the immediate aftermath she'd tried to pull together some kind of explanation, but the best that she could come up with was that she'd just…snapped. The thought of losing Parker had short-circuited something in her brain. Cate had experienced sudden, traumatic loss before, and she'd lost all ability to think rationally when confronted by the specter of that loss again. So, instead of handling it like an adult, she'd just blown it all up.

How could she explain this to Alex? He didn't know the full depth of what she'd gone through; outside of her family, Parker was the only person who knew the details of the accident. Even some of her closest friends through high school and college, who had been to her parents' house and seen pictures of her brother, didn't get the full story. Neither did the handful of women she'd dated over the years. Another reminder of all the ways Parker was so different than anyone Cate had known, and how she'd burrowed herself deep into Cate's heart so effortlessly that she hadn't even realized it until Parker was gone, and now every breath she took felt like her ribs were broken. Parker meant more to her than she could put into words.

No, that wasn't right. There was one very specific word that described what Parker meant to her, and instead of just saying it, she'd turned her back and walked out of the room.

She hugged her knees tighter. "I never told you that I had a brother, did I?"

Alex's eyes widened, his mouth opening ever so slightly. "No."

Cate took a deep breath and began, explaining everything that happened, much in the same way she laid it out for Parker: being pushed into the intersection, the truck, the sound of the deafening crash and how the glass shattered everywhere, how a piece of debris embedded itself in Anthony's neck. And how, in one brief, terrible moment, she'd relived it all over again when she saw Parker motionless on the pavement.

When she finished, Alex was silent. Cate kept waiting for the tone to drop and the sound of a dispatcher to come over the loudspeaker, but the firehouse was still, the only sound the drone of the WNBA game filtering out of the common room. Alex wiped at both eyes before speaking.

"Thanks for telling me." He wrapped his hand over her forearm. "You can always talk to me about it, too, okay? Like, in the future." Cate nodded, and Alex leaned closer with an earnest expression. "I'm serious, Cate. You can't keep this shit bottled up."

Cate unclasped her hands and placed one on the top of Alex's. "Yeah I can. Just put it all into a box, shove it deep down, and pour Jameson all over it. Works great."

Alex laughed and squeezed her arm. "Sure it does, asshole. I don't mean to armchair quarterback here, but it sure seems like Parker's accident triggered you in a way you didn't expect."

Cate thumped the back of her head against the tire again. "I think you mean armchair diagnose."

"Yeah, that. I think I heard it on a podcast or something. It makes sense, though. Hell, remember that call that really messed Morgan up? The motorcyclist and the semi? Syed had to scrape that guy off the pavement, and I'm not even exaggerating. Plus that call just a few weeks ago when you found the kid that'd been ejected from the Yukon. I bet that wasn't too far from where Parker crashed."

Cate shuddered at the memory. "You're probably right."

"I like to think so." Alex tucked his knees into his chest, mirroring Cate's position. "So…that's it? You're not even going to try to explain yourself to Parker?"

"Even if I did, I can't fix this."

"Come on, Cate, you—"

"It's over, Alex," Cate said quickly. "I broke up with her in the hospital, for Christ's sake. Not only was I a coward, I was cruel. You don't come back from that." She clenched her fists. "I can't—I can't fix this."

Alex gave her a look like he was about to start arguing, then dropped it. He sighed and got to his feet. "If that's what you think." He shrugged lightly and offered his hand. Cate grabbed it and pulled herself to her feet. Standing face-to-face, she had at least three inches on him, but she withered at the expression on his face. It wasn't quite judgmental or disappointed; Alex just looked sad. He patted her shoulder twice and turned away, tossing a parting line over his shoulder. "It's not like you to give up."

Then he was gone, striding through the garage bay toward the common room. Cate put her hands on her hips and looked up at the bright ceiling lights. No matter how hard she tried, this time she couldn't stop the tears from falling. She ducked behind the rig, keeping herself out of sight as her chest heaved in breaking sobs. The sheer force of the emotional release doubled her over, and she found herself gripping the thighs of her uniform pants to keep from pitching forward. It felt like a vise had clamped down around her chest, restricting her breathing, and the cold, clinical side of her actually wondered if she was having a panic attack. Gradually, the tears receded, and her vision cleared, and she was able to straighten. Cate scrubbed her cheeks with the heel of one hand and headed toward the common room, keeping her eyes forward like nothing had happened.

* * *

"Why exactly are you doing this?" New York Manni asked. Again. For the third time.

Parker took one last look at the Coopers and their simple yet flawless design. She felt a twinge of regret at Manni's question, but almost as soon as it surfaced, the feeling disappeared. This was the right decision, she knew it, and her conviction was reinforced even further when she realized she didn't mind explaining it to Manni. Again. For the third time.

"It's for a good cause." Her phone was lying on her desk, and she angled her head downward to speak into the mic. "What's the point of having these things if I'm just going to keep them locked away forever?"

"You could, I don't know, wear them. Like you're supposed to. Or put them on display."

Parker put the lid back on, running her fingertips around the edges of the box. She exhaled sharply, then nodded. "I could. Or I could sell them and give the money to people who really need it." Carefully, she started wrapping the box in deluxe Bubble Wrap.

"They're only going to grow in value."

"I know." Parker grinned down at her phone. "But you got me a good price."

Manni grumbled. "I did what I could. I know you wish it had been someone else, though."

Parker scrunched up her face like she'd just smelled something awful. Yeah, so, that part sucked. After the shock wore off and they'd picked themselves off the floor, Manni had set to work right away on finding a buyer for the Coopers, and despite a flood of interest, there was only one person they'd trusted to come up with the cash as quickly as Parker needed. Of course, it had to be fucking Jake, who proceeded to be a total dick about the whole thing, demanding photos and a FaceTime call to prove that Parker was legit. Manni had even jumped on to confirm the whole story about Parker hopping a flight from LA last minute. Jake was still skeptical. Parker was just about to call the whole thing off when the money hit her account this morning. She'd sent a small percentage to Manni as a brokerage fee.

"I got paid, so it's all good." Parker placed the wrapped shoebox in a larger box and began stuffing it with packing paper and Styrofoam peanuts to keep it in place. No way this one was getting a cartoon drawing. "Are you mad that I'm selling them?"

"Not mad. Surprised, I guess. There'll be other grails." Manni paused, and the weight in the silence made Parker's hands still. She inhaled, waiting for whatever Manni was going to say next. "I'm glad you like it there. It's nice to see you settled."

"Really?"

"I've known you a long time, Park, and it's always seemed like you were looking for something. Restless. You're different now. You seem happier."

"Oh. Um, thanks."

Parker grabbed her phone and left the stockroom. Late-morning sunlight spilled through the front window, brightening the entire front of the store. It was Friday, and while she'd been open for a few hours, she'd yet to have a customer. Weekday mornings tended to be slow, but business usually picked up in the late afternoon and on weekends.

She hadn't expected to like Mayville so much, and her earlier anxiety about the move and opening was now a distant memory. She couldn't even remember the point at which it happened, or what flipped that switch, just that a part of her felt like she'd always lived here. Hell, she hadn't even realized it until Manni pointed it out.

"You still with that girl?"

Parker winced, preparing herself for the breath to rush out of her lungs and a wave of nausea to hit her like it did whenever she thought of Cate. The ache was still there, but at least this time she didn't feel like puking everywhere. "It didn't work out," she said simply, looking across the street.

"Ah, shit. I'm sorry."

Parker rubbed her face. "It's okay."

"You never know, though. It could still be in the cards."

"Since when are you so full of sunshine and rainbows?"

"Boi, I've been full of rainbows since I was born." Manni laughed. "I've just lost some of my usual cynicism as of late."

"You mean you're getting laid."

"Maybe, maybe not. Look, my train is here, so I gotta go—we still on for next month? To visit?"

"Absolutely. Can't wait."

"Great. Talk soon."

Parker pocketed her phone and leaned against the window, crossing her arms. Station Two was quiet, but a few people were out on Tomlinson, idly strolling down the sidewalk. Parker wondered if they were on their way to the co-op, or maybe down to Sweetcakes, or maybe just out for a walk. She liked this neighborhood. She could be one of those people, carefree and just enjoying her day. She would walk down to get a coffee from Cora and grab a drink at Crystal's after work whenever she damn well pleased. And if the kids from the rec center needed a place to hang out and shoot the shit about sneakers, or anything else on their minds, she could offer that, too. Maybe one day, she'd even get the Barefoot Dog Walking Guy into a pair of shoes. Her future was not tied to the whims of Lieutenant Cate Wildman.

Although she wouldn't have minded if it was.

Parker pushed herself off the glass and went back to the stockroom.

CHAPTER TWENTY-SEVEN

On Saturday morning, Parker pulled up to Butler Center and nervously scanned the parking lot. No black Jeep. She took a breath, then turned off Rob's Audi and clambered out. The sting of disappointment hit her, and she realized part of her had been wishing for Cate to be there.

A few kids were milling about when she walked in, idly chatting near the bleachers or dribbling around the court. Parker was surprised to see kids here so early on a weekend, but then she realized they probably had nowhere else to go. The atmosphere was heavy and solemn as she crossed the gym, and she wondered if the news of Butler's closing had been announced yet. She quickened her pace.

Jameel's office was at the end of a narrow hallway, tucked behind what appeared to be a janitor's closet. The door was cracked. Parker knocked once and pushed it open. Jameel rose from his chair, smiling warmly.

"Good morning, Parker. To what do I owe the pleasure? It must be something urgent to drag us out here this early." His eyes crinkled in amusement, but he looked thinner than the first time they'd met. He was dressed impeccably in a beige knit button-down polo with matching linen pants, but the clothes hung off his frame in a way that suggested he was much frailer than he appeared. He looked her up and down, smile faltering somewhat. Parker took off her ball cap and raked a hand through damp hair, self-conscious about her appearance. She'd gotten up early and taken a bus over to Rob's to borrow his car, then gone to the bank right as it opened. The fact that she'd managed to pull herself out of bed in time to shower was a minor miracle in itself—a miracle that was undone when she realized she hadn't done laundry in weeks, and she ended up leaving the house in the same long-sleeved T-shirt and black joggers she'd essentially been living in for days. She was still sleeping like shit and was pretty sure that was obvious, too, but moping over a breakup paled in comparison to Jameel's very real health troubles.

Parker put her cap back on and tugged it low, hoping to hide the dark circles under her eyes. She pulled a folded cashier's check from her pocket and handed it across Jameel's desk. "Thanks for meeting me. I wasn't sure the best way to get this to you, so I wanted to do it in person."

Jameel arched a brow and unfolded the check. His face remained expressionless as he read it over, but soon the check started fluttering in his trembling hands. He collapsed into his desk chair in shock, and for one terrible moment, Parker thought she'd accidentally killed the man.

"How…?" Jameel looked up at her, face lighting up in wonder. Years melted off him right before her eyes.

Parker shoved her hands in her pockets and rocked back on her heels. Telling Jameel she sold the Coopers didn't sit right with her; she didn't want to come off as bragging. She kept it simple. "I came into some money, and I wanted to help. What you do here is more important than people realize. I don't want to see it go away."

"But this is much more than what we owe the bank."

Parker glanced down at the top of her Jordan Fours (originals, in the white cement colorway). "I know. I was hoping you could use what's left over for a scholarship fund, or maybe to expand the basketball program. Whatever you think is the most useful."

"We can absolutely allocate this to a scholarship." Beaming, Jameel rose from his chair, standing noticeably straighter. He shuffled around his desk and held out a hand. "Thank you, Parker. Truly. This is a wonderful gift."

"You're welcome, sir." Parker shook his hand. Before she could pull away, Jameel tightened his grip and curled his other hand over hers, gently but firmly keeping her in place.

"I do hope to see more of you." Jameel patted the top of her knuckles, a gesture that felt almost fatherly. "I hear your store is already quite popular with the kids. You don't have to keep bringing gifts, either. We can always use more volunteers for the after-school programs."

The kindness in Jameel's baritone triggered something fragile in Parker, and she blinked back a sudden well of tears. She nodded, focusing on the grounding strength in Jameel's hand and his warm, calloused palm. "Yeah, maybe. I'm just happy I could help with this."

Jameel smiled and dropped her hand. "I hope you consider it." He paused. "You are always welcome here, Parker, no matter who else we have on staff."

Parker's sleep-deprived brain took a moment to process the meaning in Jameel's words. He not only was talking about Cate but offering her a safe space despite what had happened between them. The trembling facade she worked so hard to maintain every time she left the house over the past two weeks was now crumbling at Jameel's gentle presence. She barely knew the man, but the unexpected care she was receiving was too much. It was almost a relief to let the mask slip.

"You're very perceptive, sir." Parker tugged the sleeve of her shirt over her knuckles and dabbed at the corner of her eyes.

Jameel offered a light shrug, still smiling. "Cate doesn't talk much about her personal life, but I'm old enough to recognize a broken heart when I see it. Two, even, as it seems." All Parker could do was nod, pressing her lips together while she put all her energy into keeping her composure. "Don't be a stranger. I don't think Cate would like that, either."

Parker opened her mouth to say that Cate had made it pretty damn clear what she liked, but Jameel's knowing look stopped her in her tracks. Cate's terrible mood must have also carried over to her shifts at Butler, similar to Josie's report that she was miserable at Station Two. Parker still took no joy in hearing that Cate was suffering so publicly. All it did was remind her of how much she cared about Cate and how abruptly it had all ended. She wiped her face one more time and gave Jameel a slight nod.

"I'll see you around, Jameel." Parker turned to leave, but just as she reached the door, Jameel called out to her.

"I like your kicks, by the way." Jameel's eyes sparkled playfully. "The Fours were always my favorite."

Parker couldn't help but grin. She looked down and kicked up her heel. "I'll get you a pair, unc."

Jameel's resounding laugh followed her out of the office and down the hall. When she entered the gym again, she already felt lighter, and she added a little hop to her step. Her sneakers squeaked across the hardwood.

* * *

When the timer on her phone went off, Cate put down her pen and let out a breath. She leaned back on the stool to stretch her back and then reached for her coffee. This was day three of the exercise, and she'd cleared the kitchen island of all other distractions, but it didn't seem to have helped. Just like the other attempts, the sentences were disjointed and she couldn't follow what she'd even been trying to express. Frustration swelled within her, but instead of throwing the leather-bound journal across the room, she closed it gently and placed her pen on top of it. She huffed out an aggrieved sigh, drained her coffee, and headed upstairs to change.

"Therapeutic journaling" was what her new therapist called it—an exercise that was apparently useful for dealing with trauma. For four consecutive days, in fifteen- to twenty-minute increments, she was supposed to write about an emotionally upsetting or traumatic event and explore her deepest thoughts and emotions around it, with no judgment. According to Matt, the new therapist, this was a path that led to "deeper understanding of ourselves" and allowed for a "different perspective on the difficulties we've faced," which ultimately resulted in a "greater sense of well-being." Cate had told him, respectfully, that she thought that was all a bunch of nonsense. Matt cocked his head and told her, just as respectfully, to shut up and give it a try.

Matt was an excellent therapist.

Cate changed into her gym clothes, mulling over today's session. Writing was about as enjoyable as a root canal, and each time she picked up a pen it was damn near excruciating. Still, she had to admit that once her immediate frustration passed, there was something freeing about writing down all the things she couldn't say, even if sometimes it didn't make sense.

A few days ago, she'd explained all that to her dad, who, after picking himself up off the floor when she told him she was in therapy again, gave her one of his patented pep talks and told her to be patient with herself. He'd given similar talks to both her and Anthony before they went off to their basketball or soccer games. She'd forgotten how much those small moments had meant to her. The conversation ended with them both near tears and Cate promising to come for dinner next week. After they'd hung up, she wished she had told him about Parker.

Restlessness and guilt gnawed at her. She laced up her running shoes and went back downstairs to pack a bag with the rest of her gear. Today she would jog over to Chevy's as a warm-up before lifting, and when she got back, she'd read through today's journal entry. When she agreed to the exercises, she assumed she'd mostly be writing about Anthony. While that was the case for the first outing, lately every time she ended up writing about Parker. The paragraphs were all a jumbled mess, her handwriting becoming less precise the more she wrote, but there had to be something of value there. If she could just figure out how to sort through it all and put together the right combination of words, she could piece together something to say to Parker. Cate had no illusions about winning Parker back, but if she apologized and clearly explained her actions, maybe at the very least Parker wouldn't hate her. After what she did, it was the best Cate could hope for.

As she reached for her phone, a text from Jameel popped up. The barest hint of a smile tugged at her lips when she read the salutation. Formal, as always, like he was dictating a certified letter. Although it wasn't her place to say anything; Parker told her once that her texts were so stiff they sounded like dispatches from a Civil War battlefield.

My dear Cate, I have wonderful news! A last-minute donation just came through. It's enough to pay off the delinquent mortgage and then some. I have a meeting with the loan officer first thing Monday morning.

Cate blinked, unable to fathom what she had just read. *What? How?*

Jameel's reply was quick. *Your friend Parker came by this morning, bearing another gift.*

You're kidding.

I most certainly am not! A brief pause, then another message came through, like an afterthought. *Even in the darkest moments, there is always hope. Keep the faith, Cate!*

The room spun. Cate grabbed the back of one of the stools at the island to keep from falling over. Her mind reeled, struggling to process what she'd been told. Butler owed tens of thousands of dollars. How could Parker possibly afford to pay off all that debt? And have money left over? Remix Footwear seemed to be doing well, from what she could tell from spending too much time watching from across the street, but surely not well enough to make such a massive donation.

Unless…

A memory sprang forward in her mind, one she tried to lock away but couldn't. She was sitting on a freezing concrete floor, Parker next to her and wrapped up in Cate's jacket like it was a second skin, holding a pair of the most boring—and expensive—shoes she'd ever seen.

No way. There was no way Parker would sell the Coopers and give the proceeds to Butler, not after the way Cate had treated her. But how else could she have afforded it? Her eyes flicked over to her messy bookshelf and the card Parker had drawn for her after the warehouse fire, still propped up against a stack of books. She couldn't bear the thought of hiding it away.

Before she realized it, Cate was out the door and running full tilt down the street. She veered right at the end of the block, almost tripping over her own feet, and cut through the park. She barreled through the middle of the park, leaping over a seesaw in midstride and almost plowing into two kids playing on the swings. At the aggrieved yell from the nearby parents, Cate threw an apologetic hand over her shoulder and kept going. All that mattered was finding Parker. All that ever mattered was Parker, and Cate had given up without a fight.

She reached Tomlinson Street in record time, Station Two looming down the block, and sprinted across the street without even checking for traffic. She reached Remix's front door and pulled.

Nothing happened.

Chest heaving, she brushed her bangs out of her eyes and tried again. The door didn't budge. Only after another breath did she notice the sign on the door displaying Remix's updated hours, drawn in graffiti-style script and decorated with bright cartoon sneakers. The store didn't open until 10:00 a.m. on Saturdays. Below the sign was the hand-drawn picture of a berry scone, and more graffiti lettering.

Yo, have you tried the new scones at Sweetcakes? Those things are mad good. Mention this ad and you'll get 10% off any bakery item!

Cate checked her watch and placed her hands on her hips. It was only nine thirty. She started pacing back and forth in front of the store. It was a typically busy Saturday on Tomlinson, with the usual foot traffic walking around the neighborhood, from Nero's Pizza to the co-op down to Sweetcakes. There was no sign of Parker's bright red motorcycle. She would just have to wait, which was almost as excruciating as this morning's writing exercise.

"Wilds!"

Cate turned. Morgan stood at the edge of Station Two's driveway, trying to catch her attention. Two other firefighters were sitting on folding chairs outside of the open garage doors. She'd been too focused on reaching Parker to notice them.

Morgan cupped her mouth and yelled, "She went that way!" Her arm pointed down the street, in the direction of Crystal's and Sweetcakes.

Cate's body snapped into action again, grateful that the probie had apparently picked up an extra shift today. She flashed her a thumbs-up and took off down the block, feeling Morgan's sunny smile on her the entire way.

Crystal's was closed, so the only place it made sense to check first was Sweetcakes. She reached the bakery's door and yanked on the handle. Unlike Remix, the door was unlocked. It also wasn't very heavy. The entire thing slammed back on its hinges and almost shattered. In that instant, an entire store full of people turned and stared at her.

The bakery was packed. The checkout line stretched the entire length of the display case. Couples, families with strollers, hungover college kids, a T-ball team—an entire cross section of Mayville's population was jammed into Sweetcakes, and every single one of them was looking at Cate. Including Parker's whole family, seated at one of the only two tables available in the back corner.

Parker, Rob, and Meagan all stared at her, wearing varying degrees of surprise. Tyson, sitting in Parker's lap, was the last to notice her dramatic arrival. He looked from his drawing and waved in excitement, grasping a bright-red crayon.

"Hi, Cate!" he yelled. She'd never heard a child bellow so loud in her life.

A gentle chorus of chuckles rippled through the line of customers. Already flushed from all the sprinting, Cate's face grew even hotter, and a trickle of sweat rolled down her temple. This was far too close to a public scene for her comfort.

"Hey, Cate." Cora appeared from the back in a flash of a bleached blond undercut and blazing white teeth. The baker's omnipresent smile flickered for an instant as she took in Cate's appearance. "Are you okay? Can I get you an espresso?"

Cate wiped her face on the shoulder of her damp T-shirt. "Yes, please," she replied, hoping the normalcy of the request would allow herself to blend into the background. That plan was dashed when the coffee arrived and she realized she'd left her wallet at home and was only clutching her keys. She'd even forgotten her phone.

"Um…" Cate blushed furiously. None of this was going according to plan. Who was she kidding? She didn't even have a plan. She'd dashed out of the house like a goddamn lunatic before thinking things through, and now she was making a full ass of herself. "I'm sorry, I completely forgot my wallet."

One of the college students snickered. Cora's bright smile didn't waver. "Oh, that's not a problem. You can owe me."

A tiny hand appeared on the counter, clutching a five-dollar bill. Tyson's voice was inescapable. "We'll get it!"

Cate glanced at the table in time to see Parker slip her wallet back in her pocket. Cora took the money from Tyson and piled the change into his palm. He dumped it all into the tip jar and grabbed Cate's hand, pulling her to the table. He grabbed his drawing and proudly held it up over his head for her to see.

"Look! It's a fire truck!"

"Yes, it is. Very cool." Cate managed a weak smile, then looked at Parker. She was dressed casually in a black long-sleeved T-shirt, matching joggers, and white-and-black sneakers. Her face was hidden underneath a flat-brimmed ball cap. She raised her head, and Cate found the gray eyes she missed so desperately, but they were stony and cool and framed by dark circles. Parker looked like she hadn't slept in weeks. Cate knew the feeling.

"What are you doing here?" Parker's voice was flat and emotionless. Her gaze dropped to Cate's tight running shorts and exposed thighs, then darted away.

"I was hoping we could go somewhere and talk. Is that okay?"

Parker shrugged. She pulled Tyson back into her lap and picked up a crayon, twirling it between her lean fingers. "What's there to talk about?"

"How much of an idiot I am."

Parker snorted. Rob kept his eyes averted, focusing on his coffee cup like he hoped it would swallow his entire face. Meagan, on the other hand, had leaned back in her chair, crossed her arms, and was glaring at Cate like she wanted to incinerate her on the spot.

"That's a start," Meagan said coolly.

Cate winced and leaned just a bit closer to Parker. "Could we step outside, maybe?"

"Whatever you have to say, you can say it here."

Sighing, Cate cast a glance over her shoulder. The tension between them all was evident throughout the small bakery. The line of customers had yet to thin out, and the sea of eyes was still trained on the table. A few people had the decency to hide their curiosity behind their coffee and scones, but some had much less tact. The college students nudged each other eagerly, and at least half of the T-ball team stared with wide eyes. Even Cora was hovering close enough to hear the conversation, wiping down the same corner of the counter so intensely it was probably clean enough to perform surgery on.

Cate's skin crawled. She hated nothing more than being put on display, being the center of attention, and this was worse than the

Mayville Reader interview and the awards ceremony combined. But she also was familiar with the concept of a penance, and if atonement could only be achieved through a public scene, then so be it.

"You sold those shoes, didn't you?" Cate asked softly. "That's how you got the money for Butler."

Rob snapped out of his trance and promptly choked on his coffee, dribbling a little down his chin. "You did what?" he gasped in Parker's direction, eyes bulging. Tyson giggled at his father's reaction.

Parker passed over a napkin. "I sold the Coopers."

Meagan's burning gaze flipped between Parker and Rob. "You sold those things? For her?" Meagan jabbed a finger at Cate.

Parker bristled and shot a look at Meagan. "No. I did it for the kids at the rec center, who didn't deserve to have their space shut down over something that wasn't their fault." She turned toward Cate, her face softening. "I had already asked New York Manni about selling them before the accident. I didn't think it was fair to go back on the sale just because you were an asshole." There was no venom or spite in her voice. She just sounded sad. Cate almost wished Parker would yell at her, or tell her to get the fuck out, or dump steaming coffee over her head—any outward bursts of anger were preferable to the obvious hurt on Parker's face. That wasn't Parker, though. Even in heartbreak, she wasn't an angry person. Not like Cate.

Still aware of the group of people staring at her back, Cate stepped forward and steepled her fingers on the table near Parker's hand. Every part of her was screaming to reach out and touch her, but Cate didn't dare move closer.

"Thank you. I know it's probably not my place to say that, but it means so much." Cate swallowed roughly. Parker glanced away. The crayon in her hand stopped moving. Tyson squirmed in protest and tried to reengage his aunt in their drawing.

"Ty, why don't you come over here and let them talk?" Rob reached over to help Tyson clamber into his lap. As soon as he left, Parker shifted in her chair, moving just a bit closer to Cate. It was subtle, but noticeable. Cate sensed an opening, a slight thaw in the icy mood of the table, and so she plunged ahead clumsily. She hadn't meant to do it like this. She hated going into a situation without a plan. All the risks needed to be assessed first, and a strategy for attack developed before rushing in. But she also knew that sometimes you had to act on instinct and run into a burning building without hesitation in order to save who was inside. She had to do this. It didn't matter that she hadn't found the right words yet. She needed to do this now, or there'd be no hope for them.

"I was an asshole. And more than that, I treated you terribly. You deserved so much better than what I gave you. I was scared and I—never mind, I can't make excuses for it." She shook her head. "And I won't. I have to own that. But I need you to know that I'm sorry. I've spent every night and day since then regretting what I did. You mean more to me than I ever thought possible—than I even knew I was capable of. And I threw it away. I know I threw it away."

Tears filled Parker's eyes, and this time Rob handed her the napkin. Moisture ran down Cate's face, and it took her a second to realize it wasn't sweat. She was crying, too. Ignoring the nosy customers, the wide-eyed stares, and her own discomfort, she knelt down in front of Parker and prayed this time she wasn't too late.

"Would you come over for dinner tonight, please? We could talk more? I want to try to explain, if you'll listen." Gray eyes finally met hers. "I want to fix this. Please."

Silently, Parker nodded, the motion so slight it was almost imperceptible, but the rest of her remained glued to her chair. She didn't need to do or say anything else. Just her agreement was enough. Cate's shoulders slumped forward as she let out a huge sigh, almost gasping in relief. There was still hope.

"Great. Thank you." She kept her eyes locked on Parker, afraid that if she looked away her opportunity would be lost. "When can you come by? Five? Six?"

Parker's lips quirked. "Seven."

"Seven. Great." Cate stood, feeling Parker watch her every move. Parker's mouth quirked again, like she was holding back a smile. Another victory, as small as it may be. Cate inhaled like she'd just been given a fresh oxygen tank.

"Wait, so that's it?" Meagan's arms were crossed even tighter over her chest, and she was still glaring at Cate, apparently determined to be pissed off on Parker's behalf. Not that Cate blamed her; she hardly deserved better. It made Cate appreciate her even more. "She rolls up in here with a Hallmark speech and that's supposed to fix everything? Hell no."

At the mention of Hallmark, Parker gave Cate a knowing look. "No. But it's a start."

Meagan huffed and tossed her sleek ponytail over her shoulder. "She better be a damn good cook, then."

Parker answered without breaking eye contact with Cate. "She is." The tears were gone, like they had never been there to begin with, and in their place was an unspoken message, an imploring look silently begging Cate not to make her regret coming over.

Cate reached forward and placed her hand on top of Parker's, reveling in the sensation of their skin touching once more. Her knees almost gave out. Who would have thought such a simple gesture could be so devastating?

"I'll see you tonight." She nodded in Rob and Meagan's direction, surprised to see an actual smile from Rob. Meagan's face was still scrunched in distaste, but she at least acknowledged Cate's gesture. She waved at Tyson, who remained aggressively disinterested in the adult drama surrounding him. "I like your drawing, Tyson," she said.

"Thanks, Cate!" he chirped like the loudest bird known to man. All three adults surrounding him reacted in various degrees of exasperation.

"Boy, stop yelling." Meagan tore a muffin in half and passed it over to him.

Cate stepped away and headed toward the door. Sweetcakes snapped back to normal like a scene out of *The Matrix*, with everyone returning to their coffee and scones like they hadn't all been staring at Cate in rapt attention. Even Cora had disappeared to the back, the stubborn spot on the counter now apparently clean enough. As she left, still gripping her coffee, she cast one last look back at Parker. She was met with a smile from underneath the brim of Parker's hat.

CHAPTER TWENTY-EIGHT

Parker took a deep breath and jabbed the doorbell with a shaky hand. In the other, she grasped a modest bouquet of wildflowers from the co-op. She was already running late but had thought the gesture was worth adding to her tardiness. Although Cate lived only a few blocks away from Remix, Parker wasn't about to show up in a sweatsuit and ball cap, even if it was a super rare Supreme hat that she got in an online bidding war versus some fifteen-year-old in Fort Lauderdale. After she'd closed the store, she took a bus back to her apartment, showered and changed at superhuman speed, then caught another bus back to the Tomlinson neighborhood. By the time she hit Cate's porch she was sweaty and flustered, almost negating the shower in its entirety, but not all her nervousness was due to being late.

The door opened and Parker's breath caught in her throat. Cate was in those jeans that made her ass and thighs rival any work of art Parker had laid eyes on, topped off with an understated white button-down, sleeves rolled up past her elbows and the buttons undone just enough to show off her collarbone and the swell of her breasts. Cate's hair was slightly longer than usual, her bangs falling almost into her eyes and dark waves curling out over her ears. A kitchen towel was tossed casually over one shoulder.

Parker swallowed. "Hi. Sorry I'm late." She raised her arm and shoved the bouquet toward Cate like a malfunctioning robot. "These are for you," she added helpfully. Great. Real smooth.

Cate accepted the flowers with far more grace than with which they had been presented. Color bloomed on her cheeks, reminiscent of the flushed look she'd been wearing when she'd burst into Sweetcakes that morning. "Thank you, they're lovely. And thanks again for coming." She stepped aside. "Come in."

Parker kicked off her Jordan Sixes (the 2018 Retro Chinese New Year—she'd changed shoes, too) and followed Cate through the foyer and into the kitchen, blatantly watching her ass the entire way. Parker scolded herself.

Part of her had been sold the moment Cate showed up at the bakery and stumbled through an adorable, mangled apology. Hearing Cate say that she was sorry and she regretted everything that happened had nearly unraveled her. That Cate did it in the middle of a packed coffee shop in front of Parker's family, despite her obvious discomfort, made the gesture resonate even more. She would've stood up and run after her if it hadn't been for Rob's and Meagan's matching glares. They refused to let Parker leave to open the store until she'd articulated a strategy for how to handle dinner. They were right. As soon as Cate opened the door, all Parker wanted to do was wrap herself up in Cate's arms and breathe in the scent of her skin, searching for that dark hint of smoke that had come to represent equal parts comfort and danger. And if she did that, she would lose herself and drag Cate to the bedroom, absolving her of anything and everything without even being asked. She couldn't do that. That was the old Parker, the person who acted on impulse without thinking of the consequences. Sex only offered temporary relief. They both deserved better. They both deserved more.

She tore her eyes away from Cate and hopped up onto the kitchen counter, nervous energy revving through her and begging for release. As Cate banged around, looking for a vase, Parker took in a scene of controlled chaos. Chopped pancetta was piled on a wooden cutting board next to a sturdy, high-walled frying pan. A pot of water was boiling on the back burner of the stove. A thick yellow mixture stood waiting as well. The dishwasher was running, and stacked on the other side of the sink were more pans and dishes to air dry. Another pile was neatly stacked in the sink.

"Busy day?" Parker asked.

Cate stretched to her full height to reach the cabinet above the refrigerator. Parker's eyes instantly went to the strip of skin peeking out under the button-down as she raised her arm. She came down with a fluted vase, filled it with water, and set the bouquet off to the side. "I did a lot of cooking today. It helps when I'm nervous."

Parker raised a brow. The only time Cate had ever hinted at nervousness was when she told Parker about the warehouse fire. "What'd you make?"

"I roasted a chicken with vegetables, braised some short ribs, cooked about five quarts of my Nonna's all-day sauce." Cate glanced over at her shyly. "Made fresh pasta, too."

"Jesus, are you planning on feeding an army?"

Cate shrugged and tossed the pancetta into the pan. The delectable smell of frying bacon filled the room. Parker's stomach rumbled. She'd forgotten to eat again. "It'll last me a while. I'll take some of it to the firehouse, too." Cate moved the pancetta around with a wooden spatula. "For us, I thought carbonara. If that's okay with you."

"Totally."

Cate nodded, staring intently at the pan. Although she was standing next to Parker, so close they were almost touching, she kept her eyes downcast. Silence fell between them. Parker cleared her throat and began swinging her legs. Cate remained grimly focused on her stove, either oblivious to the growing tension or ignoring it. Probably the latter.

Parker sighed. This night was going to end one of two ways: either she was going to throw her arms around Cate's neck and kiss her until they both couldn't breathe, or she was going to walk out and not look back. She didn't want to wait until after dinner to find out.

"Cate. C'mon." Parker leaned over and nudged her. "You're not going to say anything?"

Cate drained the pancetta, then returned it to the pan. "You're not hungry?" She grabbed two palmfuls of fresh pasta and tossed them into the boiling water.

"I'm starving. But I also think you're stalling."

Cate bit her lip, stirring the pasta with a strainer. "You might be right," she agreed but didn't stop moving. She pulled the pasta from the water and added it to the pan with a flourish, along with the egg and cheese mixture. Parker watched, enthralled by the easy grace in Cate's movements and the strength in her forearms as she turned off the heat and tossed the pasta in the pan with a flick of her wrist. Finally, she stopped and turned to Parker, leaning her hip against the stove. She bit her lip again, looking lost.

"I, um, started seeing a therapist," she said hesitantly. "I've only been a few times. He has me doing these writing exercises. I hate doing it, but I think it's helping."

Parker's eyes widened. Of all the openers, she hadn't expected that one. "That's really great. What are you writing about?"

"My brother, mostly. Trying to actually process the accident instead of just burying it. Well, at first that's what I was doing. Now…" Cate yanked the towel off her shoulder with a snap and threw it onto the kitchen island.

"Now…?"

Cate raked a hand through her hair, crossed her arms, then uncrossed them again. She planted a hand on her hip, looking down at the carbonara like it would give her the next line. Parker waited. And waited. And waited some more.

"Cate, I know it physically pains you to string together more than, like, two consecutive sentences, but you have to talk to me." Parker let out a long breath. "Or else I should probably go."

Cate's head snapped up. "No. Don't leave."

Parker threw up her arms in frustration. "Then give me a reason to stay."

Cate's gaze locked onto Parker, her eyes a dark, roiling sea of emotion. "I know. I just need this to be perfect. I need everything I say to you to be perfect."

"It doesn't have to be."

Cate shook her head so forcefully her bangs fell into her eyes. "Yes, it does. After how I treated you, it does."

Parker closed her eyes and pinched the bridge of her nose. Despite her best efforts, her patience was beginning to fray. She didn't need more self-flagellation, she needed Cate to get somewhere in the vicinity of a point. When she opened her eyes, she looked down and saw that Cate's hands were shaking. Her frustration ebbed slightly, and Parker reached out to lace their fingers together. Cate clamped down immediately on Parker's hand.

"It's adorable how bad you are at this." Parker pulled Cate's hand into her lap.

Cate chuckled, tears glistening in the corner of her eyes. She swiped at her cheeks. "I'm trying to get better."

"Is that what the journaling is about?"

"Yes." Cate let out a breath. "The first couple of times, I wrote about my brother. But then it shifted on me, and before I knew it, I was just writing about you. How amazing you are, how the whole room changes when you walk in. It's like there's a light that follows you everywhere. You make everyone and everything around you shine. I've never known anyone like you before."

Tears welled in Parker's eyes, and she wiped her own cheeks as well. "Keep going. This is good. You're really onto something here."

Cate chuckled again, but her voice was barely above a rasp. "When I saw you there in the road, blood all over your face, I thought you'd died. I didn't know what to do. What to think. It was only for a moment—a second, really—but that second felt like an eternity. I forgot everything. My training, accident protocols, all of it. I thought we were too late and…I froze."

Parker ran her thumb across the back of Cate's hand, not daring to look away from her face. "And Lieutenant Wildman doesn't freeze."

"Yeah. Exactly." Cate inched closer. "It brought me right back to the accident. All of a sudden, I was a kid again, and the person most important to me in the entire world needed help and there was nothing I could do. I know it's not rational and doesn't make much sense, but that's the best way to explain it. I couldn't fathom the thought of losing you." She took another deep breath. "And a couple days before your accident happened, we had a bad call on McChesney. We had to extricate a family from an overturned SUV and we didn't know one of the kids had been ejected. He didn't make it. I was the one who found him. So, between that and Butler closing, I just…"

Parker blinked. She had no idea what Cate had been dealing with. Her behavior in the days before Parker crashed now made perfect sense, but it didn't absolve her completely. "So you dumped me?" She laughed dryly.

The rasp in Cate's voice became harsher. "I wasn't thinking, I was just reacting. I was trying to protect myself, when I should have been taking care of you. That's what you deserved."

Parker's tears were coming faster now, too fast to wipe them all away. Cate's words settled over her like a warm blanket, soothing the ache in her chest that had plagued her since that awful moment in the hospital. Cate was so close. Parker felt the heat radiating from her body and could smell the scent of her skin. The desire to lean forward and bury her face against Cate's neck was so overwhelming she was almost dizzy. Still, there was a shard of anger that demanded acknowledgment.

"Fuck, Cate. Do you have any idea what it was like for me? I was terrified, panicking, but then I saw you and I knew I was going to be okay. I was safe. You made me feel safe. No one ever made me feel safe before. And then it all just fucking shattered." She looked down at their hands, clutching at each other so hard both their knuckles were white, and whispered, "I thought you said I had nothing to be afraid of."

Cate's features twisted in pain. "I know, baby, I know. I'm so sorry. I will never, ever push you away like that again. I promise." Cate stepped in between Parker's legs, her hands settling on the tops of Parker's thighs. "If you give me another chance, I swear I will spend the rest of my life making it up to you."

Parker inhaled sharply, holding back a fresh waterfall of tears. She looked into Cate's hazel eyes. Gold flecks shone like diamonds, drawing Parker in deeper. Cate held her gaze steadfastly, her hands sliding up Parker's thighs until they came to rest on her waist. When she spoke again, her voice was strong and smooth and full of certainty.

"I love you."

The air rushed out of Parker's lungs, and she felt herself empty out completely. Her whole life had distilled to this moment, to the sight of Cate standing before her, dark eyes glistening, wearing a look of such utter conviction that it gave Parker goose bumps. The answer to all her questions was right there, on Cate's lips. The truth, the *words*, equal parts exhilarating and terrifying and that had floated between them for weeks, were no longer unsaid. Parker had said it before in her life, on few occasions, but that didn't matter. Cate had obliterated the remnants of the women that had come before. For the first time, Parker knew what it was like to be home.

She draped her arms over Cate's shoulders and said them back. "I love you, too."

Cate surged forward and enveloped her, strong arms pulling her in. Parker buried her face in Cate's neck and inhaled. This was all she needed, all she would ever need, and when Cate pulled back enough to kiss her, Parker was never more sure of that fact.

"Meagan will kill you if you fuck up, though," Parker muttered, biting gently at Cate's bottom lip.

"That's fair," Cate muttered back. She deepened the kiss, tenderly cupping Parker's face with one hand and stroking her cheek with her thumb. Cate's other arm hugged Parker tighter, slipping around her ribs. Pain shot through Parker's side briefly, and she let out a hiss. Cate eased back, letting her arm fall. "Are you okay?"

"Just some bruised ribs from the accident. Nothing serious." Parker pulled up her shirt, displaying the yellow bruising running up her hip. Cate grazed Parker's skin with her fingertips, brows furrowed.

"I should have taken care of you. I got scared and ran instead."

"You just said you won't ever do that again, and I believe you. You are the bravest, best person I know." Parker curled her fingers in the collar of Cate's shirt. "And I need to apologize, too. I should've just gone back to Rob's when it started raining. I'm sorry."

Cate's mouth curved into a wry smile. "Can we agree that you'll start checking the weather before you go out on that goddamn thing?"

Parker nodded. "I know you hate it."

Cate tipped her head back with a groan, like it'd been killing her not to say it. "They're so dangerous. If you'd seen what I've seen, you'd agree with me." She sighed. "And it's not necessarily the riders. It's drivers who don't pay attention. Full riding gear can't protect you completely when you're clipped by an SUV that didn't look before changing lanes. Or run off the road by someone taking a turn too fast."

"That's all true."

"I don't want to ask you to give up something you love and have you resent me for it. But I just—"

"The bike's negotiable."

Cate blinked. "What?"

Parker lifted Cate's hand and kissed her palm. "It's negotiable," she repeated.

"Just like that?"

"I got it on a whim. On my dad's whim, actually. I mentioned that I wanted a motorcycle once when I was a freshman in college. I forgot all about it until I finally graduated, and then the morning of the ceremony it just showed up. My dad didn't. I guess he thought it would make up for him not being there. It's fun to ride, for sure, but it's not something I was ever passionate about. Some days it's just a reminder of how my dad throws money at things instead of actually trying." Emotion stirred in Parker's chest, and she swallowed thickly, forcing it back down. She'd never admitted that out loud before. "It's not worth losing you over."

"Are you sure?" Cate's arms slid around her again, avoiding her injured side. Parker felt the power in Cate's body even though she held her loosely, and a newfound feeling of safety washed over her.

"I'm sure. I haven't even gotten it fixed yet. It's still in Rob's garage."

"Don't get rid of it. We can figure something out."

Parker nodded. When they kissed again, it deepened and ignited, a spark against kindling that was begging for flames. Heat flared between them, but it didn't feel dangerous or wild—more like a steady, controlled burn that would feed them both. For as long as they wanted it.

She dug her heels into the back of Cate's calves and twisted her hand in the rumpled collar of Cate's shirt, drinking her in like there was nothing else in the world that would keep her alive. Cate's hands found her ass, gripping tightly, yanking Parker forward so their hips were aligned. A low noise rumbled from the back of Cate's throat.

Parker's hunger was replaced by a different need. Her fingers found the buttons of Cate's shirt, and within seconds it was on the floor. Cate grabbed the hem of Parker's T-shirt, hand brushing gently over her bruised ribs, and pulled it over her head. Their mouths crashed together, desperate and needy, like they both were trying to erase the memory of the past weeks.

"Fuck," Parker gasped when Cate trailed her lips down to the pulse point on her neck. She clutched at the back of Cate's head with both hands. "Couch?"

Without a word, Cate lifted her off the counter. Parker's surprised yelp was swallowed by Cate's lips, the kiss unbroken even as she effortlessly carried Parker over to the couch. God, she loved how strong Cate was, and how those steely muscles yielded under her touch. Cate lowered her down to the cushion and settled over her. Parker undid Cate's bra with a practiced twist of her hand and arched her back to give Cate room to do the same, letting out a satisfied moan when they came together again, skin finally touching.

"I missed you so much." Cate's voice broke against Parker's lips.

Parker traced the length of Cate's spine, fingers gliding over the slope of her back. "Don't worry. There's no way in hell you're getting rid of me now."

Cate pulled back to look at her, eyes sparking, wearing a teasing half-smile. "Is that a promise?"

Parker cupped Cate's face. She grinned. "Absolutely, Lieutenant."

* * *

Parker woke to a loud, insistent chime near her head. She fumbled under the pillow for her phone and silenced the alarm. Cate stirred next to her, tightening her arm over Parker's waist.

"It's early," Cate murmured into the back of Parker's neck.

Parker luxuriated in the feel of Cate's warm, strong body pressed against hers. The thought of pulling herself away from this woman was excruciating, but she didn't have much of a choice. Parker sighed in defeat.

"I have to grab a bus to get home, so I can shower and change before work."

"I can drive you. Or you can get ready here and walk." Cate's sleepy voice made Parker sink deeper into the mattress.

"What about clothes?" Parker barely mustered the objection. She was already debating just leaving Remix closed and staying in Cate's bed all day.

"I'm sure I have something that fits you."

"Like ten different kinds of fire department T-shirts?"

Cate's teeth grazed against the sensitive spot on Parker's neck. Her breath caught in her throat. "You have a problem with my T-shirts?"

"God, not at all." Parker shimmied closer to Cate. "I swear you wear them a size too small just to torture me."

Cate's mouth curled against Parker's neck in a smile, her hand sliding down Parker's hip and pausing just below her belly button. Heat began to pool between Parker's legs. "Maybe I do. I've caught you staring."

"It's hard not to stare at the most beautiful woman I've ever seen."

"That was smooth." Cate voice was almost a purr. "Stay a little longer. I'll make it worth your while." Cate's hand moved lower, sliding for the juncture between Parker's legs. Still on her side, Parker shifted and stretched out her leg, opening herself up to allow Cate better access. Cate's fingertips delicately brushed over her.

Parker gasped. "A-and how will you do that?"

Cate didn't answer. Her teeth went to Parker's neck again, biting harder this time, and every nerve ending sparked to life. Parker's entire body was a live wire, still alive and electric from last night. At some point they'd made it off the couch and devoured the carbonara, but after that it was just the two of them in Cate's bed. Parker was pretty sure they hadn't fallen asleep until after midnight.

She reached behind her to clutch the back of Cate's head as Cate moved down her neck and over her shoulder blade, alternating between kisses and possessive bites. Parker rocked her hips forward, urging Cate's fingers deeper. A broken whimper slipped past her lips. Cate's pleased chuckle answered, and her hand started moving faster. Parker's breath quickened. She tried to roll onto her back, but Cate kept her pinned in place, half on her side and pressed into the mattress, as Cate continued to tease between her legs. She pumped against Cate's hand, growing wetter with each stroke, until the ache for Cate's fingers inside was so much it nearly brought her to tears.

"P-please…" Another whimper spilled out of her. Parker squirmed against Cate, but it was fruitless. Cate shifted her weight and pressed Parker harder into the bed.

"Please what?" Cate's hot breath was in her ear, her voice low and urgent. Her hand stopped. Parker whined in protest.

"That's unfair."

"Tell me what you want."

"I want you to fuck me."

Cate withdrew her hand. Before Parker could object, Cate bit her earlobe, grabbed her hip, and effortlessly rolled her onto her back. Immediately Cate's mouth closed over her nipple, sucking and teasing with tongue and teeth. Parker arched into Cate, delirious with arousal and need. She gripped the back of Cate's head with both hands and guided her over to her other breast. Cate eagerly accepted the suggestion. Her tongue continued to perform unfairly wicked maneuvers, and with each swipe a new deluge of wetness painted Parker's thighs. For someone who hated talking, Cate certainly knew how to use her mouth, and Parker vowed she would forgive every moment of reticence if it meant she could wake up to this for the rest of her life.

The thought hit her like a freight train. All her life she'd jumped from one thing to another, whether it was work, school, or relationships, in a reckless search for something sustainable, but really all she'd done was chase the high of infatuation. Once the initial excitement wore off, she'd lose interest, and the pursuit would start anew. But now she'd found what she claimed she'd been looking for: something real. The thing to keep her feet on the ground. The foundation upon which to build, where she could finally find the best version of herself.

A sob threatened to break her wide open, and she choked it back just in time. Cate released Parker's nipple with a soft pop and rose up to look into Parker's eyes. "I'm right here," she whispered, as if she'd read Parker's mind. It was the most perfect thing she could've said. "I'm here. Okay?"

Parker nodded, tears pricking the corner of her eyes. She swallowed thickly. Cate bumped her forehead against Parker's.

"Do you want to keep going?"

Cate's steady presence brought Parker back into herself, and her body helpfully supplied the answer. Her hips rocked forward before she could speak. "Yes. Don't stop."

Cate held Parker's gaze, searching her face. After a moment she dipped down and caught Parker's lips in a kiss that drove any remaining doubt from Parker's mind. Cate would be there, would catch her. She wasn't going to run away again.

Cate pushed herself down the bed and settled between Parker's legs. Parker rose up to meet her and was rewarded when Cate's mouth went to her clit without hesitation. Parker's cry dissolved into a desperate whimper when Cate slid two fingers inside her. Cate's hand worked in time with her mouth, curling up and back with fierce precision and the exact rhythm Parker needed. She came after only a few strokes, in a desperate release that washed over her whole body, but Cate didn't stop. She lightened the pressure, her tongue barely ghosting over the sensitive spot, and increased the pace of her fingers. Heat built up deep in Parker's abdomen, slowly at first, then suddenly in one heady rush as Cate skillfully pulled the second orgasm out of her. Parker's entire body melted into the mattress. Cate dropped a long, lingering kiss on Parker's clit, then crawled up to lie beside her.

Parker didn't realize she'd dozed off until she heard Cate's voice again and felt her hand threading through her hair.

"You're going to be late." Cate kissed her softly. "I'll get you a towel for the shower. And some clothes."

Parker cracked an eyelid. The morning light coming through the window brushed over Cate's face, highlighting the line of her jaw and curve of her lips. Parker's breath caught at the sweet, gentle look in her eyes. She wondered again how much of a financial hit she'd take if Remix stayed closed today. She didn't have the energy to do the math. "Coffee?"

Cate kissed her again. "Anything for you."

Parker flushed and buried her shy smile in the pillow. She kept one eye open, unabashedly admiring the broad expanse of Cate's back as she sat up on the edge of the bed and reached for her shirt and underwear. Cate disappeared down the hall and returned with a plush green towel, then rummaged through her dresser drawer and came up with a handful of clothes. She placed everything at the foot of the bed. "See you downstairs."

After showering, Parker looked over the T-shirts Cate had picked out, deciding on a navy one sporting a faded Mayville Fire Academy logo that was about a size smaller than the rest. She couldn't stop the wide smile from spreading over her face when she slipped it over her head and caught the scent of Cate's detergent and, as always, the faint echo of smoke. She rolled up the sleeves so they hit the middle of her biceps and tucked the front of the shirt into her jeans.

Cate was standing in the kitchen when Parker bounded down the stairs. Her eyes roved over Parker, taking in every inch of her with a mixture of pride and possession that made Parker shiver in delight.

"I knew you could pull off that shirt." A warm smile broke out over Cate's face. "You make everything look good."

Parker smoothed down the front of the shirt, trying not to blush at the compliment and failing. "Thanks. I might have to keep this one."

"Anything you want, it's yours." Cate nudged a small travel cooler sitting on the breakfast island. Next to it was a thermos with a picture of a fire hydrant. "I made you lunch, if that's okay. Roast chicken and vegetables, with some yogurt, cheese, and crackers for a snack. And coffee."

Parker walked over and wrapped both arms around Cate's waist, tilting her chin up to look at her. "You are not of this Earth."

"I can't have you living on takeout and peanut butter and jelly sandwiches, can I?" Cate kissed her gently, tracing over Parker's jaw with her thumb. They broke apart far too soon for Parker's liking, and Cate nodded in the direction of the clock on the microwave. The store was supposed to be open in ten minutes.

Parker grabbed her lunch and coffee. "Will you walk with me?"

"I'd love to."

After Cate threw on a pair of joggers and her running shoes, they were out the door and walking toward Tomlinson, hands linked. Wordlessly, Cate took the cooler in her free hand, allowing Parker to drink her coffee.

The warm, bright morning was the absolute picture of summertime. A lush canopy of trees lined the street, branches swaying in the soft breeze off the lake. Dozens of kids were already at the playground, their yelps and screams carrying down the block. A group of bicyclists rode by in a kaleidoscope of fluorescent spandex and wraparound sunglasses. The last one in the pack gave them a jaunty wave. Parker tipped her thermos in her direction.

"I still can't believe you sold those shoes." Cate shook her head.

Parker looked around and let out a contented sigh. "I don't regret it at all. I was happy to give the money to Butler. I like being here. Makes me feel like I'm a part of something."

"Something bigger than yourself?"

"Yeah."

Cate squeezed her hand. "I know the feeling."

They walked the rest of the way in comfortable silence. Usually Parker couldn't stand that, but today she didn't feel the need to fill the space with anything. The sounds of the charming, easygoing town were enough: echoes of kids playing, the faint hum of traffic, the rustling of trees in the lake breeze. With each measured step toward Tomlinson Street, she felt more and more sure of herself. More settled. This was the place she was supposed to be, and this was the woman she was supposed to stand next to. The rush of clarity came on all at once but didn't overwhelm her. Instead, she just smiled to herself and gripped Cate's hand tighter.

They arrived at Remix a few minutes after ten. A kid was already waiting in front of the store, crouched down with his back against the door, engrossed in his phone. He popped to his feet when Parker and Cate approached, bristling with excitement. He couldn't have been more than twelve or thirteen.

"Hey, do you have the new Jordan Three Retro drop? In the stardust colorway? My mom said I could get a pair if I got straight A's this semester and I did so do you think you have any?" His words came out in a rush, bright brown eyes wide and gleaming with anticipation. Parker knew the look; she'd felt it on her own face more than once when she couldn't wait to get her hands on a new sneaker drop.

"Straight A's? That's awesome. I've never gotten straight A's, not even in kindergarten." Parker unlocked the door and held it open for the kid. "Head on inside and I'll be with you in a second."

After the kid bounded inside, Parker turned back to Cate and took the lunch cooler from her. She stood up on her tiptoes and kissed her.

"I'll see you after work?" Cate asked.

"Are you kidding? I'm going to close early to get back to you quicker."

"I love your enthusiasm."

"Will you come to dinner at Rob's?" At Cate's hesitant look, Parker added quickly, "Don't worry, it'll be fine. I promise."

Cate nodded, the corner of her mouth twitching. "Okay." She squeezed Parker's hand one last time and turned to head home. She only took a few steps before casting a broad smile over her shoulder back at Parker.

Parker waved and ducked back into the store. The kid was standing in front of her display wall, ogling the different styles. Parker clapped her hands together eagerly. "All right, young legend, let's hook you up."

EPILOGUE

Two seconds before her alarm went off, Cate woke. She slapped the snooze button and slid her hand across to the other side of the bed. It was empty. She blinked in the darkness, confused until the memory returned. Halloween was last night, and the infamous New York Manni had flown in for the weekend to hang out with Parker. They'd gone to a costume party downtown. Cate rolled over, groping for her phone on the nightstand, and started flipping through the messages Parker had sent last night, providing a steady—if increasingly incoherent—travelogue of their shenanigans. It culminated in a text that came through only two hours ago, saying they were *hme saf* and punctuated by a string of emojis that was more confounding than suggestive. Cate chuckled to herself.

She wiped her eyes, threw back the covers, and flipped on the light. She changed into warm running clothes and went downstairs. Before she headed out the door, she shot an accountability text to Meagan, who was training for the Turkey Trot half-marathon on Thanksgiving Day. Or was trying to, anyway.

An aggrieved reply came a moment later. *I'm up.*

Proof? Cate typed back with one hand while stretching her quad.

A selfie appeared on-screen: Meagan in a bright yellow sweatshirt and ball cap and flipping off the camera. *You're a masochist.*

You love me for it.

After a quick three-mile run, Cate showered, dressed, grabbed her coffee, and was out the door at promptly six twenty. The sun wouldn't be up for another hour or so, but Cate didn't mind. The air was crisp on her cheeks but it still wasn't quite winter yet, and she enjoyed the waning days of fall and the crunch of leaves under her boots.

As Cate walked, her thoughts drifted to Parker, trying to gauge the severity of the hangover sure to greet her in a few hours. Luckily, Parker didn't have to work that day; she'd updated Remix's schedule earlier that month and the store was now closed on Mondays and Tuesdays to allow herself a break. After only six months of being open, Remix's revenue continued to grow steadily, and depending on how the holidays went, Parker thought she might actually be able to hire a part-time associate in the new year. Tasha, who was at Remix just as often as she was at Butler Center, had loudly made her interest known.

A warm feeling settled in her chest at the thought of seeing Parker more often. Currently their days off together only aligned every three weeks, but it didn't feel like a hardship. Parker found excuses to pop over to the firehouse during Cate's shifts—especially around mealtimes, doubly so when Cate was cooking—and Cate always swung by the store on her runs or met Parker at closing time so they could walk to dinner together. Everything was effortless in a way Cate had never experienced before, and her fears about her work or schedule being too much, as manufactured as they were, never materialized.

Simply put, she was happy. Blindingly, stupidly happy, and it was only getting better.

As she laid a hand on the bright-red firehouse doors, she stiffened. She'd forgotten the date. Since Halloween was yesterday, that made today the first. Of November. Straightening her shoulders, she pulled open the door and steeled herself for whatever bullshit was sure to await her.

The bay was quiet. Ladder Two and Medic Two stood watching over her like silent sentinels, gleaming and motionless. She glanced up. No elaborate rigging or someone hanging from the rafters waiting to dump a bucket of water on her head. No banners, no loudspeakers, no catcalls. She adjusted the strap of her duffel and walked toward the common room.

Alex was at his locker, stowing his gear for the day. He looked over at her blandly, stifling a yawn. "Morning, Wilds."

Cate stopped in her tracks. She looked him up, then down, then up again. He was wearing his bunker pants and suspenders. And a black sports bra.

"Hey, Wilds." Morgan appeared from around the corner. She was in the same outfit, too. Omar and Syed were chatting by the coffee machine across the room, also dressed identically. Freddie emerged from the kitchen and gave his suspenders a jaunty snap when he saw her. His outfit was the only one that was any different. Instead of a sports bra, he was in a black compression top cut off at the chest, barely covering both nipples. Apparently, bras in his size did not exist.

Cate dropped her duffel and rolled her eyes. "You are all assholes."

"Something the matter, Wilds?" Cordell leaned against the doorframe to her office, ball cap pulled down low, cracking a wry smile. She, too, was clad in a sports bra and bunker pants. "Don't you like the new duty uniform?" The captain snapped her fingers, and on cue, like a trained drill team, the entire crew crossed their arms and cocked their hips, mimicking Cate's pose on the calendar.

"No, you're doing it wrong. More duck lips," Morgan said to Alex. "Like this." She pursed her lips and sucked in her cheeks so hard they indented against her cheekbones. Alex followed suit, making a high-pitched noise as he did so.

"I did not do duck lips!" Cate protested.

"Yeah. You did," Freddie said.

Cate buried her face in her hands. "I hate you all."

"No, you don't. Come on." Cordell patted her on the back and steered her toward the kitchen.

"Happy November!"

Parker stood at the end of the long table, dressed like everyone else and proudly displaying a sheet cake with the November spread printed on it. Eleven sparking candles surrounded the picture of Cate's head like a crown.

In two strides Cate crossed the room and pulled Parker into a warm hug. "What are you doing here?"

"I couldn't miss the first of the month, could I?" Parker's voice was hoarse, and she looked every bit like someone who'd been out all night drinking. Her hair was wild, and she was squinting from the bright overhead lights, but her smile was full of good cheer. She was also the only one Cate didn't mind seeing without a shirt on; the boxing classes she'd started a few months ago at Chevy's had added new definition to her shoulders and arms.

Cate cupped Parker's face and laughed. "You're a mess."

"I'm literally dying. Manni made me do tequila shots."

"I could have guessed that, based on those ridiculous texts. I can't believe you woke up for this."

"I set, like, five alarms to get here." Parker leaned closer, lowering her voice. "Look, this was the least embarrassing thing I could convince them to do, but I have no idea what they've planned for the rest of the month. I'm sorry."

"I'll consider myself warned."

"To be fair, Alex and Salt had an idea involving buckets of water and white T-shirts, and it was really hard to veto that one."

Cate laughed again. "I love you so much."

"I love you, too."

And in the middle of the kitchen, in full view of everyone, she lowered her head and kissed Parker, feeling a playful smile against her lips. A few catcalls and whistles bounced around the room, but Cate ignored them all.

"All right, Ms. November, that's enough," Cordell said. "We got a fire hazard here."

"Yeah, c'mon, Wilds," Alex jumped in. "It wouldn't look good if the safety officer let this joint burn down because she was too busy making out with her girlfriend."

"All of you can fuck off," Cate grumbled, but there was no real venom behind her words. She bent down and blew out the candles.

Cordell brandished a pastry cutter. Salt headed to the stove and started cracking eggs. "We only have an hour until we're on duty, so let's eat," the captain said. "Who wants an oblique?"

"I do!" Parker's hand shot up.

Cate reached for Parker's other hand, pulling her in to wrap an arm around her shoulder. She kissed Parker's temple, then let out a groan as Cordell started cutting the cake.

"Oh my God, I *am* doing duck lips."

Bella Books
Happy Endings Live Here
P.O. Box 10543
Tallahassee, FL 32302
Phone: (800) 729-4992
www.BellaBooks.com

More Titles from Bella Books

Jones – Gerri Hill
978-1-64247-598-2 | 260 pages | Mystery
One weekend getaway, six friends, and a deadly secret that will wash away everything they thought they knew.

Merry Weihnachten – E. J. Noyes
978-1-64247-610-1 | 292 pages | Romance
Christmas traditions aren't the only things getting mixed up when these two hearts collide beneath the mistletoe.

Sweet Home Alabarden Park – TJ O'Shea
978-1-64247-570-8 | 362 pages | Romance
She came to restore a royal estate—she never expected to rebuild her heart.

Dr. Margaret Morgan – Christy Hadfield
978-1-64247-628-6 | 286 pages | Romance
Facing the professor on campus everyone hates is terrifying—but falling for her might be even worse.

Overtime – Tracey Richardson
978-1-64247-630-9 | 278 pages | Romance
A charming romance about second chances, found family, and scoring the goal that matters most.

The Big Guilt – Renée J. Lukas
978-1-64247-657-6 | 206 pages | Romance
What if the one who got away became the one you can't have?